Sweet Serene

This is a work of fiction. All of the characters, organizations and events portrayed in this novel are either products of the author's imagination or are used fictitiously.

OPEN ME Publications

SWEET SERENE. © Copyright 2009 by Robert Hedges.

All rights reserved. Printed in the United States of America.

For information:

Bobby.Hedges@hotmail.com

ISBN- 978-0-578-01635-1 (paperback)

First published in 2009 by Open Me Publications with cooperation with Lulu.com.

WRITTEN BY

ROBERT HEDGES

For Pickle,
And everyone else who may manage to get arm's length
To all that they have ever dreamed,
And still manage to lose it all.

…may you find what you are looking for.

Part One

Halcyon Days

Austin Olsen had already eaten a slice of pizza, a hot dog covered in chili, two slices of cake, at least four chocolate chip cookies and countless glasses of fruit punch when he plunged his pudgy little hands into a bowl of assorted candies. Palms loaded, he held the sugary sweets tight against his chest as he turned back across the floor. The hefty eight-year old took three steps, bumped into Sunday's broom and then froze in place; as if he were just caught in the midst of a far more criminal act.

Something in the back of Sunday's mind warned him that no good would come from Austin ingesting more junk food; but he shrugged off the notion, convinced that someone in the medical staff would say something if they felt like he shouldn't have it. He motioned to the boy to carry on, only to watch him run across the linoleum tiled floor and dive into the inflatable moonwalk pushed awkwardly in the corner of the room. Sunday shook his head in jest and proceeded to sweep up the tiny chocolate crumbs scattered across the floor.

In the time that he had been working at WonderKids, if Sunday had learned anything, it was not to ask too many questions. He figured it was not his place to ask why the medical staff was never able to remedy any of the children. It was not his business to inquire why there was such extravagance prepared for this year's "New Admissions Day". He did not question the request to put a nametag on Steve, the coma patient; and so he certainly would never have suggested that perhaps the tubby child should lay off the snacks. Instead, Sunday simply stuck to his job, which was to transport the children when they had outings, entertain the children when there was time and clean up after the children no matter how big the mess.

WonderKids was a rarity as it was one of only a handful of similar facilities in the world. Each of the children residing in the center suffered from a strange malady, some hard-to-define disease or a condition that for one reason or another led their regular doctors, psychiatric wards and parents to give up hope on them. Some of the kids, like Austin Olsen, didn't appear ill just by looking at them. Sure, he was a round kid, but he did not look sick. Molly Rollins was the cutest little five-year old, curly pig-tails and all; but all that cuteness vanished once she started her involuntary shrieking sessions. The doctors could not cure it, the therapists could not think of what prescriptions to mix to quell her and once her parents had all they could take, she ended up at WonderKids. Steve, the coma patient, had been unconscious to the world ever since birth and much like Molly Rollins and Austin Olsen, no one could explain why. Once all seemed to be lost and the neurologists had thrown up their arms, the slumbering child was admitted to join the small band of children for whom there was no cure.

Sometimes, Sunday would try to guess as to what the cause and remedy for the children might be. He once theorized that maybe young Steve was narcoleptic and that his trigger possibly was his own name. Sunday conjectured that when his mother first called him "Steve" as he lay in her arms, the tiny infant just drifted; and with every cry of, "Steve! Oh, Steve wake up!" the poor boy fell farther and farther into a deep sleep. This idea was of course rejected and Sunday was told to clean the bathrooms.

WonderKids was staffed by a handful of doctors, nurses and assistants of varying specialties; none of whom had graduated at the top of their class or with honors. The building acted as a sister facility to St. Joe's Medical Pavilion and all major decisions and funding came down from the larger hospital's Board of Directors. Despite this, very rarely did anyone from the main building ever venture over to what they had referred to as the "Hopeless Ward". In fact, WonderKids served very much the same purpose for the medical staff as it did for the children. It was an oubliette, a place to send incurable patients and lackluster professionals to forget about them. Unless there was an issue, the Board of Directors were more apt to write the Head Physician of the facility a blank check than actually try to get involved with the oddities that were the inhabitants of WonderKids.

This accounted for the strange way money and responsibility were often allocated throughout the facility. Sunday was hired to the maintenance staff almost ten years prior, at the age of sixteen. It was not long before he was given a fancy title and made not only to perform basic janitorial needs, but also placed in charge of transportation and the procurement of any and all items needed in the recreation area, which was on the first floor and was where the children spent the majority of their time.

This meant that Sunday typically would have been in charge of planning the entertainment for the day. This particular day; however, was special, as it was "New Admissions Day". Twice a year the center would welcome a few more children whom for one reason or another had fallen by the wayside. It was typical fare for banners to be hung and snacks to be put out for the kids; but this year, no expense had been spared. An inflatable moonwalk was wedged into the corner and only inflated as much as it could be under such cramped quarters. The friendly green dragon head that rose from the top drooped under the ceiling. There was also a dunk tank that no one had yet to volunteer to climb in, a ball pit where most of the children were and as many Mylar balloons as the eye would ever care to see. According to Nurse Durby, the building's pharmacist, the latex balloons were dangerous.

As Sunday slowly and methodically swept up the last remnants of crumbs off the floor he pondered why the staff prepared such an array of activities and why he was not originally made aware of it all. He assumed that he was left out of the discussion because someone in the medical staff probably felt that since he was not a trained professional, he did not need to be included in the loop. This really did not bother Sunday too much, as he was not really one for being included in loops. When one of the doctors or nurses did request something from Sunday, it came in the form of barking demands; so Sunday preferred to stay in the periphery when it came to the staff. He felt that as long as they ignored what he did, he could ignore what they did and his days would go by that much smoother.

Back and forth, Sunday repeatedly swayed his broom. His eyes wandered to the parking lot on the other side of the giant windows. He watched as a beat-up, blue Bronco pulled into a parking space and two long, shapely legs stepped onto the asphalt. Kylie Court, the staff Phlebotomist, pushed her meticulously parted blonde hair off her shoulder, pulled on a set of elbow length green latex gloves and straightened her matching vivid green sundress before walking towards the front door. Kylie began working in the tiny lab on the second floor three months before; which was almost exactly as long as Sunday had been trying to ask her out.

Working in the lab kept Kylie fairly confined all day. She never interacted with the children and only spoke to Nurse Durby and Sunday on a daily basis. This was because Nurse Durby was her direct supervisor and because Sunday made it a point to clean the lab when he knew that she would be there. The two had forged a very close relationship which had yet to see beyond her office door.

There had been fleeting moments when Sunday proved able to work up his nerve and steer the conversation to tentative plans for the weekend; but Kylie had yet to show for one of their arranged meetings. Sunday would spend those evenings slouched on his couch, in his tiny midtown apartment; fighting back the feelings of rejection while watching the American Movies Classics Network and scribbling his woes into his spiral notebook.

This was how the custodian had spent the last weekend, as Kylie had cancelled their pre-planned date due to a death in the family. However, this did not seem like the previous occasions, in which Sunday would be taking out the trash, mopping the floor or performing some other random task on the second floor and would overhear Kylie chatting with Nurse Durby about how she got hit on by some hunk of a guy at the club over the weekend when she should have been sharing a candle lit dinner with him. On those occasions, the custodian would usually then hang his head as if he did not hear and go back to work. He would keep his distance from her, watch countless old movies and fill leaf after leaf of pages in his spiral notebook until he had worked up enough courage to talk to her again, and the cycle would continue.

Unlike those days, this particular morning Kylie had sullenness in her expression and vacantness in her eyes. They seemed tired and hollow. Despite their worn appearance, after months and months of pining and stealing glances at her day after day, Sunday still found himself captivated by her sparkling blue eyes; even from across the lot. The janitor caught himself staring, as he idly held his broom when Stew approached him.

"Blue Moon in ten." he said.

Sunday nodded in agreement as Stew added, "...and Levine wants to see you." He giggled and walked off.

Stew had been working at WonderKids as Sunday's counterpart for almost a year and aside from Kylie, was the only other staff member close to Sunday in age. Stew was a bit muscle bound and it gave him an ego that rivaled his wide shoulders. An ego so big it blinded him from the thinning black hair on top of his tanned head. He was only twenty-one and yet he already looked as if he had poorly placed plugs. Stew would often laugh at Sunday's constant misfortunes and overall bad luck. During those times, Sunday would come close to teasing him about his receding hairline, but Stew was a good guy, not to mention his only friend; so Sunday would have never have thought to actually bring attention to it.

Sunday replaced the broom and dustpan in the maintenance closet, but before he could even shut the door, the forcibly friendly, yet firm voice of Head Physician Dr. Margo Levine-Alonzo (she insisted that she be referred to by her full title) came booming over the "Hokey Pokey" playing on the intercom system.

"Mr. Sunday, you are needed in the moonwalk." She repeated it twice before adding, "Bring a bucket."

Sunday sighed under his breath every vulgarity he could as he pulled the gear from the cleaning closet. He grabbed latex gloves, and rested them on the lip of a bucket that he filled with scaling hot water, soap, industrial strength Comet, Windex, and bleach. He then grabbed an armful of washcloths. Since Sunday did not know what he was facing, he thought it wise to be prepared for anything.

Anything would have been better than what Sunday saw when he reached the moonwalk. The children had already fled the inflatable beast and had tracked little Austin chunks all over the floor. There was a huge puddle in the far left corner of the moonwalk, wedged between the wall and two of the inflatable tubes; and in that puddle sat Austin Olsen. He was wrote his name in the mess; autographing his work; or so Sunday assumed. He held his breath and made his way inside. Austin Olsen's ailment was by far one of the worst. For no reason at all, the chubby little ankle-biter was prone to erupt from every orifice in his portly body. Even a mild outburst was not pretty and this particular episode Sunday ranked as a seven.

"Austin, get out of there!" the custodian ordered.

The boy rolled over the inflated tubes and awkwardly tumbled out.

"Go get cleaned up." Sunday added as he sent him away. The custodian could only assume that the oozing orphan instead ran for more slices of pizza.

While he cleaned the mess, two things occurred to Sunday. The first was that he had to be the unluckiest man alive and second was that he was not entirely sure that what he was touching was actually little, chewed bits of hot dog. The stench from Austin's insides combined with the fumes from the cleaning solution began to burn Sunday's nostrils and his eyes began to water. He continued to sop up handful after handful of the wretched stuff. Stew appeared in the mesh window by Sunday's head and caught his attention.

"Hey, how's it going?" he asked with a malicious grin.

"You have to help me." Sunday pleaded as he pulled his face to the mesh for fresher air. His cheeks were already flush as tears rolled down from his searing eyes.

"I can't." he replied, "I'm just here to borrow your pen… and to tell you that you are kneeling in something."

Sunday looked down to see that his knee rested in a puddle hidden by the tubes. "Man!" he groaned and reluctantly gave Stew the pen. Sunday's pen had one of those little, luck trolls with big, orange hair, and he suddenly started to feel what little luck he had fade as Stew pocketed it.

Before he took off, Stew said simply, "You know, you shouldn't have mixed bleach and Windex, the fumes are dangerous."

Sunday flicked Stew off and hoped that he would see him, but knew that he would not, and went back to cleaning. Austin goo seeped into his gloves and he felt the warm stickiness slip between his fingers. It was all that he could do not to vomit. He took a deep breath to alleviate his gag reflex. The bleached ammonia air filled his lungs and suddenly everything started to go white. Sunday's head got very hot- and light… as if it had been pumped with helium. All of the sounds around him began to muffle. With eyes that stung and throbbed and felt as though they hovered over his torso, the custodian watched in disbelief as his fingers seemed to elongate. The custodian suddenly knew that he was in for trouble; his limbs went numb and with a garbled "Shit;" he collapsed face first into the puddle.

—⊙—

$\mathscr{S}$unday came to his senses a few moments later to the sound of Stew's voice over the intercom, "Now ladies and gentlemen, The WonderKids Men's Choir proudly presents *Blue Moon*."

"Double shit." Sunday thought as he rolled across the puddle and stumbled out of the moonwalk. Music began to play from the weathered player piano that rested along the south wall. He wiped the big chunks of what may or may not have once been a peanut butter and jelly sandwich off his face and slid across the floor to the nearest intercom microphone. Stew began to sing, "*bomba- dinga- dong- ding.*"

Sunday reached for the receiver and a thin strand of muck flew free of his hands and hit the wall. He grabbed the receiver just in time to join Stew for a rendition of the golden oldie. Sunday sang the verses, while Stew dropped his voice down a few octaves and sang the repetitive "*blue, blue, blue moons*". From opposite sides of the main room, they walked to the center as far as the chords would allow and hopped up on tables and chairs and "danced" as they sang. Sunday shook his hips from left to right incessantly, like a dollar store dancing Santa doll. Stew held his hands in fists, his elbows out and bobbed his shoulders up and down. The children all gathered around and cheered on the duo as though they had actual talent. They ended their tune in unison and close to the correct key. The children all clapped and laughed. No sooner had Sunday and Stew said their "thank you" for the applause; Head Physician Dr. Margo Levine-Alonzo summoned Sunday again over the system.

"Mr. Sunday, report to my office." She repeated herself and a squawk of feedback blared over through the speaker, which caused everyone to momentarily cringe.

The thought to march to the office and quit struck Sunday's mind- but it struck his mind at least once a week. He walked to the office fairly slowly; he dreaded what the woman could want and wished that he was sitting shotgun somewhere in a beat-up, blue, Bronco. Head hung down; he gazed out of the corner of his eye at the vehicle in the parking lot and sighed. Stew followed him; he assumed that Sunday was probably daydreaming about their co-worker.

"Kylie was out a while, huh? I saw that she's back at work today." He coyly observed.

"Yeah, I know. I think she was at a funeral."

"Weren't you two supposed to go out last weekend?" Stew prodded, jokingly.

Sunday found his feet dragging slower as he neared the Head Physician's office. Many of the children had taken official time-outs from their games to watch the custodian sulk towards the door. Head hung low and not in the mood to talk about getting stood up yet again, he opted not to respond to his friend.

Stew could not help but chuckle, "Remember when you two were supposed to go to that art museum and she told you that she couldn't hang out because her Dad called and it upset her?"

Sunday felt his recently flushed cheeks fill to an uncomfortable blush, "Shut up, Stew." he said.

Stew continued, his chuckle turning to a cackle, "Remember when you sank like two-hundred dollars into those concert tickets and she bailed because she was afraid her ex-boyfriend might be there?"

Sunday's pace quickened and his voice became a little more agitated as he repeated sternly, "Shut up, Stew."

Stew could not resist a final jab and as his cackle graduated to a total belly-aching-giggle-fit, he concluded, "...Nothing like an over-priced girly-pop concert to cure a broken..."

Sunday punched Stew's shoulder fairly hard and once again muttered, "Shut up, Stew." His friend could see by the custodian's tight-lipped glare that it was best not to finish the statement.

Stew slouched down a bit and grumbled, "Fine. Jeez." He paused for a second and asked, "Do you really think there was a funeral?"

They walked by the line of folding card tables. Rows upon rows of chips, dips, pretzels and popcorn sat upon crepe paper table cloths. Sunday poured some candy corn onto a napkin as he passed by, careful not to actually touch the confections with his disgusting hands.

"Of course she did. She's been out of work for a while. She looked all sad when she came back." He said, in between sugary chews.

"Besides," he continued, "It doesn't matter any way. She's out of our league."

Stew feigned outrage, "What's wrong with us?" He gasped.

Sunday stopped in front of the Head Physician's office door, turned to face Stew and threw his arms out in a grand gesture. Spittle and slime trailed from his fingertips, landed on the floor, a chair and a little on Stew's cheek. As he began to turn the doorknob, Sunday answered simply, "I have no idea."

"Mr. Sunday…" Dr. Levine boomed over the loudspeaker again just as Sunday opened the door to her office. She spun around in her chair and her big, green eyes met him through her sexy, librarian-style glasses.

"Oh," she said as she continued to speak into the microphone. She realized her error and set it down purposefully. "Mr. Sunday, I'm sending you on a special mission."

To Dr. Levine, everything was a "special mission" no matter how grueling or asinine. The staff was at her every beck and call, partly because she put on a brilliant tyrant side when she wanted to (Sunday had once said that it rivaled that floating head in the *Wizard of Oz*), but mostly because she was quite an attractive older woman. She had an incredible ability to sucker a person into doing just about anything with little more than a simple puppy dog look and a sweet, '*Please*'.

Sunday watched in dreadful anticipation as she rifled through a large stack of folders on her desk. She found the file that she required and thumbed through the pages as she spoke.

"I need you to go to the airport and pick up one of the new kids." She said as she started to cock her head to the left, a sure sign that the look was coming. Sunday was in no mood to get suckered into anything additional… so he simply gave in.

"Okay," he replied quickly, "Who is it?"

"His name is Gabriel" she said.

She continued to tell Sunday that this Gabriel child was flying in from St. Petersburg and that he needed to be picked up at the airport at exactly four forty-five. Sunday looked down at his vomit covered watch. He had a mere hour to get there. The "special mission" had begun to sound like it would be quite an undertaking, so Sunday decided to try to angle for a way out.

"I don't think there's enough time to get there. Couldn't we arrange a cab to bring him here?" He bit his bottom lip to hold in his victorious smile.

Unfortunately, Dr. Levine saw through Sunday's poor attempt and sat at the edge of her seat and leaned over her desk. Dr. Levine's brows lowered and her tone grew more serious as she asked, "Mr. Sunday, what is your job here at Wonder Kids?"

Sunday did not respond; for he could only stand silent and defeated as she continued, "Your job is to do exactly as I ask, when I ask. If I need toilets cleaned, I expect you to clean them. If I need you to run errands, I expect you to run them. If I need you to go to the farthest end of the earth to find out whom exactly put the *dip* in the *dip-de-dip-de-dip*; I expect you to do it. And do it smiling. Right now, all I need is for you to pick up this little kid and bring him back here."

Her eyes became big and batty and her voice very wispy as she concluded with, "You can do that for me, can't you Mr. Sunday? *Please?*"

Sunday simply nodded and quickly turned to run out of the door and swore under his breath over the task ahead of him as Dr. Levine added, "Mr. Sunday."

He stopped dead in his tracks and feared what she was about to add. Sunday knew that Dr. Levine was so damned cunning that if she asked him, he would surely collect, separate and label the Austin pieces scattered from the bathrooms to the moonwalk. Yet, she continued, "You might consider changing your apparel before you go out into the world to represent our fine establishment."

He looked down at his stained clothes, covered in a chunky, orange waste and nodded in agreement. Before Sunday finally turned to leave, he asked, "What's supposed to be wrong with this kid?"

Levine looked over the top of her glasses and said, "All I know is that he is supposed to be an angel."

Sunday ran back to the break room, sifted through the lockers and looked for something to wear. He found a set of blue doctor's scrubs in the last locker and hurried to change clothes. As he pulled the pants around his waist, Stew strolled and sang, "Sunday's on a mission!"

Sunday nodded wearily as he slid his shoes back on, not bothering to tie them. "Yep," He said, "And do you know what the best part is?"

"No?" replied Stew.

Sunday smiled as he slapped Stew on the back and walked towards the door; "*You* have to finish cleaning up the Austin in the moonwalk."

Stew whined and cursed Sunday's name as the custodian sprinted to the parking lot. Once outside, he climbed into his rusted minivan. Long ago, the van was a deep, forest color; but time had transformed it into a splotchy, rusted brown and faded green. Sunday had trouble backing out due to the large piece of cardboard that was duct-taped over the hole where the side-window once was. With a loud pop of the transmission and as a plume of white smoke billowed from the tailpipe, Sunday maneuvered the vehicle out of the lot and peeled onto the highway; only to get stopped in traffic ten miles down the road.

CHAPTER TWO

*T*he whole terminal bustled except the gate for arriving flight 722 in from St. Petersburg. It seemed most of the people anxious to be reunited with their loved ones had given up hope as the threat of storms delayed the flights an hour and a half. Sunday was virtually alone and well on the way of running out of ways to entertain his self. He had already doodled a nifty sign that read "GABRIEL," which took three tries due to the fact that he was not sure how to spell the name. The entire car ride and much of his time waiting was spent pondering about the kid no one seemed to know anything about. He wondered what the boy looked like, what his illness was and would he be able to pick him out of the crowd?

When the plane finally emptied into the airport and a drove of passengers filed in from the door, Sunday thought for sure that he would have trouble spotting the elusive Gabriel; and he would have, if not for the boy's wire halo, cardboard wings- complete with feathers which were crudely glued around the edges, an oversized mock-emergency parachute and bright red shoes. That coupled with the fact that he was the only passenger that ran into the room at break neck speed. He stopped in front of Sunday, eyeballed the sign, and grinned.

"I'm Gabriel." said the ten year old as he extended his hand. In it, he held a blue envelope with a Hallmark emblem on it. Sunday took the envelope and smiled awkwardly.

"I'm Sunday." he replied as he opened and began to read the card. It had a red balloon on the front in a big, blue cloud filled sky. Inside it read:

"Oh Sweet Serene, Thank You, I'm Having a Good Time." It was signed childishly, *"Love will save us. Gabriel."*

With a "hmmph," Sunday slid the card back in its envelope and tucked it in his jacket pocket.

"Thanks." He said hardly half-heartedly. He took Gabriel by the wrist and began to lead him through the growing maze of people.

"Don't you like it?" Gabriel asked.

"Yeah, it's great." Sunday said, more focused on maneuvering through the crowds towards the baggage claim than listening to the child. Under his breath he mumbled, "It's a load, but it's great."

"What do you mean?" the boy inquired.

Sunday sighed. He was not in the mood to play question and answer games with the new kid, but he also did not want to hurt his feelings. "Don't get me wrong," he explained, "I appreciate it, I just don't agree with the message."

Sunday could see that his statement was not going to be enough to quell the boy, so he opted to change the subject. "So Kid, why are you wearing the wings?"

"They wouldn't fit in the overhead." Gabriel replied nonchalantly.

Sunday was impressed that the boy had a sense of humor, "No really, what's up with the backpack?" he asked.

Gabriel reached above his head and fumbled with the crudely fashioned halo and explained that the backpack was a gift made by the children at his former facility. An overstuffed, red duffle bag fell onto the baggage conveyer. The boy reached out as far as his short arms would allow, but he could not reach his bag. A kind middle aged man leaned over and retrieved the bag for the boy before it got out of reach.

Gabriel thanked the man and reached to the side pocket of his knapsack and pulled out a Hallmark card. He handed the card to the gentleman, who immediately smiled and nodded in approval. Sunday raised an eyebrow at the notion that the boy had a stockpile of random greeting cards to hand out to perfect strangers.

"So why all the cards, Kid?" he asked, as he took the heavy red bag from Gabriel and escorted him towards the exit.

Gabriel grinned as he explained, "I like making new friends, and I like making people happy." He began to run ahead of Sunday towards the exit doors; his hand-crafted wings bobbed back and forth and tossed poorly glued white feathers into the air. Before he broke into full skip, the boy yelled back at Sunday, who had reluctantly quickened his pace as well, "What makes people feel more special than a Hallmark?"

"But your cards are all generic. It's not like you're hand picking them for everyone." Sunday argued and rearranged the child's luggage in his rapidly weakening arms.

The pre-teen spun around with a look of sheer devastation at the notion that his cards were not perceived as genuine sentiment. Suddenly, his face lit back up as he said, "Aren't I?"

Gabriel ran from Sunday, shot through the door and stopped just shy of running off of the sidewalk and straight into the evening street. He turned to Sunday, looked up into the sky and basked underneath the grey, carbon haze that loomed beneath the heavy clouds which threatened more rain from above the tall skyline that surrounded him. Arms outstretched and smiling widely, he shouted back to Sunday, who was made his own way through the door, "It's the thought that counts, right?"

Sunday nodded. As far as he was concerned the answer was good enough. He was not interested in the in-and-outs of the boy's psyche, at least not now. Perhaps one afternoon when his mind wandered while he swept or mopped or cleaned random pieces of Austin Olsen he may ponder Gabriel's condition; but for now, he had accomplished his "special mission" and that was all that mattered. With any luck at all, he thought, this would put him in Dr. Levine's good graces and she would let him coast through the remainder of his shift without further grief. Feeling somewhat satisfied, Sunday took Gabriel by the hand and they made their way back to the dented, rusted minivan.

—◎—

The car ride back to WonderKids was agony for Sunday. Gabriel, giddy to be in a new town, continuously shifted in his seat and stuck his head out of the window to say "hello" to all the cars that joined them in the gridlock of the highway. Sunday wanted to ignore him, but the boy was also full of little questions;

"What is that building?"

"Where does that road go?"

When he was not asking questions, Gabriel spoke at length about St. Petersburg and his old friends and the old nurses and how he was excited to meet his new friends and the new nurses. All the while Sunday grunted, "Mmm hmmm."

There was a brief pause in the predominantly one-sided conversation and Sunday leapt at the opportunity to turn up the radio. He began to tap his fingers on the steering wheel as if the song was a favorite, when he really had no opinion; he just wanted an excuse not to talk. After a couple of verses into the song; Gabriel, who had stared intently at the custodian since he had made a move for the knob, turned the volume down.

"You don't seem happy, Mr. Sunday." He said.

"I was happier when we were listening to the radio." Sunday dryly replied.

"See?" He continued, "You sound down in the dumps. It's like you're about to give up and go eat worms." He shifted in his seat to face Sunday, who had put all of his focus on the road ahead. It didn't seem to matter to Gabriel, who spoke as if the van were an auditorium full of admirers of odd little kids who talk too much, and they drooled in anticipation for his next statement.

"So why do you feel sad, Mr. Sunday?" Gabriel asked.

"I'd rather we didn't talk about me, kid." Sunday said most blatantly.

"Well then, do you want to know what I am in for?" The boy bubbled as he went back to bouncing in his seat.

"What are you in for, kid?" Sunday replied and tried to sound as if he were truly interested and not just mildly curious.

"I was sent to witness the word." Gabriel responded gleefully.

"You were what?" Sunday asked, quite confused.

Gabriel repeated himself, "I'm going to witness the new word of God."

Sunday was understandably flabbergasted. He glanced over at the boy, who bounced up and down in his seat with glee. "What word?" He asked. No sooner had the words spilled from his mouth; the custodian knew that it was a question that he was sure he was sure to regret asking.

"I have no idea." Gabriel happily replied, "I have to wait for the Savior to say it first." His eyes twinkled and he began to grin at the choice of conversation, and suddenly Sunday did not want to have to sit through any more of the boy's answers, especially if they were going to be overly-zealous, religious answers. Sunday noted that they were only a mile away from their destination, so he nonchalantly pushed the accelerator to the floor. The engine backfired, revved and then jolted the boys forward before it sped down the road. The duct-tape that held up the make-shift window began to give, and pulled from the vehicle, which created a loud whistle and sequential bang as the air rushed in and slammed the cardboard against the metal window edge. The noise was so great that it made it hard to hear Gabriel's glee-filled ramblings.

"...But once the Savior speaks the word, there will be such love in the world. And that love will save us all." Gabriel shouted over the noise as he tried to still be heard. Sunday figured the child to be a severe schizophrenic and rolled his eyes at the prophetic babblings of his winged passenger- an act which the boy noticed.

"You don't believe me?" Gabriel asked and then added, "Why doesn't any one ever believe me?"

"Oh, it's not just you," Sunday reassured the boy, "I'm not too big on the whole god thing."

The would-be cherub's rosy, cheery demeanor sank to an ashy, astonished expression, "Holy monkeys, Mr. Sunday! How can you not believe in God?"

"Watch the news kid, it's a scary world. And when you get older and you realize your life is constantly the pits; it's hard to imagine there being a God."

"Have you ever stopped to think that maybe people are unhappy because they aren't paying attention to the right things?" His tone clearly requested a response; yet Sunday remained silent. Instead of taking the hint that Sunday did not want to talk, Gabriel continued, "Have you ever really been happy?"

"Look!" snapped Sunday and his head whipped in the boy's direction to meet his cheery demeanor, "Not that it's any of your concern, but I don't have time for happiness because I'm too busy getting crapped on by a wicked Head Physician, nurses and kids like you!"

Sunday was furious at the notion that the little boy could get under his skin so much, "With my luck, if I did find happiness, make a million dollars, save the world and fall in love; the girl would probably fall off a cliff or something, the money would turn out to all be Canadian Nickels and the world would surely explode... You think I don't come across as happy?" Sunday demanded and motioned to the van that surrounded them; as if it were a symbol for his entire existence, "Well, I wonder why that is?"

"Well, it seems to me," Gabriel continued as if Sunday had never said anything, "Happiness could be right around the corner."

Sunday cut him off, "Look, kid, I don't feel like talking about my out look on life with a complete stranger, let alone a mental patient, and especially not a mental patient who's getting glitter all over my van with their art and craft wings!"

The boy was devastated. It appeared that the tinsel-haloed angel took Sunday's lack of belief quite personally. "But Mr. Sunday, what about Heaven, and eternity; heck, even the word itself?" Gabriel squeaked mouse-like as two skid marks trailed the van as it swerved into the parking lot and squealed to a halt in a space.

"Sounds real nice." Sunday said sarcastically and hopped quickly out of the van, "Here we are, grab your things." he added as he made his way inside, not waiting for the boy or offering to help.

—◎—

*O*nce they were back inside the walls of WonderKids, Sunday was greeted with a high pitched squeal and Stew, who stood by the door, clearly waiting for him.

"Molly started early." Stew said with a forced smile. Sunday could tell by his friend's distain that he had been drafted for the "special mission" to shut her up.

"Oh, your delivery came." Stew added, "Levine is pissed; I'd steer clear if I were you." he warned.

"She said order something fun for the kids." Sunday interjected.

"You ordered a vintage merry-go-round!" he exclaimed.

Arms weighted with the heavy red duffel bag, Gabriel entered the room, and immediately joined the conversation.

"I love merry-go-rounds! I would like to see that!" he cried. His big eyes twinkled through his unkempt brown hair. Stew could only stare at the newest and winged resident.

"Gabe, this is Stew. Stew, Gabe." Sunday said as he walked away and motioned for Gabriel to follow. The young boy handed Stew a Hallmark and ran to catch up.

Stew shouted from behind as they walked into the main room, "Thanks for cleaning all of that nasty shit, Stew. You really rock!"

Stew also called Sunday an asshole after that; but Sunday did not hear it because he quickly had to chase after Gabriel who shouted, "An indoor carnival; zounds!" and took off for the carousel, which had been set up adjacent to the now deflated moonwalk.

Two men from the rental company rolled up the giant beast and one of them picked up a small pink chunk of something- clearly something Austin had coughed up; smelled it and held back a wretch. Normally, Sunday would have laughed at the sight; but that very same odor still hung around him as well. Sunday longed for a shower. The only thing between him and the locker room shower was informing the nurses of Gabriel's arrival and staying away from Dr. Levine.

Gabriel had climbed onto a plastic orange horse, and as he circled round and round, decided to pick up on the conversation that Sunday was none too thrilled to continue.

"So, you don't think you're cut out for happiness or love, Sunday?" He asked as the ride carried him out of sight.

"Why you got a crush, kid?" Sunday asked sarcastically.

Gabriel came around the tight turn and back into view. He spoke again, "I just think you could be happier if you spent less time preoccupied with the negative."

Sunday hardly paid attention to Gabriel. He was more interested in watching the unfortunate moonwalk worker who found the rogue piece of Austin's lunch as he jokingly presented his discovery to his partner. His buddy recoiled at the odor of the object thrust into his face. To that, Sunday could not resist smiling.

"I dunno, Kid," Sunday dryly retorted, "They say the best thing about being in a bad mood is the ability to spread it to others."

"But imagine if that we did that with good moods. Lose the things that don't matter, loose the things that cause worry; what you are left with is…"

"It's not that easy kid." Sunday interrupted, "It's hard to look for good in the world when every time you turn around you're getting dumped on." He was about to say more, when Stew walked over. Sunday suddenly realized that the screaming had completely stopped. Stew tossed him a prescription bottle and smiled. Sunday looked down to see that the label read: VALIUM.

Gabriel came back into view and said, "Well, it's like it says in the Book of John…" He vanished around the corner, reappeared and continued, "This is it; this is life, it's the one you get. So, go and have fun…"

"That's the theme to *One Day at a Time*!" Stew shouted as the would-be cherub disappeared around the corner.

As Gabriel came back around, Sunday shut off the ride. The orange plastic horse came to a stop in front of Sunday and Stew, with Gabriel wobbling in the molded saddle.

"Okay… but that doesn't change the fact…" He struggled to slide off his replica steed, "…that I am very dizzy." Disheveled, he collapsed onto the floor.

Hope Daylily Margo approached as Gabriel rose woozily and tried to regain his equilibrium.

"Hey, Sunday." She smiled sweetly at him and nodded simply to Stew and Gabriel. Hope's ailment was by far a favorite of all of the children. Hope "lived life to the second power," as she described it. She learned twice as fast as anyone and matured and aged twice as fast as anyone; the ten year old girl already looked, thought and acted like a twenty year old woman; a rebellious, sullen, sarcastic young woman. What was most interesting about her; however, was that at times it almost seemed as if she could see two seconds ahead of anyone. Over the last few years, she had developed bit of a hellion side as well as a little crush on Sunday. She straightened her fish-net stockings under her grey and black, Catholic school uniform in a manner that she was sure Sunday would notice.

"Who's the new kid?" she asked.

"I'm Gabriel." He replied and handed her a Hallmark from his bag.

"What the fuck is this?" Hope inquired as she looked oddly at the card.

"Just take it" interjected Stew.

"And don't say fuck." Sunday added. Hope winked at him; her grey, wise eyes outlined by a thick black liner, and nodded a thank you to Gabriel.

"I heard Levine is out to kill you." She giggled as she nudged Sunday, "Personally, I would have liked a computer; but the merry-go-round is cool."

"Don't you have homework to do?" he responded.

"Yes," she stated wittily, "I have a midterm to write... on a word processor." She tossed her long, straight black hair over her shoulder.

"Maybe next time, we'll get a computer." Sunday said.

Hope suddenly snapped at attention, much like an attentive gazelle or some kind of meerkat, "Well, you've got about three seconds to figure out how to save your ass, or there won't be a next time."

No sooner had Hope finished speaking, Dr. Levine's voice came over the intercom, "Mr. Sunday, if you're in the building, please report to my office-NOW."

"Shit." Sunday mumbled.

"Don't say shit." Hope smiled coyly as she scolded him mockingly.

"Don't say shit." Sunday repeated to her, but less mockingly. He turned to Stew and motioned to Gabriel; who curiously took in his new surroundings.

"Watch the kid, I'll be back." Sunday sighed, and turned to make the arduous walk to the Head Physician's office.

"Like hell," Stew said from behind, "I wanna hear this."

"Ooh, me too!" bubbled Hope cynically. Without turning around, Sunday heard them begin to follow.

"Can I come too, Mr. Sunday?" shouted Gabriel gleefully as he trotted quickly to catch up.

"Sure, why not?" the janitor gritted through his teeth; and posse' in tow, approached the ominous office door.

Sunday stood outside that door for what seemed like an eternity. Each time he brought himself closer to actually knocking, he quickly retracted his hand, fearing what fate had in store once that door was opened. As he smiled up at the terrified and defeated custodian, Gabriel knocked three times.

"Thanks." Sunday glared at the little boy, who simply nodded with pride as if he had actually assisted in some grand way.

A sweet, "come in" could be heard from the other side of the door. Sunday motioned for the tag-alongs to wait outside and reached for the cold brass doorknob. Head Physician Dr. Margo Levine-Alonzo's office had always reminded Sunday of one of those trophy rooms that overly proud parents have set up for their do-good children. Awards of merit, any merit at all, plastered her walls: Diploma from Emory University, Diploma from West Atlanta High School, and a whole wall dedicated to perfect attendance certificates and candid shots posed with various pseudo-famous people, like the local late night news anchor woman. She even had her completion of C.P.R. training framed and displayed. The only thing different from Dr. Levine and one of those uppity parents, was that Dr. Levine had no kids. These were all her accolades, her accomplishments, her arm draped around the smiling newswoman in the photo. Sunday rarely saw Levine leave her office and he often imagined the room as her own little chamber of solitude where she could sit and waste her time away reliving her past achievements. If she were anything like him, he thought, most days she probably spent her time all alone, wondering where she too went wrong.

However, Dr. Levine was not alone when he opened the door. A nun in her early forties and a teenager sat in the two leather chairs facing Dr. Levine's large mahogany desk. The Head Physician rose from her oversized, burgundy leather chair as soon as Sunday entered and the nun followed suit. Sunday apologetically nodded to the holy woman, who was attired in a simple grey dress; the kind that Julie Andrews wore in *The Sound of Music*, complete with that white, head-thing. Over it she wore a black, leather jacket and a black sash with an intricate green cross-like emblem sewn into it. In the breast pocket, Sunday could see that she had a pair of dark, aviator-style sunglasses. The nun had deep, mocha skin and eyes that looked worn well beyond her age. They were tired eyes that peered over Sunday and sized him up. It made him uncomfortable and he could not bring himself to move more than two steps from the door.

"You wanted to see me?" his asked meekly as his voice cracked.

Head Physician Dr. Margo Levine-Alonzo stared him down and then began to look over the large piles of files and papers stacked high upon her desk; her eyes cold an unmoving through her strangely seductive librarian-style glasses. Sunday's first instinct was to run; run to Mexico, run anywhere and start a new life, but then she spoke.

"You are one piece of work, Mr. Sunday." She said.

"I can explain..." he began.

"First things first." Dr. Levine said, "This is Sister Mary Rochelle. She brings us a select number of the children."

Sunday extended his hand and the nun shook it with a surprisingly tight grip. He had often wondered how the facility had found the children that were not referred from other hospitals or from parents who were all but willing to leave their offspring on the doorsteps with nothing save a small packed suitcase. For the custodian, it felt as if a small mystery had come to a close. The only problem was the answer only led to more questions... like why is the seemingly intelligent, clearly street-wise woman would still bring admit children; when not a single resident had ever recovered. More importantly, why did a nun need a gun? Sunday noticed as she released her grip of his hand that beneath her leather jacket was holstered a white handled hand gun.

Sunday decided not to ask. Instead, he inquired, "How do you do?"

Sister Rochelle nodded.

"…And this," Dr. Levine continued, "is Callym Rafferty, he's being placed here, all the way from Dublin."

The young man didn't move from his chair. Not only were most of his fingers covered with bandages, but he was hand cuffed. Around his chalky neck was a choke-collar with a chain that ran from his throat to Sister Rochelle's right hand. His otherwise motionless face curled ever so slightly at the corners of his lips. His milky eyes, though they had no pupils, squinted a little; as if he were smiling. Sunday figured immediately that the boy was an applicant for the psyche ward.

Dr. Levine swiveled her chair back towards Sunday, held up a finger and began to speak condescendingly, "Now, on to the pressing matter of the carousel."

"I can explain the carousel." Sunday started to say but was instantly cut off as the Head Physician continued her rant.

"Sunday, I believe what we have is a failure to communicate. I want something, but I don't get it. I feel like I give you an order, and I'm presented with something that only barely falls into the wheelhouse of what I had asked for. And what do you get?"

Her question was clearly hypothetical, for as soon as Sunday began to answer, she cut him off again, "You get what we have today, not to mention last week's Zimmerman Pork Incident."

"I can explain that too…"

"There's nothing to explain. That was an awful lot of sausage for a Jewish man." Dr. Levine said.

Sunday could tell that the Zimmerman Pork Incident was too fresh in the Head Physician's mind to rehash his side of the story which led to the ruining of the children's exercise tumbling area that now contained the merry-go-round. Instead, he sighed under his breath, "That was an awful lot of sausage for a Christian man." A comment at which the nun began to giggle.

Dr. Levine shot a glare at the Sister Rochelle, who quickly put a finger to her mouth. It comforted Sunday that despite her apparent surliness; even the holy woman was not immune to having the Head Physician get under her skin.

"I'm concerned that maybe I have given you too much responsibility…" Dr. Levine continued.

"No, no." Sunday interrupted, "Look, after the Zimmerman Pork Incident, I figured that we needed something for the kids that wouldn't be as messy and as difficult to scrub meat stink out of. If you think about it, the carousel is quite practical."

Once again, Sister Rochelle began to laugh.

"Well, you are in luck. The directors saw the delivery guys unloading that thing, and thankfully they sent old Wayland Puttey down here to bring me this." She tossed an envelope to Sunday who looked over the warning notice from the Board of Directors. "Anyone else and I don't know what would have happened; but I was able to sweet talk him." Dr. Levine said with a slight smile.

"Yeah you were!" Sunday said in jubilation as he thought perhaps he was in far less trouble than he had previously assumed.

Dr. Levine's smile got even wider as she added, "I even got him to ride the monstrosity. He loved it." She too began to giggle.

A wave of relief rushed over Sunday, and he could not help but laugh a little too. He felt his stomach relax and his body became less tense. Suddenly, the Head Physician's tone changed again and she started to arbitrarily arrange the many folders.

"Of course, Mr. Sunday, even though the Board of Directors up at the hospital approve of that… thing." Her fingers motioned the carousel, "I feel that we need to make a few changes."

Sunday's throat got tight and he found it hard to swallow. "Effective immediately, we are putting someone else in charge of supervising your team. Someone who has more of a medical background."

"Well, what am I supposed to do then?" Sunday asked; a little devastated at the notion that he was still had been punished despite the approval of the giant merry-go-round.

"You will continue to handle the transportation and janitorial needs for this facility." Dr. Levine said, "And you will train your replacement. And you will do it with a smile."

Just then Kylie Court emerged from the Head Physician's private bathroom. She smiled slightly at Sunday as he dumbfoundedly exclaimed, "Really?"

As a phlebotomist, Kylie had spent much of her time working on the second floor. She was used to only having to deal with the children one at a time and in short, silent doses. The thought of her actually surrounded by the hoard of them at once made Sunday wonder if she was actually up for the task. Nevertheless, he was thrilled that he now had an excuse to spend some time with her.

"Stellar." Sunday said, trying to fight back a huge goofy grin. He was pleased that there was at least a bright side to his demotion.

"Splendid." Said Dr. Levine, "Now that we have all that cleared up, where's Gabriel?"

Suddenly, the office door flung wide open and in ran the winged child, wide-armed, straight at the Head Physician. He gleefully wrapped his arms around her. They all exchanged a cheery, "hello" and the young angel handed her an oversized hallmark. As Kylie greeted the youngster, her sweet southern accent rang in Sunday's ears like beautiful church bells. Gabriel passed out Hallmarks and hugs to everyone in the room as if it were Valentines Day. Gabriel paused a second before he handed Callym his Hallmark. Once he finally did, the white-eyed boy's brow slightly rose as if somewhere deep inside; he was saying "thank you".

After the "hellos" and hugs, Dr. Levine suggested that Sunday lead an impromptu tour of the building for the new guests and so that Kylie could see the facility from his side. He exchanged a short gaze and a small smile with Kylie then a voice from behind him rang, "I'll do it."

Hope stood propped in the doorway. She had a look about her as if she had just been challenged to a hideous dare. Sister Rochelle looked Hope up and down, a little disapprovingly, and directly asked Levine, "Is she an employee?"

"Resident." replied Hope dryly, "But I've been here just as long as Sunday has."

"I think it's a splendid idea." Gabriel cheered.

"That's fine." agreed Dr. Levine, and with a quick eat-shit grin from Hope, the group filed out of the office. Sunday had turned to follow, when the Head Physician stopped him.

"No more headaches, please, Mr. Sunday." She said. The custodian nodded graciously and she added, "I'm counting this as strike two."

Not wanting to push what little luck he had, Sunday thanked her and turned to catch up with the tour.

St Joseph s Medical Pavilion

525 East Peachtree Lane

Atlanta, GA 30031

404-985-3364

To: WonderKids Head Physician Dr. Margo Levine-Alonzo

RE: Warning For Excessive Entertainment Expenses

Dear Head Physician Dr. Margo Levine-Alonzo,

We, the Board of Directors for St. Joseph's Medical Pavilion would first like to state that we value the unique skills you provide our corporation. However, it has been brought to our attention that WonderKids, Inc., a division of St. Joseph's Medical Pavilion has recently exceeded its monetary allotment for entertainment for the residents for this fiscal year while under your supervision. Head Physician Dr. Margo Levine-Alonzo, please note these expenses include but have not been limited to:

- The purchase, delivery and eventual removal of multiple pieces of foam padded exercise mats and equipments.

- Numerous movie tickets.

- Shetland pony rental (2)

- Rental of medieval costumes (2, sized small)

- Purchase of stated medieval costumes, due to damage.

- Revocation of $500 deposit for Shetland ponies due to breach of contract (for details, please refer to legal files titled: *The City of Atlanta vs. The Horse Jousters of East Peachtree*).

- The rental of large barbecue grills.

- The purchase of various snacks and beverages outside of the allotted cafeteria budget; including a large order from Oskar's Sausage Palace and Pork Emporium.

- The rental of numerous carnival items.

- The purchase, delivery and installation of one refurbished carousel.

Please consider this an official warning that any further questionable expenses will result in the re-evaluation of all funding to WonderKids, Inc. and subsequent employee performance evaluations. Head Physician Dr. Margo Levine-Alonzo, we encourage you to take the necessary steps required to ensure that further inquiries are not needed.

[Dictated, but not read.]

Sincerely,

Arthur J. DeQueau, PhD

Arthur J. DeQeau

Wayland Puttey

W. Puttey

William A. Augustine-Chrystine

W.A. A-Chrystine

Francis Benginton III, PhD

Francis Benginton

Thomas Swindle, Esq.

Thomas Swindle

Martha Swindle, PhD

M. Swindle, PhD

The Seventh Seat

(Director Not In Attendance)

Astor VonVanderbraun, PhD

Astor VonVanderbraun Ph

Marvin Perry Snell

MP.Snell

ST JOSEPH S MEDICAL PAVILION   525 East Peachtree Lane
                                      Atlanta, GA 30031

CHAPTER THREE

Lilac. Or maybe...Vanilla?

*S*unday thought to himself as he breathed in the scent of Kylie's hair while they stood tightly pressed into the small elevator along with the would-be angel, complete with fully expanded cardboard wings; the hardcore nun and the zombie-child, who was bound at the hands and feet, as well as their sparse, yet space consuming baggage. Hope had suggested that the tour begin on the top floor so that the boys could drop off their belongings in their new rooms. Once Sunday realized that the quarters would be close, he intentionally positioned himself to be next to Kylie for the trip up.

Maybe it's some kind of lilac/vanilla blend.

He wasn't sure what the scent was, or whether it was coming from her hair or her perfume or what but he savored it. Kylie looked up at him and smiled awkwardly. For a moment, Sunday was afraid that the sound of his deep breathing was audible. He felt the familiar knots that would tend to appear in his throat, stomach and knees when ever he was around her and his mind began to run wild.

What if she heard me?

What if she heard me and now thinks that I am some kind of hair fetishist?

Should I say something?

What should I say?

Has too much time passed for me to say anything?

Maybe lilac and vanilla is just the natural scent of beauty.

Say something.

Do something.

At least smile!

Sunday forced a smile and searched for something to say; however it was Kylie who spoke first, "I hope that you aren't too mad at me for taking this position. They didn't tell me that you were being demoted because of it."

Sunday could tell by the tone in her voice and from her caring expression that she sincerely hoped that he was not angry about their current situation. Not that it mattered; she could be lying for all he cared… he was simply ecstatic that his dream girl was thinking of him in a non-clean-the-trash-bins kind of way.

"It's okay, honest." He replied with a wink that he regretted as soon as his eyelashes met. *So cheesy*, he thought to himself, *never wink again.*

"At least it gives us a chance to get to know each other a little better." She said; winking back as her nervous smile turned to a genuine one, pleased that there was no bitterness between them.

Sunday blushed and smiled back. *Forget what I said about the winking*, he thought.

Hope pushed her way through the doors, and while facing everyone, drug her fingers over the buttons along the side and pressed the top button marked 5. As the metal doors slowly slid closed, she forced a cough to gain her small audience's attention and began to speak in an artificial tone much like a stewardess for a large airliner.

"Welcome to the WonderKids elevator." She began, "This is the only wheelchair accessible way to the upper floors. This elevator provides access to all five floors, as well as the basement." Gesturing towards the laminated certificate on the wall, she continued, "As you can see, this elevator was last inspected by S. Hoffman, who makes his 'n's' look like 'z's' on January of this year. You may also notice that this elevator was installed in 1975…"

"Can you keep it to relevant information, please, Hope?" Sunday asked.

"It is relevant," the young woman defiantly rebutted, "You see…" She began, addressing everyone, "You may have seen the large twin spiral staircases when you came in. They are the main means of getting up and down; and they were built long before 1975. As a matter of fact, this building was the original St. Joseph's hospital during the Civil War. General Lee himself was treated for an infraction of the knee and re-learned to walk by going up and down those very steps."

"That's amazing!" Kylie exclaimed, "I've been here all this time and never knew that."

Sunday leaned to her ear and whispered, "That's because it's not true."

Kylie looked at him, incredibly embarrassed and somewhat astonished that the scantily clad, sarcastic young adult would lie about such a thing. He thought it was adorable and couldn't allow Hope to tarnish her childlike expectations or ruin her opinion of her new job so soon. He leaned back towards her ear, took a quick breath of her lilac and vanilla scent and said softly, "Well, the Civil War thing might be."

Hope coughed again, demanding complete attention. Once Sunday and Kylie both looked back to her, she continued, "Here's a cool tid-bit. When you arrived, you might also have noticed the large fountain at the front of the main pavilion. In the center of the fountain is a statue of St. Joseph holding a cross in one hand and a bible in the other. That statue is based on the original, which can be seen in the front of our building. Unlike the fountain statue; however, the original is missing its arms. Rumor has it that they were used to break down the front doors during the battle for Atlanta; but the truth be told, one day the janitor put way too many bags of trash in his van so that he couldn't see and backed right into it. He knocked it over, causing its current dismemberment."

Everyone laughed and assumed that it was a joke. Sunday once again leaned over at Kylie and whispered shamefully, "Unfortunately, that was true."

The elevator doors opened and Hope faced the small crowd and boldly demanded, "No talking during the tour!" She waved everyone down the long hallway and ushered them past the many doors which lined either side of the hall.

The walls of the boy's floor were a faded blue, except in the corners and where the ceiling met the walls; tiny patches where the paint still retained some of its original vibrant shade. Every door had a construction paper tag with four of the children's names written on it. Some doors also had posters, Velcro dart boards and numerous other decorations. Behind each door was a small common area with old couches and chairs, a shared bathroom and two bedrooms, which each contained a set of bunk beds. Some doors were opened and gave view to children who sat on the couches and worked on homework; other kids in other rooms simply played, talked, and generally did the things that kids do.

Gabriel ran up behind Sunday, tugged on the custodian's pant leg and whispered, "I think I have seen that Callym kid before."

"I doubt it," Sunday whispered back, "Unless you've been to Ireland." The custodian's answer seemed logical enough, but Gabriel did not look convinced.

"All of the windows are lined with safety bars, and the children are paired up two to a bedroom." Hope explained, "Which is cool. Roommates are good because it takes two people to dismantle the windows."

Sunday scowled at Hope, wanting to once again remind her that she represented the facility; but he knew that the notion was futile. Defeated, he looked to Gabriel and directed him to place his bags in the first room on the left. Since they were roughly the same age and since Gabriel had pestered him since their introduction, the custodian decided that the worst punishment he could dole out would be to make the boy bunk with Austin Olsen and force him to deal with the thin layer of vomit and mucus that would soon cover all of his belongings.

Gabriel giddily ran towards the door that listed Austin's name and flung open the door. Sunday could hear him introduce himself to the other two children who bunked in the adjacent room. He assumed Hallmark cards were distributed.

Sunday determined that it would be best for Callym to room with Steve since neither child seemed to be conversationalists. He placed the boy's belongings in the common room, making sure that the nun noted where the room was and made a reach for his pen to add Callym's name to the door.

"Oh, Sunday" Kylie said she began to fumble around in her small purse, "I think I may have something that belongs to you." She rooted around inside the bag and finally produced the little troll pen. Sunday reached out and grabbed it, maybe a little more greedily than he had intended.

"I've been missing this!" He exclaimed, amazed as he lovingly stroked the fuzzy hair on top of the grinning troll's head, "How did you know that it was mine?"

"You just seem like a guy who's in need of a little luck." She laughed, "Plus, that Stewart guy told me it was yours when he lent it to me."

Is it her soap?

There is definitely a hint of vanilla.

Gabriel ran up beside them, wrapped his arms around his new- found friends and said, "Sunday doesn't need luck, he just needs to believe."

"Believe in what?" Kylie asked.

Sunday's eyes rolled up into their lids. He knew from the ride from the airport that Gabriel was about to embarrass him.

"Believe in anything really, so long as it makes him happy." The boy explained, "He's a morose guy, he needs some love." His tinsel halo bobbed as he tilted his head and winked at her.

Sunday bit his lip to keep from saying anything, though he had plenty to say. He tried to think of a subject that would quickly and permanently get them off the topic of him and his problems when Gabriel yipped, "Ooh, a troll pen! Can I see it?"

Sunday finished writing Callym's name on the door and happily handed Gabriel the pen as he hoped that it would silence the young boy's rants. Immediately fascinated by it, Gabriel walked ahead, spinning the pen so that the troll's hair flared out in a fluffy orange sunburst. Sunday took a moment to admire Kylie's porcelain skin and realized that he should probably say something or risk looking extremely creepy again.

"Thank you again, that's just amazing. It's my favorite pen." It was all he could muster.

Hope walked between them and bumped both of their shoulders. "No talking during the goddamn tour." She barked and pushed them toward the open doors of the elevator.

"Watch the "goddamns" around the nun, huh?" Sunday suggested as the young woman brushed by. Sister Rochelle and Sunday both gave Hope a disapproving look; but the unwavering young lady merely walked backwards and waved on the rest of the party to catch up to continue the tour.

- ◦ -

$\mathscr{T}$he group took the spiral stairs down to the girls'
floor. The layout for the girls' dormitories was similar to the
floor above, however the walls were purple and retained their
deep hue. Instead of posters and dartboard, the walls were
filled with paper flowers and inspirational blurbs tacked to
corkboards. The group walked down the hall and took note of
the glittery and bubbly way all of the names were written on
the doors until they reached the only door painted red; a deep,
blood red. Dark and large calligraphy spelled out:

HOPE DAYLILY'S ROOM

KEEP THE F___ OUT

Over the "UCK" was a giant smiley face sticker that
Sunday had put on when Hope went through her I-deserve-
my-privacy-and-I-refuse-to-censor-my-feelings phase.

"To your left you will see my room," Hope explained,
"as the "oldest" patient here at Wonder Kids; I'm the only one
with their own room. The most important thing to take from
this tour is stay away from this room. I'm serious, keep the
f…"

"We can all read the sign, Hope." Sunday interrupted.
He smiled a forced smile at Sister Rochelle, in hope for
approval, or at least acknowledgement of his effort. She only
shook her head slightly.

They all circled around the small hallway and walked
back toward the stairs, passing room after room. Sister
Rochelle mumbled something only audible to her catatonic
captive. Sunday sighed under his breath afraid that the nun's
poor opinion of the facility could lead him to more office time
with Head Physician Margo Levine-Alonzo. The only two in
the group who seemed content with the tour thus far were the
wide eyed Gabriel and the motionless Callym. Sunday
concluded that he would get the same effect from each of the
boys if he presented them both with a simple granite rock.

A beeping came from Sister Rochelle's watch and she
pulled her end of the chain taut, which caused the leashed lad
to stop. She reached into her leather jacket and removed a

small, black leather case. She ran the zipper around the edges and produced a syringe and a tiny vial filled with a cloudy, blue liquid. She rolled up the boy's sleeves, exposed his scar-riddled arm and slowly pushed the needle into the boy's vein. Hope watched as if entranced as a tiny bit of Callym's blood went into the syringe and turned the liquid purple before the nun pushed the plunger, injecting the child with the concoction. The milky whiteness of Callym's eyes suddenly swirled like they had been shaken and his body went as limp as an unused marionette puppet. The nun silently replaced the syringe, zipped the case closed and placed it back in her jacket.

"Um," Hope said, with a befuddled shake in her voice, "This concludes the tour of the fourth floor. Please make your way back to the stairs."

— ◎ —

*T*he middle floor of WonderKids housed the classrooms. Moderate sized classes sat on opposing sides of the hall. The children's artwork was taped to the doors of the classrooms for the younger kids. Pictures of crayon colored, multi-racial stick figures who all held hands under a crudely drawn sun; a purple unicorn that galloped on what may have been a rainbow; abstract pieces in which rudimentary triangles intersected with multiple circles...*perhaps it was a pizza?* Classrooms for the older kids did not have such décor.

Hope stopped in the middle of the hallway and continued her stewardess ruse, "These are the classrooms. If you like, you can attend classes at the Catholic school down the street. But, if for some reason you decide you can't, or if a school setting isn't right for you, the staff holds classes here during the week. You'll learn the same material; and all the tests are open book." She laughed at her own joke. When no one joined in, she continued, "And you miss the chance to get asked to the winter mixer." Once again no one laughed. Hope gestured toward Callym and asked, "Can he even hear me?"

Callym slowly and quite eerily nodded. Sister Rochelle concurred and added, "He can hear you; he's just heavily sedated."

Hope clapped right by the boy's head. Callym hardly responded at all. "I'll say." She finally agreed, "Well, in that case, let's move on to the medical floor."

—◉—

*U*nlike the rest of WonderKids; which always seemed to have the lingering smell of sweaty, playing children no matter how hard Sunday and Stew tried to scrub it away, the second floor was always kept surprisingly clean and smelled of ammonia and iodine. The odor was reminiscent of the actual hospital up on the hill. On either side of the long hallway were various examination rooms, the nurses offices, Kylie's former lab office and a small emergency room; for any serious problem that should occur.

After they passed all of the nurses' offices, Hope escorted them into Examination Room 1. The examination rooms all resembled a traditional medical room. A giant padded chair rested in the middle, a long metal arm extended from its base and held an overhead spotlight. A smaller chair on wheels sat beside it and the cabinets that lined the walls were blue Formica. Sister Rochelle led Callym by his chain leash and inspected the countertop by running her finger over it. She studied the lack of grime that was lifted up and gave an approving nod.

Hope stood just in front of the vacant patient's chair, hands once again clasped and explained, "WonderKids is first and foremost a care center for freaks and nut- bars." she began, "All of the children are required to have at least a short physical once a month. Some of the kids need more; some of them are in here every day." Hope explained.

"How often are you in here?" Gabriel chimed in.

"More than once a month." Hope replied dryly in a tone that showed she did not want to talk about her treatments. Due to her condition, Hope was subjected to intense physicals once a week; and ever since she hit puberty at age six, they seemed to take a toll on her. Instead of delving, she led everyone into the next exam room, which happened to be occupied.

In the large chair in the center of the room sat Heavy Paul. Paul was a skinny-looking fourteen year old. He had choppy shoulder length hair, wore baggy clothes that suited his skateboarding fascination, and his skin was a powdery aqua blue-green. Two I.V. needles ran from his left arm to a large shiny drip bag hanging nearby. Nurse Durby noted his readings on a clipboard. She was so entranced in her work that she paid little attention when the bunch entered the room behind Hope. Either that or she just didn't care.

"This is Heavy Paul." Hope explained to the guests. Paul lifted his arm and waved, "Paul has been with us since he was eight, and over the last two years has become quite the extreme sportsman. Skateboarding, biking, you name it, Paul does it."

"Why is that boy blue?" Gabriel whispered up to Sunday.

"That's because he's a freak too." stated Hope, "We're all freaks. Just like you. We're all just a bunch of screamers, pukers, sleepers and losers. There was even an invisible guy at one time, but I haven't seen him in a while." She smiled at Gabriel, "He was shy. You know, kept to his self."

"I have a rare condition," Explained Heavy Paul, "My body doesn't receive the same electric impulses the normal body does. When I first got here I couldn't move. I was in a wheel chair and everything."

Sunday looked down at Gabriel who rummaged through his backpack in a rush. Then he looked over at Kylie, who smiled at him. He awkwardly smiled back.

"Once a week I come up here and the nurses pump a thin liquid brass into my tissue; the metal conducts the impulses and I can move." The azure boy continued.

"And now he's fast as shit." Hope testified.

Sunday nudged her ribs and whispered through his teeth, "Language, Christ!"

"The only problem is that I get all sweaty and it tarnishes my skin. That's why I'm blue." explained Paul.

"Why do they call you Heavy Paul?" asked Gabriel as he handed the boy a hallmark. He held one out to the unresponsive nurse. Once he realized that Nurse Durby was not interested in him, he finally set it down on the counter.

"He weighs like two-hundred and sixty pounds." said Hope.

"It's all the brass." Paul grinned.

Sister Rochelle nodded again, smiled at Heavy Paul and left the room. It was her signal that she was ready to move on. Hope led them to the end of the hall. A large locked door led to the pharmacy and a giant double paned window that gave view to shelves upon shelves of colorful little bottles.

"Welcome to Pill Alley." said the gleeful Hope, "This is where the nurses keep everyone's medicine. Here you'll find your uppers, your downers, your gigglers, your criers, your touchers, your hazers, your feelers and fliers."

Sunday didn't like the way Hope's eyes tingled as she went down her list. She looked over at the lucid Callym and sized him up. Sunday could tell she was devising some sort of devious scheme.

He had often suspected that she occasionally snuck into the pharmacy to sample the children's medications; so he was not surprised when she coyly asked, "So, what are you on?"

Sister Rochelle answered for the boy, who had yet to change expression, "He's on a high dosage of Lithium Validemerethyzine."

Hope recoiled at the sound of the treatment, "That's not a real drug."

"It is for Callym." The nun responded, "It's the only thing that keeps him… quelled."

Hope's mischievous twinkle in her eye immediately faded and Sunday could see that at that she truly felt sorry for the boy. Hope crouched down to look him in his milky white eyes and sweetly said, "I think there's someone you'll want to meet."

Hope pointed out the fire route and noted that it was oddly enough the best place to sneak smokes and then led the party down the final set of spiral stairs. Gabriel's little legs scurried down the steps as he led the line and looked in his bag frantically for the perfect Hallmark. Hope, who was directly behind him, informed the boy, "You should probably just save this one."

Halfway to the second floor, Kylie and Sunday fell back a few steps, "You having' fun?" he asked.

Kylie had an expression of sheer astonishment and wonder as she nodded. "It's funny; this place seems like a whole other world when you aren't stuck on the second floor."

"It's definitely different." Sunday agreed, "But the kids like it." He added as he motioned towards Gabriel.

"Speaking of Gabriel," she asked, "What's his deal anyway?"

"He's an angel." Sister Rochelle interjected in a dry voice from behind them as she led Callym slowly down the stairs; the chains that bound his feet clanged and rattled as he raked them across the stone steps.

Hope held the door open, and Gabriel's attention was immediately drawn back to the carousel and the laughing children riding it. As Callym descended the stairs, Hope took his hand and said, "This way."

Sister Rochelle looked back approvingly as Hope led the vacant child off. She placed her hand on Sunday's shoulder and said, "The facility is lovely, but someone needs to keep an eye on that young woman."

Sister Rochelle's demeanor seemed that of steel, with equal parts coldness and hardness and it visibly intimidated Sunday to where he felt the need to oblige her, not out of duty or respect, but because he feared what the consequences of crossing her would be. He gulped and nodded emphatically.

Amid the frolicking children in the main room, Austin Olsen jogged to the group. Sniffling through his rubbed red nose, he greeted them. Sunday saw out of the corner of his eye that Gabriel was already rummaging in his bag.

"Austin, this is Gabriel. He's your new roommate." He said, introducing the two children.

Austin said hello and Gabriel offered him a bright green card. Austin extended a sticky, doughy hand and took it.

"How are you feeling?" Sunday asked.

"Just the sniffles; not as bad as before." Austin snorted and went for a Kleenex in his pocket, "not even close to the quickening."

"Quickening?" Kylie asked.

Austin looked up at the Assistant Nurse and explained, "Sunday says that one day I will just empty out... or explode. We call it the quickening."

"Well, it sounds like Sunday has all the answers." She winked.

"He's the best." proclaimed the portly boy.

Sunday blushed and grinned awkwardly. Just then a bubble formed out of Austin's left nostril and popped. He smiled blushingly, cupped his hands and caught the stream of mucus that began to pour from his nose as if a faucet had turned on inside his head. He did not need to say anymore. Sunday asked him to get cleaned up and then suggested that he show Gabriel to the carousel. The winged boy exclaimed, "Really! What about the rest of the tour?"

"Austin can show you the rest." he suggested, and the two boys ran off, already seeming like long time friends.

Sunday and Kylie caught up with Hope and her audience outside of the room that currently contained the comatose boy. Multi- colored streamers still lined the door. They walked inside the room, and Hope moved to the foot of the bed. She was flanked on either side by Mylar balloons. She focused on Callym, whose milky gaze was fixed on the gentle sway of one of the shiny, metallic balloons.

"This is Steve." She whispered the name, "He's been asleep all his life. He just dreams."

Callym slowly moved his head to look upon his lulling peer, his lips parted and the faintest hint if a grin emerged... and sort of froze that way.

Sister Rochelle picked up Steve's files and began thumbing through them, "Why do you whisper his name?" She asked.

"Well, he's been in a coma since he was born;" Hope began, "and Sunday's theory is that Steve is narcoleptic..." Sunday felt his stomach tighten as all eyes shifted to him, "...you know like the goats?"

Sister Rochelle nodded and looked back down at the file, a little more intensely.

"Anyways," Hope continued, "Sunday believes that the word Steve is the trigger. I whisper because I believe him."

"Thanks." Sunday mumbled, only half meaning it.

"No problem" She bubbly replied.

"It's his birthday today, too." Kylie added.

Sunday and Hope exchanged a glance. It was clear that this was new information to them. Sister Rochelle was now buried in the documents in front of her. Kylie continued, "Yeah, I found out last week it was his birthday. That's why we have the moonwalk and the ball pit and everything today. I talked Head Physician Dr, Margo Levine- Alonzo into getting a few things to celebrate for him."

Sunday was floored. It sounded like just the kind of manipulative maneuvering that he had used to get the merry-go-round. If he had any real doubts about her performance as his supervisor, they were now gone. "That's brilliant." He complimented.

As is whatever that scent is.

Hope suggested the tour conclude in the play area, and she led Kylie and Callym, by his leash, out of the room. Sunday lagged behind to check on Steve. He had little idea how to read all of the gauges for Steve's little tubes; but he faked it to look a bit more professional to the nun, who continued to flip through Steve's file.

"You know him don't you?" Sunday finally asked. The holy woman nodded.

"You brought him here didn't you?" he asked and she nodded again.

"Why did you bring him *here?*" he said.

She closed the file and looked at Sunday straight in the eye.

"I get a file; like this one" she held it up, "and I find the kids and take them where it says to take them."

"Who sends it?" Sunday asked, but got no answer. Sister Rochelle's attention was back into the file. He tried another question, "Who pays for all of this? Why these kids? Where are Steve's parents?"

Sister Rochelle simply put her finger over her lip in a shushing manner. Sunday sighed and turned to look out the window and watched Callym thoughtlessly sway slightly back and forth, more like a plant than a person as Kylie readied him for the carousel.

"Sister?" he asked, "What's wrong with him?"

She looked up and smiled mockingly, "Maybe he's narcoleptic."

"No, Callym. Why…"

The nun cut him off, "…is he sedated? Let's say that Steve really is narcoleptic, and Gabriel is a perfect angel… well, then Callym is the exact opposite of both." She closed the file and walked out the door.

— ◎ —

*S*unday found the girls on the merry-go-round. Hope rode on the black horse and gave Sunday a sarcastically enthusiastic thumbs-up as she held the long chain that led to Callym; who sat upon the purple, plastic steed directly behind her. They were followed by the giggling duo of Austin Olsen and Gabriel who rode side by side on green and blue plastic ponies.

"This is great!" Kylie said as she rounded the corner, riding the only unicorn on the carousel; "This was your idea?" Sunday blushed and nodded a modest yes.

"Nice job." She complimented, "…and narcoleptic name triggers. You're quite impressive."

Sunday could only think to say, "I try."

She winked and orbited out of Sunday's view. As they completed their rotation, he caught Hope's eyes as they locked onto his; then her gaze darted to Stew, across the room. A split second later, his voice came over the intercom, "Ladies and Gentleman, Wonder Kids proudly brings you…"

Sunday grabbed Kylie by her gloved hand and said, "Come with me. You're gonna have to learn to do this."

He walked her over to Stew and the small gathering of children that already began to sit cross-legged on the floor. Sunday climbed on the table where Stew stood as his co-worker announced the song, "For the Longest Time."

As the music spilled from the nearby player piano the children cheered all throughout the facility. It was clear that this was a fan favorite. Stew handed Sunday the panel's second intercom receiver and from the table top they began to sing, "*Whoa, oh, oh, oh; for the longest time.*"

A forced falsetto came from Stew as he attempted the backing vocals, "*Ti-ime!*"

Kylie sat with the gathering group of children on the floor as the men sang and danced to the song. Hope watched from the back of the crowd; arms folded. It was difficult to tell just by looking at her if she enjoyed the spectacle or if she felt embarrassment for the guys. Like two bumbling fools, they shuffled about the table with the confidence of Fred Astaire.

"If you said goodbye to me tonight;

There would still be music left to write.

What else can I do?

I'm so inspired by you; that hasn't happened for the longest time..."

After the song had ended, and bows had been taken; Sunday noticed Sister Mary Rochelle standing outside of Levine's office. She nodded approvingly, and walked back in the door. New found friends, Gabriel and Austin trotted over to where Sunday and Kylie stood. Gabriel smiled ear to ear and exclaimed, "That was amazing."

Austin, who now wore Gabriel's wire and tinsel halo agreed, "I told you the guys are great."

Sunday raised one eyebrow, "What is on your head?" Sunday asked disapprovingly.

"I'm an angel too." The tubby child replied.

Sunday snatched it off his head and gave it back to Gabriel, "You're a touch-stuffer is what you are."

"A what?" Kylie giggled.

"A touch stuffer. One who touches stuff." Austin replied, "But I am not one, I was an angel."

"We only have room for one." Sunday added, "Now, go play."

The two boys ran off, and Kylie shouted after them, "It was nice meeting you!"

"And at some point I want that pen back!" Sunday followed, suddenly remembering that the little boy still had it.

For the first time, Kylie and Sunday were absolutely alone. There was a brief moment of silence between the two as they listened to Head Physician Dr. Margo Levine- Alonzo give her traditional welcoming speech to the new residents and staff members. It was essentially the same speech and the same motherly tone that Sunday had heard her use every "New Admission's Day", with the only changes being the names of the new individuals. He began to mouth along to the speech, much to Kylie's amusement.

"Hello all, this is Head Physician Dr. Margo Levine-Alonzo. I would like to welcome you to WonderKids' New Admission's Day. As you have hopefully already seen, WonderKids is dedicated to ensuring development and growth, while taking special consideration for each child's special needs.

Today we welcome Gabriel and Callym to the family. As a resident of the facility, I will see to your education, health and care with the assistance of my skilled staff, which I am confident you will find loving and attentive. As a resident of the facility, I would like you to take advantage of my open door policy. If you ever wish to speak to me, about anything at all, just knock on the door that reads HEAD PHYSICIAN MARGO LEVINE- ALONZO, PhD. As a resident of this facility, it is likely that you haven't had the best of home life. Perhaps your parents couldn't care for you as you needed; perhaps you were moved from hospital to hospital. As a resident of this facility, I hope that you learn to love your new home as we all have; but most importantly, as a resident of this facility, I hope you know that you are now part of our family.

The same goes to our new staff members. Today we welcome to the family Owen Drislensen, our new accountant; Elaine Weir, who will be replacing our former Phlebotomist, Kylie Court, who has been promoted to Director of Resident Affairs."

Everyone began to clap and Sunday could see that Kylie was turning a bit red. He faced her and joined in the applause.

"Seriously, congratulations." He said once the congratulations had stopped. She bashfully nodded in acceptance, squeaked out a small "thanks" and stared at her shoes. Sunday rummaged through his mind for something witty to say. Meanwhile, the Head Physician continued with her introductions;

She's so cute and modest.

She smells just like what heaven should smell like.

"New staff members please be aware that you too are now considered family and I want to also encourage you to feel free to come to me when necessary. Appointments can be made a day in advance."

While he searched for the perfect thing, Sunday watched Kylie turn to admire the children who were attentively staring at the speakers as the Head Physician spoke. He took the opportunity to really take her in and attempted to etch her image into his mind. He got lost somewhere in the smooth curves of her silky neck and suddenly, found words spilling out of his mouth, "Simply amazing."

He recoiled at his error, and for a moment thought for sure that he had just made a fool of himself. Kylie turned back and pointed to the children, "They are just so adorable."

"You know," she added, looking around, "this place is…" Sunday was relieved to see that she too was a word searcher.

"…Stellar?" he suggested.

"Yeah." She agreed, "I like that."

Sunday shrugged modestly, "The older kids keep me up with all the new slang."

"Maybe you can teach me some tomorrow when you teach me more about working on the floor?"

His heart skipped a tick, and then dropped, "I don't know how much training Levine is going to let me give you."

Kylie got feigningly serious and tossed her head back, "I'll just have to go insist on it." Without missing a beat, she began to walk in the direction of the Head Physician's office. She stopped and turned back to Sunday and added with a smirk, "You know, the singing… that was kinda cute."

"You're gonna need to make an advanced appointment." He teased. He knew she heard him, because she stopped mid-step, looked back at him and giggled.

"Stellar." Sunday whispered to himself as he watched her walk off, her hips sashaying to the left and right. After a ridiculous amount of time just watching her walk, Hope, who had apparently been eaves dropping, snuck up behind him. She put her hands on her hips, and jauntily tossed her hair from left to right.

"Stellar." She said in a false bubbly voice. Before Sunday could even think of a retort, she brushed her hand down Sunday's arm and said, "I'll see you later."

He was a little embarrassed that she was mocking his best abilities at being charming and got an uneasy chill down his arm where her fingers had gently caressed him.

"Don't forget to write that report!" he called to her.

Hope turned around and pointed towards the speaker, "Apparently, you aren't the boss of me anymore."

She directed his attention back to Kylie, who was waiting by the Head Physician's office door. Once she heard Dr. Levine say, "...so once again, this is Head Physician Dr. Margo Levine-Alonzo. Welcome to WonderKids;" she knocked on the door, winked at Sunday and walked in. Hope looked back at Sunday, shook her head and strutted up the spiral stone steps to her bedroom.

Sunday felt fortunate that no one was paying much attention to him at that moment, because there was no containing the goofy smile that had come over him. The custodian felt a long forgotten feeling- a sort of verge-of-happiness feeling that accompanies anticipation of something special. It was the feeling that awoke children on Christmas Eve, the feeling that he imagined awoke Billy Joel on the night that he wrote that song, the feeling that awoke Sunday from his regular monotony. He finally felt that there was something to look forward to, some kind of silver lining to his typically grey existence.

Lilac and vanilla. God bless that lilac and vanilla.

CHAPTER FOUR

*C*allym Rafferty stood motionless, expressionless and silent; a lone wallflower in the recreation area where the other children frolicked, filling the room with glee and rambunctious noise. His lack of irises made it hard to tell what he was focused on, but he appeared to be staring intensely at something. His head cocked to the side, strained from the weight of the loose chains which draped down from his neck and wrists and linked his feet together at the ankles. They seemed excessive to Gabriel and Austin Olsen who had been observing the young man for at least twenty minutes.

It began as simple, childish curiosity as the two boys initially stole quick glances from the ball pit once Austin noted that Callym had yet to move since he had been taken off of the carousel. A few minutes and a few dares later, the duo had inched and crept their way directly in front of him, astonished that with the exception of the rising of his chest as he inhaled, Callym had not wavered in the slightest.

Austin swayed his hand in front of Callym's face but the boy did not flinch, "It's the weirdest thing." He commented.

"I swear I've seen him before." Gabriel said with a frustrated tone, "I just can't seem to place it."

"I don't see how you could forget a kid like this;" Austin sniffled as he bravely took a few steps closer, "he's so creepy."

Austin moved his face inches from Callym's, and still Callym did not acknowledge his presence. The chubby child noted how the cloudy, white liquid that filled Callym's eyes swirled and twisted around.

"His eyes freak me out." He said as he turned back to Gabriel, and then with a mischievous grin added, "Hey, I dare you to come touch him.

"What?" Gabriel asked innocently.

"Come here and touch him. I bet he's all cold and leathery." Austin teased.

Gabriel hesitated and adjusted his backpack straps. "C'mon don't be a chicken. Touch him." Austin prodded.

Gabriel shrugged and enthusiastically replied, "Okay." He stepped up to Callym and reached out his finger, but could not bring himself to touch the boy.

"Do it." Austin whispered.

"I'm gonna;" Gabriel replied as his finger quivered mere fractions away from Callym's pale cheek, "don't rush me."

"Sorry, I'm excited." said Austin, who was so overwhelmed with anxiousness that he too had begun to shake.

"It's okay." Gabriel replied. He took a deep breath, gulped and prepared himself for the daring task of moving his index finger millimeters to its target. Just as the tiniest tip of his finger flesh reached Callym's cheek… unexpectedly, Callym blinked.

The movement startled both Gabriel and Austin to the point that they jumped backwards and shrieked. "That scared the you-know-what outta me!" Austin panted as he hunched over and waited for his heart to slow back to its regular pace.

"I know; me too." Gabriel agreed.

"Is he cold and leathery?" Austin Olsen asked.

"No;" Gabriel commented while straightening his cardboard wings, "maybe a little cold, but he's more greasy than leathery."

"Gross." Austin Olsen concluded.

Both of the boys kept a safe distance, awaiting the statuesque Callym to lunge at them at any moment. Once they determined that Callym would not be moving and that it was safe to step forward again, Gabriel asked, "Do you think he even felt it?"

Indeed, Callym did feel the tap of Gabriel's finger, and were it not for the Lithium Validemerethyzine which prevented him from acting on any impulse; he would have relished nothing more than to hear the dull thud of the two boy's heads as he smashed them together over and over again until there was nothing left, save two mushy lumps. However, the strong, blue concoction that coursed through him made it impossible for his brain to tell his body to attack. Having been robbed of his own will for so long, Callym had gotten used to serving the time in the prison that was his mind by replaying old memories and allowing his thoughts to run wild.

He imagined himself jumping at the boys, maybe pulling the fat one to him by the hair and biting into his thick ear while with his other hand his fingers would dig into the angel's face until he had blinded him.

He found himself lost in scenes of his home Ireland; lost in memories of life on Camden Street, the masses of people bustling about, running the random errands of their simple, modern existences all around the backdrop of Dublin's ancient architecture. He remembered The Cake Café on Pleasants Place. The recalled the sweet smell of cakes and cookies baking in the hidden ovens which were located behind the glass counter. He remembered reaching over that counter when Old Lady Olivia O'Lannigan was not looking to steal a couple of icing covered sugar cookies, placing them in his coat pocket and running through the Daintree Building to the far end of the courtyard. There he would perch behind the benches and slowly eat his pilferings.

He dreamed of taking hold of the chains that bound his wrists and how if he could, he would wrap them tightly around Sister Rochelle's throat until all the air had escaped her. He imagined how her body would tremble as he squeezed and how her eyes would bulge, roll upwards and eventually grow very still. He pictured himself releasing her lifeless body as it fell in slow motion to the ground. Maybe next he would steal a car and drive it all the way to Mexico… or Canada. Either way, he was sure that he would leave a fiery path of destruction in his wake all the way to the border.

Callym thought back to the lush ivy that lined Iveagh Gardens and entangled the stone carvings of the gods which were scattered through out the park. He remembered the rows of old Georgian houses along the back of the park. He recalled the widow who lived there and how she used to leave bag upon bag of unattended garbage. He remembered the smell and the rats that would plague the trash bins.

He imagined himself a Nazi lieutenant, in full regalia, abducting and torturing a small family. He imagined himself a Mongol, burning a village while he mowed down the inhabitants. He imagined pulling the lever which dropped the floor and hung an innocent cattle driver, the assault of an elderly woman and the killing of an adorable puppy. He imagined these things and saw himself awash in a pool of blood.

Callym Rafferty recalled the mildewed smell of the burlap sack that he used to gather the rats and the way the rodents crawled upon each other as he tied the bag closed- the shrill squeaking that came from the sack as the creatures attempted to fight their way to freedom. He remembered running back through the center of the park and hiding deep in the garden's maze. It was there that he reached into the sack and removed a milk carton and a squealing creature and placed them both on a rock. Illuminated only by the moonlight, Callym crushed the animal with a small craft hammer.

Callym watched, unable to tell the two boys who continued to stare at him that their behavior was rude. He was unable to ask to play. He was unable to ask the staff to sing another song. He was unable to tell Gabriel that he too thought that the boy appeared familiar.

He thought back to how he held the dying rodent over the milk carton and watched it twitch as the blood ran from its broken body. Once he no longer felt a pulse, Callym tossed the corpse over the wall, reached in the bag and repeated the process until the bag was empty. In the end, he had overflowed the milk carton and carried it down Camden Street to White Friar Church, dripping a scarlet trail behind him.

Callym envisioned himself a soldier in a great battle. He fought mighty enemies along side an army of vicious demons. He saw himself push a rapier through a soldier's silver armor, his white garb quickly staining red as he fell to the fog covered ground. Callym swung his sword in an arch and beheaded another member of the silver army. He saw himself engaging in battle with the winged child who stood in front of him wearing a similar silver chest plate- blade of fire clashed against blade of fire.

He summoned all the will he had. He had past the apex of the effects of the chemicals that had hold of him. He knew that if he focused enough he could perhaps force his body to perform a simple task. Maybe at least scare the boys again before Sister Rochelle would return with another syringe and he would once again be completely captive to his mind.

Callym remembered how he past by the endless rows of candles, the relics of St. Valentine and proceeded to the Shrine of St. Albert. It was here that hundreds of the Sunday Morning faithful would place their hands in the water and touch the liquid to their foreheads, hearts and lips in the hopes to be blessed; and it was here where Callym emptied his milk container.

His mind played visions of war; bayonets clanging against bayonets, anguished cries of newly orphaned children who sat in blood-soaked streets as tears streaked their soiled faces. A symphony of terrifying sounds echoed in his head and provided the soundtrack and the young man could do no more than accept it all.

"I'm sure he feels it." Austin Olsen burped, "Unless he's like zombie or something." He reached out and touched Callym's earlobe, "He doesn't react to anything!"

Just then, using all of his effort; Callym rolled his head towards Austin Olsen's and frighteningly flashed a menacing, stained-toothed smile.

— ◎ —

Sunday and Stew completed their regular custodial checklist and teamed up to finish cleaning the final remnants of the party trash, cutting up and ribbing each other the whole time. All the while, Sunday stole glances to the Head Physician's door in the hopes that Kylie Court would reemerge. When the main floor was finally clean, the custodians played a round of paper-rock-scissors to decide who would send the children to their rooms for the night and who would take out the garbage. Sunday choose paper and had taken the garbage bags down to the basement and threw what materials he could into the incinerator. The rest went in the dumpster outside.

When he finished, Sunday walked over towards the Head Physician's office, to let her know that he was clocking out and so that he could see Kylie Court and tell her goodnight. As he approached, he heard the muffled sound of arguing. He quietly approached closer and attempted to decipher what was being said. Once he realized that this was impossible, the custodian slowly and stealthily turned the knob and inched the door open.

Sister Rochelle paced within the office and as she debated with the Head Physician, who wanted to lower Callym's medication upon his admission.

"...Without his medication, that boy is prone to fits of rage, violent mood swings, suicidal tendencies and God knows what else. I highly recommend keeping him on that regiment." She said forcefully.

Head Physician Dr. Margo Levine-Alonzo sat behind her desk and stated directly, "There is not one child in this building that is put on medication without a documented and valid reason. I am not in the business of doping these kids all willy-nilly, just to keep them complacent; and I am most certainly not comfortable injecting that child with an uncertified substance." She folded her hands on top of Callym Rafferty's file and leaned back in her overstuffed chair. "I'll tell you something else, you have a better chance of me crawling up under that habit of yours and making you feel like a natural woman before I go approving the order to keep that boy chained."

Furious, the nun slammed her hands down on the desk, "Look, you have zero chance of curing this boy. This place is nothing more than a dumping ground for these kids, and you know it." She calmed herself slightly, stood back up, folded her arms and appologized, "I'm sorry Margo; I didn't mean that."

The Head Physician nodded forgivingly and the nun continued, "I have spent time with him, and I am begging you. For your own good, and as a favor to me, keep that kid on that medication, and keep him on a very short and tight leash."

"Sorry to interrupt." Sunday said as he knocked lightly to make his presence known, "I just wanted to let you know that I was taking off for the night."

Head Physician Dr. Margo Levine-Alonzo waved him on. Sunday was relieved that she was too engrossed in her debate with Sister Rochelle that she failed to assign him some sort of last minute task. He quickly turned to exit the room before she could change her mind. He nodded to the nun, who nodded back at him as he closed the door.

He circled the main floor twice before he determined that he was not going to be able to tell Kylie Court goodnight. Disheartened, he waved to Stew and made his way through the double doors that led into the parking lot. Sunday looked up and counted the handful of stars that were not obscured by the bright lights of the city. The night sky was a luminescent blue and the moon glowed hazily through a patch of deep grey clouds. As Sunday gazed upward, he heard a voice come from across the way.

"Hey!" Kylie shouted as she hovered over the raised hood of her beat-up, blue Bronco, "What do you know about cars?"

Sunday walked over to her and offered to look at the engine. Even though he knew not thing one about the mechanical workings of the vehicle, he rubbed his chin and toyed with valves and hoses. In between "mmm hmms," he inquired, "So, did you give Levine a piece of your mind?"

"What?" she replied, "Oh, honestly… no. I chickened out. I did finish my 401K forms" she quipped with a thumb-up.

Sunday laughed and fiddled with a belt until he felt secure in saying, "Yep."

"What is it?" Kylie asked.

"Looks to me like you need a lift." He waited for her to laugh at his attempt at cuteness or at least the notion of having to ride around in Sunday's van. He was utterly shocked when she accepted. They walked to the van; Sunday opened the passenger door for her and drove her home.

Sunday's Notebook

Oct. 12   Colossus Pizza: (770) 123-1052

Well, here we are. My first notebook entry. i was told this would help give me new perspective. So far, the only perspective i have is that this is kinda girly. Dr. Shayam said that it didn't matter what i wrote as long as i tried to write something everyday. Right now, i have really nothing to say at all. so i guess we can start by writing about what i am doing. Right now i am watching tv. Not crappy tv. News.

i just saw a news article on tv about a pop star and her latest party exploits. Is that even news? Do we really live in a world where this is the top story of all the things that happened in the world today?

Other stories on today's news:

Shooting in Marietta

Mugging on MARTA   **Shopping List**

Scandal and disapproval of the president   **Coke**

Political strife   **Milk**

More political strife   **Pop-Tarts, grape**

Starlets try to quell political strife   **Sandwich turkey**

by adopting war-torn babies   **cheese**

Football star gets DUI   **cereal**

Storms are here to stay   **soap, shampoo, etc.**

Falcons loose

Celebrity gossip, celebrity gossip, celebrity gossip

i've decided that the news is depressing. Are we really this far gone? i feel empty having seen it.

Oct. 16

Hello again notebook,

Bills   ive been doing this for a few days ive still no idea

rent— $800   what im supposed to gain from all of this. ive sat and

van note— $250   stared at the blank pages until i just ramble just like

insurance— $115   i am right now. Looking back, this week i have given

internet/cable— $150   plot summaries for 3 sitcoms, wrote about how

electricity— $70   i hate traffic, how the news is depressing and don't

credit card— (pay next month)   see how any of it is supposed to help.

Total— $1115   from now on, im going to write my entries in haiku.

Today

Today was shitty.

Im not being dramatic,

Austin crapped his pants.

Could be Worse?

Nothing works for me,

Id stay in bed, but it broke.

But could it be worse?

I Wish

Oh God, how I wish

That the Wonder Kids would bathe,

Smells like spleen spirit.

Ode to My Notebook

Spiral and loose leafed;

You should have eighty pages

...but I tore out three.

JOBS

~~Driver, ABC— Mon thru Fri~~

~~Temp Agency— 1) 777-1221~~

~~Janitor—~~

(Orish)

N is because this will Never work.

O you are the Only one for me.

T is for the Time we have shared.

E is for Every line ive written

B is for the Binding on your spine.

O is for Orgasm, cause it's funny.

O is for Orgasm, see it's funny.

K, maybe im the only one who thinks
            it's funny.

Oct. 21   —Why don't they make grape Pop-Tarts anymore?

Unicorns   This Morning

Leprechauns were real,   I heard no alarm

Unicorns used to exist,   Still dressed in yesterday's pants

They were delicious.   (@every other day)

                                    This Afternoon

                                Im master of mops

                            Sticky kids and sticky floors

                              Filth and funk be warned.

Later on today   Night before 3

Daydreams while dusting   Molly has the flu

I fight fires, a cop, space-man   She screams out of frustration

Anything but this.   I cant hear a thing.

                                      Tonight

                                Lazy, lounging night

                              Heated Hot-Pocket dinner

                                 Me, TV and beer

                              Later while im buzzed

                            Saw the news today, oh boy.

                              Brother kills brother

                                Maybe its just me

                            But it seems were all off track

                            Where'd we put the maps?

        Emus   On Dating

  These birds are kick-ass   Sure, Stew saw her first

  Goofy looking but loyal.   Are there shotgun rules for love?

  Just don't piss them off.   I thought all was fair.

Just Before Bed   The Girl at the Bar

Now I lay me down   I bought her a drink

Alone (again), left to dread   I asked for her name, number

Monday with the dregs.   "no habla ingles"

                                    I need to find something, soon.

Nov. 11

So today Dr. Shayam asked me how my writing was going. i told him that i was having a hard time getting into the swing of it. i showed him the my entries i had made and he didn't seem pleased. He insinuated that I wasn't taking this seriously. Then he called me Slick. He calls me Slick and I don't take things seriously! Whatever.

He did however give me some pointers. First off, apparently i need to lay off of so many haikus. Sorry, i liked them too.

Secondly, he told me that the best thing to do was not to think too much about what I should be writing. Just to write what ever was on my mind.

Blah, blah, blah.

Finally and most importantly, he told me that i should imagine that i am writing to a long, lost and distant friend. i told him that i didn't have one. He suggested that i make one up. So starting tomorrow Notebook, you will be known as Diane. You are a childhood sweetheart who moved to Sydney to be an Australian soap opera star. We hooked up once at summer camp when we were 13, but it didn't work out (because we were 13).

It was shortly after that that you started to look gigs as a sock model. For a while you exclusively modeled orange fashion socks. Once your Times Square billboard unveiled, the offers rolled in. At 17, you left Georgia for good, to play the part of Ursula on Australias wildly popular, "Koala Restless". We shared one kiss before you left and it was amazing.

We have kept in touch ever since then by writing daily letters, which we stuff into bottles and throw into the sea.

That's right: I gave my notebook a back story. How's THAT for taking things seriously?

Dec. 7

Diane,

We decorated for Christmas today at work. Stew and I strung up the lights, hung wreaths and even painted the windows with this spray on artificial snow. In the end, I thought it looked great. We had the kids make long popcorn strands that we draped all throughout the facility, until Dr. Levine told us we had to take them down because she was afraid that it would attract insects. Can you believe that, Diane? Attracting insects in the middle of December?

It really ~~preturned~~ perturbed me. Here we were, trying to do something nice for these sick little kids, they spend hours making the thing and he forces us to remove it. You know, sometimes I wonder why I stay. I'm sorry, I'm just venting. Here's your daily haiku:

<u>Why?</u>

Can someone tell me?

Why the Helen Keller jokes

Are always funny?

Diane,

Do you ever feel like you aren't doing what it is that you are supposed to be doing? I've been working here for years and years and I always justified staying because I was helping these poor kids. But more and more I feel like I am just not doing what I should be. Stew says that if I am unhappy, I should quit and find something that I will enjoy. The thing is, I don't know what I will enjoy. It's not like I have some amazing skill or talent that will translate into a high-paying career. I'm a custodian for crying out loud.

I don't know, I just I feel stuck today.

I don't know how long I can take it if things keep up like this.

Feb. 3

Diane,

Things are looking up!

I know that I've been terrible; constantly complaining about my job and my station in life. I flipped through the pages for the past months and all I can say is☺ wow! I was such an Eyeore.

But I think all that is about to change. I was doing my regular tasks, helping install the new foam mats and padded equipment for the kids new play area when the most beautiful woman I have ever seen came in. I don't mean pin-up beautiful or model beautiful— but beautiful in a way that I can't describe. She pulled up to the building in an old Bronco. A real piece of shit.

After talking with Stew, I learned that she's the new Phlebotomist (something to do with blood. I'm going to have to look it up to learn more). Her name is Kylie Court. When I asked what he thought of her, Stew agreed that she was cute. He didn't seem too interested though; which is great. There's nothing worse than two guys chasing after the new girl.

I haven't had a chance to say too much to her; but I did say hello and she waved back and smiled. I myself, have found myself daydreaming about her ever since.

Kylie Court

Blonde hair, eyes of blue

I need to learn more of you

Thank you for the smile.

Not creepy sex dreams or anything. But dreaming of taking her out to dinner, giving her flowers, anything to see that smile again.

Call it a crush, call it ridiculous, call it what you will☺

Whatever it is; I can't wait to go to work tomorrow.

$\mathcal{S}$team rose off the street in front of Rudy's Fish and Bait. The offices and adjacent fish tanks looked as if they were once a gas station; renovated so that the pumps were replaced by twenty concrete tanks, each the size of a twin bed and filled with assorted fish of varying shaped and sizes. The signs that hung above them predetermined the fate of the fish that inhabited each tank. Fish destined to become bait were separated from those that would become cat food or Ravenous Rudy's famous fish sticks (they were shaped like farm animals). Behind the tanks and offices sat two massive, overflowing dumpsters. Garbage bags lined their bases; many had been disemboweled and strewn across the grounds by the countless stray cats that roamed the area. The strays had been permitted to eat from the trash and the uncovered cat food tank. Some ran in to what Sunday expected was their home; a rusted out hole in the siding of one of the five trailers that sat in the rear of the property in a semi-circle which faced the back of the office. Sunday swore to himself then and there that he would never eat a Ravenous Rudy fish stick ever again.

Most of the trailers in the backwoods neighborhood were rusted on the bottom and little holes formed in their aluminum siding; all accept the trailer that sat in the first lot on the left. Kylie signaled Sunday to turn into its gravel driveway. The trailer was positioned right next to the dumpsters and was the closest to the fish; yet it seemed most captivating. Not only for its baby blue color, but also because it was the only trailer with a patio. It was the only trailer with a storage shed complete with a little built-in porch swing. It was the only trailer on the lot with a fully grassed lawn; and the only trailer that appeared to be affected by what looked like a massive pipe burst, which sent the sewers spewing above the ground. A black puddle started at the fence and ran the length of the yard and ended just under the swing. It covered the once green grass and created a bog right off the tiny blue trailer's doorstep. The stench and sludge aside, this was still clearly the envy home in the small makeshift trailer park.

Sunday stopped the van; it shuddered and chattered before it finally exhausted itself to a complete rest. Sunday took one step out of the vehicle and felt the sludgy earth beneath him. The storage shed, it seemed, had become a mating ground and kitten nursery for the numerous strays. The lingering, choking odor of opened garbage, mackerel, and enough sewage that no amount of soap could ever clean festered in the air and caused the kittens to cry. A tiny black cat crossed Sunday and trotted over the mud covered rocks that littered the yard and hopped onto the patio. It sat at the base of the steps and purred twice.

"That's exactly what I need." Sunday thought.

"Hi kitty!" laughed Kylie as she climbed out of the van and ran up to her front door. She lifted the kitten into her arms and brushed her tangled hair away from her cherubesque face. A myriad of Christmas lights wrapped around the cracked painted lattice and illuminated the porch in an array of color. Candles and flowers gave off the faintest scent under the pungent odor of Rudy's Fish and Bait. Random decorations were placed in the vacant space around the newly painted wicker furniture.

Kylie sat down at the patio table, brushed aside her troublesome hair once more and smiled at the sight of her home. Sunday simply watched, amazed that like an orchid, someone as beautiful as Kylie Court could survive in so much muck.

"It was really cool, you know," Sunday said awkwardly, "what you did for Steve."

Kylie looked up from petting the kitten and flashed Sunday a true and genuine smile. Sunday had never seen Kylie smile this way before and for the first time, he noticed that she had the slightest hint of dimples.

"Do you really think so?" she asked.

Sunday nodded. Hands in his pockets, he looked around and hoped for something to trigger in his head that he could say that would allow him to hang around just a second longer. Once he had determined that to her he just looked like he was idly standing there, he finally gave up and said, "Well, it looks like you're okay here…"

Kylie interrupted him, "You're leaving?"

Taken aback, Sunday's voice cracked as he replied, "No, I can stay. Sure, I can stay for a minute."

Sunday hopped up onto the porch and Kylie offered him a seat on the wicker chair. Sunday sat down and further took in his surroundings. He noticed that there were dense cobwebs in the corners of the patio covering and saw that the trailer across the way was actually being held up by a series of cinder blocks. Kylie excused herself and walked inside.

Sunday tried to shake the familiar tight knot out of his throat and cease the shaking in his legs. He performed a breath check and attempted to straighten himself up. After some time, Kylie kicked open the door, a lit candle in one hand, two wine glasses crisscrossed the fingers of her other hand and a bottle wedged under her arm. She had changed into an old hockey jersey and a pair of slightly oversized pajama pants, which were rolled at the top in a kind of makeshift belt. She situated the candle on the little table, sat down next to Sunday and poured them each a glass of a pinot noir.

Sunday put the glass to his lips and slowly let the liquid swim over his tongue. Fireflies sparkled in the night and a cool breeze wafted the odor of fish and sewage past him. It took a couple of breaths before he became accustomed to it.

"So, you really liked the birthday party idea?" Kylie asked again and set her wine glass down on the small table.

"Yeah," Sunday once again stated, "The kids loved it. And that's the important thing, you know?"

"Once I saw in his file that his birthday was the same day as admissions day, I just felt the need to do something special." She explained as she slid a little closer to Sunday.

"I think it was a great use of entertainment expenses." The custodian replied encouragingly.

"Working in the lab all day; it just started to seem like the kids were just samples, not people. And that's not why I started working there. I want to help people, you know? Did you know that I'm not even aware of most of these kid's conditions?"

Intently listening to her, Sunday noted how Kylie's mouth formed words with a subtle, southern twang as her top lip curled upwards ever so slightly. Her blue eyes darted from left to right as she proceeded to get more passionate about the subject, "That's why I jumped at the chance to move to the main floor. I wanted to feel like I was actually doing something helpful for those kids, not just monitoring their diseases."

"It's the only part of the job that's worth it." Sunday agreed.

Kylie's tone changed as she quickly added, "And I took part of that away from you. I am so sorry Sunday, honestly."

Sunday stopped her from apologizing further, "It's alright. I'm glad that it's you that's replacing me."

"But I don't want you to be demoted." She started.

"Then it sounds like you have yourself a pickle." He teased.

Kylie shot upright, "Did you say pickles?"

"Yeah." Sunday admitted, "Like in baseball."

Kylie hopped up from her seat, "Doesn't matter; now I'm craving them." She disappeared back into the trailer.

"Okay." Sunday called into the open door, "Look, those kids like me because I'm just like them. For every bad thing that has happened in those kids' lives, they have seen mine take the bad stuff as well. They like me because I'm unlucky and they can relate."

Kylie returned with a jar of pickles. She opened the jar and offered it to Sunday.

"Pickles and Pinot?" He asked sourly as he respectfully shook his head.

Kylie pulled out a pickle and ate it from the bottom in order to catch the dripping juices before they wasted themselves to the floor. She then took a large gulp from her glass which emptied it. After removing the cork from the bottle to refill her glass, she concluded, "Then I should fit right in."

"Why, do you have issues too?" Sunday felt more at ease as the wine went down. He spent less time worrying about what Kylie thought about him and simply began to enjoy their time together.

"Of course, doesn't everyone?" She said as she winked and slid even closer to Sunday's spot on the seat. They reclined themselves so that they could admire the sparse stars that hung over the distant Atlanta skyline. A faint glow from the city could be seen through the trees, creating a luminescent haze of blue between the land and the dark night. The moon seemed fuller in the sky as the wine bottle emptied.

Sunday and Kylie drunkenly wrapped arms around each other, told favorite stories, shared their mutual love of Muppets and basked in the moments when neither of them would talk. The whole time, Sunday thought to himself how amazing it was that Kylie was not only sharing details of her life with him, but also wanted to know the details of his. Not once while he sat next to her did he have his regular thoughts of being trapped in a hopeless existence. She rested her head on his chest until their arbitrary ramblings faded into a mumble and together they eventually fell asleep under the cover of the rickety patio.

$\mathscr{S}$unday woke to the blinding, white glare of the sun in his eyes, the putrid odor of the foul yard as it began to bake in the morning heat and Kylie's perfect head resting on his chest. His body was tense from sleeping in such an awkward position, but he was in no rush to move Kylie away to stretch. He glanced down and watched her head slightly rise and fall with each breath that he took. Sunday leaned over her to get a glimpse of her slumbering face. Her eyes were closed somberly, her lips slightly pursed; she was beautiful as she slept. The sun cast a beam of light from Sunday's watch onto his face. Squinting, he looked down, noticed the time and suddenly the peace of the morning was gone.

"Damn it," He moaned, "We're gonna be late." Sunday gently nudged Kylie. She jerked her head up in a horrified manner that startled the custodian.

"Good morning, Pickle." He added and chuckled at Kylie's hair which stood up in places.

Kylie cooed in appreciation at her newly appointed nickname. It made her feel accepted and it was cute. She nodded as she rubbed the spot on her cheek that had been pressed up against Sunday's chest. "Oh, we fell asleep out here?" She groggily mumbled.

Sunday nodded and took the opportunity to crane his body back in a grand stretch. Kylie yawned and opened the screen door, "Hang on, I'll come with you."

The door slammed behind her and Sunday was once again left alone on the patio. She immediately poked her head back out to ask, "Is that okay?"

Sunday nodded and said, "Sure." He ticked his toes inside his shoe like a bomb's timer running down for he knew how late they were going to be. Kylie reappeared ten minutes later and looked more radiant than the sun that had so rudely ruined their slumber. She wore a bright, orange sundress with giant lilies printed on it. She already had put on her matching orange, elbow-length latex gloves. A "wow" spilled out of Sunday's mouth as she handed him a coffee mug with a Marriott logo on it and a faint trace of lipstick around the rim. Sunday graciously took the mug, turned the stain away and took a sip. It was the worst coffee he had ever tasted, but he still forced a smile.

"Thanks" he choked.

"No problem." She smiled, "Sorry if it tastes weird. Sometimes the water acts funny."

Sunday immediately thought of the sewage and the smell of the yard and set down the mug.

—◇—

Sunday and Kylie arrived at WonderKids twenty minutes late. As they snuck in, Sunday noticed that the merry-go-round was still very popular with the kids; many of them had formed a line to take turns at riding the whimsical, plastic animals. Head Physician Dr. Margo Levine-Alonzo had already locked herself into her office for the morning, which gave Sunday time to take a quick shower. He saw the clothes that he had worn the day before still wrinkled on the floor, festering and soppy. Picking them up with the tips of his fingers, Sunday said a last goodbye to his favorite shirt and threw the whole lot in the trash.

He stood in the shower for quite some time and relaxed under the hot water that ran over his head and down his body. Even after he had lathered, rinsed and even repeated, Sunday could not bring himself to shut the shower head and join the worker world. Only when his fingers began to prune did he finally climb out and steal a fresh pair of grey scrubs to wear. Upon entering the main room again, he quickly located Gabriel and Austin Olsen.

"Where's Stew?" he asked Austin.

Hope came up from behind and put her arms around Sunday's neck and said, "He's soundproofing Molly's room. We ran out of Valium."

She had a devious smile that made Sunday doubt that they had actually run out of Valium. Hope propped her elbow on his shoulder and kissed him on the cheek. Sunday felt a sudden, burning awkwardness inside. He looked around to make sure that Kylie had not seen. He was pleased to see that she had not.

"Oh, and you'll love this," Hope giggled, hopped up and down merrily and continued, "Levine took that creepy kid off his meds this morning."

"Callym's awake?" Suddenly, Sunday had a new interest in the catatonic boy from the day before.

"Yeah, he's on the second floor. Psych ward." Hope pointed to the ceiling. Sunday smirked; within the first seconds of meeting Callym; he had pegged the kid for the psychiatric ward.

"Did you meet him?" asked Austin.

"Yeah." replied Hope, "He's twitchy."

A loud squawk filled the room from the intercom. A soft, southern and unsure voice came over the system, "Ladies and Gentleman, the Wonder Kids choir proudly presents..."

Sunday turned to see that Gabriel and Austin had already started to run off to watch the song, and said to Hope, "I'll be back." adding, "Play nice."

The custodian trotted over to the children, who had gathered around Kylie. She sat on the edge of the player piano and awkwardly held the intercom microphone. She looked at Sunday straight in the eyes and announced, "*Baby, It's You.*"

Kylie voice started out shaky and nervous, as if there were some chance she might get booed out of her performance. However, the children's cheers boosted her confidence and by the midway point, she hit every note perfectly in her lovely, twangy tone. She began to shake her hips, toss her hair and truly get into the song;

"Is it true what they say about you?

They say you'll never, ever, never be true.

It doesn't matter, what they say,

You know I'm gonna love ya any old way.

What can I do?

What 'bout you?

She crossed her arms at the wrist, pointed at Sunday and sang, "Baby, it's you."

From inside her office, Dr. Levine even grabbed her microphone and joined in with the backing "la la's". Sunday thought to himself, *"This is going to be a good day."*

Kylie finished her song to the roars and applause of the children. Sunday stood and clapped, assured that their new commander-in-chief was a welcomed addition. Brimming, Kylie blushed then curtsied. Sunday took her by one hand and helped her down from the piano.

"Incredible." Sunday determined.

"Really?" asked Kylie, surprised.

"Are you kidding," exclaimed Sunday, "You even got Levine singing!"

Kylie ran her gloved fingers down Sunday's arm and smiled a thank you. He, in turn, turned red and said, "Um, I should probably go check on Stew. Do you think you have everything under control?"

Kylie's eyes widened at the thought of being left unattended with the children for the first time. She shook her head back and forth slowly and pouted.

"I can't. I'm not ready." She pleaded.

"Just let them play, keep them happy and if someone makes a mess... call Stew." Sunday joked which brought the dimples back to Kylie's face, "Don't worry about a thing," he added, "You'll be fine." He winked at her and made his way up the spiral stairs.

Sunday reached the second floor. The fluorescents that scattered the ceiling in the hallway were sporadic and ill illuminating. The lights in each examination room were brightly and harshly lit and spilled into the dark, flickering hallway. He knew that he should check-in with Stew a few floors above, but he also knew that Callym was un-medicated somewhere on the second floor. Curiosity took over and Sunday suddenly found himself skulking down the second floor hallway.

The doctors and nurses of the second floor rarely had much to say to Sunday. Whenever he would have to clean the medical floor, he usually spent that time in silence, unless one of the children spoke to him. Sunday understood the concept of doctors distancing themselves from patients, but he found it rude that they also distanced themselves from him just because he emptied the trashcans.

Sunday quietly crept past the first examination rooms. His shoes squeaked to a halt when he heard the unfamiliar but unmistakable voice of young Callym. It was scratchy and forced from years of atrophy; meek, gravely and slow… oddly mature. Sunday slouched down on his haunches just short of the cracked doorway and listened.

"What I am trying to say is that I have memories of things I shouldn't have memories of." Callym hacked a cough to clear his voice and continued, "I have visions of periods of time like I was there, as if I watched it happen. I can describe the Salem Witch trials like it was yesterday. And that's not all; I have the same memories about things I simply couldn't have. I can give you details about the battle between God and Lucifer like I lived it. I can describe the fire that lit the heavens when God's sword struck Lucifer and sent him falling to hell, I can tell you how the air smelled on that day." The boy began to scare Sunday, not only because he appeared to be eerie and schizophrenic, but also because he sounded very sincere. Sunday pressed his head closer to the crack in the door.

"I could tell you just about everything except the meaning of life, and I shouldn't. I'm a kid and I know I'm a kid- I shouldn't have these memories, I shouldn't be haunted like this. But I am. So you tell me, am I crazy?"

"Those are probably hallucinations manifesting themselves because of all the drugs that those nuns had you on. I'm shocked you were coherent at all." The doctor replied.

"…I *asked* the nuns to put me on those drugs." The child's voice held defiance under its frailness, "I couldn't take how I felt anymore."

"And how do you feel now, Chief?" Sunday could tell by the overly buddy tone that it was Dr. Randall Shayam. Dr. Shayam was the elder of the two staff psychiatrists. Sunday had met with him a few times in the past to discuss his bad luck. Dr. Shayam suggested that Sunday keep a notebook, as this was his favorite prescription. With the number of diaries, journals and notebooks floating around WonderKids, the custodian would not have been surprised to learn that the doctor was on a paper company's payroll. The hefty old man was from Israel and called everyone "pal," "buddy," "chief," or "princess". He was one of those guys who looked over his glasses. Sunday edged his head closer to the door so that he could peer inside.

Callym rapped his fingers against the plastic chair that he awkwardly sat in. "I need to be in chains." He said nervously.

"And what makes you say that?" asked the doctor.

There was a pause before Callym spoke, "You know how people have that thing that tells them not to do… wrong?"

"A conscience?"

"I don't know, I don't think I have one."

"Everyone has a conscience, Ace." Sunday held in a small chuckle over Dr. Shayam's latest addition to his repertoire of friendly titles.

"Look Doc," the boy explained in a strained, rasped voice, "From the moment I could remember, I have had only one kind of thing in my head. Evil things- and I'll be damned if it doesn't make it worse that there is no rhyme or reason for it."

"What does that have to do with you needing to be in chains?" the doctor pried.

"I'm trying to explain," Callym said in an agitated tone. From the other side of the doorway, Sunday could tell that the boy was beginning to get frustrated over his inability to convey the nuances of his condition, "I'm sure that you have a voice in you that says, 'look both ways before crossing the street, don't park in handicap spaces, don't forget the eggs and generally just do good.' And I'm sure that that voice looks out for you and keeps you relatively safe and happy. If you see someone standing on the side of the train tracks, I'm sure your little voice would say 'leave him alone.' Well, my little voice would say 'I wonder what happens if you push him?' And since there is no voice to tell me to generally just do good; I get frustrated and the next thing I know, I am doing something horrible."

"Do you feel happiness in doing these things?"

The boy's voice became more agitated, there was no anger in his tone, more of a frustrated sadness, "I don't feel happiness. I don't feel anything. I don't feel that things I do are wrong until after I do them; then it feels like all the pain that is caused by my actions fills me. That's the only true emotion I ever get to feel."

"I'm telling you it's the medication."

"It's not the medication; the Lithium Validemerethyzine made me numb and kept everyone safe. It's just how it always has been. I don't feel the happiness in things, it's just emptiness…" The boy sobbed, "…it's just too much. Then the next thing I know, I am doing something evil and for just a moment, all the pain and suffering and torment that it causes… *that's* what I feel." Callym took a deep, cleansing breath and sat upright, "Then the emptiness creeps back in and so it goes, and so it goes."

The custodian had become quite intrigued in his spying state; when the elevator dinged and Kylie and Hope stepped into the hallway. He shot up from his crouched position and his shoes squeaked loudly on the immaculate floor.

"We wondered where you were!" Hope said louder than she needed to. Sunday was certain that she made enough noise to make their presence known because the talking in the examination room abruptly ceased.

"What are they saying?" Kylie whispered. Sunday was surprised to see her so interested.

"Is he crazy?" Hope asked. Sunday put his finger to his lips to shush them.

Moments later, Callym shuffled out of the room. His baggy black cargo pants were frayed at the bottom from continuously being raked across his untied black shoes. He wore one of the break room scrubs under a tattered black and blue flannel robe. As if a current ran through them, Sunday, Kylie and Hope shot to attention.

"Hey Callym, how are you feeling?" Sunday casually inquired, his arm aloofly propped up on the wall. Through his neglected hair, Sunday could see that the milky substance that swirled in the boy's eyes had gone. Callym's crystal blue grey eyes met Sunday's; they would have scared the hell out of him, the faintest grey with tiny incandescent blue specks, outlined by the thinnest black circle, had they not looked so morose. And yet, a cold chill ran down Sunday's spine as he answered a gritty, "I'm tired."

"Maybe you should get some rest, sweetie?" Kylie suggested kindly.

The boy looked at her coldly, fidgeted his fingers and monotonic and matter of factly replied, "I could sleep until the world burned and I still don't think it would help." Callym threw open the stairwell door and headed to the main floor.

Once the door had shut behind him, Hope exclaimed, "Damn, that kid is messed up!"

After Sunday was sure he was out of earshot, he whipped his head to Hope and snapped, "Be louder."

She gave him an offended look and before she could explain, Kylie jumped in, "I asked her where you were. I missed you a little."

Suddenly, Sunday forgot why he was upset. Hope, however, did not and she flicked him off. Just them, Dr. Shayam stepped out of his office. Once again, the trio froze like students caught smoking on the side of a school.

"Hey buddy," he said, looking at Sunday over his wire rims, "Keep an eye on that kid, okay?"

"Okay." Sunday nodded.

"I'm serious, I'm not sure if he's entirely... stable. They had him highly medicated."

"We know." Hope chimed.

"He seems like a good kid, but there's no telling what coming off of all of that will do. Levine should have weaned him off slow, but you know how she is about these things. He should be fine. I've got him working on a notebook." The doctor smiled and retreated back into his office. With a simple nod, Sunday and the ladies went back to the elevator and pressed the button for the fourth floor.

—◉—

$\mathcal{T}$he dormitory floor reeked of wood shavings and hot foam and the shrill sounds of power tools echoed through the hall. The trio walked into Molly's room, where the little girl pouted upon her bed. Meanwhile, clad in a sweat-stained, wife-beater t-shirt and a pair of tight and slightly out of date jeans, Stew stood on the top rung of a ladder and tacked up panel after panel of giant foam pads to the wall. Sunday rapped on the open door, "What's going on?" he asked, announcing their presence.

"Stew won't let me play in my room. I want to play." Molly huffed.

Stew threw down the staple gun and pleaded, "Honey, I told you; as soon as I'm done you can play in your room. You can listen to music as loud you want. You can scream all you want because you don't want to sleep. You'll be free to do as you please; just let me finish."

Kylie knelt down and picked up the staple gun. Stew straightened himself us, heaving out his chest like a proud bullfrog as he took it from her.

"You have everything under control?" Sunday asked.

Stew climbed down off the ladder, and wiping the flop sweat off of his brow said, "No, but I should have it finished shortly after lunch. Can you go and take care of the regular stuff downstairs?" He discreetly nudged Sunday in the ribs, noting that he was trying to ensure that the custodian would be able to spend more time with Kylie.

As the trio left, Stew shouted, "You've got the next big project, asshole." Sunday shot him the bird from behind his back and escorted the girls back to the main floor.

—◉—

he girls palled around the main floor while Sunday preformed his routine duties. Hope went in to detail about all the children's personalities and maladies which gave Kylie a bit more insight into the children that she had worked with for so long, but had spoken so little to. Meanwhile, Sunday took out the morning trash, cleaned the tables and swept the floors. Once the chores were completed, he made sure that the kids were safe and noted the severity of their conditions for the day.

By hanging out with the children, Sunday was often able to gauge which one's illnesses would give him the most trouble for the day, and be able to plan accordingly. It was typically the highlight of most days and how he often justified staying at WonderKids. For a part of the day, between the cleaning and the crying; the custodian got to play. He hung out, played videogames, watched cartoons, shot hoops, asked questions and would now get to ride a merry-go-round.

He hopped onto the carousel and began to chat with Heavy Paul and Callym who rode side by side. Paul informed Sunday that his track coach wanted him to try out at least as an alternate for the pole vault.

"It's really the only problem I have. I feel ok, I'm just nervous… 'Cause you know, I weigh so much." He looked down sadly, "I'm seriously afraid I'm going to snap the pole."

"Do you want to do it, Paul?" Sunday asked. The young man nodded. "Then try, what's the worst that will happen? You fall?"

"I fall hard." Paul explained.

"I heard it only counts when there's a possibility of falling hard." Sunday suggested. Heavy Paul looked up, his eyes welled with a hint of aqua-marine tears and he nodded in agreement. Sunday continued, "Look at Callym; yesterday who would have thought he'd be all up and shuffling around. With the amount of that stuff they had in him, it's amazing that he hasn't crashed. And here he is; off his meds and doing fine."

Callym leaned forward, and softly spoke, "I didn't ask to take the fall, brother."

Sunday gathered that Paul was going to be alright, so he turned his attention to the mysterious new resident, "So, you wanted to stay on your medication?"

"It's... better if I'm on it." He stated.

"The shakes?" Sunday asked; noting that Callym constantly fidgeted with his fingers, touching the fingertips repeatedly to his thumb and occasionally biting at the edges.

"No. That won't go away.... It's... just safer for all concerned." With that, he slithered off his plastic stallion and walked off into the play area. Sunday saw him maliciously and what seemed without provocation, shove one of the children in the chest, causing him to flip backwards over the bench he was standing in front of. Sunday rose off his steed in an attempt to chase him down and at least get him to apologize; if not find out what lead to the outburst. Suddenly; however, the lunch bell chimed and Callym was left momentarily off the hook as Sunday was forced to navigate through the herd of children rushing into the cafeteria.

— ◎ —

*T*he meals at WonderKid were prepared everyday by two Czech brothers. The oldest, Vladimir Zelkovinivich, was in his sixties, was short, over weight, loud, ill-tempered and had a salty and thick handlebar moustache which curled at the ends. His taller, thinner brother, Mica; was just as loud, and had the same moustache. Neither of them spoke a word of English. Meals were served with a side of incomprehensible cursing, but the meals were amazing; even the peanut butter and jelly sandwiches where incredibly delicious. The Zelkiviniviches added a hint of honey to the peanut butter, heated it and spread it over two lightly toasted piece of thick homemade bread, and coupled it next to thick fruity grape jelly; cut cornerwise. Sunday grabbed two as he nodded past the brothers. They argued back and forth; flailing their arms and setting out apples, bananas and a multitude of other side items.

Austin Olsen and Gabriel stood in line a few children behind him. Austin grabbed a handful of sandwiches and piled them high on his tray. Sunday was about to intervene when he overheard their topic of discussion.

"See, I think Sunday's problem is he doesn't see the good an anything, and that's why he is the way he is." Gabriel declared.

"Yeah, that makes sense." Austin agreed.

"And he has to see it before he can be who he wants to be." Gabriel said as he reached for a bag of chips and an obscene amount of ketchup.

"That makes sense too." Austin nodded and grabbed a fistful of spicy French fries.

"And I think he likes Kylie, but he's too afraid to say so."

"That makes sense too!" said the amazed Austin.

That was all it took for Sunday to lean back out of the line and shout at the two boys, "Hey!"

"Austin, what did we say about other people's problems?" he asked sternly.

Austin squeakily apologized; Sunday accepted it and then added, "It's no big deal. Why don't you set one of those sandwiches back?"

To which Austin responded sarcastically, "Other's people's problems…"

The cold glare Austin received assured him that calling out Sunday's hypocrisy was not a good idea. He forced a grin and slowly set two sandwich wedges back on the tray.

"*Silly, chubby bastard,*" Sunday thought and turned the rest of his angst on young Gabriel, who was still happy as could be; unaffected by the recent outburst in the lunch line.

"You." Sunday pointed, "You and I are going to have a talk later about minding our own business." He looked the boy square in his cheery eyes to let him know that he was serious. "Alright?"

The little boy seemed neither remorseful nor scared; he was simply cheerful, usual Gabriel. Sunday tried to shrug it all off, and continued down the lunch line.

The custodian joined Stew, Hope and Heavy Paul on what had been known as their side of the "grown-up table". The cafeteria at Wonder Kids had many similarities to a high school lunch room. The same white tables arranged in two columns, the same orange and blue plastic chairs, the same gathering of cliques. However, here the small tribes were rarely judging. The children sat with their friends and often chattered between tables.

The medical staff sat at one end of the "grown up" table, and for the most part kept away from everyone else. Callym walked that lonely lunch path to find a table for himself. Kylie had decided to eat lunch with Gabriel over at Austin's table and they sat with the other pre-teens, one table away from Molly and the younger kids. Callym stalled at both tables, but the rabble-rabble-rabble of the children as they gawked was enough for the boy to see that he should move on. Gabriel got up and met Callym halfway across the floor. He extended his tiny arm, inviting the dreary teen to join them at their table. Callym timidly smiled and thankfully sat down. Sunday was relieved. Not only that Callym was being accepted by somebody; but also that he was not going to end up at his table.

"So, Kylie is looking hot, huh?" Stew said; his mouth half full of peanut butter.

Sunday nodded and examined his sandwich. Hope smirked, but did not say anything.

"What's she like?" Stew asked.

Sunday shrugged and took a bite of his semi-warm sandwich, "I dunno, she's cool. We haven't really had time to talk."

"Maybe you should." Hope suggested. It was then that they all overheard the soft spoken words coming from the neighboring table. The nurses were still speculating Callym's condition as if they were all members of a bridge club. Rumors of vandalism, rage and all-out hedonism circled the table. Sunday's legs twitched as he fought back the urge to defend the kid. It seemed to him that it was one thing that Callym's mere presence gave him the willies; it was another thing for the people who were hired to try to fix the boy to be caught saying such slanderous things. He almost spoke out, but their rumor mill went from one extreme to the next as the gossip turned to Gabriel. The medical staff all sang the praises of Sunday's least favorite resident. He blocked out their conversations before all the sugary fluff sullied his appetite.

"So, are you going to?" Stew asked.

"Going to what?" Sunday asked back.

"Talk to Kylie." Hope batted her eyes.

"What for?" Sunday responded defensively and tore a huge, drippy bite of his sandwich with his teeth.

"Get her story. Aren't you interested? Look at her." Stew said as he stuffed his mouth with more of his sandwich.

Sunday blushed and quickly changed the subject, "So, when are you supposed to be done with the soundproofing?" he asked.

Stew's face fell as he was reminded of his current mission. Hope, however, called the custodian out, "You are such a pussy."

"What?" Sunday exclaimed.

"Just go talk to her." Hope said as she too joined in the taunts.

"Go talk to her." Stew ordered.

"You should." Heavy Paul added.

"Just go talk to her." the nurse that sat closest to the group demanded in a perturbed tone.

Sunday tossed down his sandwich, "Fine." he said defiantly and rose from the little plastic chair, "I'll go talk to her."

As he approached Kylie's table, a knot appeared in his throat and the palms of his hands began to go cold and clammy. As he got closer he picked up pieces of what Callym was saying.

"...a lot of nightmares; but I had them before the drugs. I had them on the drugs. They never ended while I was on my meds; but it helped me... and they help me. You can learn a lot from your dreams." He raised the straw to his chocolate milk to his dry, chapped and sad lips. He had the entire table on edge.

"I learned so much about myself… everything while I was on my Lithium Validemerethyzine." He added and swallowed savoringly as if the experience of drinking chocolate milk was somewhat foreign to him. He examined his cardboard carton and then took another sip.

Sunday walked up behind Kylie and looked over to his table. Stew held a big, thumb-up, while Paul looked on smiling and Hope threw her hands up with rocker horns. Sunday leaned over Kylie and for a brief second took in the smell of her again. The scent of flowers and sweetness danced in his nostrils.

"Sorry to interrupt…" He almost whispered it. Kylie spun around in her chair.

"Oh, did you want to get down to business?" She asked. Sunday stood awkwardly, slightly taken aback.

"What?" he asked.

"Is there something we need to be doing?" She specified.

"No." Sunday mumbled, "I just wanted to see if you wanted to get some ice cream and take a little walk."

She nodded and told the kids that she would meet up with them later. As she got out of her chair, Sunday looked down at her angelic lunch mate and reminded him, "Little talk later, kid."

Gabriel nodded, at which Sunday added, "And after lunch; I want my pen back."

Sunday looked over one last time as they walked to the back of the cafeteria and saw that Stew spoke something to Hope, who was not smiling. Instead, she simply stared at Sunday and Kylie with a sour expression. Sunday took Kylie behind the lunch line and food counter, past the Zelkoviniviches, who screamed incoherently as they passed them and walked into the kitchen area. The brothers turned their attention back to each other as Sunday waved a hello and held the door to the walk in freezer for Kylie.

The walk-in freezer was flanked on either side of its arctic steel walls by two rows of shelving which held all that the Zelkoviniviches would ever need to feed the children.

Sunday propped his foot on the bottom shelf and hoisted himself up to reach the top shelf. He rummaged through a box barely in his reach, hopped down from the shelving, and handed Kylie one of the ice cream cones that he had procured. "Nutty Buddy?" he asked.

She took the ice cream cone, they exited the freezer and Sunday led her out of the emergency exit and into the courtyard.

CHAPTER SEVEN

The courtyard that rested behind the facility was nothing more than a few tall shrubs to block the view of the dumpsters from the parking lot and the statue that Sunday had ruined. Multicolored flowers sporadically lined the bushes and a simple, rarely used, wrought iron bench sat in the center. Sunday and Kylie Court sat on the bench for a moment. Long enough to un-wrap their frozen treats and begin to eat them. Sunday watched, slack-jawed as Kylie's tongue slid over the vanilla ice cream that capped the top of the cone. She took his hand and rose from the bench and she led them beyond the courtyard and the parking lot, over small slope that led down to a tiny duck pond that rested just off the property.

"Can I ask you a question?" Kylie asked.

"Can I ask questions back?" Sunday replied and licked his ice cream, just barely catching a drip before it reached his hand.

"Of course." She smirked. A little dimple formed in her cheek.

"Then okay." Sunday agreed.

"Does that Callym kid…?" Kylie said offhandedly, "…Freak you out?"

"God, yes." Sunday chuckled.

They reached the pond and took a seat under the lonely willow tree that rested at the bank. The noon day sun reflected in the water, a broken circle that danced between the ripples. A family of ducks swam along the shallow bank and bobbed in and out of the water.

"All the kids seem great," She continued, "There's just something…"she shivered, "about that kid."

Sunday nodded as he looked up at the web of branches and dewy white leaves that canopied overhead. "I know."

There was a comfortable silence for a moment; Sunday took in the fresh air and if even for a second, felt genuinely at peace knowing that he was getting paid, however little, to sit there with a beautiful woman and just relax. He found a tiny rock and skimmed it across the surface of the water. The stone hopped across the pond and left many ripples which slowly spread out until they met each other. They watched the tiny, circular waves grow smaller and smaller until the water once again grew still. Kylie broke the short silence and said, "It's your turn."

"Questions, right." Sunday replied as he snapped out of his daze. He stumbled as he tried to think of a question, "Um... What's your favorite color?"

"Seriously?" giggled Kylie, "Pink. You?"

"Blue."

"Did you really break that statue?"

Sunday only nodded, "Okay, my turn. Beatles or Elvis?"

Kylie answered without a pause for thought, "Elvis."

Sunday could tell by the way she answered that she had a fondness for the king.

"Blasphemy!" He cried.

"I take it you're a Beatles man." She said.

"Through and through." He said proudly. There was a brief lull in the conversation, and Sunday sat upright and rested his head in his hands. He looked at Kylie out of the corner of his eye, "Not a Beatles girl? And you were so close to perfect." He teased.

Kylie shoved him jokingly and Sunday toppled over onto his side. "I'm serious," he said in between chuckles, "We could have had something special." He sat back up and feigned a sigh, "Oh well, Obla-dee-obla-dah."

"Life goes on. It's my turn." Kylie paused, looked Sunday straight in the eyes and said with a smile, "Will you call me Pickle again?"

Sunday chuckled, "Always, if you like."

They sat very close and once their mutual laughter settled, Kylie hesitated for a moment and then asked, "So, what's up with Hope?"

"What do you mean?" Sunday asked.

"I think she likes you." Kylie teased. Sunday felt a slight blush, and quickly took the defensive.

"It's just a fascination from the ten-year-old in her." Sunday said.

"She's ten?" Kylie exclaimed.

Sunday explained Hope's ailment to Kylie. He told her how shortly after he started working at WonderKids, a baby was found on the doorstep. At least that is what he was told. The little baby did not cry; instead, she smiled all night long and took in her new surroundings. The staff had all agreed to name her Hope, and Head Physician Levine-Alonzo insisted that she take on Margo as a last name. Kylie became more interested in the history of her newest friend as Sunday told her of how they soon learned that Hope aged twice as fast as any one. He told her of how they would celebrate Hope's birthday every six months and how the hospital and a panel of judges had never really decided if Hope could be considered an adult.

"...which explains her wild side." Sunday concluded, "She's smart. I like to think she acts out like she does because she knows she can't get in trouble... or she wants to force them in to making a decision."

"To think, I've seen that girl every other week since I've been here and all I knew was that she hated her physicals." Kylie said baffled.

"The doctors don't divulge too much to you either, huh?" Sunday asked.

"Not when it comes to..." she struggled to find the most appropriate way to phrase her thoughts, "the kids with the stranger illnesses."

"The Wonder Kids." Sunday laughed.

"I just studied their blood."

"Well, you'll learn tons down here." Sunday smiled.

"I can't wait." Kylie replied.

Sunday told her about the children, about Austin Olsen and his inability to control his orifices and how once he had an incident that was so bad that the carpet had to be stripped from his room and replaced with linoleum. He told her stories of inappropriate times in which Molly Rollins would scream and how Heavy Paul used to have to be carted around in a modified wheelbarrow. He told her tales about the toddler who lacked a torso, the girl whose large mouth spanned the length of her stomach and of Steve Swindle; the coma patient who had not been awake a day of since his birth. Kylie listened to Sunday describe each of the children and finally concluded, "That's so sad." She softly and sweetly added, "It's your turn."

Sunday pondered a moment over what he should ask, and what may be too personal or out of line. Clearing his throat, he asked, "You haven't said much about the funeral last weekend; are you doing okay?"

Kylie's demeanor dropped and she slightly nodded and suggested, "I'm okay I guess. You know, no one has asked me that since I've been back." Kylie was growing more and more fond of the custodian as she began to see how kind and concerned he was for her.

"Did you want to ask me anything else?" she flirted.

"That counted as your question." Sunday flirted back and added, "Yes I do."

"Make it good." Kylie requested.

He reeled over a deeply thought provoking question. After a brief pause, Sunday asked, "Why did you punk out on me before?"

Kylie did not respond right away; instead, she hung her head down and fiddled with her latex gloves. Sunday felt very awkward as he had not intended on upsetting her. He reached out and came very close to touching her shoulder in order to comfort her, but he hesitated inches from her skin. Her expression had fallen; in a broken voice she finally said, "Ask me a different question."

She craned her neck and looked over at Sunday. Her eyes had begun to well up with tears. "I just can't talk about it. Just know that I am so sorry. I never meant to hurt your feelings." She said sincerely.

"It's okay" Sunday lied, "We never planned anything serious."

His heart went out to her, but he did not know what to think. Although he could see that she was truly aching, he could not help shake the thoughts of the conversations that he had overheard after those weekends when he would get stood up. He wanted to ask her about it, but he did not want to disturb her any farther and risk ruining their so-close-to-perfect day.

Kylie wiped away the water from her eyes and said softly, "Please know that I am sorry, and know that I really like you."

Those four simple words were able to shove away all of those questions that still Sunday still held; and although he had no idea what to say in return, in that moment, everything thing seemed as it should be. He smiled at her and they both stared out at the hazy Atlanta skyline and tried to ignore the distant shouts from Heavy Paul.

CHAPTER EIGHT

"Chew, Chew, Chew!" the children chanted as Austin Olsen crammed the fourth consecutive sandwich into his mouth. Peanut butter and jelly ran down his round chin as the boy forced his jaws up and down. With each compression of his mouth, more of the rich spread was forced out of the corners of his lips and trailed across his cheeks. The children pounded on the tables as Austin forced swallow after swallow. He shook his head, looked to the ceiling and took down the last bite. As he opened his mouth to show that it was empty, the entire cafeteria filled with cheers.

"That was incredible!" Gabriel exclaimed from across the table.

"It's all in the cheeks." Austin boasted as he puffed out his face like a blowfish.

Molly turned from the smaller children's table and said, "So what's your deal, new kid?"

"What do you mean?" Gabriel asked innocently and squeezed packet after packet of ketchup onto his tray.

"She wants to know what's wrong with you." Austin explained, smacking his mouth.

"Oh." Gabriel said, "I'm an angel."

"So, you're crazy?" Molly replied.

Gabriel looked confused, "No. I'm a real angel." He took a potato chip, covered both sides with ketchup and ate it.

"Where are your wings?" one of the other children from the younger table inquired.

"They're attached to my backpack." The boy answered innocently.

"No; real wings. Angels have real wings." Molly insisted.

"Not on Earth. I had to be born just like everyone else to get here. No halos, no wings." Gabriel said.

Many of the children refused to accept this idea and there was a barrage of insults and proclamations of shenanigans hurled at the boy.

"It's true, honest." He pleaded.

"Bull." Molly declared.

Sitting across from Gabriel, Callym leaned back in his orange plastic chair and repeatedly tapped the tongs of a fork on his empty tray. He looked up and through barely parted lips and said, "He's telling the truth, sister."

An abrupt hush swept through the cafeteria as the children all turned their attention to the strange new resident. Callym set down the fork and continued in his coarse, tired voice, "God used to be big on spectacle. Winged angels parting the sky with trumpets and swords of fire, raising the dead, walking on water;" Callym's eyes darted around the room, never actually focused on anyone; instead looking through everyone. He began to tap the fork again, "But people, being the simpletons that they are, focused more on the spectacle and not his message."

Gabriel nodded in agreement; somewhat amazed that Callym was so intuitive, "That's right! So God made it rule that there are to be no more miracles. No more wings, no more halos!"

Just then, Stew appeared at their table. He spun a plastic chair around, sat down backwards in it and faced Austin. "Religious discussion, awesome!" he gave a sarcastic thumb-up, "But there are bigger fish to fry." He slammed his palm down on the table and exposed a fresh twenty dollar bill as he lifted it.

"Alright Olsen, the sandwich thing is impressive." Stew said he stared down the chubby little boy, "But I've got twenty that says you can't up the ante."

Austin picked up the bill and inspected it, "What do you have in mind?" he asked inquisitively.

Stew grabbed the pepper shaker which rested in the center of the table and unscrewed the cap. He poured a small pile into Austin's hand. Austin looked at Stew with an unimpressed look. "You want me to eat this? That's child's play." He said defiantly.

Stew shook his head, "No, I want you to snort it."

"Oohs" and "Aahs" came from all the children who had crowded around the table. A sparkle filled Austin's beady eyes at the notion of the challenge. Without a word, he reached out and shook Stew's hand. The cafeteria burst into applause. Kids began to bet desserts, paper-route salaries and toys with one another over whether or not Austin would succeed.

"Oh, and just to make sure it's fair." Stew said as he lifted Austin's milk out of the boy's reach. Suddenly, the children scrambled and every carton of milk was quickly removed from the vicinity.

Austin breathed deep and took another look at the money on the table. The children began to chant his name. The boy nodded and pressed his nose into his open palm. The room was alive with cheer. Stew's smile showed that despite his defeat, he was completely impressed. Austin lifted his head back up, his nostrils flared red and burned all the way to the tip. He began to cough profusely. The lunchroom grew full of laughter. Tears poured from the boy's eyes as he lost control of his non-stop coughing.

"It burns… so bad!" he gagged. A thin line of drool fell from his bottom lip to form a pool onto the table.

"Here, this will cancel it out." Molly joked as she held out a shaker of table salt. Without hesitation and despite the many cries of "No," Austin immediately took a large pinch and sniffed it. His face turned a turnip purple and he began to squeal. Stew finally handed the boy his chocolate milk and amid the applause of the children said, "Well worth it."

Austin smiled between choking gasps and tucked the twenty dollars in his pocket. He put his hand to his temple and exclaimed an understated, "Ouch."

Molly spun back around from her table and asked, "So Gabriel, if all that angel stuff is true; then what is the message that people haven't seemed to figure out yet?"

Callym stopped tapping and sat back up in his chair. His gaze fixed upon Gabriel as the little boy said, "I don't know; the Savior is coming and they will tell us." Callym's head hung low; clearly disappointed that Gabriel did not have the answer. The young boy then added, "But I do know this; when it happens, love will save us all."

Depressed, Callym barely audibly muttered, "Bullocks."

Gabriel overheard this and reached across the table to touch the teen's hand. His thin fingertips gently brushed over the top of the pale, white hand. Callym recoiled; startled.

"Every life can be saved." Gabriel stated.

Callym rapidly rapped his fork and his leg began to shake as he listened to the self-proclaimed seraphim continue to speak, "It's all about finding what makes you happy."

"What makes you happy?" Callym echoed. The boy peered around the room. He looked down at his lunch tray and then gazed back up and stared coldly at Austin Olsen. His eyes rolled up into their sockets and with a whip of his arm, slung his lunch tray straight into Austin's face. The plastic struck the boy so hard that he fell backwards out of his chair. Sandwich crust and chip bits were cast into the air as the tubby pre-teen hit the linoleum floor with a dull thud. The children began to scatter from the table like a troupe of bewildered ants. Callym leapt over the table and threw his arms around Austin.

Stew jumped over a chair and grabbed Callym to hold him down. Nurse Durby and an assistant quickly ran to help subdue the teen. Callym flailed wildly, kicking his legs and swinging his arms. Stew struggled to pin the boy still. The assistant grabbed hold of his arms tightly as Callym clenched his hands and thrust the fork he was holding deep into the her wrist as he eerily shouted, "No, No, NO!"

Stew called to Heavy Paul to find Sunday as he pinned Callym's arms down with his knees. The blue-tinted teen ran as fast as his weighted legs would carry him, flung open the double doors and hurried out into the courtyard.

CHAPTER NINE

*K*ylie gently knocked on the door to the observation room. She turned the knob cautiously and opened the door as quietly as possible. The small room was nothing more than a table and a few chairs that sat darkly behind a special mirror which looked into the psychiatric exam room. A computer sat in the corner and ticked out various readings. Head Physician Dr. Margot Levine-Alonzo sat in one of the chairs and listened intently to the conversation in the other room. Two large files rested in front of her. She whispered a hush to the pair, and waved them in. Sister Mary Rochelle stood in the back of the room; her leather clad arms crossed. Kylie and Sunday sat down next to Dr. Levine and looked through the window and into the next room where Gabriel and Callym sat at a table with Dr. Shayam; both hooked up to numerous sensors that fed information back to the computer.

"So what happened?" Sunday softly asked.

Dr. Levine held a finger to her lips and pointed to the window. Dr. Shayam's voice came muffled but audible in the room as he spoke to the boys, "So, what were you feeling before you hit young Austin Olsen?"

Callym's vacant eyes roamed the room as he spoke, "Nothing. I saw the tray and I wondered what kind of damage it would do to that kid's fat face. Next thing I knew I was swinging it at him."

"Why?" the doctor asked.

Callym did not look up from his fidgeting fingers, "There wasn't a reason. It just seemed a thing to do, so I just did it."

"And the fork?"

"Same thing." Callym answered.

"It never occurred to you that it was wrong?"

"Wrong how?" Callym retorted.

"What I'm trying to ask, Ace" the doctor explained, "Wasn't there a moment where you realized the pain you'd cause them?"

Callym rocked back and forth in his seat, his lips curled up in an evil smirk, "Why would I? They're just sacks of flesh, just like everyone else."

"They are God's children." Gabriel stated.

"They are God's playthings, just like all of us." Callym argued, "He's not high on some cloud, looking after us. He doesn't care. If he did, he wouldn't let me feel so hollow all the time."

From inside the observation room, Sunday whispered, "What's he talking about?"

Without taking her eyes off the two-way mirror, Dr. Levine silently slid Callym's file over to Sunday in an effort to quell his questions. He opened it and began to study the various charts and notes, but no matter how he examined them, he could not make sense of any of it. "This looks like Chinese to me." he said softly.

Kylie took the file from him and began to review it. It did not take her but a brief moment before she found something interesting in the contents of the papers. Her eyes grew wide with surprise and she said, "According to his file, Callym has a blood type I have never seen before." she looked to Dr. Levine, "Did you see this?"

Dr. Levine handed Kylie the other file in front of her, which Kylie studied in a similar fashion. Sunday leaned over towards her and began to read over her shoulder, in the hopes that something in the large stacks of papers would make sense to him. Kylie's mouth dropped as she said, "Gabriel has the same blood type?"

"That's why we moved them to the same facility." Sister Rochelle explained as she set a long sheet of paper from the computer's printer in front of them. She pointed to a steadily increasing line on the chart. The peaks of the line exceeded the numbers on the chart. "This is Gabriel's brain pattern. His brain is responding to just about any stimuli with near euphoric synapses."

"I could have told you that." Sunday stated, unimpressed.

Kylie noted the second line on the chart which was considerably lower on the chart and made a slight decline. There were several severe downward spikes to it. "According to this, the only time Callym's brain triggers anything it's in a very negative way."

Sunday slowly began to put the pieces together, "So whatever is wrong with Gabe, Callym has the same type thing, just with opposite reactions?"

Completely entranced with the evaluation in the opposing room, Dr. Levine nodded that Sunday was correct, and shushed him.

"How did you feel afterwards?" Dr., Shayam asked, continuing his questioning.

Callym glanced up; his grey eyes locked onto the doctor's, "Horrible." He said simply.

"How do you feel now, Buddy?" Dr. Shayam probed.

Callym looked back down and shrugged, "It wouldn't have happened if I had my medicine."

Sister Mary Rochelle leaned over to Dr. Levine, "I told you not to take that kid off his medication."

Dr. Levine held up a hand, "Roxie, don't start."

Sunday smirked at the nickname and briefly envisioned his boss and the nun as old college buddies; staying up late with wine spritzers, watching Golden Girls or Highway to Heaven or something and talking all night about girly things. He would have liked to have cracked a joke, but was too captivated to actually say anything. Instead, he continued to spy on the children's conversation. Dr. Shayam prodded at Callym, "Tell me about what happened while you were on the Lithium Validemerethyzine."

"Nothing happened." Callym replied, "When I was on it, I couldn't react to those sudden urges to do bad things. So, I was a zombie, but that's a damn site better than walking around in this living hell."

"What do you mean by living hell?"

Gabriel chimed in and cheerfully added, "There's not really a Hell."

With a disheartened expression on his face, Callym said flatly, "There's not a *heaven*. Heaven was lost a long time ago. There's a *hell* in all of us."

"I assure you that there's a heaven." Gabriel rebutted cheerfully.

Dr. Shayam thumbed through the papers in front of him and responded, "That doesn't make sense boys. If Gabriel is an angel, and you are…"

"…a hell-spawn? Possessed?" Callym shouted, cutting off the doctor. "…Just a troubled teen? Look through the files, doc. They won't help you. You have no idea what's wrong with me. Or this kid!" Callym screamed as he pointed to Gabriel. "Or any of the kids in here! You're a hack and you couldn't possibly understand!" The boy rose from his seat, leaned across the table and glared at the blank faced, befuddled doctor.

"Maybe you think I'm wrong?" Callym questioned, "Then tell me what's wrong with me! Tell me I am a normal kid and I can be fixed. Tell me what's wrong with me, you hack-loser!"

He slammed his fists violently on the table and pushed the file across the table. Papers scattered across the surface and onto the floor. He sat back down in his seat, took a long, wheezing breath and said knowingly, "You can't do it because you are just like everyone else, and not a single one of you are willing to listen to what's really going on!"

Dumbfounded, Dr. Shayam meekly finished his thought, "If there's no Heaven or Hell then where do you think you come from?"

Despite the sudden outburst, Gabriel grinned. His expression widened at the question and he pointed skyward. The doctor looked confused, asking, "But he said there is no Heaven?"

"Do you believe in Heaven?" Gabriel asked.

"I believe in an afterlife which leads to reincarnation." Dr. Shayam replied.

"Well, it wouldn't be fair to you if there was just one Heaven and it wasn't all you imagined, would it?" Gabriel inquired.

"So are you saying that there are many little Heavens, Chief?" The doctor was visibly relieved that some form of order was reappearing in the room. Gabriel answered came only as a toothy grin and a wink.

Baffled, Sunday turned to Dr. Levine and asked, "Shouldn't he be trying to get to the bottom of their illness instead of placating them?"

"Are you a trained professional or are you the janitor?" Sister Rochelle snapped mutedly.

Stunned, Sunday brokenly replied, "No… I'm…It just seems to me… What I mean is…"

Before Sunday could properly string a sentence together, Hope abruptly flung herself into the room. She had a fearful look in her eye that Sunday knew meant that she had sensed trouble and that he was about to have to spring in to some sort of action.

"Grab the kids." he ordered and relented to his duties.

"I'm on it." Hope shouted, as she darted back out the door. She ran into the psychiatric room and had the two children on their feet before Dr. Shayam could think to object. Pulling the tiny sensors from them, she escorted the boys out the door.

Dr. Levine and Sister Rochelle looked confused; as did Kylie. Before Sunday could explain, Stew's voice hastily announced over the intercom. He sounded out of breath as he urgently huffed, "The soundproofing is not completed. The soundproofing is not completed. You have approximately…"

That is all he had time to say before a sonic shriek filled the building. Sunday put his hands up to Kylie's ears to block the chilling sound. She threw her hands up and wrapped her fingers around his, adding to her protection as they ran out of the room and down the emergency stairs.

Every window that lined the exterior of the first floor had been shattered from the high pitched squeal. Shards of glass scattered all across the floor in a myriad of dangerous angles. Sunday examined the damage as he corralled children to follow him. Since Stew was left to finish the soundproofing job, the realization struck Sunday that it was he who would to have the "mission" of replacing the panes later that night. Feet crunched over tiny bits of broken glass as the group ran to meet up with Hope and her company of children; "Put half in your car." Sunday commanded.

While they ran outside, Gabriel asked Austin, "What is that sound?"

Austin replied in a snuffled shout, "That's Molly."

CHAPTER TEN

$\mathcal{S}$unday's van cruised down the vacant street, sputtering and throwing up random pillars of smoke behind it. Kylie Court sat in the passenger's seat and watched as the wall of trees that lined the highway sailed by. Gabriel and Austin Olsen had claimed occupancy of the center seats while four children sardined themselves into the back. Off-key and almost shouting, the children sang along to the radio. Sunday was impressed at their ability to all seem to sing the same wrong verses and welcomed the humor of their incorrect words. After a few moments of listening to the juxtaposed whoosh of the wind through the cracks of the windowless hole and the children's gleeful cries of, "Jennifer has a Dixie cup..." Kylie turned to the children and giggled, "I don't think that's right at all." Sunday half-smiled as the van suddenly filled with laughter which eventually faded out and left the sound of the air that crept from outside.

"So, what exactly happened to the window?" Kylie enquired.

"A renegade Sprite bottle." Sunday explained. Apparently, the answer was not clear enough because Kylie looked unsatisfied.

Just then, Hope sped along side of the raggedy minivan. Her deep red, classic convertible Beetle crammed with Heavy Paul, who sat shotgun, one of the younger children in his lap and Callym in the back with at least four other children. Hope had snuck out on her sixteenth "birthday" and got her driver's license. Despite the court's lack of a ruling on the girl's actual age, she bought a car with what she said was allowance money. Sunday told her as long as the nurses did not find out; she could keep it parked down the block, with the understanding that he knew nothing about it. She cued Kylie to roll down her window and shouted, "Where are we going?"

Sunday thought for a second and shouted back, "Where do you take a dozen Wonder Kids?"

Hope smiled and screamed back, "Follow me." Her tiny vehicle sped ahead and as she pulled away a gummy worm flew from the back of her car and splattered onto the van's windshield.

"Son of a…" Sunday exclaimed as he turned on the wipers; which only pulled the candy and smeared a jelly rainbow across the glass, "Austin I know you're holding." Sunday said.

Without further discussion, the tubby snack-smuggler doled Twinkies, Sno- balls and an assortment of sweets to the rest of the children. Sunday turned to Kylie and explained, "You're about to find out what happened to that window."

He floored the gas pedal and after a short while caught back up to the convertible. The children pulled the cardboard window free and lobbed their candies at the passengers, the windshield and the doors.

"Moving food fights? That's what broke the window?" Kylie asked as she cowered in her seat from the rogue pasties which pelted the panes of glass.

"Sort of childish, huh?" Austin asked as he handed her a chocolate snack cake. Kylie examined the treat and looked to Sunday, who approvingly nodded for her to toss it out of the window. Timidly, she inched the glass down and with a squeak, threw the treat towards the trunk of Hope's accelerating car. Kylie quickly rolled the window back up and began to laugh uncontrollably.

Hope raced ahead so fast that Sunday knew his rickety vehicle could never keep up; and they were once again assaulted. More gummy worms, half chewed Oreos, even a slice of cake exploded and stuck to the van.

"We had cake left?" Austin exclaimed longingly as icing began to obscure Sunday's view of the road.

Suddenly, a giant textbook rose from the back of Hope's car, arched in the air and struck the front of the van with a shocking "BANG". It rolled over the hood and smacked the windshield which left a long spider web crack. Kylie jumped out of her seat in shock of the sound and the children briefly screamed. From the convertible ahead, Sunday saw Callym's arms rise up like a red-handed criminal. He kept his arms elevated and his head hung low for the remainder of the short trip as the rest of the children tossed assorted candies at each other.

—◉—

The windshield of the rusted minivan had been powdered with so much confectioners' sugar, gelled with candy worms and obscured by the long vein-like split in the glass that by the time the vehicle had pulled under the ivy wrapped stone archway which led into Our Lady of the Holy Spirit Monastery, Sunday had dropped his speed to a slow crawl. He pulled into the lot and parked next to Hope, who sat on the hood of her car. Her passengers had already emptied from the vehicle and begun a game of tag.

The monastery rested on a large grassy field which was encased on all sides by a circular perimeter of dense Georgia woods. To the east of the sprawling, green grounds and pushed back behind the monks' home was Hope's tiny Catholic High School. Its meager stone campus held almost 300 students, all of whom purchased their supplies at the monks' bookstore, which sat directly in front of the school. The shop offered textbooks, Bibles, Bible-related textbooks, Bibles on tape, Bible-related textbooks on tape with narrations by William Shatner, tiny religious trinkets and the monastery's locally-renowned fudge and handmade bread.

On the west end of the field was the monk's modest two-story living quarters which overlooked their peacock sanctuary and pond. A crudely fashioned chicken-wire perimeter lined the surrounding woods and permitted the majestic birds to roam freely on the grounds, safe from predators. In the center of all of this was Our Lady of the Holy Spirit's chapel. Its gothic stone structure immediately drew the eye. Ivy and kudzu slinked up the corners and twisted around the iron bars that protected the framed arches of the stained glass windows. Callym sat on the rounded rear of the convertible and blankly stared out at the building which was both too glorious to be a church and to meek to be a cathedral.

"All right kiddos, listen up!," Sunday shouted; which prompted the Wonder Kids to pause from their play and immediately turn their attention to him, "We are going to be hanging out here for a while. We will stay until I hear that they have Molly under control. At that time we will load up and leave- without any tears. Understood?"

The children nodded in unison as if they had been repeatedly drilled to do so. Pleased by the response, Sunday continued;

"There is a playground behind the school and there are birds to look at by the water. There is to be NO swimming in the water. There is to be NO running around the church. There is to be NO pestering the priests."

Gabriel's hand shot up as he interjected, "They're monks Sunday."

"Whatever." Sunday replied, "Leave them alone. There is a little gift shop with really good bread and candy and stuff. If you have money, you can go in. If you don't have any money, then you don't need to be in there. If you do go in, where do your hands go?"

The children all shoved their hands deep inside their pockets. Sunday nodded in approval, "That's it. Stay within earshot of my voice and be safe."

Gabriel's hand went up again, "How do we know how far you can yell?"

"Just don't go so far that you would have to worry about it." Sunday sighed, exasperated with the boy.

The children scattered and Sunday shouted after them adding, "Remember, this is Jesus' house, so don't act up. If any of you act up, I will pull off each and every one of your faces, switch them around and sew them back onto someone else's head!"

Gabriel stopped mid-stride and yelled back, "Mr. Sunday, I don't think that's actually possible."

Fuming, and with hands clenched in frustration, Sunday ordered, "Just go!"

Once the children had all dispersed, Sunday turned his attention to his windshield. He ran his fingers over the crack and shook his head hopelessly. Hope stretched and slid off her hood.

"This can't be my life." He sighed to her.

Hope smiled supportively and shifted her hand down his back in a comforting manner. Sunday ran his hands over his face and with a deep breath, pushed away his frustrations along with his hair. He leaned against his battered vehicle, began to look around the monastery and attempted to allow the peacefulness of the place to calm him. Wind rustled the leaves above him and he could hear the constant chatter of the cicadas in the trees sounding out to the ones in the grass all around him. A pleasant, white-noise that grew more pronounced as the children ran farther away. Just as Sunday thought he had found peace, a brown thrasher flew overhead; its white droppings fell to the ground and spattered on his shoe and the hood of his van. Disgusted, he tried to clean his shoe by moving his foot back and forth through the grass; an attempt that only worsened the problem by smearing it around.

"Why here?" Sunday asked Hope as he lamented over the stained leather.

"Why not?" she replied, "It's free, it's a nice day, the kids can get some God. There's a playground... and if the any of them fuck up, these guys *have* to forgive them."

"I think it was a great idea." Kylie Court chimed in.

Hope smiled graciously to Kylie and shot Sunday a triumphant grin.

"And I have to say," Kylie continued, "I'm really impressed at how the kids look up to you. I don't know if I'll ever be that good with them."

"Oh sure you will." Sunday said, reassuringly, "You just have to learn to…"

"…be an asshole." Hope quipped.

Sunday held up his middle finger, "I was going to say, you just have to learn to identify with them."

"I'm afraid they'll resent me, or I'll end up talking down to them all condescendingly." She confessed.

"Just remember to talk to them like you would anyone else. They will accept you. I promise. In the end they just want a friend."

Comforted, Kylie giggled, "You really think they will accept me? Make me part of the club?"

"Oh, you've got to be damned to be one of us, girl." Hope warned and with a nonchalant wave, walked towards the peacocks.

"She runs hot and cold; doesn't she?" Kylie asked.

Sunday agreed, but added, "Don't let her intimidate you."

Kylie shook her head, "She doesn't." She motioned for Sunday to follow her and he immediately slid off of the trunk of the convertible.

Kylie led Sunday across the grass and through a secluded trail which opened up to an un-manicured portion of the property which opened into a small cemetery. The thick yellow mist of southern pollen hung above the tall grass and weeds as the two carved their way through, agitating the vapor which burned Sunday's eyes and gave began to give him the sniffles.

"I owe you an apology." Kylie said after they had walked for a few minutes in silence.

"What?"

"You asked me earlier today about standing you up all of those times." She said sheepishly, "You've been so sweet to me; especially since I've been back, I just wanted to...like, explain things to you."

"You don't need to..."

She put her finger to her lip, "Yes I do."

"It's no big deal..."

"I want to."

"Okay."

Kylie Court stopped and turned to Sunday. He halted, faced her and squinted from the sun's rays which spread from behind her like a heavenly aura. She toyed with the end of her latex glove and said, "You have to understand. It was never anything you said or did." She looked to the ground, "I...um... I have *serious* intimacy issues."

Not knowing how to respond, Sunday simply nodded.

"I mean serious." She continued, "It took me years to get to the point where I could have people so much as touch me. I still have troubles touching people." She noted her color coordinated gloved hands.

"No shit?" It was all the custodian could think to say.

"I wanted to go out with you- honest. A couple of times, I even got all dressed up, made-up, ready to go... but in the end, it was always the same. I would freak out and end up locking myself in the bathroom."

From the way that she spoke, Sunday could tell that what he was hearing was rarely revealed. He knew that he needed to say something; something important and relevant. Now that he knew that his picture-perfect dream girl was flawed, for some unexplainable reason, he found himself increasingly drawn to her. He needed to know more.

Before the right thing to say could come to him, they were waved down by a monk who walked towards them, kicking up a flume of yellow dust as he approached. As he neared, Sunday noted the man's size. He was well over six feet tall and had wise, comforting eyes set far in their wrinkled sockets. His wispy, white hair crisscrossed atop his head in an unattended fashion. He wore a brown cassock that exposed only his calloused, liver-spotted hands. He brushed them against his knees and extended his hand to them, his smile revealing his extraordinarily white-teeth smile.

"Hi, Father." Sunday said as he took the monk's firm hand.

"Brother." The white-toothed monk replied.

"Excuse me."

They exchanged niceties about the weather and the grounds.

"Did you arrive with that group of children?" The monk asked.

"Yes;" Sunday answered, "We're from WonderKids. We needed a place to take the children for a little while. A couple of the kids are students over at the school and..."

"Ah yes, I thought I saw Ms. Daylily Margo."

"That was her." Sunday confirmed.

"Lovely girl." The white-toothed monk nearly choked on the words.

"Yeah, I'm sorry about that." Sunday stated as he apologized for the young woman's rebellious behavior.

"Think nothing of it, child. We were all young once." The old man surmised as he passed by. He wished them a fine day and added, "The choir will be rehearsing soon; I recommend listening in the chapel while you are here... And please make sure to try some of our handmade bread. God bless you both."

Sunday and Kylie said friendly goodbyes as the holy man continued to walk towards the buildings. They opted to skew their course and began to stroll towards the breaking of dogwoods that led to the water.

"So, where were we?" Kylie finally asked.

"The bathroom" Sunday said, hoping he was not making too light of the conversation.

She let out a slight tee-hee and summarized, "Yeah, so it wasn't anything you did, I just couldn't get past thinking about an end-of-the-night-kiss or something with out freezing up."

Sunday asked, "What about all the times you told Nurse Durby about the guys in the bars that hit on you?"

Kylie appeared slightly astounded that Sunday was aware of the bars, "You know about that?"

Sunday nodded and immediately grew fearful that Kylie may think he was stalking her; but instead she explained, "I… I lied about that too." She stopped, shocked and suddenly realized the number of deceptions that were needed to hide her condition. She straightened up and as if Sunday were a support group told him directly, "*Wow-* I'm a liar."

"Well that's… Wait… Did you say thinking about end-of-night-kisses?" The custodian pondered.

Kylie Court blushed and nodded. A warm feeling that he could not define wrapped around the custodian. He felt in that that moment the urge to lean forward that happens when a first kiss is imminent; yet he knew that based on the knowledge he had just received, he would be unable to act on the impulse. Thinking of how to properly take advantage of what was surely a fleeting anomaly in time that was not likely to happen again, the custodian said as coyly as he could, "Well then I guess you are forgiven."

—◉—

*H*undreds of dogwood trees stood in military-style rows, their trunks twisting around themselves until branching into a million white flowers. Here and there, benches were placed between the trees; some faced the pond, others faced the buildings across the rolling, grassy yard. This was where Sunday and Kylie found Callym Rafferty, who sat in the middle of one of the green benches, a bag of seed in his hand and surrounded by birds.

All around him tiny thrashers, pigeons and sparrows landed at his feet and on the bench beside him as he rustled the bag and tossed handful after handful of the brown pellets to the earth. Eerily, however, Callym paid no attention to the creatures that he fed. Instead, just as he had done in the parking lot, he stared blankly at the church across the way. He purposelessly placed his hand in the bag, rustled around and raised a palm full of seed which he held out. Almost instantly, a sparrow landed in his hand and began to feed.

"That's pretty cool." Sunday said as he and Kylie walked behind the bench and leaned upon it, facing the adjacent pond where Hope Daylily Margo and a small band of children were gathered.

Callym did not answer, nor did he turn to acknowledge the two people whose backs were now propped up on either side of him. Similarly, Sunday did not turn to face the boy as he said, "Callym, I think we need to talk about the book."

Rustle, rustle.

"What book?" Callym carelessly rumbled.

"The book you threw at my windshield."

"Hmph." The boy growled.

Click.

Sunday looked over at Kylie and nodded. With her watching, the pressure was on to make headway with the boy, "Well, listen. I know we were all throwing things out of the cars, and I know that sometimes things can get out of hand; so we can let the windshield slide."

Rustle, rustle.

Click.

Sunday looked to Kylie for approval and received a smile. He smiled back and continued, "But I did see you hit that kid in the main room and I heard about what you did to Austin Olsen."

Rustle.

Crick.

Rustle, rustle.

Clack.

Callym did not respond.

"We need to talk about it." Kylie added as she attempted to coax the boy to talk.

Crick.

Rustle, rustle.

"Why?" he finally creaked.

"Because you hurt them, Callym." Sunday explained.

Clack.

Crack.

Rustle.

"So?"

"So? So, you can't just go around hurting people."

Rustle, rustle.

Click.

"Why?"

Kylie Court was astounded by the boy's lack of concern, "Because it's wrong." She said.

"And because I won't tolerate it." Sunday added.

Rustle, rustle.

Click.

Rustle, click.

Clack.

Sunday had had enough of the boy's preoccupations with the bag and said, "Will you leave those bir…"

His words lost themselves in his mouth as he turned around to look the boy in the eyes. Callym held in his hand a young, tiny bird. He slowly tilted his head to look at Sunday and as he did, squeezed the bird until its neck snapped horrifically at an awkward angle, the small bones protruding from the bloody down feathers.

"Holy shit! What are you doing?" Sunday shouted.

Kylie spun around to see what the child was up to and gasped in terror.

Sunday pulled the boy up and lifted him from around the bench. Wanting to scold him, but not quite sure how, the custodian could only barrage the child with half-sentences and curses. He looked around and saw up the hill that Gabriel and Austin Olsen were walking towards the church steps.

"Kylie, will you take him up to the church and get him cleaned?"

She nodded, "What are you going to do?"

Sunday looked at the numerous dead birds strewn out in front of the bench. Surely, no good would come from anyone happening by them. He knew that he had to bury them, toss them in the water, throw them in a trashcan; anything to dispose of them quickly.

"Clean up this mess so that we can avoid a much bigger mess."

—◎—

Sunday found Gabriel and Austin Olsen on the front steps to the chapel. In between them sat a white bag of the monastery fudge. A chocolate-colored ring lined Austin's lips and trickles of the substance ran through his fingers and down his plump wrists. Gabriel munched on a piece while he straightened the wings of his backpack.

"Have you two seen Kylie and Callym?" Sunday huffed breathlessly.

"Ergh durgh." Austin replied; his mouth wedged with fudge. He indicated the stone archway to the main doors of the chapel that loomed over their heads. The double doors were a reddish stained wood and stood at least fifteen feet tall. Sunday found them extraordinarily heavy as he struggled to pull one side open. Gabriel and Austin attempted to follow him through the door, but Sunday whipped around, pointed at

Austin and snapped, "You look a train wreck, stay here." He added to Gabriel, "You can come in, but behave and be quiet." As much as the child irritated Sunday, he did not dare deny the would-be angel God's front door.

The two stealthily walked into the alcove, which was tiled with white marble. A Celtic cross composed of irregular black tiles centered the floor. Red linen drapes surrounded the walls, and separated the room from the actual church; two matching silver and ivory holy water basins marked the entrances in the cloth. The basin on the right had been toppled and shattered; its contents soaked the floor. Gabriel knelt down on one knee and dipped his finger in the puddle of holy water.

"He's definitely been in here." Sunday whispered.

With moist fingers, Gabriel touched his forehead, heart, then each shoulder blade and then rose from the ground. Sunday parted the red linen and entered the sanctuary. A breeze twisted and furled the fabric as they passed and entered the large vacant room. It looked just as he would have envisioned: the empty uncomfortable pews, the still light that passed through the stained glass; illuminating strange colorful shapes on the smooth spotless floor, the tiny unmanned flames of a thousand candles, sad paintings of saints and martyrs, gruesome life-sized replicas of the tortured Christ, wrapped in gold, silver and white silks. Gabriel walked beside him and inspected the intricacies of the angels and saints romanticized in the stained glass artwork adorning the windows.

In the third row of pews Sunday saw Kylie and Callym watching the choir rehearse. The plain-clothed octet was led by a guitarist who wore tinted glasses and a black, collared shirt with white etching, like the bank robbers that fought the Lone Ranger used to wear. A road-worn looking man played a stand up bass while a gentleman in a button-up shirt and tie tapped away on the church's organ. They were accompanied by a drummer and four women who all looked as if they could have been sisters.

Sunday noticed that Callym now appeared complacent, content in taking in the melodic sounds that bounced throughout the stone walls:

"Well, Mary wore three locks of chain;
On every link was Jesus' name.

Singin' Pharaoh's army got drownded,
O, Mary don't you weep."

Gabriel walked down the fourth row of pews to whisper in Callym's ear, "Aren't they great?"

The young man slowly nodded as the heavy door opened and Austin Olsen trotted in, licking the remaining fudge off of his fingers. He slipped in the puddle of holy water and his shoes squeaked loudly. The hefty child wiped his stained mouth on his sleeve, joined his winged roommate and showed Sunday his clean hands before he sat down.

Kylie motioned to the upper balcony and suggested that Sunday and she watch from above. Sunday nodded in agreement and leaned over to the three boys, "I'm right behind you, so watch yourselves."

The children in the fourth row nodded in understanding, while the lone occupant of the third refused to turn his attention away from the choir.

"Well, one of these nights around 12 o'clock,
This old world is gonna reel and rock.
Singin' Pharaoh's army got drownded,
O, Mary don't you weep."

There were only a handful of pews in each row of the stone balcony. Sunday and Kylie Court sat in the middle to ensure the best view of the boys below. They could see that Gabriel and Austin were deep in a hushed conversation, while Callym had yet to move. And this was exactly how Sunday wanted it.

"He started twitching before I brought him in, he knocked over the water bowl and as soon as he heard the music, he stopped." Kylie reported softly and added, "It was the strangest thing."

"I'm sorry I dumped him on you like that."

"It's okay. I guess I need to get used to it anyways." Kylie said optimistically. "What did you do with the birds?"

Sunday thought about how he had picked up the victims and placed them in his shirt, basket-style as he had seen Austin Olsen do with food so many times before. He recalled carrying them across the clearing and behind the dogwoods where the alignment of the trees obscured the children at the pond's ability to see him. It was there that he set down the birds and began to kick at the ground with his heel. He loosened the earth until a small but long trench had been dug. He rolled each corpse into the shallow gulley with his sneaker until they were all in. He then attempted to cover them back with the dirt, stamping it down as to mask the area, only to realize his error after he had further crushed the creatures and a sticky, muddy gunk had collected on the bottoms of his shoes, which he then had to clean off by rubbing his soles with a stick and repeatedly dipping his foot into the far end of the pond where no one would see.

"O, Mary don't you weep, don't you mourn."

"Do you really want to know?" he asked.

Kylie shook her head and said, "What do you think is wrong with him?"

"You understood the charts better than me." Sunday laughed.

"To hear those two kids talk... do you think it's possible that..."

"They were sent from the Great Beyond to witness prophesies of the second coming? No."

"I know; it's silly. They just sound *so* sure. And when Gabriel told me that he was glad I was here because it was a good sign for both of us, I felt that too."

Sunday was shocked to hear that Kylie was had begun to buy into the little boy's delusions. He looked down at the church below and was equally shocked to see Callym kneeling at the foot of the altar.

Kylie leaned over to Sunday and whispered, "You said you overheard me talk to Nurse Durby?"

Sunday nodded.

"Did you overhear anything else?"

"Why, do you have more secrets?" Sunday lovingly ribbed.

Kylie nodded, almost guiltily.

The custodian was caught off guard by her response; and in an attempt to appear aloof asked, "Is mom not really dead or something?"

His lips began to curl into a smile, but he immediately saw the flush expression that had swept Kylie's face.

"Brothers and sisters don't you cry,
There'll be good times by and by.
Singin' Pharaoh's army got drownded,
O, Mary don't you weep. "

"Are you kidding me?" She demanded.

"I didn't mean…"

"You think I would *lie* about my mother dying?"

"No…I didn't… Stew said…"

"That's sick, Sunday." She angrily screamed as tears raged from behind her eyes. She rose from the pew to storm out and added before she left, "You really are an asshole."

Sunday stood up to chase after her, but was sidetracked by the scene below the balcony which caused an abrupt absence of music and required his immediate attention. He listened, disheartened at the loud, dull thud of the large front doors as Kylie quickly escaped through them. To Sunday, it might as well have been the dull thud sound of his last dream being crushed.

CHAPTER ELEVEN

"Well, old man Satan he done got mad,
Lost that soul that he thought he done had."

$\mathcal{C}$allym Rafferty closed his eyes and listened to the melodies and harmonies that filled the church, finding satisfaction in every note. He had heard an expression long ago about music saving savage souls and while he did not know anything about that, he was certain of its charm over the empty ones.

He sat on the cold pew and thought back to all his favorite pieces of music. Chilling concertos from long lost gothic conductors, sullen sonatas, heavy metal riffs. He cued select sections from his memory that matched the tone of the song played by the choir until he felt Gabriel's stare on the back of his neck. He turned his head slightly to acknowledge the boy who failed to say anything.

"Aye." He answered, though there was no question asked.

"Aye, what?"

"Aye, we've met." Callym said flatly.

Gabriel elatedly whispered, "I thought so!"

"When? Where?" Austin Olsen added, in effort not to be excluded.

Faced fixed forward, Callym explained, "We met briefly in Dresden, Saxony in early winter... 1945."

"That's impossible." Austin suggested.

"That's only the beginning, brother;" the pale pre-teen responded, "There was a couple of years during the crusades where we were both living in the same Turkish village, a short encounter over the course of a weekend in 33 A.D., we clashed swords over two-hundred-thousand years ago and before that I'm pretty sure we were friends."

"Why don't I don't remember any of this?" the winged child responded, overlooking the blatant discrepancies in date and time.

"You will. The older you get, the more memories you will recover." Callym predicted.

Pleased to have found a kindred spirit, no matter how different, Gabriel prodded the young man further, "So, are you here to witness the word too?"

"Aye."

"Do you know who the Savior is?"

"No."

"Do you know when the word will be spoken?"

"Not when. Where."

"Really! Where?"

Callym did not respond.

"O, Mary don't you weep, don't you mourn."

"Where's the word going to be spoken?" Austin Olsen had become so involved in the conversation, that he repeated Gabriel's question. Once the boys realized that they were not going to receive the answers they sought, Gabriel changed the subject.

"I'm loving this trip back, how about you?" he whispered cheerfully.

Callym slowly shook his head, "I'm not from where you are. Being here isn't fun for me. There are many rules. And it's *painful.*"

"Why don't you just go back?" Austin innocently asked.

"You have to die." Callym and Gabriel said in unison.

Austin was a little embarrassed to have asked about what was apparently obvious common knowledge for his peers. Trying to save face, the portly child meekly added, "What about exorcisms?"

For the first time since they had begun their conversation, Callym turned to look at the boys behind him. Though he said nothing, it was clear his mind had begun to churn. He smiled at the boys and slowly turned back around in his pew, once again faced the practicing choir, closed his eyes and lost himself in the flashes that invaded his head.

—◉—

Bleak.

*I*t was the only earthly word he could use to describe the surroundings. There was no landscape, only a dense, dreary grey. There was no ground, only dust and ash. There were no pits of fire, no rivers of blood or lava; there was nothing. Perhaps an occasional shriek or cry would pierce the void, maybe a brief breeze of rot, but that was it. It was a place that by design depressed any soul damned to reside in it. And it was a place of his own design.

He had no memories of a better, happier place- a Heaven, but he was sure that he had once been there. Then again, he knew that it may have just been this place creating falsities to torment him. That is how it was in this place; the only pleasant things existed as unattainable entities and most usually they were merely fleeting fabrications or mirages of the mind. However, for some reason these memories seemed genuine. He knew that he had battled against a mighty army. He remembered that he had rallied with the small band of rebels hell-bent on making their demands known. He remembered the distain that he felt. He remembered the war and he remembered the fall.

He recalled being overpowered by an armory of angels and an intense light. After that he and his comrades fell, fell, fell. They fell for what seemed a millennia, picking up speed, racing towards the unknown. As they descended, their souls scorched and twisted. Like a sponge, they were squeezed of all that they valued. Squeezed until the only thing left was a residue of melancholy that maybe there had once been something better, but here in the wasteland, it was long out of reach.

Bleak.

From the fog he heard the call… maybe *felt* is a better word, "YOU WILL BE BORN A HUMAN CHILD. YOU WILL FIND THE SAVIOR AND YOU WILL WITNESS THE WORD. THEN YOU WILL RETURN.

While there, your soul will retain its cursedness. You shall not harm the Savior. You shall not prevent or alter the proclamation of the word. You shall not conjure miracles. You shall not commit Suicide..."

This continued; commandment after commandment, what he could and could not do, what he could and could not say, what he will experience and what he was not allowed to experience. He knew that he could not object to the charge, he could not question the laws for it was willed- it was The Will; it was Destined and undisputable. As soon as the voice had subsided, he was whisked away in a black bolt only to find himself forced towards a thin white light.

He tried to speak, but could not. He was covered in a pasty gel and wished to rid his body of it, but he had no control over his arms or hands. When he opened his eyes, he found that he had lost all control of his limbs, his voice, everything. He found himself trapped in the body of a newborn boy in a small hospital on the outskirts of Dublin. He tried to tell the masked man who held him to release him, but could not. From his soft skull to his tiny, tiny toes, he experienced a searing pain that felt like a thousand angry claws ripping the skin from the inside out and that refused to subside.

While the bleak, grey void was not a place to be homesick for, this rebirth left him confused and helpless and he loathed the feeling. He knew that he was now constrained to the slow crawl of time and that he would be imprisoned for a lifetime... and he knew that a lifetime spent in a body would feel much, much longer than he was accustomed to. A lifetime in the fleshy shell; a lifetime with this inner pain.

This is no better of a place; this is no better an existence.

He was passed from the man to a sweaty, weeping woman on a bed. He squirmed, but was unable to object. The woman held him uncomfortably, and as she said, 'His name is Callym'; he cried.

—◎—

Austin Olsen marveled at the notion of angels and devils and some magic word or phrase that would save everyone; and though he was not sure what everyone needed saving from, he was hopeful that whatever it was and whenever it happened, his disease would be cured as well. He barraged Gabriel with questions regarding the details of his task and the general nature of angels, "Why do you need to watch this special person say these special words?"

"Just to be along for the ride, I guess." Gabriel answered.

"And you remember everything?"

"No, just pieces of things."

"Neat! How will you know the Savior guy when you find him?"

"I guess I just will."

"He could be anyone?"

"Yep."

"Could it even be me?"

"I guess it's possible."

"What about Callym?" Austin teased.

"I think he's just along for the ride too." Gabriel noted.

It would have possibly tickled Callym Rafferty to think of himself as the savior of the human race, had he been listening to the boys behind him. Instead he glared at the altar, lost in thought and engulfed in the choir's song. He wondered to himself if it was possible that all of these nightmarish memories from other times and places could be explained away. Perhaps it was due to an overactive imagination or the side effects of a strange brain tumor or perhaps he was possessed, as the fat child suggested. It seemed highly unlikely.

If only there was a way to get rid of it.

He sulked, stuffed his hands into his coat pockets and dropped his head.

"God gave Noah the rainbow sign,
Said, "No more water but fire next time."

Singin' Pharaoh's army got drownded,
O, Mary don't you weep. "

His bandaged fingers slid over the thin plastic tip of the emergency syringe of Lithium Validemerethyzine that he kept on him at all times. The boy had long since given up on the ideas that it was a medical condition that was the cause of his plight. He was certain that if it were, one of the doctors, examiners or psycho-analysts would have found evidence of it in at least one of the hundreds of tests they had preformed on him over the years.

Callym slowly rose from the pew and inched to the aisle. Austin Olsen and Gabriel both fell silent and watched, mouths agape, as the young man knelt on both knees at the foot of the altar, which was covered in the traditional silk cloth and draped with a red liner. Above it hung the church's traditional, depressing rendition of the Savior nailed upon a crucifix. The molded, agonized Jesus looked down from his wire elevated cross, upon the teen with weary, plaster eyes. Callym hung his head down solemnly; his shoulders heaved up and down as if he had been crying. Suddenly, he rose, stretched his arms outward and screamed, "Is this who I am; one of your brilliant disasters? Fuck you! Fuck you and fuck them for all of this!"

The musicians stopped mid-song at the unusual disturbance; their gasps of shock and dismay echoed the now silent chapel. From the balcony, Sunday saw Callym unzip his pants and begin to urinate on the altar. He sighed for he knew that he would have to wait to catch up with Kylie to apologize and sprang to stop to the boy. However, before he could run down the staircase, the alcove and the aisle to reach him, the white-toothed monk appeared from a door on the right side of the altar. Callym's focus was broken as he took notice of the monk, who walked beside him and placed his hands on the shoulders of the troubled boy.

Callym collapsed into the man's arms, "It's not fair." He whispered.

Gabriel scrounged in his backpack and pulled out a couple of Hallmark cards and the troll pen then began to scribble in them, while Sunday once again found himself apologizing to the holy man.

"Your Holiness…" He began.

"Brother." Gabriel corrected.

"That's right." Sunday replied, "I am *so* sorry. He's with us."

The old man nodded and embraced Callym, who turned back to the crucifix and screamed, "It's not fair!" The teen broke free form the monk and ran back to the altar.

"Are you out there? Are you listening? Slag off!" He shouted at the foot of the statue of Christ and fell back to his knees.

"Don't feel bad, Callym," Gabriel pleaded as he held a get-well card over the sobbing teen's slumped shoulders. Callym swatted away the boy's hand along with the card.

"Why shouldn't I feel bad, Gabriel?" Callym demanded, "I have had to live like this, seeing others experience happiness, love, acceptance and feeling nothing myself but indifference, hatred and pain."

Callym's words began to break as his seldom used vocal chords gave out, "No one believes me; and they would rather focus on not believing than on helping me to find a way to *feel*."

"I believe you." Gabriel said honestly.

Callym brushed off the boy's attempt at friendship and said, "You *have* to believe me, you are just like me- you just didn't get the shit end of the stick like I did."

He sprang from his position and once again attacked the altar. "Why won't you help me?"

He shouted to the heavens, tossed the religious items from their surface and ripped at the cloth. Sunday wrapped his arms around Callym and locked them at their side until he stopped thrashing around. Once he was released, the boy fell limp onto the floor.

The white-toothed monk calmly approached; he did not look the slightest bit agitated over the ruined room. He held a hand out to Callym and said, "There is help here if you want it."

Callym sobbed and rubbed his grey eyes dry. He looked deep into the old man and could tell that he sincerely wished to help. The young man took the monk's hand and lifted himself off the floor.

"You believe that there is something wrong with me?" Callym asked.

"I believe that we can help you." The monk promised.

The holy man nodded at Sunday and his sidekicks and shooed them toward the door. Callym began to weep into his hands as the holy man sat down beside him. Gabriel's eyes were fixed on the scene in front of him as he bent down to set a hallmark on the floor. Sunday grabbed him by the loop of his backpack and lifted him up. The monk turned and then knelt down beside Callym and rested his hands back on the child's sulking shoulders.

Austin hustled to keep up with Sunday and Gabriel as they exited the building. Sunday turned to the boys and said, "That kid is going to be the end of me."

He sat on the top of the stairs, looked at the sun's deep orange streak through the heavy clouds and listened to the cries from within the chapel. Gabriel plopped down beside him and watched inquisitively as Sunday rolled his head in a large circle, cracking the vertebrae in his neck.

"Do you think the monk saw his card?" Gabriel asked.

Sunday did not answer; he mumbled something foully, stretched out his legs, stood up and began to walk towards the water. The boys sat up and began to follow.

"Sunday, do you think he'll get it?" Gabriel shouted from behind as he hurried his little legs. Sunday nodded at a couple of passing monks and then instead of answering the child, grabbed him, spun him around and pulled the troll pen from the backpack's side pocket.

"Mine." He said.

Austin trudged along a few paces behind them, "Where are we going?" he huffed.

"I'm dropping you two yahoos with Hope and Heavy Paul and I am going to apologize to Kylie." Sunday said, not breaking his stride until he had reached the group gathered by the small pond.

—◇—

The reflection of the late day sun rippled off of the small wakes in the monastery pond. A handful of geese had taken residence on the bank and bobbed their heads in and out of the water as they searched for an early evening snack. The smaller children turned cartwheels in the heather while the older children gathered around Hope on a nearby picnic table just a few feet where the trees broke from the shore line. From across the water, Sunday could see the marble slabs of the cemetery and Kylie sitting by them on a bench. Even from that distance, she appeared lonely and full of sorrow. The sight tore at the custodian and he wanted to call out to her from across the water; however he was suddenly bumped by Austin Olsen, who ran haphazardly towards the water as a rogue peacock chased him.

"Help me, help me!" he screamed.

Feathers unfurled, the bird charged after the boy until he stumbled over his bumbling feet and splashed down on the water's edge. The occupants of the picnic table began to clap and cheer.

"It's not funny; help me out!" Austin whined as he undulated to and fro and pivoted back and forth, like an overturned turtle trying desperately to right his round body. Heavy Paul and Gabriel ran down to the boy's aide, each grabbed an arm and hauled the soaking lump to his feet.

"We weren't laughing at you;" Paul said to Austin who had begun to shake himself off, "We are testing Hope, and she said that once you got down here you would fall in the water."

"That's amazing." exclaimed Gabriel.

Austin was not as impressed. Shaking himself off like a soggy dog he said, "Anyone could have guessed that. What else do you have?"

Hope thought for a moment and said, "The church bell is going to ring in three…two…" Just then the chimes of the steeple bells rang in the distance. Hope smiled at her accuracy.

"Incredible." Gabriel gushed astonished.

"Come on, you could have been looking at my watch." Sunday teased.

Hope closed her eyes and concentrated intensely. Her eyes darted about under her eyelids as she focused on future events. After a few seconds, she opened her eyes and said with a snap, "Heavy Paul's going win the state title for the pole vault."

Hearing the prediction, Paul's blue face lit up with hopefulness.

"That's over six months away. You've never made a prediction that far ahead before. Are you sure?" Sunday asked.

Hope sat up on the edge of the table, smirked and wagered, "I'll bet you fifty bucks."

Sunday nodded in agreement and asked, "Alright girl, what about me?"

Hope stood up and walked over to Sunday. She moved close to his face, stared deeply into his eyes and focused all her being onto him. Sunday stared back awkwardly. He watched as her eyes darted back and forth and read his life's story as if it were written far behind his pupils. She began to inch closer to him; so close that he could feel her warm breath on his neck as her brow scrunched in intense concentration. Unblinking, she fixed on him until they were so close that they almost touched. Suddenly, she pulled away; her expression fell as if the tale she were reading had thrown her a twist she had not expected.

"What?" Sunday asked, "What did you see?"

Hope looked as if she did not want to reply at all. She craned her neck and said, "I'll tell you another time."

Gabriel took this as an opportunity to chime in, "I know Sunday's future!"

"Oh, what's that?" Hope prodded him on playfully.

"Well, it's actually from a passage in Leviticus. But I think it suits Sunday well." Gabriel began, "Everybody's got a special kind of story, everybody finds a way to shine. It don't matter that you've got not a lot. They'll have theirs, and you'll have yours, and I'll have mine. And together we'll be fine....."

Sunday swatted at the boy, "That's not Leviticus; that's 'Diff'rent Strokes'." He stated bluntly.

"It still makes sense though." Gabriel said defensively.

Hope suddenly turned to Sunday. Her bewildered look immediately told Sunday that something was wrong. Cryptically, she ordered, "Sunday, you need to go to the church, now. Paul, go get Kylie."

Not seconds later, a strange and angry growl echoed over the hill which prompted everyone to follow the young woman's commands. Sunday began to sprint up the hill, unsure of what he was running towards and unaware that Gabriel trotted behind him as fast as his legs would allow. As he approached the chapel, the sound grew more prominent. Sunday leapt up the stone steps in one great leap and flung open the heavy doors. He took a few steps inside and his shoes gave out and squealed over the holy water still spilt upon the marble floor. He tossed open the drapes, finally lost his footing and fell to one hand. As Sunday stood, he looked up and saw Gabriel standing beside him.

"It was coming from somewhere high." He smiled, referring to the sound.

"What are you doing?" Sunday barked through a whisper. The shrill sound from another scream ricocheted from behind a door that sat across the balcony walkway. Gabriel smiled and scurried towards a staircase leading towards the sound.

"Gabriel!" Sunday cried out as he darted up the stairs to follow the boy. Rushing past the few rows of pews, across the walkway and through the door, Gabriel stood in a long, narrow hallway and inspected the many closed doors that flanked either side all the way to the building's end. Sunday caught up to him and grabbed him by the back of his neck.

"What do you think you are doing up here?" he demanded. Before the boy could answer, a monk emerged from one of the doors. Sunday released the boy and smiled.

"Excuse me, sir;" He said, "You haven't seen a little boy: this tall, with creepy eyes… screaming? Have you?"

The man nodded, "He told Brother Linus that he was in turmoil."

"He's the priest from before." Sunday said to Gabriel as if they were suddenly the Hardy Boys gathering clues.

"Monk." The man corrected.

"Why is everyone so hung up on that?" Sunday inquired.

"Do you know where they are now?" Gabriel asked. The monk pointed to a door on the far end of the hallway and they made a move towards it.

"You can't go in, though." He cautioned, "They are conducting a very private session.

Sunday smiled and waved to him as he turned and continued to the door which had a box window centered in the upper half. He peered inside and saw that the room was quite small. There was barely enough room for the twin sized bed, the simple nightstand and the wooden chair that filled it. Callym Rafferty lay upon the bed and squirmed to free himself from the straps that bound his arms and feet to the frame. The white-toothed monk hovered over him, sprinkled him with holy water and chanted, "*Sic liminaca pom suffaretaca.*"

Sunday was not sure that was what he really said; for it was all in comprehensible gibberish to him.

"I can't see." Gabriel whispered as he struggled on his tip toes to view into the tiny window. Sunday lifted Gabriel up for a moment so he could take a quick peek inside. The monk began to chant louder:

"*Pardo lificilta baraca sin pificilta da! Pardo lificilta baraca sin pificilta da! Demons leave this child!*"

Callym screamed and thrashed about. His teeth were gritted tightly, his eyes wide and evil, and he had a terrible look of anger on his face. The monk commanded again, "Demons leave this child!" and tossed more holy water on the boy.

Gabriel grew heavy in Sunday's arms and he had to lower him; "You weigh a ton, kid." he said as the boy's sneakers touched the ground.

"What's happening now?" he whispered.

Sunday peered back through the glass. Brother Linus had stopped chanting. He had placed down the holy water and spoke softly to Callym, who was panted and tried to gain control over his lungs after all of his thrashing about and screaming.

"… There is nothing happening, son." The white-toothed monk gently explained, "I think it's possible that you simply are not possessed."

Callym lifted his head off the pillow as high as possible, to lock eyes with the holy man, "I have to be. I have seen hell. You have to help me."

The monk sympathetically smiled at the poor boy, his huge teeth a glimmer. He reached over and began to unfasten the belts that held Callym's right arm to the bed.

"I'm sorry. I just don't know what else to do." Brother Linus said softly and moved to unlatch the boy's leg.

Callym took his now free hand and worked the latch for the other arm. As soon as he had released his arms and his right leg was unbound; Callym launched off the bed at the monk with speed that never would have been expected from the slow moving teen. He grabbed the old man by his robe as he was in mid-movement; and even though his left leg was still bound to the bed's frame, he lunged forward to throw Brother Linus against the wall. The bones in Callym's lower leg began to snap and break as they were forced into a full 90 degree angle in the wrong direction. *Crack, Crack, Pop*; went the boy's limb; the sound mixed with the surprised cries of the gasping monk into one ghastly noise. Callym's knuckles went white as his grip tightened around Brother Linus' neck. Shocked, Sunday quickly began to attempt to force the door open.

"Find something to do! Tell him to make it stop! You promised!" The boy demanded in a wicked tone; his leg broken to the point where he could freely get his face inches from the old man's. Callym's eyes were locked on those of his prey as a thin strand of drool poured from his teeth-gritted mouth. The white-toothed monk's terror-ridden expression turned a pale purple as his airway began to completely close off. He thrashed around helplessly beneath the boy's knuckles as they tightened around his jugular.

"Stop!" Sunday shouted and began to ram the door in an attempt to dislodge it. Callym paid no attention to the custodian on the other side. Instead, he squeezed on the old man until his eyes began to bulge and roll up into their sockets. Meanwhile, Sunday slammed over and over against the decades old door, until it bent from its hinges and he was able to pry it far enough away so that he could fit through.

The interruption surprised Callym enough to release his grip on the man, who dropped to the floor and put his hand over his throat and attempted to find air again. Not knowing what else to do, Sunday cocked his arm back and punched Callym hard across the cheek. The boy collapsed across the bed, his arms dangled over one side; his mangled leg over the other. Sunday unlatched the unconscious boy and pulled him off of the bed. The monk from earlier burst in to the open doorway and knelt to the aide of Brother Linus.

"What happened?" he asked.

"Everyone's just gotten a bit overzealous." Sunday grunted as he lifted Callym into his arms.

He rushed to exit the chapel and ignored the white-toothed monk who called for them to wait. Callym's lifeless leg dragged clumsily behind Sunday and smacked steps, roots and every other obstacle that it met along the way back to the van. With each dull thump, Callym winced in pain until it proved too much for him and he passed out on Sunday's arched shoulder.

Gabriel, meanwhile, fumbled behind them and attempted to lift Callym's limp leg from off of the ground. Sunday cocked his head and warned, "See what happens when you try to convince people your condition is more than what it is?"

The young cherub did not respond; he simply shifted Callym's legs in his arms so as not to lose grip. However, Sunday could see through the beads of sweat that were gathering on the boy's frustrated and confounded brow that his message had been received.

Heavy Paul was fastening the children into their seats when Sunday and Gabriel met him at the van. Hope had already filled her car with the remaining tykes and had taken off for the highway. Sunday thrust Callym from off of his shoulder and into Paul's arms and caught his breath. Disappointment slapped him once he saw that Kylie had left in Hope's convertible. Despite the current commotion, Sunday still desired the opportunity to right things with her.

"What happened?" Heavy Paul asked as he shoved the motionless teen into the back seat.

"Callym wore out our welcome." Sunday replied.

"What happened to his leg?"

"It doesn't matter. Let's just get him in the car and get him back home."

Gabriel shouted, "Shotgun!" and hopped up into the seat beside Sunday as the custodian repeatedly tried to get the old engine to start. It took a few twists of the key, but finally the machine roared to life. Sunday made a last minute seat belt reminder, pushed the gas pedal to the floor and sped out from under the arch of Our Lady of the Holy Spirit Monastery.

"How are we doing back there?" Sunday called back to Heavy Paul whose blue hands pressed down on the pale child's fracture.

"It's pretty gross, Sunday. You're going to have to burn this seat." Paul stated, "And he's waking up."

Callym moaned softly as he groggily came back into consciousness. The children squished in the middle seat began to inquire what happened.

"He fell." Sunday said as he tried to block out all the havoc and focused instead on the road through the cracked windshield.

He could feel Gabriel's glance on him. The young boy had a disapproving look, like he was ashamed to be the only one to know that Sunday was not being honest. Sunday put his finger to his lips and motioned for the boy to keep quiet.

Austin poked his head between the front seats, "Is he going to be okay?" he sobbed; his mouth full of food and chocolate icing lining his pudgy lips.

"Are you eating the food fight ammunition?" Sunday snapped.

Austin took a big gulp and explained, "I'm nervous. I eat when I'm nervous." Tears rolled down his plump, sticky cheeks.

"There's nothing to be nervous about. Just calm down." Sunday said and peddled the car towards a low laying sea of black rain clouds.

"But Callym's in trouble; and you said that if anyone gets in trouble you were going to pull off our faces!" Austin cried as he gasped for air between whines and wiped the errant mucus trailing down from his nose with a disgusting sniffle.

Sunday shook his head and found it hard not to giggle a little, "No one is going to lose their face, Austin." He said assuredly, "I promise."

CHAPTER TWELVE

*R*ain pummeled the parking lot. It fell sheet after sheet while Head Physician Dr. Margo Levin-Alonzo waited under the overhang; Sister Rochelle by her side. They both had their arms crossed and stood a few feet behind their small entourage of medical staff at the ready with a gurney, some kind of IV and an unnecessary crash kit. They watched as Sunday's van half-hydroplaned around the corner and into the parking lot. Before the custodian could even put the vehicle into park, they had placed Callym onto the stretcher and raced him inside. Sunday climbed out of the vehicle and ran after them.

"What happened, Mr. Sunday?" Dr. Levine demanded as Sunday caught up with her and the already at work medical team inside the elevator.

"He snapped his own leg." The custodian explained.

Sister Rochelle added coldly, "We were called just as soon as you left the monastery. Why did you leave?" The door opened to the second floor and they began to run down the hall.

"He snapped his own leg." Sunday repeated.

"You didn't call the hospital?" The nun delved.

Sunday stopped running; Dr. Levine and Sister Rochelle halted as well. "Am I being interrogated?" he demanded, "Look, the ambulance would have taken ten minutes. I got us here in less time, and the hospital probably wouldn't have all that psycho shit you had him on."

Sister Rochelle boasted to the Head Physician, "I told you not to take that boy off of his meds."

"We're not going to get into this again tonight, Roxie." Dr. Levine quipped.

Sunday was relieved that the subject of the boy's medication had taken the focus temporarily off of him as the nun retorted, "We're putting him back on them *tonight*."

A nearby nurse nodded and began to follow the team who had set up in the emergency room. They lifted the mangled teen from the stretcher and onto the operating table.

"A third of what he was on, Missy." The Head Physician ordered. The young aide nodded and started off again.

"Wait!" The nun yelled. The nurse stopped and Sister Rochelle turned back to the Head Physician. She lowered her tone, "Honey, we've been in this business long enough that you should know by now that you aren't going be able to fix this boy."

Dr. Levine looked at her old companion; her face filled half with disgust, half filled with heartache and said, "We've been in this business long enough for you to know that something like that would never stop me."

With that, Sister Rochelle silently walked back to the elevator. Her anger was evident in every step. As soon as the sliding doors closed and the nun was out of earshot, Dr. Levine summoned the young nurse one last time and said, "Half his dose, Missy."

The young woman nodded and hurried off. Dr. Levine looked back at the custodian and shook her head, "I don't know what to say, Mr. Sunday."

"It wasn't my fault." He insisted.

"It doesn't matter. That monk didn't call *us*. He called *St. Joe's*... And he was directed to the office of William A. Augustine-Chrystine. We got the call from Mr. Augustine-Chrystine himself, Sunday. And he said that he was making it issue number one that the Board of Directors vote Monday to cut funding for WonderKids due to high overhead and lack of returns. We have a little over a week to cure one of these kids or they are going to shut us down... He wants to turn this place into the William Augustus Augustine-Chrystine Quarantine Center."

"Honest, Dr. Levine, I left because I was trying to keep this low profile." Sunday explained as a terrible guilt that he felt he did not deserve began to overtake him.

Undeterred, the Head Physician sighed and said, "It's raining pretty hard. You should probably get to work on those windows."

"I'll be here all night!" he protested to the woman who had already begun to walk away from him.

Dr. Levine turned three-quarters of the way back to the custodian and with an empty, disenchanted expression blankly replied, "Then you'll be here all night."

—◉—

All of the children had been sent to the cafeteria for dinner, which left the main room clear. And very wet. The rain had fallen more fiercely and had soaked the floor. Stew had already swept up the shards of glass in Sunday's absence and had set aside large plywood sheets from the basement to board up the windows. The custodian walked across the empty room and went to grab a poncho from the utility closet, slid the plastic jacket over his head and grudgingly made his way to the first vacant window.

There is a certain solace that can be found in a good southern rain; something quelling in the tapping sounds of the droplets hitting the wind-rustled leaves of the region's many, many trees. The beauty of the sky as it gives off an amber hue just before the pace quickens. Even at its hardest, there is a lulling effect a southern storm can possess as the water splashes onto a soaked street in rhythmic waves that is unlike the rain of any other place in the world.

After spending an hour in the Wonder Kids parking lot, Sunday had only two windows covered and felt nothing quelling as the pounding rain stung his exposed skin. The poncho served little protection and his clothes had become heavy from saturation. Streams of water rolled from head to toe and the custodian constantly had to brush errant beads of rain from rolling into his eyes. The entire process was very tedious and frustrating. Sunday's mind was weary from replaying the evening's strange events. He could not shake images of Kylie and the anger and sorrow in her eyes as she screamed at him, scenes of the boy shouting at the head of the altar, threatening the white-toothed monk, and most of all; he kept seeing his lack of hesitation in breaking the bones in his own leg. It haunted the custodian as he ran his hand through his wet hair and steadied the third board.

The time slipped away and the rain became more ominous. The worsening winds numbed Sunday's knuckles and beat against him, which made it nearly impossible to rush through the job, as he so desperately desired. He looked across the building at the many gaping holes he had yet to fill, and grumbled.

Sister Rochelle walked from the elevator doors and crossed the wet tiles over towards him. As she neared, he noted the straight expression across her face. He steadied the board and inspected the nails that held it in place. Satisfied with his work, he stepped through a hole to greet the nun.

"How is he?" the custodian asked and shook the beads of rain off like a wet, shaggy dog.

The nun walked past him to one of the numerous empty sills, reached her hand deep in her leather jacket and pulled out a pack of cigarettes. She looked out at the clouds, slid out one of the thin menthols, wedged it between her stern lips and lit it.

"The doctors are finishing now." Sister Rochelle began, "He sustained a six inch spiral fracture. They pieced the fragments together as best as they could. The leg is being held together by a thick metal sleeve and surrounding pins. At least that's what they said. He may have to keep the pins forever." She paused to exhale smoke out of the room. "I just don't know."

"What?" Sunday asked.

"What can be done for that poor boy?"

Sunday forced a reassuring smile, comfortingly touched the nuns arm and said "We'll figure it out."

Sister Rochelle nodded, "I hope so."

Shortly thereafter, the cafeteria doors flew open and a flurry of children emerged. They dispersed in little cliques that gathered around the merry-go-round and packs that scattered here and there; all of which avoided the giant pool of water that had spread to almost half of the room.

Stew walked out through the double doors and crossed the puddle over toward his damp cohort. He handed Sunday a grilled cheese sandwich, "I would have brought more, but Austin got back in line for seconds before I could get to anything."

Sunday gratefully accepted the sandwich and took a large bite. The bread had already begun to sag from the onset of heavy downpour; but the custodian gladly sent it straight to his grumbling stomach. Stew grabbed a corner of a board and helped steady it in the frame. "So...," he began, "So far I've heard he fell, I heard he jumped out of a window and that you *threw* him out of a window. What happened to that kid?"

They bolted the window in place and walked to the next pane. "That creepy little shit ransacked a church, literally cursed God and convinced some priest..." Sunday said.

"Monk." Gabriel rang out as he joined the maintenance workers.

"Don't start." Sunday warned and then continued, "He convinced some *monk* he was possessed... and then he broke his own leg trying to strangle the guy when he couldn't exorcize him." Sunday shoved the rest of the now ruined sandwich into his mouth and forced it down his throat.

"I guarantee you that Gabriel kid had something to do with it, too." Sunday added in a whisper so that the child could not hear him.

"Oh, he seems harmless." Stew replied.

"He's a pain in my ass." Sunday mumbled.

"...And Kylie?"

"Don't ask." Sunday griped as he turned his attention back to the boards. He hammered the corner in place and then asked, "How long did Molly scream?"

Stew suddenly got excited, dropped his corner of the board and ran back inside through the window hole. The board swayed from its fixed point and splashed to the ground. Stew returned with an overly complacent Molly Rollins. Sunday could see that her eyes lacked irises and were a cloudy white.

Stew happily explained, "This is so cool! Nurse Durby has been playing with that stuff that they had that Callym kid on, right? So, we're out of Valium and Molly's screaming her brains out; so Nurse Durby gives her like a fifth of Callym's dose of the stuff mixed in some juice. Next thing you know…" He gestured to the little girl, who was calmly held his hand.

Aside from her colorless eyes, Sunday could see nothing extraordinary about the child. With a shrug, he replied with and unimpressed, "So?"

"So!" Stew continued, "I was finishing up the soundproofing with her just standing there. She hardly answered anything I said to her. But then I told her if she wanted me to finish faster, she could help by sweeping up. So she leaves right? And what does she do? She sweeps the whole damn place! That's when I realized, she's become like some kind of trained monkey!" He crouched down next to her and added, "In fact, hey Molly, be a monkey."

No sooner than a finger could snap, the little pig-tailed girl's body hunched over and she began to clap her hands and shake them over her head like some kind of primate. She hopped around and leapt at Stew's arm in an attempt to scurry up him as if he were a tree.

Sunday laughed, "That's amazing! Do you think they'd let us give it to all of the kids?"

Stew shrugged and chuckled at Molly as she scratched at her underarms and eeked.

"Let me try." Sunday said, "Molly, sweetie, do a little dance."

The child immediately stopped her monkey business and began to prance about. As Sunday suggested dance styles, from the waltz to the robot, to the moonwalk, Molly altered her moves seamlessly. This continued until Sunday requested the running-man. As Molly jogged heavily in place, her foot hit the wet floor and she slipped and fell.

One of the children saw this and realized that sliding across wet linoleum is a dangerous kind of fun. The youngster glided across the room until he wobbly lost his balance, fell on his back and slid across the floor. Soon after, another child attempted to beat the previous record and crashed onto his rear just past the point where the first child lost balance. It was not long before a very unsafe game had broken out.

"We can't let the kids stay down here." Sunday reasoned.

"What do you think we should do?" Stew replied, "They're all hopped up on chocolate-covered caramel and peanut butterballs. They aren't going to go peacefully."

"You had chocolate-covered caramel and peanut butterballs?" Sunday asked enviously, devastated that he had missed out on such a wondrous delight.

"With nougat." Stew added.

"Bitch." The custodian whined as he felt the rumble return within. Knowing that the soggy sandwich would not subdue his hunger for long, he quickly developed a craving for the tempting confections.

Gabriel watched the men toil over the wet window and debated what to do about the impending danger of allowing the children to play off their sugar highs, as well as what the consequences would be if they locked them up in their rooms for the night. As they weighed their options the familiar buzz of feedback from the intercom filled the facility.

"Attention little kiddos," rang Kylie's soft voice from the speakers mounted on the ceiling. Sunday looked up and saw her standing on the piano. As a group of kids gathered around she explained, "The floor is wet and it's really not safe for playing."

Stew smiled at his companion and they watched as the sugar-wired children booed her. Sunday could tell by the way her tone changed that the reaction had gotten to her. His heart went out to her and rooted her on as she continued, "But it only seems fair that you get a song before we send you off."

Stew and Sunday simultaneously stopped mounting the board and held it still as they looked on and anxiously waiting for what Kylie had planned. She sat upon the edge of the instrument and took a deep breath. Nervousness read across her brow while a handful of children joined her in a small gathering. Kylie nodded to herself, raised the microphone back to her lips and softy sang to the small audience;

"What do you get when you fall in love?

A guy with a pin to burst your bubble

That's what you get for all your trouble.

I'll never fall in love again."

Her voice flowed angelically throughout the room, as more and more children stopped their games and gravitated to the source of the southern belle's song. Sunday looked on as Kylie's confidence grew; her voice amplified and she began to smile at her young, captive audience. The ravaging clouds above must have been just as entranced, because the rains suddenly ceased.

"She is something else." Stew noted and Sunday agreed, crushed by the guilt that he felt over having had upset her. Her eyes shifted to Sunday and she shot him a terrible glare.

"What do you get when you fall in love?

You only get lies and pain and sorrow

So, for at least, until tomorrow

I'll never fall in love again

Oh, I'll never fall in love again."

"And she is pissed at you!" Stew chuckled. Once again, Sunday reluctantly nodded in agreement.

By the end of her song the only child not on their feet clapping was Hope, who Sunday noticed was nowhere to be found. The custodian went back to the window work and saw that Gabriel still stood nearby and watched him. He could tell that words sat upon the boy's tongue and he could see that the child was having difficulty collecting his thoughts.

"What's on your mind, Gabriel?" Sunday asked, unenthusiastically.

His tiny face scowled a bit, "Why is it that you can tell Mr. Stew about what happened and you expect me to lie?"

"Look." Sunday explained, "I told Stew what *happened*. You want to tell everybody that Callym is the devil or something. That isn't what *happened*. I told you before, spreading that around is no good for anybody."

Sunday suddenly realized that he was speaking to a doe-eyed child and stopped defending himself, "Besides, Stew and I are employees here. I'll tell him what I think is necessary."

Gabriel motioned as if he wanted to interject, so the custodian quickly cut him off with a parental, "When *you* work here, you can tell people whatever *you* want."

Albeit with a child, Sunday was satisfied with his victory over the quarrel. Gabriel's eyes showed a look of defeat, but also determination. Sunday suspected that the conversation would have picked back up if it were not for Sister Rochelle, who threw open the front doors and screamed, "There's a child on the roof!"

A veritable circus suddenly unleashed. The children wailed around, some laughed at the fact they no longer had to go upstairs, some slipped in the puddles on the floor and most of the children shrieked. Stew and Kylie chased after the herd as they scurried and made way to the parking lot. Shouts of "stop" and "wait" held no power over the curiosity of their excited minds.

Sunday struggled to set down the heavy pane that he held as he watched the population of the building evacuate for the second time in a day. With a sigh of, "Fuck it," he dropped the board onto the pavement, slid across the wet floor and hurried up the stairs to its apex.

*S*unday shimmied up the maintenance ladder that led to the roof. When he reached the top rung, he found two bobby-pins lying beside the picked lock. He flipped the hatch open and could hear distant sounds of "Don't jump!" from the street below. He hoisted himself up to the top of the building and saw Hope who sat on the ledge and stared up into the cloudy sky. He was not sure what he should say or do, but the custodian knew he had to say or do something. Slowly, Sunday eased his way to her.

"We're not high enough; you'll just break your legs." He finally said.

Without turning to face him, Hope softly replied through broken sobs, "Not if I dive."

Her straight-toned reply startled Sunday and left him speechless. He wished that he could see her face. He was pretty good at reading Hope and if only he could have seen her eyes, he would have had a better gauge as to how serious she actually was.

"True." He finally replied.

Hope patted the ledge beside her and invited him to sit, "Nice night, huh?"

He eased himself to the edge of the building, sat down beside her and gazed up. The clouds rolled over one another like overlapping, black sheets and in the patches of sky where they had dispersed, a canopy of flickering lights glistened above them.

"There aren't a lot of stars." He noted thoughtlessly.

Hope turned to Sunday, caught a tear as it trickled down her cheek and said, "I'm not going to jump."

"I know."

"I like to come up here to clear my head sometimes."

"I've done that before."

"I know."

"Do you want to talk it out?"

Hope sighed and looked to the sky. She said nothing for a moment then finally whispered, "I'm speeding up, Sunday. I found out last week. There's a good chance I'll age even faster."

She began to cry again, "I'm going to look and feel eighty when I'm supposed to look and feel like I do now."

Sunday tried to do the math, but he could not. Hope slammed her fist down hard onto the building's ledge. The impact made a dull smack.

"It's not fucking fair Sunday; it's just not fair." She objected.

The custodian put his hand to his mouth, unsure of what his next step should be. He fumblingly draped his arm around her and rested her weeping head onto his chest. They sat in silence, listened to the commotion below and watched the peaceful skyline as a new wave of clouds threatened toward the building from off in the distance.

Just then an idea hit Sunday, "You know what we're going to do?"

Hope sat up and looked at him, very interested. Her worried face longed for an inch of hope and she anxiously whispered, "What?"

"We're going to call tonight your very last birthday." He said excitedly.

"But it's not my…" She began.

"It doesn't matter. Tonight is the very last birthday you will ever have. From now on, we just won't worry about how old you are, how old you look, how old you think you should be. After tonight, you are just Hope. You can be what ever you want to be."

As Sunday unveiled his impromptu plan it progressively sounded more and more asinine to him, but Hope ate it up. Her frown, though it did not melt away, definitely subsided. She tightened her arms around his neck in a grand hug.

"You like that?" He asked.

Hope nodded.

"Good." The custodian exhaled a sigh of relief and rolled his head around, stretched his weary neck and caught a brief sight of the stars before they vanished once again under the dark blanket of clouds.

"It's my last birthday and there's no cake." Hope observed semi-sarcastically. The thought of food rumbled Sunday's stomach.

"Yeah, we missed out on peanut butter balls too." He mournfully noted.

"Bitch!" Hope agreed. She smiled at Sunday, winked and fell back to onto his chest.

The custodian looked down at his dangling feet and the heads of the spectators floors below. Among them, he spotted an apprehensive Kylie, who wrenched her hands in fret. Hope saw this and said, "You know, she likes you too; don't you?"

"I don't think so. Just between you and me, I really screwed up this afternoon."

"I know."

"Oh, you do, do you?" Sunday laughed uneasily and wondered what else may have been discussed on the ride home.

"Yep;" Hope replied, "And I think you should just apologize."

"How do you apologize for alleging that some one lied about their really dead mother being dead?"

"You'll figure it out." Hope said assuredly.

"You know," Sunday noted after a brief moment, "It's only right that you should get one last gift."

Hope sprang upright; her pink tongue wet her cherry lips as they curled to a pseudo-version of her normal malicious grin.

"Now it's not wrapped." He stalled as he stuffed his hands into his coat pockets. He fumbled around and produced his orange-haired troll pen.

Hope carefully reached out to take it. She examined the little plastic man and noted his silly grin, the gem where his belly-button should have been and the stress-induced bite marks.

"I can't accept this; it's like your magic feather."

"No, it's yours."

Hope tossed her arms around the custodian and kissed him lightly on the cheek, just to the left of his lips. Close enough to his lips, in fact, that he could taste her fruit-flavored lip gloss. As if she were never upset in the first place, Hope gleefully hopped up onto the ledge, silenced her audience below and then shouted, "I'm coming down!"

A collective sigh swept the crowd which was followed by grand cheers that rose to the rooftop. Sunday glanced down to see that the children had started to dance and jump with glee across the wet asphalt as Kylie Court collapsed to her knees in relief.

Hope added, "Now go back inside and go to bed so Sunday can finish cleaning!"

Another roar rose up but this time of boos, not applause. Sunday joined in the grumbling as he stood up and felt the strenuousness of the day in his body. As the custodian moaned, Hope descended down the ladder, stopped before she vanished from Sunday's sight and said, "Just apologize to her. She likes you too."

Sunday shook his head and reviewed the evidence in his mind that led him to believe otherwise, "I don't think so."

Hope smiled, said, "You'll see," and slipped down the ladder.

— ◎ —

*G*low-in-the-dark stars and a couple of clown nightlights illuminated Austin Olsen and Gabriel's bedroom. Two small desks were placed in opposite corners; Austin's covered with a small stack of notebooks, an assortment of candy bars, a half-finished soda, a lamp and a few scattered baseball cards. The only things on top of Gabriel's desk were a lamp, a bible and the standard-issue notebook. His winged backpack sat on the floor next to it. Austin had plastered the walls with posters of sports and music heroes, a couple of science-fiction characters and a black-light poster of a dragon. Gabriel had only tacked up a construction paper cross which was posted in the center of the east wall.

Kylie Court and the boys knelt on the University of Georgia Bulldogs rug at the foot of the bunk-bed and faced the craftwork cross. They looked towards the green glow of the plastic heavens and prayed;

"Now I lay me down to sleep…"

After she had tucked the boys in, Kylie walked out into the hall and was immediately encountered by Sunday. He held a bouquet of make-shift aluminum foil roses in his hand and said, "The Bacharach was incredible; you have an amazing voice."

"Mmm Hmm" She replied in a tone that revealed her distain.

"Look Pickle, I owe you an apology." He said as he held out his lackluster token, "They're not much, but I didn't have time to stop..."

Kylie took the bouquet and waited for Sunday to continue.

"I am so sorry. So sorry that sorry doesn't even sound like a strong enough word... It's just..."

"Yes?"

"It's just... I get very discombobulated around you. Sometimes the words just don't come out the way they are supposed to; and that was the worst..."

Kylie offered a smile and said, "Sunday, why don't you take me out after work and we can pretend that it never happened?"

Sunday had never felt so relieved, "I'd like that." He sighed, "There's a bakery right down the street that has the best... well, everything."

Kylie agreed and they made plans to meet after he had completed his window repair and she had finished her bedtime rounds.

"You were great on the roof." She complimented.

"It wasn't anything; it's just about knowing how to deal with Hope."

"Well, from where I stood it was very heroic."

Sunday had never thought himself as heroic before, and the notion tickled him.

"Well, we should get back to work, so we can get out of here." She suggested.

Sunday agreed and watched as Kylie began to walk downstairs to tuck in the girls. She paused, feigningly smelled her foil flowers and asked, "I discombobulate you?"

The custodian nodded and confessed blushingly, "I like you."

Kylie Court blushed back and replied, "I like you too."

—◉—

*B*oards had been placed, boxes crushed, bathrooms sanitized and floors buffed; the only thing left for Sunday to do was to conduct his final rounds. He stood silently in the hallway of the fifth floor and listened for sounds of horseplay. As he tiptoed across the floor, he heard the faintest sounds of giggles coming from the door tagged, "Austin/Gabriel".

He found the boys sitting cross-legged on the floor as they played a board game. Sunday knocked on the door as he opened it and ordered, "Put it away guys, it is way past lights out."

The boys whined but complied. Sunday supervised as the children packed away the game and climbed into their matching rocket ship bedspreads. Pulling the sheet under his chin, Gabriel asked, "Mr. Sunday."

"Yes."

"Are you mad at me?"

Sunday hunched down to the level of the lower bunk and explained, "You tried my patience a little today, that's for sure; but no kid, I'm not mad at you."

Gabriel exhaled a sigh of relief, squirmed in his sheets to get comfortable and exclaimed, "Gee, that's fantastic."

Just then a glurgle came from somewhere in the depths of Austin's insides and the boy hopped from his elevated mattress and hurried into the shared bathroom. Moments later the slopping sounds of retching could be heard.

"You guys may want to consider switching bunks." Sunday noted.

"The board game was to determine that very thing." Gabriel replied.

As Austin returned and climbed back into bed, Sunday flipped off their light and added, "Well, you can start it up again tomorrow."

—◎—

A thin sliver of light slipped out from under Hope's red doorway along with the sounds of a rock song that Sunday had never heard before. He knocked on her door and waited for the young woman to unlock it. She opened the door, turned and sat on the edge of her bed. Hope's room was clad in burgundy reds and deep black. The room was riddled with posters of bands that Sunday vaguely recognized, paintings she had done and a thousand other trinkets. Sunday eyed the girl and immediately noted her shifty eyes. He had known Hope long enough to be aware when she was plotting something and judging by her body language, he suspected that she was up to trouble.

The custodian looked all around the room, but saw no sign of foul play. He walked over to her closet and flung open the door. There was nothing in it but her array of torn fishnets, miniskirts and various articles of black and leather. He eyed her carefully as she innocently sat down on the corner the bed. He was sure she had something to hide; however, her medicine cabinet proved to be clean and he did not smell cigarette or marijuana smoke. He walked over to her and put his nose close to her mouth.

No smell of alcohol.

He tossed aside his suspicion due to lack of evidence, sat next to her and asked, "Are you holding up okay?"

She nodded and asked in return, "Did you work things out with Kylie?"

Sunday nodded and replied with a grin, "I'm supposed to meet her after rounds."

Hope hopped up, grabbed his arm and pulled him to the door, "Then what are you waiting for? Finish up and go!"

She hurried him out of the room and closed the door behind him before he could say anything more than, "Lights out."

—◎—

$\mathcal{T}$he final stop of Sunday's rounds was on the medical floor. The hall was vacant to the point were it sort of sent chills through the custodian. He walked over to the glass window and looked into Callym Rafferty's room. The boy lay asleep in the recovery bed, various tubes and wires extended from his body. His blue and purple, bruised and battered leg hung suspended by cables. Three steel crescents wrapped around the outer portion of his leg, two on the inner. Each crescent was fastened to him by long screws that sank through his skin and into the metal sleeve that held his shattered bones together.

Through the glass, Sunday could see that the boy shook to the point of near convulsion. The custodian lightly rapped on the door and whispered, "Callym?"

He received no answer. Sunday walked to the edge of the bed and lightly nudged the boy. Callym's eyes shot open; they were back to the medicated, cloudy white. His capillaries; however, were now bloodshot.

"Callym, how are you doing?"

The custodian received no answer. Sunday looked around to ensure that he was alone. He whispered in the young man's ear and said, "Callym, I want you to say you're sorry for the trouble you caused tonight."

The custodian had hoped that the medication would force the boy into an apology, but instead, Callym leaned forward and mumbled grimly, "I see a red door."

After the short phrase, he collapsed onto his pillow and fell back adrift from the rest of the world.

"Must be some trip, kid." Sunday noted as he quietly shut the door.

CHAPTER THIRTEEN

The steam from Sunday's third cup of coffee no longer rose from the glass for the liquid had cooled to a sugary lukewarm. The custodian played with the graham-cracker crust of his mostly eaten cherry cheesecake. He raked the fork across the creamy, white and pink swirls and etched a kind of grid. He listlessly looked across the booths of Ms. Lovett's Cakery. The only other customer was a young woman in a flack jacket with an oversized purse that rested on her table next to her plate of blueberry pie. She silently read a book on miming. The young woman must have felt the custodian's eyes on her as she glanced from her book, looked him over and disappeared back into the pages.

Sunday's bites had grown progressively smaller the longer he had waited; he raised a bird-sized morsel to his mouth, slowly chewed and eyed the empty parking lot as he anxiously awaited Kylie's arrival. Mrs. Lovett passed by his booth and topped his cup of coffee.

"We're closing shortly, honey. Would you like anything else tonight?" She asked.

Sunday shook his head and methodically poured sugar into the mug without looking. Mrs. Lovett pulled her check pad from her flowered purple apron and set the bill on Sunday's table and they both watched as the young woman across the booths trapped herself in an imaginary box.

Audrey Hepburn sat on the edge of the overly-lit window sill and lulled away at her guitar, carefully picking out the notes, subtly singing *Moon River* as George Peppard adoringly watched from above. Meanwhile, Sunday sprawled in his second-hand recliner and licked peanut butter off of a spoon.

"That's all I am asking for!" He said to the paint chipped walls as he longed to be part of the Technicolor world where dialogue was simple, drama was lackadaisical and the topsy-turvy universe always seemed to correct itself in the end. Instead, he was trapped in his one bedroom apartment, surrounded by his bargain bin décor, dirty dishes, shattered expectations and half-assed dreams.

After being stood up yet again, the custodian had spent the remainder of his night drinking heavily and bingeing on old movies and junk food. He attempted to write his thoughts out in his standard issue notebook, but just was not in the mood to try to put his emotions together in a cohesive manner.

By the time Audrey Hepburn had hopped out of the cab and into the rainy streets of New York and frantically ran up and down the backdrop as she cried out for her cat, Sunday had sobbingly reached for his phone. Misty eyed, the custodian watched wide-eyed as miraculously and in true, vintage Hollywood style, Audrey Hepburn found the waterlogged feline and the fairly-tale ending that she never even knew she wanted. Stew answered on the third ring.

"Dude, what's up?" He said hurriedly.

"Hey man, not much. I was just thinking…"

"Jesus man, are you watching old movies?"

"No." Sunday lied.

"Dude?"

"Okay, yeah. I had a shitty night; just answer a quick question."

"Sunday, I'm kinda in the middle of a date." Stew tried to explain.

"Fine. That's excellent. I am very happy for the two of you…" Sunday drunkenly hiccupped, "I got stood up for my date…hic… so… you can just answer my question… and I'll let you go."

"Fine." Stew relented. Sunday could hear him apologize to someone on the other end of the phone.

"Do you think that, like, everyone gets a happy ending?"

Stew sighed and said, "Dude, are you okay? Do I need to swing by?"

Suddenly, there was a light knock on Sunday's door. Sunday jumped to his feet and said quickly in to the receiver, "Someone's here, I have to go. Don't come by here! Enjoy your date!"

He tossed down the phone, hopped over the back of his couch and rushed to let in Kylie Court, who he assumed must have had a breakdown and finally worked up the nerve to swing by. It did not occur to the custodian that Kylie was unaware of where he lived until he threw open the door and saw Hope standing in the entryway.

"You look miserable." She said concernedly.

Sunday shrugged and asked, "What are you doing here?"

"Don't tell anyone... but I'm going to Nashville for a couple of days to see a Mike Farris show."

"Damn it, Hope..." Sunday began to scold.

"No, no, no. You said it yourself; I am old enough to do what I want."

"Fine;" Sunday gave in, "But why did you have to come over here? It... like, makes me an accomplice or an accessory or something." Sunday added.

Hope gave him a sympathetic smile and continued, "I had a feeling you would need some company."

Sunday sort of nodded, shuffled back into the room and waved Hope inside. He plopped back into the recliner, finished of his glass of whisky and asked drunkenly, "What am I doing wrong?"

"I don't know, sugar." Hope replied softly as she stepped behind him and began to massage his shoulders. Sunday started to pull away but her penetrating fingertips paralyzed him. He closed his eyes and he sank into her hands. She ran them through his hair and tilted his head back under her will. She replied, "I think she's a fool."

Hope took the empty glass from Sunday's hands and walked over to the small counter that separated the living room from the small corner that served as the kitchen. She made him another drink, brought it back to him and as she leaned on the back of his couch, continued to caress him; her finger tracing his brow.

Starting to relax, Sunday closed his eyes and said, "Thanks, Hope."

"I'll take care of you."

"Mmmm" Sunday moaned as he sipped his drink and sank deeper into his alcohol and massage induced trance.

Hope spoke softly into his ear, "She couldn't care for you like I could anyway."

Sunday felt her soft lips touch his and recoiled instantly as he realized her motives. "Whoa!" He cried, stunned.

Hope withdrew and sunk her head down in embarrassment. Sunday felt horrible and suddenly remembered the new information he had about her condition. He touched her cheek and said apologetically, "Hey, it's alright. It's okay."

"You said it didn't matter." She quipped, "You said my age didn't matter! If you don't believe it; then how am I supposed to?"

"It's not that…" Sunday began.

"Then what?" She begged gently.

Sunday said nothing. There was nothing that he could say. He wanted to tell her that he was dating Kylie; but he knew that it was not true. Hope stepped closer, her eyes more intense. Sunday felt her hand slip slowly down his arm.

"Just one night." she pleaded through pursed lips.

In that minute, something inside Sunday wanted her, but something inside Sunday also knew better. Despite what he may or may not have believed, something inside him said that she was too young. That is what he said to himself as her hands pulled him to her and she pressed her soft wet mouth to his. The taste of peppermint and cigarettes filled his mouth as her tongue rolled past his lips.

Sunday believed what he had said; he did not see her as a ten year old. It had been a long time since he thought of the young woman as a child. But still, something deep in his head continued to chime a faint, almost indistinguishable caveat.

She's still too young.

Her fingernails raked down his back as she sucked on his bottom lip, her hands slid into his. Fingers entwined as she raised them up to her chest and rested his palm over her breast. Sunday felt the ebbing thump of her heart.

She's still too young.

He relented, returned her kiss, took in her breath and caressed her chaste breast. She put more force behind her lips and kissed him even harder... faster. Her fingers trickled to his hips and she traced tiny circles across them. Sunday's hands dropped slowly down the sides of her body and grabbed her hips. She nibbled on his ear and whispered a myriad of things that led him to once again question his conscience. He thought about how he had watched her grow, how she had written him little love poems when she was younger. Images of Kylie crept into his psyche as well in one whisky-colored haze until Sunday was unsure of what was real and what was in his head. He felt fingertips run down his leg. Somewhere in the swirl Sunday sensed apprehension, but these thoughts were whisked around with all of his other thoughts and he allowed himself to accept her advances and he began to kiss down her neck.

She's still too young.

She slipped her hand into the waist of Sunday's pants, pulled him close and pushed him so that he fell on top of the couch. As she climbed on top of him, her legs straddled his and she began to lick a circle around his navel.

She's still too young.

She slithered up his chest and kissed him deeply. Sunday traced her lips with his tongue and she moved his hand up under her shirt. He felt the warmth from her firm stomach, over her exposed breasts, her nipples grazed his fingertips. Her skin was sweaty and hot; as if just beneath it she was filled with a liquid mixture of sex and fire. Sunday could no longer keep his eyes open; his mind reeled as if he spun in place. Everything around him moved clock-wise, sideways and sway-ways, though he knew that he was still. Hope sighed through slightly parted lips and he felt her hands move around his hips to unbutton his jeans.

She sucked on his tongue, he ran his hands down her bare back and as her hand slid lower still, he heard the metal tabs of his zipper slowly being pulled...

She's still too young...

Part Two

Let It Flow...

May 17

Diane,

Last night was a **strange** one.

Dr. Levine called me this morning and asked if i had seen Hope. i told her about the concert in Nashville. It took a lot of convincing, but i think i finally convinced her to let it slide and to remember that she's more of a woman than Levine would like to believe. I can't blame her for freaking out, though. She's always treated Hope like a daughter.

After being stood up from Kylie Court one too many times, i think i am finally through pining for her. Granted, it took some help from Hope, and in order to get to this place, there's a chance i made a huge mistake...

When i woke up this morning Hope was gone. She didn't say goodbye or anything. I know she said 'one night'... but something feels off.

I'm just not sure what I'm supposed to do next.

Someone once said, "you can do what you want"

Well, how? How? HOW?

The things we've lost

Time has taken much

Of all the things we have lost

I miss grape Pop-Tarts.

Diane,

Remind me to look up the number to their corporate office phone number for after I have saved enough to turn my internet back on.

May 18

Diane,

It has been 2 full days since Kylie stood me up. Still no apology. Not even so much as a phone call. Ive been tempted to get in the van and drive past her fish trailer☺

Ive found myself getting angry when i think about it. I cant tell if its me being mad at myself for thinking about her, or if I am mad at her. All i know is that when i do, i also start thinking about Hope.

Emotions are the damnedest things.

What do you call it

When you don't feel quite as bad

But you don't feel good?

i keep picturing us on Monday, exchanging all these inconspicuous nods to each other. i haven't pinpointed how that makes me feel. I'm also not sure how im supposed to handle Kylie on Monday either.

Maybe I'll have a better idea of what and how I should be feeling when i see her on Monday.

That's what I'll do. I wont worry about it. I am sick of sitting around this dump. I will go out tonight. I will have a nice dinner— from a place that doesn't have a drive through. Maybe I will go to the Masquerade. I will have a couple of drinks and I will enjoy some local music. After that, maybe I'll get something from the Cakery☺and then head home (maybe via the fish trailer.)

I will figure it all out later.

CHAPTER FOURTEEN

*W*illiam Augustus Augustine-Chrystine gained notoriety in the medical community when he became the youngest valedictorian Emory University ever had and then became the youngest Assistant Director ever for the CDC. He spent seven years working pro-bono in Uganda in the seventies, was part of the medical team that isolated the genome that determines male pattern baldness, co-created invisible bandages and had claimed to have invented early versions of erectile dysfunction pills, but had lost the lawsuit which would have granted him credit and subsequent fame.

It was these accomplishments that allowed him a seat on the Board of Directors at St. Joseph's Medical Pavilion. Mr. Augustine-Chrystine was both a medical genius and a narcissist and the loss of the lawsuit caused him to shy away from his past achievements and devote all of his time and his substantial wealth to ensuring that his name live on via a wing of the hospital, where he had long ago decided to end his esteemed run in the medical profession. As he approached forty-five, he felt the time that he had left to leave his mark on the city slipping from his grasp.

The other members of St. Joseph's Medical Pavilion's Board of Directors had equally impressive resumes. Arthur Jefferson DeQueau was a Neurosurgeon from St. Paul who had once, during Vietnam, performed a tumor removal in less than twenty minutes using only the wiring and parts from a rotary phone, a 12 Volt battery and a roll of duct tape. He was tough as nails, spoke in an almost humorous accent and was the current Chief of Medicine for the entire Pavilion as well as the Head of the Board of Directors.

Thomas Swindle was one of Atlanta's most respected medical lawyers. His career peaked in the eighties when the Atlanta Journal and the Atlanta Constitution named him the city's most eligible millionaire bachelor. Shortly after that, he met his wife Martha, who at the time was an up and coming obstetrician and that year they had a summer wedding. A decade later, when she became the head of the Pavilion's Maternity Facility and gained a seat on the Board, the couple donated the money initially needed to fund the opening of

WonderKids, which led to the unanimous vote to offer Mr. Swindle an open seat as well.

Wayland Puttey, the philanthropist, made his millions marketing fried cola; which was nothing more than funnel cake mix and soda syrup. His family owned the land that St. Joseph's was built upon and his seat had been handed down to him; as was the case with Marvin Perry Snell, whose family had once owned the rest of the land in town. Marvin Perry Snell was the youngest member of the Board and had only just recently graduated medical school with a specialty in ears, nose and throat. His goal was to invent a tiny vacuum that could be inserted into the throat to swab and clean the lungs.

Francis Benginton III was a genius in the field of pharmaceutics and treatment studies and Astor VonVanderbraun was a world-renowned surgeon and ten years prior was Ms. November in the *PhDs of the World Swimsuit Calendar*.

Twice a month, these pillars of the community would gather in their large conference room on the top floor of the hospital building. The room held a fully stocked bar and a long black table with nine black leather chairs, was lit by expensive, executive track-lighting and wired for every luxury one could imagine, all via one convenient remote control.

Holding the device and wearing an out of style, three-piece, pin-striped suit, William Augustus Augustine-Chrystine stood in front of the Board of Directors and ran his fingers across his pencil thin moustache. Behind him, an overhead projector displayed an artist's rendering of the medical facility which included the WonderKids building, the courtyard and the maternity ward.

The rat-faced man smiled a crooked-toothed smile to his fellow co-chairs and said, "Ladies and gentleman, as you know, this fiscal quarter the only division of St. Joseph's that is not coming in under budget is the WonderKids facility. In fact, this year it appears that the WonderKids facility will be exceeding their budget.

I have taken the liberty of pulling their records, which you will find in front of you. As you will see, in the years that this facility has been open there has not been one patient who has been cured. Not to mention the recent increase in questionable activities and incidents at the facility.

Ladies and gentleman, I propose that we put forth a vote to officially shut down WonderKids to make room for…"

The thin framed man pressed a button on the remote control and a new rendering of the pavilion appeared on the screen. However, in this image WonderKids had disappeared. In its place was a grand building that appeared twice the size and countless times as impressionable. A beautiful walkway lined with shrubbery would link the building to the main hospital, the limbless statue had been removed from the drawing as well, replaced by a lovely gazebo.

"…The William Augustus Augustine-Chrystine Quarantine Center."

As the wiry man unveiled his proposal, there was much discord amongst the other members, especially the Swindles.

"You plan on naming it after yourself, Mr. Augustine-Chrystine?" Dr. VonVanderbraun asked.

Mr. Augustine-Chrystine adjusted his wide bottomed tie and pouted, "Since most of the funding for the project would come from my foundation and since my connections to the Center for Disease Control will be essential in assuring that we have the nation's foremost center for handling dangerous epidemics; yes. Yes, my name will be on it."

"What would you propose we do about the children?" Marvin Perry Snell inquired.

"As it stands right now;" he said coldly, "we are running a glorified orphanage. I propose we transfer the minimal care children to local orphanages and the more specific-needs children would be sent to sister facilities. Surely, the Organization understands the importance of economic stability."

"I don't know, Mr. Augustine-Chrystine…" Dr. Swindle added worriedly.

"It would bring in more money…" Dr. Binginton noted.

"And money is the bottom line." William Augustus Augustine-Chrystine agreed; the alignment of his pointed rodent-like teeth askew as he assuredly grinned as he thought, "*I WILL have my building.*"

—◎—

*M*onday came too quickly and brought with it more dreary weather. The sky was heavy with dark clouds that swelled with their load and looked as though they could rupture at any moment. For the time, however, it was dry and the ground was newly dusted in the yellow of the pollen from the early morning breezes.

Sunday reclined in his van and viewed the sunrise-silhouetted outline of the city in the distance; the shadows of the buildings stood in front of a backdrop of gold as the sun's glow pierced the clouds. He had woken with a distinct feeling that it was a special day. The weekend had left his mind reeling, and since he could not determine if his instincts were alerting him to a blessing or an omen, he had decided to delight in the day as it came to him.

Sunday enjoyed his toaster pastry breakfast while he listened to the classic comedy routine being aired on Album 88. He had heard it announced as he pulled into the parking lot that after the routine, the disk jockey would be spinning the Dial of Dean Martin, and the custodian decided that he would wait to go into work until he found out what song would be played. He noticed both the battered, blue Bronco in the parking lot and the absence of Hope's car then reminded himself of his promise to take the day in stride before he could allow his mind to spiral around the two women again.

The van's speakers sang out with the crooner's rendition of "*Sway*" and Sunday decided to stay in the vehicle just a moment longer. He closed his eyes and envisioned dancing on the distant golden clouds, dressed in the most debonair of suits while the woman at his wrist wore an equally fanciful, flowing gown. He tried to picture the face of his partner but the images switched from Kylie Court to Hope as the couple coiled on the clouds. Before the indecisiveness could get the better of him, Sunday turned off the radio, stepped out of the van and made his way into work. However, his attempts at calmness were quickly squelched as he approached the building and saw crudely taped to the windows and doors of the facility numerous signs of various size and color that read:

Warning:
Steve Free Zone

The custodian's heart sank as he pondered what possibly could have happened to the comatose child. He rushed inside and began to search for answers. His blood churned rapidly from somewhere near his knees. He scoped the main floor; far too frantic to notice that the children played per their daily pre-class routine. He ran to the back of the facility and found Stew in the storage room draping long lengths of medical tubing over his shoulder.

"Dude! What the hell happened to Ste-?" Sunday's question was cut short by an open handed slap across his mouth.

"Sorry, man;" Stew explained, "All I know is that we aren't supposed to say that word."

Sunday rubbed his sore lip, "But he's okay?"

"As far as I know; but you'd have to ask Dr. Levine or your dream lover if you wanted to know more… and once again, I'm sorry about your face."

"No worries." Sunday replied as he felt his pulse return to a regular pace.

Stew began to rummage through an unlabeled box and asked, "Have you seen the harness?"

"What are you doing?" Sunday asked.

"If anyone asks, you should just tell them that we found a way to free up quite a bit of space in the basement; but really, I think I'm about to invent the coolest game ever."

"I'm intrigued."

"I have no doubt that you will approve."

"So, you said that Levine is in her office?"

"Yeah, and Kylie's on the medical floor… Hey, so how did your night end up anyway?"

"I'm sorry if I ruined your date."

Stew accepted the apology and added, "You got off the phone pretty quick…"

Sunday was reluctant to answer, so he stalled and finally changed the subject, "Coolest game ever, huh?"

"Just make sure you find your way back here in a few minutes;" Stew replied and noted the tubing.

— ◎ —

A gathering of children congregated in front of Head Physician Dr. Margo Levine-Alonzo's office door, their tiny ears pressed to the wood. Among the small group was Austin Olsen, who whispered what little he could decipher to Gabriel, who in turn whispered the information to a wheelchair bound Callym Rafferty, who in turn sat indifferently. Instead, the young man stared at his body's new metal additions and the tubes that ran from his swollen leg to an IV bag which hung from a pole attached to his chair.

"What are they saying now?" Gabriel whispered.

"Something about animal fish statements, I think. I can't tell." Austin relayed.

"Okay, Austin says that the suit guys are talking about fishing or something." Gabriel whispered to Callym, who merely grunted.

Sunday spotted the spies, shooed them away from the door and barked, "What are you kids doing?"

The children stood in unified silence, each wondered if they were in trouble and toiled over the consequences of telling the custodian what they were eavesdropping on. Finally, Callym broke the silence and said scratchily, "Two suits walked in five minutes ago."

"It was Mr. Puttey and Mr. Augustine-Chrystine." Austin added.

Sunday gulped. It was a strange enough occurrence for one of the board members to show up, but for two- and after the warning about shutting the facility down; Sunday did not want to think about what the worst of situations could lead to. The custodian needed more information.

"What are they talking about now?" he asked.

"Animal fish statements." Gabriel answered.

"There's no way that's right."

"Well, that's what I heard." Austin said defensively.

"Fair enough. Do you know anything about St… the kid who doesn't wake up?"

"We've been calling him Gene." Gabriel added happily.

"No." replied Austin.

"Okay, here's what we're going to do." Sunday explained, "I'm going to find out what's going on in here. I promise that I will tell each of you what I find out as long as you can all promise me not to worry about it and do what ever your doctors need you to do, okay?"

The children nodded.

"And don't spy on this door." He added.

"Oh, we can't promise that." Austin Olsen answered honestly as Sunday tapped on the Head Physician's door and tiptoed inside.

The room was lit solely by an overhead projector that displayed an image of the proposed modified version of St. Joseph's Medical Pavilion sans the WonderKids building. Dr. Margo Levine-Alonzo sat behind her desk and faced the projection. Sunday could not tell if the flushed look on her face was one of anger or worry, but he could see that Sister Rochelle was furious by her scowl as she stood cross-armed behind the Head Physician and attempted to stare a hole through William Augustus Augustine-Chrystine. Beside the rat-faced man sat Wayland Puttey, who looked almost ashamed to be in the room with his co-chair as they completed their presentation.

"…Because of these annual fiscal statements and the lacking success rate, the board is considering the following alterations to the Medical Pavilion. As you can see, WonderKids would of course need to be removed to make way for the expansive new quarantine center."

"We were told that if we could cure a child, that there would be reconsideration;" the Head Physician defiantly noted, "We do believe that we are making headway with one of our patients."

"Dr. Levine-Alonzo, I'm afraid the gears are already in motion. The Board has decided to reconvene next Monday to make a final vote; so do not be surprised to see members showing up to inspect the facility between now and then." Mr. Augustine-Chrystine said pompously and immediately began to repack his briefcase.

"Do you really expect the Organization to agree to this?" Sister Rochelle snarled.

William Augustus Augustine-Chrystine's head darted up from his file packing and he retorted, "I expect the Organization will be reasonably convinced that our thinking is the most intelligent for the future success of St. Joseph's Medical Pavilion."

"It *is* a very impressive PowerPoint presentation." Wayland Puttey shamefully admitted.

Sunday slinked into the corner and hoped that he could go unnoticed until the meeting had finished. Mr. Puttey turned the lights back on and said, "I think I am first going to inspect the craftsmanship of that carousel."

"Suit yourself, Wayland." Mr. Augustine-Chrystine replied un-emphatically as he double clasped his case.

Sunday tried to hold it in, but the director's eagerness to ride the merry-go-round tickled him, which prompted him to giggle and suddenly there was no escaping that his presence was known. Sunday feared that he would be reprimanded for interrupting, but instead was dryly welcomed.

"Good to see you, Mr. Sunday." The Head Physician said, "Have you seen Hope this morning?"

Sunday knew that he should have told the Head Physician that he had not seen the young woman, but he hastily decided that he owed it to Hope to cover for her, "Yes, I knocked on her door when I arrived. She slept in late and was heading to school."

"That's good to know." Dr. Levine said relieved. Sunday imagined that the Head Physician probably did not sleep much that weekend, as he assumed that she worried and wondered of the whereabouts of the young woman that she treated as her own.

"I will personally be performing my tour of the facility today." the rat-faced man smirked as he made his way towards the door and added, "So; I will no doubt see you at lunch time."

Wayland Puttey hesitated a moment before catching up to his co-chair. He looked back into the office and said, "For what it's worth, I truly hope you find a way to help one of these kids in a very profound way."

After the men had left, Sunday walked to the desk and said, "I'm sorry to interrupt, but…"

Dr. Levine composed herself and interrupted him saying, "No, that's fine Mr. Sunday; I needed to speak to you anyway. As you gathered, we are in the direst of times and I need you to make sure that everything runs smoothly while the Board Members are here."

Sunday nodded and asked, "So, what's going on with…um…Gene?"

Dr. Levine began sorting through her stacks of files and replied, "You will have to speak to Ms. Court for more on what's going on; but she has asked that we not speak his name in this building until further notice. It sounds absurd; but at this point, absurd is just about all we have left."

She sighed and began to well up with fret. Sunday could only nod. He had never seen his boss so emotional before and he suddenly felt compelled to side with her, without the need of her sweet, little 'pleases'. Sister Rochelle comfortingly placed her hand on Dr. Levine's shoulder. The nun's expression could have been chiseled out of ice.

"Don't worry; we will take care of everything." Sunday said as he backed out and slowly shut the door only to be immediately bombarded by inquisitive children.

"What did they say?"

"Are they going to shut down WonderKids?"

"Did you learn anything about the fish?"

"What did you all hear?" Sunday asked and attempted to hush the barrage of questions that he had walked into.

Austin hiccupped and replied, "We think that we heard something about a duck and a fun warranty?"

Sunday chuckled and said, "Not even close."

He motioned for the children to gather around him and he squatted down to meet their eye level. Huddled by the group, the custodian stated in a hushed tone, "Okay, here's what's going on. The Board of Directors are going to be touring the building because they are going to vote later on what they want to do about the building."

The children gasped and gulped in fear. Sunday was quick to calm them by adding, "But don't worry. We aren't going to let that happen. The doctors are going to be working real hard to work things out. All they have to do is show improvements in just one of you, alright?"

"But what if they can't fix us and they still shut the place down?" a child asked.

The children all nodded in agreement, the sight of which tore at the custodian. He placed his arm around the nearest child and replied, "The worst case scenario would be that the doctors and nurses and all of us grown-ups would have to find new jobs and you kids would all go to new facilities."

"They want to split us up?" Austin shrieked and a sudden discord rang through the circle of children.

"Hey, nothing is going to happen." Sunday assured, "Everything will be fine. I'm telling you that there's nothing to worry about. Now all of you go play; Stew has a new game we are going to try out in a little bit. Go have some fun before classes start."

He watched as the children involuntarily dispersed to play in various corners of the main room and crossed his fingers that he had been able to convince them that everything would all work out in the end, even though he was not convinced himself. Austin and Gabriel lagged behind with Callym.

"Do you really think we'll be okay?" Austin sniffled.

"It sounded like if the doctors can figure out a way to understand what's wrong with one of you it may be enough to stop it." Sunday replied caringly, "You just have to hope things will work out."

"Not hope;" Gabriel chimed, "You have to believe! It's like I was telling Mr. Sunday before, you have to find something that you can believe in with all you are and things will all work out in the end."

"Now's not the time." Sunday said in an attempt to stop the boy's sermon before it could get out of hand.

Just then, Wayland Puttey, who had witnessed the custodian's conversation with the children climbed from the carousel, approached them and said, "I must say that I am impressed with your rapport with the children. Are you also the one responsible for the carousel?"

Sunday shook the man's hand and responded respectfully, "Thank you, sir. And yes sir, I am."

Wayland Puttey knelt down and asked Austin directly, "Do you know who I am?"

The chubby child nodded and the chairman continued, "Good. If the other board members see more of what just happened here and more of that right there," he pointed to the merry-go-round, "then I can assure you that I will do everything that I can to sway them to vote against the Quarantine Center."

He shook Austin's hand, formally excused himself before he trotted back to the carousel and called out, "I said five minute rule!" as he attempted to keep the children from taking his spot on the plastic ponies.

—◈—

*H*ope's room provided no clues as to where she was or when she would return. Sunday checked the dresser tops, the vanity, everything short of rummaging through her drawers. He called her cell phone and waited and waited until her voicemail began and he heard a recording of Hope that said almost seductively;

"Hello, this is Hope's voicemail. Hope missed your call, so you get to talk to me. Lucky you. Why don't you tell me your name, cutie? You can give me your number, tell me what you're wearing and maybe tell

me a little something sexy and if you can make me beep, maybe I'll have Hope call you back."

The machine beeped and Sunday replied into the receiver, "Hey Hope's voicemail. It's been a while. I've missed you. Don't tell Hope this, but I like you so much more than I like her. I wish I could talk to you everyday. Maybe run away with you... tell you my dreams and you can tell me yours... But if you see Hope tell her to check in, Levine is already looking for her and I don't know how long I can stall."

He was about to hang up, but quickly added, "Oh, and here's your something sexy;

'Roses are red, a deep crimson hue;

If I were a recording, oh the things we would do!'"

Sunday stepped out into the hall and locked the door behind him so as to prevent others from snooping around as he just had. On the other end of the floor, he saw Stew suspended from the rafters by a thin cable and an old fabric harness. He was screwing metal hooks into the ceiling.

"What are you doing?" He called out.

"Come over here and give me a hand." His friend replied as he spun from his wire.

Sunday made his way to the other end of the floor and pulled Stew back towards the banister. Strewn around his feet were multiple lengths of rope, the medical tubing, a net for volleyball and numerous piñatas. Stew began tying the piñatas to the net with the lengths of rope.

"What exactly are we doing?" Sunday asked.

Stew's eyes sparked deviously as he explained, "We are about to invent Ultimate Piñata. See, I cleared out like ten of the piñatas that were taking up all the storage space down stairs, we tie them to the net and run the net from this end of the banister, over these hooks and then to the other end and let them hang over the gap. Then, we are going to take this medical tubing and tie it to the banister one floor below, thus creating a make-shift slingshot. The object of the game is for the children to bust the piñatas using the slingshot and candy will rain from the top floor to the main level where the other kids will be waiting below. Pretty cool, huh?"

Sunday inspected the elaborate set-up and shook his head, "We can give it a try, but I don't know... I personally think it needs more piñatas."

Together, they tied the crepe paper animals to the net, lashed it all to the wooden banister, walked the opposite line to the other end of the floor and tied it off as well. Once the lines were secured, Stew hoisted the piñatas over the side of the banister where they dangled from the net in different lengths that went as far down as the second floor and tucked sections of the net onto the hooks. Sunday helped Stew back over the banister and while the two men leaned over the railing to revel in their handiwork, Mr. William Augustus Augustine-Chrystine stepped out of the elevator, a smug look on his rodent-featured face as he quickly approached them.

"What on earth are you two doing?" He demanded.

Sunday pushed himself off of the railing and replied, "Just setting up the morning activity for the kids before they head to classes. We have one organized game every morning to wake the children up a little, get them excited for the day. Some of these kids... it takes a minute for them to warm up to other people. We find that the organized activities help."

"So, creating this monstrosity is in your job description?

"Cleaning and entertaining." Stew saluted sarcastically.

Mr. Augustine-Chrystine sized up each of the custodians. He spent an extra moment to stare down Sunday and finally asked, "Where did all of these... things come from?"

"They're piñatas, sir." Sunday noted.

"How much do the piñatas cost us?"

"We bought them in bulk, sir." Stew answered.

"That's right, sir. There's a cost break when you buy like fifty."

The custodians ribbed each other as both men tried hard not to laugh. The board member did not look pleased. His black beady eyes darted to Sunday, "You are the one who ordered the carousel, aren't you?"

"Yes sir." Sunday confirmed simply.

"And the pony rides?"

"Yes sir."

"And the pork…"

"Yes sir."

"And the foaming fountain?"

"Um… Sir;" Stew interjected, "That was both of us; and to be fair, we were really only trying to clean it."

Mr. Augustine-Chrystine wrung his fingers together, looked the custodians over one last time and said, "I'll be keeping a close eye on both of you."

As the rat-faced man walked away to continue his inspection of the facility, Stew nudged Sunday and said, "Dude, that guy hates you."

"Yep;" Sunday agreed, "So are we ready to play?"

Stew looked over their work and said, "We just need to find something to use as a projectile."

Sunday began to laugh and said, "Round up the kids and I'll be right back with the projectiles."

—◎—

*T*he announcement went out over the intercom that a Level 3 Game was being organized, and all of the children were instructed to grab their Level 3 Gear from the Level 3 Lockers, which were a series of red gym lockers that sat next to the storage area. The children quickly dressed themselves in the special garbs, which consisted of rain galoshes, heavy raincoats, catcher's knee and chest pads, industrial cleaning gloves, goggles and one of an assortment of helmets that ranged from football, mining and Viking styles.

While he clasped the buttons of his safety raincoat, Austin Olsen asked his companions, "Which one of us do you think they will be able to cure?"

"Definitely not you, Slugsly." Peter Tertiary, one of the less likable of the WonderKids suggested. Peter Tertiary acted aggressively towards just about everyone and appeared much too muscular for a young teen his age.

"Shut up, Pete." Austin shot back, "Seriously, what do you think will happen to us?"

Gabriel clicked the brakes onto Callym's wheelchair, began to fit the young man with a hockey mask and said, "Mr. Sunday said we have nothing to worry about. I think we can trust him."

"I just wish there was something that we could do to help." Molly Rollins added.

The children finished their preparations for the game and attempted to brainstorm ideas that could help the doctors heal them, only to realize there was little that they could do.

Stew's voice came over the intercom and said, "All children wanting to play Ultimate Piñata, meet by the piano right now!"

The children raced to meet the custodians, who had laid out a blue tarp directly under the hanging piñatas. The children lined up military style and awaited instructions. Stew inspected the children's gear as he explained the rules of the game, "You are about to experience the birth of the future of games. Ultimate Piñata. When the game starts, a team of three will follow me upstairs where a 'slingshot' has been created; the rest of you will join Mr. Sunday down here to retrieve the treasure. Team One will use the 'slingshot' to launch these compact disks that Mr. Augustine-Chrystine donated... by failing to lock his LeSabre, into the piñatas that hang high above you."

The children noted the stack of easy-listening disks and the festive animals that hung above their heads. Stew resorted to 'my grandma and your grandma were out hanging clothes' to decide the captain of Team One. Austin Olsen was determined the winner and he selected Gabriel and Callym to be the other two shooters. Wayland Puttey grew curious and joined Sunday and the children on the main floor while Stew escorted the trio upstairs to the slingshot. Sunday handed him a helmet and secured a perimeter under the firing zone.

"Did I hear you say that Mr. Augustine-Chrystine donated something for this game?" he asked, quite astonished, as he fastened the straps to tighten his baseball helmet. Just then, the rat-faced board member descended the staircase to watch the game. He found an out of the way spot along the wall and sipped his latte.

"It's probably best if you just pretend that you didn't hear anything." Sunday suggested.

Before too long the children on the main floor began to cheer as silver disks rocket upward and sliced into the cardboard bodies of rainbow colored horses, giraffes and elephants. After a few initial direct hits, candy began to rain from the top floor of the building. Sunday reminded Team Two to secure helmets and goggles and sent them to scoop up the candy as more fell upon them.

"It's working!" Sunday yelled to the upper floors.

Stew leaned over the railing as disks rose to the roof from behind him and yelled back, "Of course it is!"

Austin and Gabriel had worked out a system wherein one of them would man their end of the slingshot, while the other loaded Callym's end for him and then they would switch. While they took aim at the targets that hung above them, their conversation continued.

"Imagine if we could help the doctors by curing ourselves. How cool would that be?" Austin asked as he launched a copy of Amy Grant's 'Heart in Motion' into the neck of a festive lion.

"It would be cool." Gabriel, who had yet to make a connecting hit, agreed and handed Callym a copy of Boy Meets Girl's 'Reel Life' to fire skyward.

"How would you even start?" The creepy, young teen mumbled and released the CD with such precision that he decapitated a unicorn. The screams of glee could be heard from Team Two below as a bevy of candy fell upon them.

"Research, I guess." Austin replied as he moved to help the young man reload.

Sunday shouted up to Stew, "Congratulations, man. This game is great!"

Stew leaned over the railing again and saluted his co-worker.

"Why am I finding so many Wilson Phillips CDs down here?" Sunday asked as he held up a broken disk.

"That's not the half of it." Stew shouted back and laughed, as more projectiles flew through the building, "I've never seen such an extensive Amy Grant collection."

"At least not from a dude." Sunday agreed.

William Augustus Augustine-Chrystine grew purple with rage. "Are those my CDs?" he demanded.

"They were donated." Wayland Puttey chuckled as he helped the children gather the cascading sweets.

Austin watched Callym accurately pierce the belly of one of the low hanging elephants. Crepe paper trickled through the air as a flap pulled free from the bottom of the beast and small chocolates rolled out.

"Where would you suggest we start the research?" he asked the chunky child.

"Geez; I dunno." Austin replied, "I guess it would depend on what you were trying to find out."

He handed Callym another disk and went to switch places with Gabriel, who watched as the copy of the Hanson's CD sailed through the air only to smash into the wall on the other side.

As the pieces of the disk showered to the floor below, Mr. Augustine-Chrystine grew furious. He stormed over to Sunday and shouted, "This is serious young man. Theft and destruction of personal property;" through gritted, crooked teeth he continued, "I will have your ass."

Suddenly, with a swift whiz through the air, an ABBA disk soared between the two men and sliced the edge of Mr. Augustine-Chrystine's cup; hot latte poured from the gash and leaked onto the chairman's slacks, which abruptly and effectively ended his tirade. As the scalded man screamed, Callym wheeled himself to the banister, glanced over the edge and smiled satisfyingly.

The children picked up the remaining candy from the ground, pocketed their portions and set aside shares for the gunmen above. They yammered to each other over their loot as they removed and replaced their Level 3 Gear. The bell sounded to notify the children to ready themselves for classes or for the school bus. Callym watched the hurly-burly around him as the children grabbed backpacks and lunches; he stroked his finger along the side of the emergency syringe in his pocket and thought to himself;

Research?

—◯—

$\mathscr{O}$nce the facility-schooled children had reported to their morning classes and the Catholic school attendees had left for the bus stop, Sunday knew he would be able to return to his questioning in regards to Steve. He emptied the last bit of compact disk shards, candy wrappers and crepe paper into the trash bin and wiped clean the puddle of latte with paper towels, which prompted him to laugh once again at the thought of the weasely looking man having to rush home to change his pants. Sunday tossed the wet rags into the bin and hurried up the spiral staircase to locate Kylie to inquire about what it was that she was working on.

The custodian only had to follow the sounds of pop music to the middle laboratory. He spied Kylie as she shook her hips and sang along while she curled over a microscope. Images of brain scans lined the light boards on the walls and her table was cluttered with papers, test-tubes and her morning breakfast which consisted of a Cakery blueberry muffin and a Diet Coke that she reached for without looking up from the eyepieces of the magnifying device. Sunday watched her silently and tried to place where his feelings for her fell. At that moment, as he leaned more towards disdain than adoration, she raised the can upwards, wrapped her heart-shaped lips around the straw and sipped. Suddenly and almost effortlessly, Sunday found himself completely infatuated with her again. He stole one last gaze and gently rapped on the door, startling the young woman.

"Jinkies!" she gasped.

"Sorry, I didn't mean to…" Sunday began.

"It's okay." Kylie giggled, straightened herself up and replied, "You just caught me off guard."

"I saw all your signs about… Gene;" Sunday said taking a couple of steps into the laboratory, "What are you working on?"

"First things first," She demanded and walked to meet him halfway across the room. She took his hands in her red latex gloves and continued, "I'm *so* sorry that I stood you up on Friday."

"It's okay." Sunday stumbled.

"No;" she retorted, "It's not. I swear to you, I was completely excited about going;" She noted her muffin, "You see, I even went later this weekend and I *love* the place, but that's beside the point. The thing is, I had an episode and I ended up locked in the bathroom for hours."

While his heart went out to the girl and her debilitating condition the sight of the Cakery muffin set off a twinge of anger or perhaps a strange jealousy deep in the recesses of his psyche. Not towards anyone particular; simply at the knowledge that she was able to pry herself from the bathroom and found the means to visit the Cakery; yet at no time thought to call him. He wondered if it was even possible to be jealous of a muffin. All he could muster to say was, "Aw."

"Yeah;" she replied, "I got really down on myself. Then I started to think about how much trouble WonderKids is in, and I decided that I should occupy myself by trying to help figure out a cure for one of the kids." She handed Sunday a file that he was unable to understand, "I decided to focus on Gene; specifically, your theory about him. It was my way of saying I'm sorry."

Sunday blushed and said, "You're forgiven." Deep down he wanted to tell her not to waste her time with his silly daydream theories.

"I ran a couple of tests, called in a couple of favors, stayed here all weekend and it turns out that there maybe something to it." She pointed to a graph on the chart and smiled proudly at the custodian.

"I don't know what this means." Sunday admitted.

Kylie flipped the pages in the file and explained, "See, all these patterns provide strong evidence of some form of narcolepsy. Which means we maybe able to combat it."

"That's great!" Sunday exclaimed, "That should save the building."

"I don't know," Kylie replied worriedly, "If we are right, it may take a couple of months before we have the kind of proof that they are looking for. I don't know if we can stall that long."

Sunday could see how heartbroken she appeared over the thought that discovery may not be able to save the facility; it was just as Dr. Levine looked in the office earlier that morning. The custodian simply could not tolerate those sour faces. He scratched at his chin and thought about ways in which he could help them. After a moment, he smiled at Kylie and began to search through the desk drawers.

"Don't worry; you keep doing what you're doing. I think that I have a way to buy you plenty of time." He said as he pulled the yellow pages from out of the desk drawer.

CHAPTER FIFTEEN

*C*allym Rafferty wheeled his chair to the elevator, where he was expected to go up to the third floor for the first day of his new tutorings. He had been unable to shake the thoughts about researching his condition ever since the chubby tyke had mentioned it. He wondered where such information could be obtained. He ruled out public book depositories and had serious doubts about finding any success in medical libraries either.

He realized that in order to cure his illness, he would need to identify it. The young man had spent enough time in hospitals to know that the proper way to identify an illness was to look into the symptoms. His previous psychiatrists and doctors had all regarded his symptoms as signs of schizophrenia and he assumed that since the regular medications had already failed him, he would have to look elsewhere.

A sharp pain pierced his leg and he felt a dull ache in the places where the metal rods ran through his skin and muscle and into the metal sheath that now supported his lower leg. He pressed the button on his IV regulator, watched as a dosage of morphine twisted through the tubes and flowed into his arm and he waited for its effects to set in. It occurred to him that he would need assistance if he were to attempt to leave in his condition.

The elevator doors slid open just as the thought suddenly struck Callym whom he should enlist to help him. He watched the sliding doors close, looked around to make sure that the coast was clear and rolled towards the front entrance to the facility. Once he was past the double spiral staircase, he spun around and inched backwards slowly until he had reached the double doors.

The handles for the doors were just out of Callym's reach from his wheelchair. He leaned as far as his body would allow with his leg extended straight out, but he could only brush it with the tip of his longest finger. The morphine began to take hold and a lethargic wave soaked through him. He struggled to reposition his wheelchair and attempted again, this time approaching the chair from the side. As he wheeled himself forward, the door began to ease open. Gaining a triumphant second wind, the young man strained his arms to keep the door from closing while he awkwardly pivoted his chair in directions that made it possible for him to finally prop the door open with his elevated leg.

Once outside, Callym took long and heavy breaths and then quickly rolled to the side of the building as a means to conceal his presence. He skated to the edge of the facility and peered around the edge. Once he determined that it was safe, he rolled his chair down the paved road.

—◉—

The students of Our Lady of the Holy Spirit Catholic School stood at the front of the entrance to the medical pavilion and awaited their bus. Due to the location of the stop and because some of the children were actually enrolled in the special needs classes, all of the students from WonderKids were made to ride the short bus to school. This troubled many of the children, who would sit behind the large, white sign and hide between the hedges until their ride arrived.

Austin Olsen had just recently reached the age where he lamented the bus like the older children so he grabbed Gabriel by the wrist and led him to a spot on the ground that would assure that he would only be visible via rearview mirror.

"So, you… have all kinds of… insights into things, huh?" Austin Olsen asked his companion as he slid off his backpack and sat on the ground.

"Yeah, I guess." Gabriel replied.

"Cool. Can you explain something to me?"

"Maybe. What is it?"

"Okay; in *The Terminator* movie, John Connor sends Kyle Reese back in time to save his mother from being assassinated by a robot, which would mean that John Connor would never be born. Kyle Reese and John Connor's mom have sex and she gets pregnant with John, meaning that Kyle

Reese is John's father. My question is; doesn't that mean that there had to be an original past where John Connor didn't exist?"

"I have no idea what you are talking about?" Gabriel replied.

"*The Terminator!*" Austin exclaimed, "See, Kyle Reese was born years after John Connor and after the apocalyptic war that is the background for the future subplot. That means that at some point someone else would have been humanity's savior and would have sent Kyle Reese back in time for some other reason where he would have met Sarah Connor for some unknown reason and then conceived John Connor."

"You aren't making any sense." Gabriel insisted.

"Exactly!" Austin replied excitedly.

"I've never seen it." Gabriel confessed, "But in my experience, saviors come from the most unlikely of places so it's best not to question their existence."

Austin Olsen gasped, "How could you have never seen *The Terminator?* It's only like the best movie ever!"

"I guess I missed it."

Austin wrung his hands in eagerness, "We'll have to fix that."

Just then, Peter Tertiary and a few of the other older children arrived at the bus stop. He told jokes that Austin Olsen did not understand, but somehow could tell that they were dirty. Peter walked over to the hedges to take his designated daily spot and saw that Austin and Gabriel sat with their backs resting on the sign.

"What do you think you're doing, squirts?" Peter sternly growled.

Austin's skin crawled as he answered, "Just waiting for the bus."

"Yeah, well the retards all stand to wait. You're in my spot, Snot-bubble." Peter said as he kicked over Austin's backpack.

"Hey, that's not nice." Gabriel insisted.

"Oh, what are you gonna do about it, little fairy." Peter taunted as he turned his attention to the young boy, specifically his winged backpack, "Maybe I should clip your wings for you little fairy."

Suddenly a grizzled shout came from behind them, "Oye!"

The children looked up to see Callym Rafferty rolling towards them rapidly. Once he neared the group, he pressed his hand against one wheel and skidded to a halt, which left two tiny, rubber tracks in his wake. He came to a stop and his body leaned over and his head hung forward as the morphine slowly lured him to lucidity.

"What do you want, Eddie Munster?" Peter demanded.

"I think you should leave the kids alone. Aye?" Callym suggested groggily.

"Why would I ever do that Cripple McCreepy?" Peter asked as he puffed up his chest.

"Because if you don't I'll tell everyone right now why it is that you act like such a braying ass." Callym said coolly.

"What are you talking about?" Peter asked and coldly walked over to the pasty, young man.

Callym rolled towards him and stared with crystalline eyes. He snarled at the red-haired boy and said, "I'm talking about your parents. Your father was a star quarterback and your mother was a beauty queen. They were happy." He rolled a bit closer and continued, "Until you were born. Your parents went broke trying to figure out what was wrong with you. Your dark secret."

"You're looking to get your ass kicked, freak." Peter Tertiary said and flexed his bicep.

Callym did not shudder; instead he wheeled closer and spoke much louder, "Your dark secret that under your pimpled skin doesn't lay thick, strong muscle. Isn't that right Peter?"

Peter turned white, took a step backwards and pleaded, "Shut up."

Callym advanced; his eyes boiled in fury as he yelled, "It is pus; yellow, sticky pus. Inside you're grosser than Austin and that's why you pick on him; because on the inside you are thoroughly disgusting."

"Stop." Peter begged.

Callym's voice dropped and he calmly continued, "What you don't know is that after your parents finally had to turn you over to the WonderKids, your mom got fat, your dad became a drunk and beat her."

"Stop it." Peter repeated.

"He got drunk and beat her so bad that she had to wear a hood to go outside."

"Dude, cut it out." Austin requested as he saw that Peter had begun to cry.

Callym refused to relent, "She smothered him in his sleep, Peter; and now, she is in jail. They are going to send her to the electric chair; all because of nasty, pus-filled you, Peter. All because of you."

Peter Tertiary fell to his knees, a broken wreck and sobbed into his hands. Across the street, a MARTA city bus pulled to the small covered bench station. Callym spun towards Gabriel and Austin Olsen who both looked on, slack-jawed at the weeping bully.

"Gabriel, I need your help." Callym announced and motioned the would-be angel towards him.

Gabriel skipped over to the wheelchair and said, "Callym, we appreciate you helping us and all; but that was a little uncalled for."

"I know." Callym replied, "Come closer, I need to talk to you privately."

Callym stuffed his hands into his pockets, thumbed his syringe and whispered into the boy's ear, "I want to do some research to learn more about what's wrong with me. I think that it will help me figure out how to cure it. Which, you know; will also help the building."

Gabriel hopped up with joy, "That's great Callym!"

"Here's the thing, and please understand that I can only ask you once. As you can imagine, I can't get around on my own too well, so I need someone to come along. I figure since you and I have the same kinds of symptoms, you are the perfect candidate. So what do you say?" Callym explained and smiled as pleasantly as he could muster.

"Gosh;" said Gabriel, "I'd love to, but today is my first day of school. I can't miss that. I already have Hallmark cards ready for my new classmates."

Callym sighed disappointingly and mumbled to himself, "I told him, I told him, I'm sorry." He locked his hand down on top of Gabriel's wrist and pinned the boy to the arm of the wheelchair. He slid out the emergency syringe and jabbed it into Gabriel's hand. Gabriel's eyes grew wide and he squealed in pain. The wheelchair-bound, young man pressed the plunger so that a tiny amount of the liquid entered the boy. He pulled him close and whispered into his ear, "I want you to walk me over to the MARTA bus and we are going to get out of here."

Gabriel's eyes began to cloud over. He walked around to the handles of Callym's chair and despite Austin Olsen's cries, began to push the young man toward the street. As his pupils completely faded to a milky white, the winged child sang, "The wheels on the bus go round and round…"

— ◉ —

*K*ylie Court laughed as Sunday detailed the plot to buy her more time to work on her cure while he hung up the phone. She was relieved that the custodian had been gentlemanly enough to forgive her for once again abandoning him at the last minute. Just the thought of it made her sick to her stomach and she was glad to have him around. Recently, she had noticed that for some reason, she felt more and more at ease around the custodian.

She pulled a slide containing a red spot of blood from the child once known as Steve. She held it up to the light, examined the thin translucent fluid and placed it under the microscope. Sunday replaced the phone book, leaned against the desk and watched as Kylie began to examine the cells that floated and spun around each other in the sample. She longed for him to say something, anything; so much so that the anticipation caused the back of her neck to tingle. Once the sensation had finally driven her to the point where she could no longer take it, she flipped her blonde hair so that she could subtly play at her neck and broke the silence as she inquired, "So, if I told you that I was thinking about trying something else from the Cakery's menu tonight after work, what are the chances that I might see you there?"

She looked up from her work to see that her question had made the custodian blush. She quickly turned and put her face back towards the microscope as so that he could not see her smile.

"I...um... I guess that might be possible." He said as coyly as he could.

Kylie felt tremendous happiness, but was afraid that if she showed or expressed how she felt it would ruin the moment or scare Sunday away. She wanted to let him know that she would not stand him up again, but was afraid to bring down their playful mood. As breezily as she could, Kylie added, "Just so you know, I'll be there regardless if you show up. I'm going for the baked goods not for you; so don't be afraid to show up- I'll be there."

Thankfully, Sunday laughed. Kylie demanded to herself that she would not cancel this date. She would not spend another night cursing her reflection in linoleum tiles. Even if she had to show up, hyperventilating into a paper sack, she would show up at Ms. Lovett's Cakery. She would eat iced, sweet somethings and would enjoy time with Sunday. She wanted another night with him like the one they shared on her porch. She hoped that she may get to know more about him in a similar manner that evening, if she could only overcome her own obstacles. They were unable to make further plans; however, because Sister Rochelle, Head Physician Dr. Margo Levine-Alonzo and Austin Olsen crashed into the room, each of them with a look of terror written on across their expressions.

"What's going on?" Sunday asked as the nun shut and locked the door behind her.

"We have a huge problem, Mr. Sunday." Dr. Levine said, "I need you to go on the most important of missions."

"What happened?" Kylie inquired.

"Callym and Gabriel left the bus stop and got on a MARTA bus!" Austin exclaimed, "Oh, and now I have missed the bus."

Sister Rochelle looked as though she were prepared for battle. She held an old-school motorcycle helmet and carried a black, messenger sack. Through stern lips she relayed her orders, "According to Margo, there are two busses that stop across the street. One goes downtown to the Capital building, but stops at the train station first. *Jesus, we pray that they don't take that bus.* The other one runs past the school and goes all the way down to Stone Mountain. I'm going to take the path of the first bus, you take the other."

Sunday nodded and Dr. Levine added, "I can not stress to you guys how absolutely necessary it is that this information doesn't leave the people in this room. Austin, I'm going to have Ms. Court take you to school; you can't say anything about this to anyone, okay?"

Austin saw the panic that engulfed the Head Physician and agreed. Sister Rochelle approached Sunday as if she were a drill sergeant and said, "Mr. Sunday, there is no telling what Callym Rafferty is capable of. Some days he is self-sufficient and able to regulate his own injections, other days if he is not constantly supervised he can be a considerable danger. It is important for you to remember that at all times. Do not let his age or his size fool you; this young man is capable of unspeakable damage."

The nun pulled a basic black handled pistol from out of the satchel, released the clip and inspected the chamber. Kylie gasped once at the sight of the weapon and once again at the sound it made as the nun slid the clip back into place. Sister Rochelle replaced the weapon and tossed the bag to Sunday.

"This is yours. Don't be afraid to use anything in that satchel." She instructed.

Sunday looked into the bag and saw the gun, a few extra clips, a butterfly knife, a rosary, a Zippo lighter, a compass, a tiny book of maps, a few pens, a new notebook, a walkie-talkie, a pocket bible and a handful of other trinkets.

"Is it really that serious?" Kylie asked.

Sister Rochelle looked at the young woman as if she were half-crazy. She said sternly, "I will say it again; Callym Rafferty is dangerous. Do not be afraid to use anything in that satchel."

"It's best you go now, Mr. Sunday." The Head Physician suggested as she held the door open for the nun.

"Austin, go get your bag and I'll meet you downstairs to take you to school." Kylie said and then added, "What you did was the right thing to do. I'm proud of you."

The chubby child smiled and ran out of the room to ready himself for class. Sunday thumbed through the bag and threw the strap around his shoulder. He winked at Kylie and shrugged, "I guess it never ends."

"This is insane. Are you going to be okay?" She asked, visibly concerned.

Sunday smiled and nodded, "Yeah, I seriously doubt I am going to need a knife or a gun or a compass to find these kids. I'll just go look in the arcades and the ice cream shops and I'll be back here in an hour."

"Well, just in case..." Kylie said as she stepped towards the custodian and looked into his eyes. She placed her latex-lined hands on the sides of his face, looked into his eyes, pulled him close and whispered ever so softly, "For luck."

Kylie closed her eyes and ever so gently and ever so barely touched her heart-shaped lips to his.

CHAPTER SIXTEEN

*T*he public bus maneuvered clumsily between the narrow city streets along its route. The twenty or so passengers bounced about uncomfortably as the long, ad-plastered vehicle rolled over the countless potholes and large metal slabs which were used to cover even more potholes. Callym Rafferty's wheelchair was locked in place behind the driver, in the space reserved for the handicapped. He shifted in his seat and the IV lines that dangled from his body bounced and shook back and forth with each severe jostle that the bus made.

Gabriel sat next to Callym, white-eyed, hands folded in his lap, motionless and awaited his companion's next command. The effects of the small dose of Lithium Validemerethyzine had fully engulfed the boy and he no longer felt compelled to indulge any impulse at all. Lost in his own mind, Gabriel did not even act on his desire to pass out greeting cards to all of the passengers.

Callym turned to his sidekick and began to run down his agenda for their spontaneous excursion; but since he knew first-hand that one of the side effects of the Lithium Validemerethyzine was extended periods without speaking, he essentially held the conversation with himself.

"Like I was saying; I think we need to get to the root of what our conditions are before we can figure out what they are specifically... I know, I thought that too; but you and I both have been tested enough that I think that we can rule out most neuroses or delusions of grandeur."

An elderly woman with bags from a local craft store stared at the pale child as he held a conversation with his winged companion, who had yet to blink, let alone speak. Callym acknowledged her gaze with a drool-lined grimace. Horrified, she turned her attention to the objects that passed out of her window. Callym found pleasure in her reaction and raised his chest in pride. He returned his focus to Gabriel and continued, "Where was I? Ah yes; so, here's what I'm thinking. Instead of wasting a lot of time thumbing through a bunch of flippin' books to try to find what is wrong with us; why don't we try to either eliminate or confirm the possibilities of what we *think* might be wrong with us…"

"The question is: where should we begin? I don't know. I don't know that either. Why would you ask me that? Let faith lead us? Let faith lead us?!" Callym looked back to the elderly woman and asked, "Can you believe this guy?"

The elderly woman gave the young man polite and nervous smile and silently turned back towards her window. Callym laughed and patted Gabriel on the knee, "At least you keep the conversation lively... Let faith lead us... ha, ha, ha."

The bus reached a station and came to a stop. A small group of Hindu men walked from the rows behind the boys and exited the vehicle. Callym shot Gabriel a baffled glance and chuckled, "Maybe you are onto something after all... Let's get off of this bus, I have an idea... Follow those guys."

Gabriel rose from his seat as if he were hypnotized and rolled Callym to the exit.

— ◎ —

The stealthy duo tailed the men a few blocks down the suburban sidewalk. They kept an inconspicuous distance as they passed by fast food restaurants, strip malls and overly manicured entrances to gated cul-de-sac neighborhoods. Callym craned his head back towards Gabriel who mechanically manned the handles of the wheelchair and said to the drugged child, "You gave me the idea. Let's follow these guys and see if we can get a non-Judeo/Christian view on us. For all we know, there are no angels, no devils and no possessions in their religion. That might eliminate the possibility that we are actually what we feel we are. Then we can move forward from there!"

He looked for Gabriel to show any sign that he too shared in the excitement; but the child remained confined to his mind. Callym watched as the group of men crossed the street in the direction of the Walgreen's and suddenly felt terribly disenchanted. He clenched his fists in rage at the thought that allowing Gabriel's so-called faith to lead them had left them follow a group of bargain shoppers.

"Aw, to hell with your faith." He said and slammed his fist onto his armrest.

As Gabriel pushed the wheelchair further towards the intersection, Callym's view widened and from behind the store he saw a beautiful stone Hindu temple that filled his vision. The massive, white structure appeared blatantly out of place amid the super-saver groceries, the video rental stores and the suburbia that engulfed it from all sides. It appeared as if someone had dug the building and its surrounding grounds from their foundations and transported the whole mass from India straight to Middle-of-Nowhere, Georgia. The grand building had five tall pinnacles and multiple spires that reached high above the other buildings that surrounded it.

"Dumb flippin' luck." Callym mumbled as the duo ventured closer.

It took Gabriel much effort to guide Callym's chair through the long, ramped walkways which lined the stairs that ran through impressive verandas that lead to the front of the temple. The boy shuffled his feet and pressed onward as the wheels chattered over stone; everything appeared to be made of imported stone. What was more impressive was that almost every inch of stone had a design carved into it. Tiny imperfections and chisel marks also suggested that each piece of marble or limestone or sandstone had been hand shaped. Gabriel could not say anything to note it, but he felt as if he were walking in the closest thing to Eden that he could remember. They arrived on the second row of steps that led up to the entrance and came upon a row of cubbies and were instructed to remove their shoes. A looping recording of chants played through speakers hidden in the fauna. Even though he only wore one shoe, Callym ordered his companion to help him oblige and they continued the remainder of the path sock-footed.

They passed by lovely gardens and a long reflecting pool that directed them to the entrance. At the front of the large archway stood a sign that read:

Shri Swaminarayan Mandir
Welcomes You
All Donations Welcome!

The boys passed by two security officers who looked as though they wanted to stop the children from entering, but after they exchanged confused glances with each other, the guards waved the children in. Once inside, Callym and Gabriel were overwhelmed with the majesty of the temple's grand foyer. Columns upon columns of intricately carved stone, statues on every wall, the white marble all but glowed under the soft, azure-tinted lighting. Callym asked Gabriel to wheel him around the room for a moment so that he could appreciate the building to its fullest.

"Someone here is sure to be able to help us." He insisted.

From elsewhere in the large domed room, chimes rang which notified everyone inside that it was a time for prayer. Callym stopped a gentleman who wore a simple white robe to ask what was going on.

"Pradakshina," The man explained in a whisper, "It is where prayers for the spiritual and the mundane are fulfilled."

The man bowed to the boys and continued towards the gold-trimmed altar which was brilliantly juxtaposed against a backdrop of white marble and colorful decorations.

"Did you hear that?" Callym asked his walking, yet mute chauffeur, "Spiritual and mundane. I'd say that we fall into one of those categories. Let's go see if your so-called faith gets us any answers in there."

The children went to the back of the room and watched as the men walked in a circle. Callym shrugged and ordered Gabriel to join them.

"What are we doing?" Callym asked the white-robed man.

"Meditate." The man whispered.

The boys fell into line and silently traversed the circle until Callym's mind had grown numb. He watched as one-by-one, the men in the ring fell into a pleasant meditative trance. Before long, Callym appeared to be the only fully cognitive person in the room. It frustrated him to no end that he was unable to reach the state that everyone else had seemed to achieve so easily.

He closed his eyes and tried to concentrate, but all that he could focus on were flashes of villainy, veiled in shades of violent red. He fought his urge to scream or thrash about and pressed the button on his portable morphine device. He tightly grabbed the sides of his armchair and waited for the drug to work as the winged boy behind him carted him around the room another rotation.

This is pointless; you are wasting your time.

Callym watched as an elderly man in robes of gold, green and red crept into the room, his head hung in thought. The man silently walked past the circle of men and neared the adorned altar, where he knelt down with his head to the floor and chanted quietly.

"That's the man we need to talk to if we're going to learn anything in here." Callym whispered to his companion.

You won't learn anything here.

The boys continued to follow the lead of the meditating men until the Pradakshina had ended. Once the group had dispersed, Callym instructed Gabriel to wheel him closer to the softly chanting elderly man, who was still in the middle of his prayer. Gabriel parked the chair right next to the man who kept his head to the floor and his eyes shut tight. The boys sat silently as the man completed his ritual and as they waited Callym once again began to feel the morphine wear off.

He hasn't even acknowledged you; he doesn't want to talk to you.

Callym coughed rudely and said, "My name is Callym Rafferty. My associate and I had some questions about your organization."

The elderly man remained with his head to the ground; eyes closed and continued his prayer.

If only you weren't in this chair, you could pull him up by his white hair.

Finally, the man rose to his knees, turned to the boys and situated himself so that he sat cross-legged in front of the children.

"Organization?" He asked pleasantly. Placed deep in the wrinkled recesses of the man's aged face were bark-brown eyes that advertised the man's friendly nature, "My apologies, I am Swami Subramuniyaswami. How can I help you children?"

Swami Subrawhat? This bloke doesn't even have a real name.

"Nice to meet you." Callym said as he forced a friendly smile, "As I was saying, my friend and I are ill. Very ill."

Callym noted the concern the Swami displayed as he began to look over the boys, "Don't worry. We aren't contagious or anything. The thing is; we aren't exactly sure what is wrong with us. We were looking for answers."

"This is a very good place for that, young man." The Swami assured.

That's what they all say.

"Indeed." Callym continued, "We were told that taking part in the little circle prayer thing would bring us enlightenment, but it didn't work."

Swami Subramuniyaswami chuckled heartily and explained, "It can take a lifetime to reach enlightenment, young man. In fact, few ever truly will. Many of us never fully achieve it."

Sounds like a pyramid scheme.

"And it is worth noting that the Pradakshina is usually preformed after one pays homage to the deities."

See, he's just looking for your money.

"Deity?" Callym asked.

The Swami gestured towards images of three figures that sat amid lotus flowers, "I assume by your friend's wings that you are both Christians."

Callym shrugged and allowed the man to proceed, "We believe in the same God; however, we believe this higher entity manifests itself in various forms. Brahma, Vishnu and Shiva."

Their gods have blue skin and eight arms!

Are you kidding?

There's an elephant head on one of these guys!

"Our religions aren't really all that different when they are thoroughly examined." The Swami added with a grin.

"Indubitably, sir what we are wondering is, are there any instances of angels, demons, possessions or anything like that in your religion?"

"Of course." The elderly man answered, "We believe there are spirits of good and these are also deities, under the same Creator. We also believe in the transverse. Evil spirits, known as diatyas or rakshas."

Gabriel tapped his chair-bound companion on the shoulder in a reminding manner and continued to stare white-eyed in place. Callym recognized the boy's request and asked, "Where do you guys fall when it comes to souls being reborn?"

"We do believe in reincarnation." The man noted.

Well, maybe there's something here.

Callym wheeled himself closer to the man, "So, what if someone were somehow... *inhabited* by one of these evil spirits. What would someone like you...you know, do?"

The Swami chuckled boisterously and patted the pale young man on the shoulder, "You know, I'm guessing you're having strange feelings. Sometimes you feel rage and yet you don't fully know why. I'm guessing that you sometimes act without thinking or regard to your actions. Is this correct?"

A bit dumbfounded, Callym nodded. Swami Subramuniyaswami added, "This is perfectly natural for a child your age."

Damn it, he doesn't understand.

"I don't think you follow..." The boy began.

"Trust me, young man. I suggest that you find a quiet place to just relax and clear your head. Look around at our astounding Mandir. This temple is beautiful not only to pay glory to the Creator, but also because as humans we require tranquility for true meditation. By surrounding ourselves in beauty, it is easier to achieve a deep level of meditation. Trust me, child; spend some time in a park and reflect. It will make all the difference."

It sounds like bullocks to me.

I wonder where their faith would fall if you tore this place to the ground?

This old man is of no use to you.

You should take his eyes. See if he can meditate if he can't see the beauty.

Callym felt his mind take control over his body and he began to fidget as he tried to keep himself from causing a disruption. He tapped Gabriel on the hand and said, "We need to go, now!"

The young man suddenly lunged from his seat towards the friendly Swami. His pale, lanky arm reached as far as he could extend, his fingers inches from the cross-legged man.

Gabriel grabbed his companion and pinned him to the back of his seat and wheeled him backwards towards the exit. Callym squirmed for a second, relented and waved goodbye to the Swami who placed his hands together and bowed his head towards the boys.

"I hope that we will see you both again very soon." He called to the children as they walked back into the large marble room.

— ◎ —

*P*ush My Buttons Arcade's acne-faced clientele had not seen Callym and Gabriel enter or leave, as was the case with the darkly-dressed, emo kids that skipped school at Spare Change Billiards. The ticket taker at the multiplex had not seen them, nor had the truants at the bowling alley. Sunday had run out of places to look and had resorted to driving aimlessly in the direction that he was assigned. He kept the van at a decent speed and continuously glanced left and right for signs of the children or a road or establishment that may look tempting to a pair of gallavanting miscreants.

Even though things seemed to be falling apart back at WonderKids, Sunday found that he was enjoying his day. He was complimented by a board member while another one was humiliated, there was progress with Steve…Gene, he had made up with Kylie and they had plans for later. Real plans. She had promised; and he was getting paid to basically drive around. The break from the sweeping and scrubbing and screaming far outweighed the cost of all the gas that he wasted.

The custodian cranked up the radio and began to sing along. He was in such good spirits that he did not even bother to refrain when he arrived at a red light. A horn caught his attention and he looked over to see two women who laughed at him from inside their car. The woman who sat shotgun mimicked him by singing into her hairbrush. Sunday blushed but continued to sing all the way through the duration of the light. He passed a sign which noted that he was approaching the mall and he decided to check it out. Even if the boys were not there, he could possibly find something good to get for Kylie.

Is that too much?

That's got to be a faux-pa, getting a gift for the girl who stands you up.

Might as well go check it out anyway; they could be there.

And you never know… if I see the right gift…

As the custodian strummed his steering wheel like a guitar, he fanaticized about the night and wondered what he might say to her and how the night might go. Would he get another kiss? He licked his lip and thought about the kiss that she gave him for luck. Although he barely felt it, to Sunday it was the most epic experience of his entire existence.

From inside the black messenger bag, which rested on the seat next to him, the custodian heard a voice, "Sunday are you there? Sunday are you there? This is Sister Rochelle. Over."

Sunday reached for the bag and shuffled inside for the walkie-talkie as he navigated the road with one hand. He found the device and responded, "Sunday here….um, over."

Sister Rochelle's static-covered voice responded, "Any luck?"

"None yet, but I'm about to check out the mall. I have a good feeling about the mall."

"I've found nothing here either. The good news is they have not been to the subway station on this side of town, so they couldn't have gone deep into the city. Over."

"That's great…Over."

"Keep me updated of what you find at the mall. Over."

"Will do." Sunday responded and set the walkie-talkie down.

Sister Rochelle's voice crackled back through the machine, "Mr. Sunday."

Sunday picked it back up and quickly said, "Sorry, over."

"No, not that." She laughed, "I just wanted to thank you for your help."

"Don't mention it." He replied.

"From what I have seen, you are an asset to the Organization." The nun said sincerely.

Sunday grinned. The icing on his day seemed get sweeter, "Thank you ma'am." He replied.

He replaced the device back into the bag, turned up the radio and tried to go back to his daydream about the kiss. He tried to image what an actual kiss from Kylie would feel like; it would surely be an event that could light a night sky but it was something he simply could not wrap his head around. Suddenly, his strumming stopped and he started to ponder the possibility of her not showing up at all. Could he really stand another night like that?

The custodian parked his van in the mall lot next to a brand new VW Beatle, which reminded him of Hope and he began to wonder how she would really react if she learned that Kylie and he were dating- if they were, in fact, dating. Either way, he was anxious to put an end to his new, bizarre, love-triangle. He picked up his cellular phone and dialed her number. Once again, the call was sent to her voice mail. He hung up before the recording ended and tossed the phone onto the seat beside him, where it landed next to the black messenger bag. Sunday picked up the satchel, looked through it, pulled out the gun and held it close to his lap in case any shoppers happened by. In the bag, he also located a shoulder-style holster, much like the nun's own accessory. Sunday debated wearing it under his jacket, but decided that it would be better just to leave it in the van. He packed the gun back in the bag and pushed the lot under his seat. The custodian retrieved his cell phone, opened it and typed a text message to Hope that read:

Where R U?

— ◎ —

$\mathcal{G}$eneral Lee's great, granite eyes stared blankly at Gabriel as the mesmerized child answered back with a hollow gaze. The Sky Bucket carried the children along thick metal cables, past the large carving of Southern Civil War heroes in the side of the dome shaped mountain on their way to the top.

The boys were informed by the park rangers that the apex of the mountain was the most peaceful and secluded place in the park during that particular time of the day. Since Callym Rafferty was in no shape to climb the massive rock, they had opted to ride the swaying bucket to the peak. The higher the rickety, metal box rose above the well-manicured lawn and pond, the more Callym's impatience intensified. He had grown frustrated with not being able to get around on his own, not being able to act upon his thoughts and being a prisoner to the chair had become just as tormenting as being entranced by the strange, blue concoction. If the Swami was correct, then maybe meditating on the top of the mountain would cure him of the terrible visions that filled his mind and the wretched voices that tempted him to do wrong. In the very least, he had hoped to gain some enlightenment to help him understand the condition better.

The Sky Bucket came to the end of its cable and Gabriel rolled Callym onto the rocky, grey surface. Aside from the operator who sat inside the booth near the cables, the boys were alone. From their position, they could see the neighborhoods below, the city's skyscrapers off in the distance as well as the rolling, grassy fields that were broken up by lush forests in the other direction. Too high up to hear the roar of the highway traffic below or the sounds of the good ole' boys who played flag-football in the lawn, Callym approved of both the ranger's and the Swami's advice. He instructed Gabriel to roll him over to the fence that ran along the designated safe area in search of the perfect spot to begin their meditation.

That perfect spot sat roughly one-hundred feet on the other side of the safety fence. A granite slab rose slightly above the rest of the rock and leveled off at a plateau with enough room to park the wheelchair. From that vantage point, Callym Rafferty assumed he would not only be able to see the landscape for countless miles, but he would also have a view straight down the face of the rock, past the carvings to the pond and gardens below. He craned his neck back and looked to his companion and said, "Gabriel, don't you think that spot over there is perfect?"

The winged child nodded slowly.

"We're going to need to get on the other side of this fence." Callym coaxed.

Gabriel turned to check if the Sky Bucket operator had paid any attention to them, only to see that the man was preoccupied with a magazine. He rolled Callym to the fence and began to tug at the metal meshing. After some finagling, the fence finally gave and the boy was able to pull loose the corner of the fencing from the rod that held it in place. Gabriel folded back a corner of the fence that was large enough to wiggle Callym under. They had acquired a few scratches from the metal on their way under, but the children successfully made it onto the restricted side of the mountain.

Gabriel knelt next to the wheelchair on the plateau and per his companion's instructions, began to pray. Callym closed his eyes and waited to feel whatever it was that the Swami had alluded to. The spring breeze carried the clouds westward and pushed its way through the leaning trees; their rustling the only sound that Callym could hear besides the tapping of his fingers on the armrest of his chair.

Though he tried, the pale, young man could not cope with the peaceful stillness of the park. His eyes closed tighter and he fought back the rage that slowly tried to capture him. As he looked to Gabriel who blissfully prayed, he rocked back and forth in his seat, frustrated that he too had not found the same experience. He balled his hands into fists and began to beat his temples in anger.

Work!

Work!

Work!

Please Work!

From somewhere deep inside, the voice spoke back, "It will never work."

Callym shook his head in disapproval, but he could not stop the flood of rage that suddenly overwhelmed him. He gripped his chair, succumbed and let it fill him with wild whims of mayhem.

It will never work because God does not care about you.

He's dead to you, and you are dead to him.

In the back of Callym's cornea, he saw images of fires which consumed buildings; he heard the screams of mothers and children as their flesh blistered and burned and their lungs filled with the black smoke of their livelihood.

You're better off forgetting all of this.

Heads on posts, miles upon miles of them- a forest of sharpened trunks with meaty tops that filled a valley of heather, painted in blood. Dead eyes rolled upwards into open lids, crusted lips frozen agape and white with the bleaching of the sun.

Do what you want, damn the consequences.

There are no consequences.

Callym looked to his winged companion for support and saw that the boy had begun to stir from his drug induced slumber. His pupils slowly returned from under the dissolving, white fluid. Gabriel coughed, shook his head and stretched as if he had just awoken from a long, rejuvenating nap.

"I missed my classes, didn't I?" he asked.

Callym nodded and replied, "I didn't want to inject you; I asked you first."

"It's okay, I guess." Gabriel said as he searched his now clear mind and tried to separate the things he saw while under the spell of the Lithium Validemerethyzine from the real and the imagined, "Were we in a castle?"

"It was a temple." Callym replied, and shushed the boy.

Puzzled, Gabriel whispered one last question, "What are we doing now?"

Through gritted teeth, Callym explained, "You are helping me; now pray."

Gabriel saw no issue in that, so he lowered his head and began to recite a prayer, "Hail Mary, full of grace; the lord is with thee..."

Callym closed his eyes as well, listened and tried as hard as he could to block the things that echoed inside.

You are only fooling yourself, boy.

There is no escaping who you are, Callym.

Give up.

Callym shook his head and focused on the winged child beside him. Gabriel faced heavenward, removed a rosary from his pocket and began to count off his prayers on the little linked beads. By the time he had reached the halfway point of his rosary, the child appeared seemingly content. A serene expression swept Gabriel's face and as the sun broke momentarily through the clouds, it seemed as though it had occurred solely for him.

Callym looked on, jealous that his companion had clearly reached the meditative state that he so desperately desired. He closed his eyes once again and attempted to pray.

"Our Father, who art in Hea…" He murmured, but was unable to finish. No sooner had he spoke the words, the voices in his mind grew louder and more intense until the young man could no longer concentrate.

LOOK AT YOU, YOU ARE *PRAYING!*

DO NOT FORGET WHO YOU ARE, BOY.

SPAWN OF HATE; YOU ARE VILE.

LOATHSOME, SOULLESS, YOU ARE BILE.

YOUR HEART IS CORRODED AND CAKED WITH CRUD,

AND PUMPS VENOM THROUGH YOU, INSTEAD OF BLOOD.

STOP THIS FRIVOLOUS, SILLY GAME;

YOU ARE WICKED AND CAN NOT BE SAVED.

GOD IS NOT LISTENING; LEAST NOT TO YOU,

SO GO AND DO WHAT YOU WERE SENT TO DO.

YOU ARE HELL, CALLYM! IT IS YOUR JOB TO SHOW THEM.

SHOW THEM ALL.

THERE IS NO ESCAPE; IT IS THE ONLY WAY.

SHOW THEM ALL.

Callym could take no more. He screamed and tore at his face with his bandaged fingers, "Stop it! Stop it!"

The cries broke Gabriel from his meditative state and he dropped the rosary to the ground in shock. Callym struggled to rise from his seat and tangled himself in a mess of tubes, then finally collapsed back into the chair.

"Why damn it! Why!" The young man screamed to the sky, "Why are you allowing me to be tormented?"

Gabriel rose from his position and attempted to comfort his friend by patting his shoulder. Callym quickly snapped at the child's hand and swatted it away with feline speed. He pivoted his chair, rolled closer to the winged boy and forced the child backwards to edge until he had lost his balance on the plateau and fell to the hard ground.

"Don't you dare placate me! He *loves* you." He glared at the boy then threw his fists to the sky, "This isn't fair!"

Callym collapsed into his seat and a tear rolled down his chalky cheek, "Just let me roll off the side and be done with me."

Gabriel sat up, brushed off his jeans and checked to make sure that his wings were intact. He stepped towards the distraught child and said, "Oh, but Callym, you know we can't commit suicide."

"Then just push me." The boy somberly pleaded.

Gabriel could only stare blankly at the boy's request. He saw no reason why anyone would want to leave this wonderful place, so he had no idea what to say. He tossed off his backpack and checked to see if he had any sort of Hallmark that could assist him.

"Callym?" He timidly said; only to be responded to by a series of groans.

Gabriel stepped back towards the boy and kindly suggested, "Maybe we just need to find someone else to talk to."

Suddenly, the boys were disrupted by the calls across the mountain top from the Sky Bucket operator who had finally noticed that they were in the unrestricted area. The boys saw the man run towards them, already nearly out of breath.

"Shit." Callym said.

"Are we in trouble?" Gabriel asked; his face flushed with concern.

Callym used his good foot and kicked off the parking break and said, "Not if we get out of here now."

Without a further thought, the pale, young man began to wheel himself along the fence, towards the walking path. Gabriel trotted behind and gasped to keep up as the chair gained speed as it continued down the mountain's domed slope. With a grand leap, the winged child took hold of the handles, rested his feet on the back metal brace of the chair and tried to help Callym steer the vessel as they rapidly escaped the park employee who had just reached the edge of the fence;

only to see the children drop off a small ledge and out of his sight.

The boys dashed over large slaps of granite; they chattered, skidded and sailed as the chair gained inertia and propelled them faster down the face of the mountain. Gabriel's cardboard wings flapped and flopped behind him and the boys both screamed. The out-of-control wheelchair clipped a stone and abruptly changed course, which sent the children in the path of a patch of trees. Gabriel lowered his left foot and dug his heel into the ground, which slowed them down and allowed him to alter their direction just enough to narrowly miss the trees and topple over the wheelchair.

The boys lay on the grey stones, bruised and scraped. Callym Rafferty had fallen out of his chair and had become tangled in his IV tubes. Blood trickled from a small cut on his forehead and his clothes were tattered from the fall. The young man felt a stabbing pain in his broken leg and feared that more damage had been done. He looked down to see that the metal crescent shields which screwed into his legs had worked. Though they now had terrible gouges and scratch marks on them, they had successfully protected his fragile limb from further injury. Callym rolled onto his back and began to laugh maniacally.

Gabriel meanwhile, dusted himself off and hobbled over to help his companion. He set the toppled chair upright and assisted the cackling teen back into it. Panting heavily, he untangled the IV lines and huffed, "Like I was saying... gasp... Maybe we need to talk to... someone... gasp... sensitive... gasp... to our needs."

Callym rolled the wheels of his chair back and forth to ensure that there was no damage to the axles and replied, "What did you have in mind?"

Gabriel took hold of the reins, began to push Callym the rest of the way down the hiking trail and said, "What about Brother Linus?"

Callym stuffed his hand in his pocket and felt around his emergency syringe, contented to learn that the instrument had not been damaged in the crash, "From the monastery?" He asked.

"Yeah. He promised to help you."

"I tried to strangle him."

Gabriel shrugged off the statement; noting, "He's a holy man, he *has* to forgive you. He promised."

Callym repeatedly pressed the button on his morphine dispenser until he saw the liquid flow through the tubes. Once the pain killer reached his arm, he responded, "We can give it a try."

CHAPTER SEVENTEEN

*L*ittle Miss Molly Rollins hid on the top step of the second floor of the facility, a small handful of pepper in her clenched hand. She checked to see that the hallway was clear and held her nose under the small mound. She fought the urge to sneeze, brushed the spice from her hand and rubbed the residue into her eyes. Tears fell down her face as she covered her mouth to hold in a scream and contained it to only an audible "Eep". Molly dried her eyes with her sleeve and walked down the medical hallway until she reached Pill Alley.

Nurse Durby stood on the step ladder and shelved the new shipment of medications. She slid the ladder down its track and placed the contents of the box that she held into the empty slot between the penicillin and the placebos. She continued this up and down and from side to side until her box was empty.

The nurse climbed down the rungs and turned to grab another box from the counter, only to be startled at the sight of the red-eyed little girl that stood pitifully in the doorway.

"Good Heavens little one, you nearly scared me out of my socks." The nurse exclaimed.

"Sorry about that." The child apologized.

The nurse picked up another box, climbed back up the ladder and said, "What can I do for you, honey?"

Molly put her hands behind her back, crossed her fingers and said, "The pollen keeps making my eyes itchy."

"Oh, your poor thing." Nurse Durby said while she restocked the gauze.

Once the boxes of gauze had been placed, she pulled herself across the row and picked out a bottle of seasonal Visine to give to the child. She climbed down and handed it to Molly, who grabbed the nurse's arm to pull her closer. The little girl kept one arm behind her back and while keeping her finger's crossed whispered embarrassedly, "Nurse Durby, I also think I had too much peanut butter balls with caramel because I haven't pooped in like two days."

Nurse Durby smiled comfortingly and walked back to the tall shelves. After a moment of searching, she returned to the little girl with a travel sized bottle of liquid laxative. She instructed Molly to take it immediately after she ate lunch and she would be fine.

"Thanks Nurse Durby, you're the best." Molly said. The pig-tailed child uncrossed her fingers and as the lunch bell rang, she reached out to hug the woman.

—◉—

William Augustus Augustine-Chrystine had returned to the WonderKids facility wearing a fresh pair of pressed slacks and a determined, spiteful scowl. He sat in the cafeteria with the faculty-taught children of first-period lunch, shoveled forkful after forkful of salad into his crooked, rodentesque teeth and wiped errant dribbles of dressing off of his chin with a napkin which he had tucked over his tie.

From the tables across the large room, Molly Rollins watched the man with disgust. She picked over the creamed corn that filled the tiny square compartment of her lunch tray, too furious to eat. She spied him as he sipped on his brand new, steaming hot latte and dabbed his pencil-thin moustache dry.

"Look at him, sipping on his drink. Smug, ugly weasel." Molly said to the children at the table and not to anyone specifically.

"Who are you talking about?" One of the children asked.

Molly pointed across the table, "Mr. Augustine-Chrystine. He's the one trying to shut down WonderKids."

The children within earshot of the pig-tailed little girl turned to steal a glance at the man, whom had been joined by Mr. Wayland Puttey and Dr. Margo Levine-Alonzo. The Head Physician set down her tray and before she even took her first bite of meatloaf, turned to her superiors and said, "I hope you know that I am fully committed to fighting you on this; even if I have to get the courts involved."

Mr. Augustine-Chrystine nearly choked on his lunch as he laughed at the woman, "Oh, you go right ahead and try, Margo; you go right ahead and try."

"You can't just put it to a vote and kick all these people to the street." She implored.

Mr. Augustine-Chrystine motioned to his associate, who clearly had no interest in getting involved, "Dr. Levine, we most certainly can and we most certainly will."

He slapped Wayland Puttey on the back for added emphasis. He paid no attention to the fact that the man sulked, helpless despite his desire to side with the Head Physician. Dr. Levine saw that she was outnumbered and hung her head towards her lunch tray and began to eat quietly.

Molly Rollins slammed her fork down. She could not tolerate to see the closest person she ever had to a mother-figure relegated in her own lunch room; especially not by a nasty man in a terrible suit.

"I've had it." She announced angrily, "We can't just sit here and let him get away with this. We have to do something."

"What can we do? We're the faculty-taught kids." A child asked.

"Yeah, we kind of suck." Another agreed.

Molly motioned for the children to huddle closer and softly said, "I've been putting a plan together, but I need someone to start a distraction."

"What kind of distraction?" One of the younger children asked.

"It doesn't matter, but we have to get Mr. Augustine-Chrystine to not pay attention to his coffee for a few seconds."

The children of first-period lunch whispered back and forth and brainstormed potential ideas that they could use as distractions. They ruled out a fake fight, since two kids would have to deal with being put on restriction; which also ruled out food fights, fire drills and just about everything else that was suggested. With little other options, Molly pulled out the Visine and the small bottle of laxative and handed them both to one of the older children.

"You guys just make sure that these get poured into that latte." The pig-tailed girl said bravely.

The kids at the table each promised that they would do their part and wished Molly luck. She summoned all the courage contained in her petite body and rose from the table. She saluted her friends, who in turn saluted back. The little girl took a big gulp from her 2% milk, nodded and began to run around the perimeter of the cafeteria. Once she reached her top speed, she stretched out her arms and began to shout.

"I want to be an Airborne Ranger; I want to live a life of danger!"

Once she reached the front of the lunch room, she leapt upon a chair, stepped onto the table and ran between the children's trays as she sang.

"I want to die in the old drop zone; box me up and ship me home!"

By the time Molly jumped from one table to the next, the cafeteria has become alive with commotion. Dr. Levine stood up from her chair, chalk-faced and panicked. She scurried around the room and tried to regain order, embarrassed that she had apparently lost control in front of the board members. Meanwhile, Mr. Augustine-Chrystine rose from the table, cautious not to soil another pair of slacks. The rat-faced man surveyed the room; ready to pounce to a pants-safe-area at a moment's notice.

The facility-taught children of first-period lunch passed the Visine and laxative vials from one set of hands to the next, until they reached the table closest to the board member. Molly Rollins continued her distraction, kicking up creamed corn as she stomped across the tables and watched out of the corner of her eye as a couple of kids poured the contents of the bottles into the board member's cup, unnoticed.

Seeing that the mission had been accomplished, Molly stepped down from the tables in front of the flustered Head Physician and put her hands over her head. As soon as the young girl surrendered, the rest of the children quietly sat back down to their lunch trays and calm immediately returned to the cafeteria.

Dr. Levine was near tears. She took the pig-tailed girl by the arm and asked, "What are you thinking? You know that this isn't the time…"

Molly threw her arms around the Head Physician, buried her face into the woman's open knit sweater and began to cry. In between muffled sobs the young girl replied, "I'm just trying to help."

"This is outrageous!" William Augustus Augustine-Chrystine shouted as he brushed down his slacks to ensure their pristine appearance.

"I'm handling it, sir." Dr. Levine replied assuredly and prayed that her sweat was not visible.

The rat-faced man's face puckered up in disapproval and he took a long, deep gulp of his latte. He licked his lips and took another sip. Many of the children in the lunch room had to put their hands to their mouths to conceal their smiles of satisfaction.

"I certainly hope that you are planning on punishing this young miscreant." Mr. Augustine-Chrystine noted and finished the cup of latte with a final chug.

Wayland Puttey squeakily interjected, "William, I'm sure she was just having some fun. No harm done."

Molly Rollins looked up to the Head Physician and said courageously, "I did what I had to do and I even though I believe you will thank me later; I will take what ever punishment that comes to me."

Dr. Levine looked down at the girl, quite confused. The faculty-taught students of the first-lunch period rose from their seats and in unison saluted the young girl as the Head Physician escorted her into the office.

Once the Head Physician and little miss Molly Rollins left the lunch room a very loud, very juicy gurgle could be heard from somewhere within William Augustus Augustine-Chrystine's insides.

—◎—

The subway car for the eastbound MARTA train jostled across the rail. Throughout the compartment, the standing passengers held onto the railings to maintain their balance, while the seated passengers bounced up and down. They wore suits, business dresses, ripped jeans and faded tees; a variety of personalities all confined to the same sticky box and each pretended not to notice one another. The hot, stagnant smell of stale urine hung in the air, which forced the passengers to either breathe in short, choppy breaths or through their mouths.

Callym Rafferty and Gabriel sat in the middle of the car and watched the other riders, all of whom seemed to be searching for ways to occupy themselves without disturbing those near them. Callym desperately felt the urge to force open the doors and push one of the passengers out, just to see what would happen. Luckily for the passengers, Callym's state prevented him from acting upon his impulses and because of this he began to twitch in his seat. He stuffed his hands into his pocket to keep from fidgeting and tapped the plunger of his emergency syringe with his fingertip. He turned to his winged companion who happily observed a young father tend to the newborn child that rested in a blue, plastic stroller. Gabriel smiled and slid off his backpack.

"Hey Gabriel," Callym said as he cleared his throat, "When you were…you know…drugged, did you have any visions?"

The would-be angel pulled a Hallmark card out of his bag and handed it to the father, then turned to Callym and exclaimed, "Yes, as a matter of fact I did."

"What did you see?" the pale young man asked.

"Jeez, I saw a bunch of stuff. I saw the waterfalls of the Great Garden, I saw an amazing pyramid, but it wasn't in the desert. It was in a forest. Indians had built it. What are they called?"

"Mayans?" Callym asked.

"Yes! That's it!" Gabriel shouted, which gained him sideways glances from a few of the other passengers, "I saw that, and of course I saw Jesus."

"Of course, you did." Callym said smugly. He paused a moment and asked, "Did you see anything from the future."

Gabriel giggled in response, "Of course! I know lots of things about the future."

"Like what?" Callym inquired.

"Future stuff." Gabriel replied simply.

"What kind of future stuff?"

"I can't tell you that, silly. The future's a secret."

"I just wanted to know if your vision of the future matched mine."

"We'll just have to wait and see."

"Do you know who *it* is? Do you know what's going to be said?" Callym agitatedly asked.

Gabriel said nothing further; instead he held his index finger to pursed lips in a shushing motion.

Callym sulked in his chair and then added, "I guess it doesn't matter anyway. There is no way that these people will even accept the Word, even if they were to hear it. Look at them, they might as well be robots; they hardly accept themselves."

"That's not fair." Gabriel exclaimed, "People deserve more credit than that."

"Why? What makes them so special, anyway?"

Gabriel defensively said, "Doorbells, sleigh bells, schnitzel with noodles..."

Callym moaned in disgust and grumbled, "Pfft. Those are just a few of *My Favorite Things*, you rube."

"Okay," Gabriel replied, "What about love? These people treat love cooler than any other living thing, and you know it."

Gabriel smiled broadly, crossed his arms as he assumed victory. "Check and mate." He thought.

Callym glanced around the boxcar at the idle passengers and noted a lonely man who stood in the center of the cab, held the metal rung with one hand and an overflowing gunny-sac of kitchen gadgets in the other. The man wore a vibrant, blue polo-shirt with an embroidered, yellow lightning bolt and a logo that read "POWER DICER". He stared thoughtlessly at the ads plastered to the inner walls and sighed.

Callym tapped Gabriel, pointing out the man and asked, "What can you tell me about that guy?"

Gabriel observed the man and searched his brain. After some thinking, he finally said, "His name is Wallace

Reed, but he goes by Wally Ray Reed at work; he sells and demonstrates easy-to-use vegetable dicers in department stores. He talks fast and smooth and wins over his audience into purchasing the gizmos. He's a top seller and he likes his job, because for hour stints at a time, he gets to feel like he's a somebody.

He's thirty-two, he doesn't date often because he's shy- unless he's talking about kitchen cutlery. He scored decently on his SATs, his parents are still married, he likes dogs, but only small ones and he hates it when people dress them in sweaters."

"Very impressive." Callym Rafferty said, rather pleased. He nudged the boy and gestured towards a darling, young woman in jogging apparel and asked, "Do you see that girl? Her name is Celia Crowe; she's twenty-seven, she's originally from Tempe and she hosts pleasure parties."

"What is that?" Gabriel asked innocently.

"She puts together grown-up lady parties. She too is shy and she too is single. Her father left when she was three and her mother dated many men throughout her childhood. She lost her virginity at a college dance when she was nineteen to a boy who never called her again.

She dated a well-to-do banker, who proposed to her. He cheated on her with her maid of honor. She left home and moved here to start anew. So far, she has only made one friend; unless you count her pet goldfish."

"Can we?" Gabriel asked.

"No." Callym replied simply, "She likes acoustic rock music and reality shows. Her favorite color is orange and she had eggplant for lunch."

Gabriel clapped and said, "That's great! What does it all mean?"

As the train dove into a tunnel, Callym reclined as far back as he could in his wheelchair and said, "Since we have been on this train, he has glanced over at her four times. She's checked him out six."

"Amazing." Gabriel said, happily.

"I bet you anything that they won't speak to each other. Two people who are clearly interested in each other; yet held back by their societies' insistence that they leave each other alone, lest they risk looking a fool. How's that for your theory on human's and love?" Callym replied pessimistically.

"You don't think that they will get together?" Gabriel asked with genuine concern in his tone.

Callym shook his head slowly. The boys watched the two passengers steal glances back and forth with one another, as each missed the other's gaze by mere seconds. The train exited the tunnel and the car flooded with light. The cutlery salesman shifted the heavy bag in his hand and looked back towards the young hostess.

"You really want to bet that they won't get together?" Gabriel asked breezily.

"Sure." Callym replied, "In fact, if they get together on this train I will let you call WonderKids to check in when we get to the monastery."

"What if you win?" Gabriel asked.

"I punch you." Callym said, matter-of-factly.

Gabriel weighed the stakes, extended his hand and said, "Deal."

Callym took the would-be angel's hand, shook it and the boys continued their ride and stared blatantly at the two selected passengers.

The subway train neared its next stop and Wallace 'Wally Ray' Reed began to make his way towards the sliding doors. Callym cackled, slapped Gabriel on the chest and said excitedly, "He's about to leave! It looks like you are going to loose, brother."

Wallace Reed stole one last glance at Celia Crowe as the train pulled into the station; only this time his eyes met hers, for she too had tried to steal one last glance. Celia blushingly looked away quickly and Wallace feigned checking his watch. The doors slid open and Wallace Reed looked down, sighed at his inability to be proactive in time and joined the line of people that slowly shuffled out of the train.

Gabriel saw this and clasped his hands together and closed his eyes. Almost instantaneously, a boxed Power Dicer fell out of the man's bag. Wallace failed to notice and sulked past the sliding doors. Celia Crowe, however, did notice the box fall as she had allowed herself one final view of the man before he became just a fleeting moment in her day. She waited to see if he would realize that he had lost the item, and part of her actually hoped he would so that she could justify not being able to work up the courage to talk to him. When she finally concluded that he was not going to return for the dicer, she sprang from her seat, grabbed the item and hurried to catch the man right outside of the boy's window.

"See?" Gabriel said cheerfully, "I knew they'd get together."

Callym snuffed and said "They aren't on the train; you still loose."

From out the window, Gabriel watched as Celia Crowe handed a very grateful Wallace Reed his merchandise and after a few awkward silence seconds, waved to him goofily and returned to the train. As she walked through the doors, the would-be angel saw the look of self-loathing on the woman's face. She plopped back into a seat and moped while she waited for the train to start moving again. Callym apparently saw this too, for he giggled an evil, pleasured giggle.

"Hopeless, hopeless, hopeless. Get ready to get socked, brother." He said and cocked back his fist as the bells chimed, which noted that the sliding doors were about to close.

Just then, Wallace Reed returned and stood in the middle of the door's path, preventing it from fully closing. He searched the train and saw Celia Crowe with her head down.

"Excuse me, miss?" He announced.

The young woman turned and became overjoyed to see that he had returned. She rose from her seat and met him in the doorway path.

The boys watched the two of them talk and fumblingly attempt to quickly exchange proper introductions.

"Um... My name is Wally...er... Wallace Reed."

"I'm Celia."

"Hi."

"Hi."

"I'm... um... not very good at this."

"Me either."

The conductor came over the intercom and ordered that everyone stand clear of the doors so that the train could leave the station. The boys suddenly became very invested in what would happen between the two strangers.

Wallace Reed bumbled and finally found the courage to say, "I would like to ask you out, can I get your..."

That was all that the man could say before Celia Crowe grabbed him by the polo collar and pulled him out of the doorway and into the station, which effectively made her miss her train as well as broke her long bouts with shyness. As the subway train pulled away from the station, Gabriel saw out the window as the two strangers stood on the platform and kissed.

Gabriel laughed in celebration, "How do you like that?" he giggled.

"It wasn't technically in the train." Callym remarked.

Gabriel gasped and replied, "You aren't going to count it?"

"What do you think we should?"

"It was half in."

"It was half out."

"Mostly in."

"The kissing part happened out."

"Well, then what should we do?"

"How about you get to call and I get to punch you."

Gabriel pondered the proposal and after a bit of thinking, he extended his hand and said, "Deal"; only to be struck across the face by Callym's tightly balled fist.

—◎—

Mid-day shoppers littered the mall; small packs of consumers, lone housewives, high school truants and bored stoners milled the walkways, loitered the food court and roamed from store to store; all taking advantage of the lesser crowds. Sunday had circled the mall twice and spoken to at least one employee of just about every shop in the building, but there were no signs of the missing children. The custodian leaned over the second floor railing and scouted the crowd below. In his hand he loosely held a small, blue bag that contained a trinket that he picked up for Kylie, partly as a way to say thank you for her work with the boy formally known as Steve's ailment and partly because he had begun to feel sorry about his recent affair with Hope.

He felt a rumble in his stomach which he was not sure was being caused by his ravenous hunger or the overwhelming stress and guilt that had been bottled up inside. He decided that he would take one last look around the building so that he could stop at the food court to calm his stomach and then he would be on his way.

The custodian studied a happy looking couple as they passed by. The man placed his arm around the woman's waist and she offered him a piece of her pretzel in return. They looked completely content, Sunday thought and imagined that their days must have been spent lackadaisically and full of laughter and love. He wondered if he would ever know a feeling like that. What was he doing wrong?

He was distracted from his daydream by the vibrations of his cell phone from a number that was listed as 'unknown'.

"Hello?" He asked.

From the other end of the receiver, he heard the gruff and blunt voice of Sister Mary Rochelle, "Where's your walkie-talkie?"

Sunday responded, stuttering, "I...uh...I'm checking the mall right now. I...um... thought it best not to bring all that stuff into such a public place."

Thinking that his answer was decent enough, the custodian coolly sighed; however, the nun's response once again put him on edge as she said, "I thought I told you to keep that bag on you at all times."

"Yes ma'am. I'm sorry." He said sheepishly.

"Listen," the nun continued, "I just heard from Dr. Levine-Alonzo that Gabriel called the facility just five minutes ago. He says they are at the monastery."

"That's great!" Sunday exclaimed into the receiver.

"I am inside the perimeter and it will take me some time to get there. How fast can you get there?" She asked.

Sunday looked down at his watch, realized that he would have to skip the food court and said, "I can be there in less than ten minutes."

"Excellent." Sister Rochelle stated, "I will contact you when I get closer."

"Will do." Sunday sighed.

"…and Mr. Sunday…"

"Yes, ma'am?"

"Keep that satchel with you."

—◎—

$\mathscr{B}$espectacled in dark sunglasses, the choir director led his musicians in a practice session. Each had a Hallmark in their hand or nearby in their possession. Gabriel watched wide-eyed as the group fine-tuned their rendition of *Amazing Grace*. Sunday found the boy in the same pew that he had sat in a few days prior; his cardboard wings protruded from the back of the bench, which gave him away. Sunday sat down next to the child, dropped the black satchel from his shoulder and immediately spotted the swollen purple and blue patch under the boy's eye.

"What in the world happened to you?" The custodian whispered sternly.

Sunday lightly touched the tender spot. Gabriel winced and explained, "I made a bet and I lost; but I won."

"Well then I am happy and sad for you." Sunday replied unenthused.

They sat and listened to the music for a moment, then Sunday proceeded to grill the child and asked, "Where's Callym?"

Gabriel explained that when they had arrived, the young man sought out Brother Linus and he and the white-toothed monk were discussing Callym's condition in one of the rooms in the small cathedral.

"What were the two of you thinking?" Sunday demanded.

Gabriel shrugged and said innocently, "We were trying to help."

"Kiddo, there's a good way to help and a bad way to help. This wasn't the good way."

"I know. I was drugged." The young child explained, "Callym wanted to find information that could prove that I am an angel and that…"

"That will be enough." Sunday moaned. He had grown tired of the children's constant insistence that their delusions were real, "There is no way that you are an angel."

"Why is that?" The young child inquired.

"Because they don't exist. You aren't anything other than a regular kid with a few issues."

The choir completed their song and the audience of two clapped.

"Sure they do." Gabriel said happily, "Lots of people believe in them. Angels *are* real. So are demons, we learned that today."

Just then, the leader of the choir turned towards the custodian and asked in a thick, southern drawl, "You with that creepy kid in the wheelchair?"

Sunday nodded and said, "Yes sir."

The musician shook his head in sympathy and said matter-of-factly, "That boy's the devil."

Gabriel looked up at the custodian and giggled proudly, "See?"

Sunday did not acknowledge the child, instead he said to the singer, "Yeah, sorry about that. You guys sound great by the way."

The musicians thanked him and began to practice another song. A short time later, the door to the side of the altar opened, Brother Linus entered as he cheerfully led Callym's wheelchair into the church. They smiled and carried on as if they had become blood-buddies while they were in the back room. Sunday rose to meet the white-toothed monk, extended a hand in gratitude and said, "Thank you for looking after the boys."

The monk smiled and replied, "It was my pleasure. It was delightful."

"Seriously?" Sunday asked.

The white-toothed monk nodded. Sunday was confused. It was odd enough that the pale, young teen had an expression about him that could almost qualify as happiness and that the white-toothed monk seemed so cheerful, pleased and outgoing towards the boy who nearly had killed him just days prior, but something else seemed inherently wrong; yet he could not quite figure out what it was. He cast the feelings aside; simply happy that every one appeared safe and that there had been no collateral damage.

"I also wanted to apologize for the other day…" the custodian began.

"Think nothing of it, son." Brother Linus insisted, "I was just as much to blame. The notion that young Master Rafferty could be possessed captivated me and I admit that I was hasty and overstepped my position."

"Well, okay then." Sunday replied, relived, "Thank you."

"Yes, thank you." Callym said as he smiled from his chair.

"Anytime." Brother Linus said, as he mussed the young man's jet black hair, "I hope to see you very soon."

Sunday watched slack-jawed as the wheelchair-bound youth agreed. Callym rolled towards the custodian and said, "We can go now."

The custodian shrugged and radioed to Sister Rochelle that he had the children and that they were safe.

"I'll be there in twenty minutes." The nun said through the walkie-talkie.

A hollow rumble echoed from within Sunday's stomach and he hunched over in hunger pains. He spoke into the device and asked, "Can you meet us at the Cakery instead? I'm starving."

The nun agreed and Sunday told the boys to say their goodbyes so that he could finally find something to eat.

— ◎ —

𝒯hick, sugary syrup trickled off of the sticky bun and pooled onto Sunday's plate. He took a bite of the sweet, warm biscuit and let it dissolve in his mouth. He moved onto his berry pie and then took a large gulp of coffee. Callym and Gabriel sat across from the custodian and silently spooned ice cream into their mouths. Upon entering the Cakery, Sunday had made a deal with the boys that they were allowed a double scoop if they promised that they would not make a sound, at least until he had finished eating. Gabriel had chosen a scoop of mint-chocolate chip, a scoop of bubblegum flavor and topped the whole thing off with sprinkles, chocolate and cherries. Callym ordered two scoops of vanilla and topped them with hot fudge.

"You kids have a lot of nerve." Sunday said as he took another bite of the gooey dish, "You know how serious things are back at the building. Neither of you have been here a week and already you are putting us all at risk."

The children listened to the custodian's scolds and occasionally took small, slow bites of their ice cream, which reminded them not to speak a word.

"And to get that monk involved again!" He continued, "I don't know what you said to him, but rest assured it all stops now. I don't want to hear another thing about angels, devils, possessions or saviors. Starting now, they do not exist."

Gabriel frowned, took one last bite and pushed his ice cream to the center of the table. He could no longer enjoy his delicious treat if it meant he could not defend himself.

"I'm sorry, but that's ridiculous." The boy said, "Just because you don't believe in anything doesn't make it not so. It says right in the Bible that Jesus told his people that what ever they believe will be made a reality. That's why there's a hell, a purgatory, duck-billed platypuses and why it's entirely plausible that we are what we say we are."

"So you're saying that just because the Bible says it then it has to be true? I don't buy it."

"Well, someone does, because I'm telling you I was born into a human body to witness the Word!" Gabriel said defiantly. The young boy had never felt such frustration and it bothered him tremendously.

"You know what else the Bible says?" The winged boy added, "It says you suck, Mr. Sunday. You suck."

He let out a relieving 'grr' and stuck out his tongue, which made him instantly feel much better.

Callym, who up until this point had surprisingly kept his end of the ice cream bargain, pointed across the sparsely filled Cakery at the young, female regular in the flack jacket and finally spoke, "What in Hell is that woman doing?"

The table turned its attention to the woman who sat alone, her oversized purse once again resting on the table. In front of her was a large piece of triple-layer German chocolate cake, a large cup of black coffee and a small, half-empty bottle of whisky. She held her fork and stared at it suspiciously. She manipulated the utensil so that it wiggled around between her two fingers as if it were alive.

"She's a mime, leave her alone." Sunday answered.

The children watched, fascinated as the fork spun around the street girl's fingers and danced across her table as she chased it with her hand, barely touching it with the tip of her finger.

"She's yours?" Callym asked without wavering his fixated stare.

"Not *mine*. *Mime*. It's like a clown, but more annoying." Sunday corrected, "Leave her alone."

The young woman sprang from her seat, grabbed the fork with both hands and held it tightly, moving her hands around the table as if the utensil fought for its freedom. She raised it high over her head and with crossed eyes and great force, she stabbed deep into the layers of her cake. The boys laughed out loud as she slunk down in her seat and wiped the imaginary sweat from her forehead.

From within the black satchel that rested beside Sunday, he heard the muffled voice of Sister Rochelle, "Sunday, Sunday… Do you copy?"

The custodian rifled through the sack to grab the walkie-talkie as the nun said again, "Sunday, Do you copy? You better have that bag with you, mister."

Sunday pressed the talk button and responded, "Yes, I'm here."

Sister Rochelle's voice sounded much cooler as she said through the device, "Good, I should be at there in a few minutes."

"Great, see you then." Sunday said and placed the walkie-talkie back into the sack and rested it beside him. He sighed and unwillingly returned his focus back to Gabriel, who had left the table to hand the woman a Hallmark card.

The young mime accepted the card happily and searched her table for something to offer in return. Without speaking, she held out her half-empty bottle of whisky.

"No thank you." Gabriel said as he generously shook his head.

She eyed her fork suspiciously, removed it from the cake taking a portion of the frosted, spongy dessert with it and offered it to the boy. Gabriel leaned in to take the bite and the fork once again began to dance around in the woman's hand. Gabriel followed it with his open mouth up and down, left and right. Finally, the mime gained control of the fork and with two hands slowly began to move it towards the boy. She stopped short as her hand hit an invisible wall. She attempted again and again to the delight of the child. The mime shrugged and took the bite herself, stabbed the fork back into the cake and banged against the barrier that was not really there.

"Hooray!" Gabriel cheered and clapped.

The young woman held up an index finger and began to search through her large purse. When she finally pulled her hand out, she held a crumpled stick of chewing gum. It was missing the outer wrapper, so there was no telling what kind it was. Gabriel gleefully accepted it.

"I'm Gabriel." The winged child said.

The woman thought for a moment and then went back into her purse and pulled out her driver's license. Next to a terrible picture of the girl in which her hair was a deep purple, the ID shown her name: Jezebel Charlene Costello.

"Nice to meet you, Jezebel." Gabriel nodded.

Sunday slid from their table and went to regain custody of the young boy. He grabbed the child by the back of the backpack and said, "Tell the nice mime lady goodbye."

"Goodbye." Gabriel waved.

Jezebel Costello waved back and blew the young boy a kiss as he was pulled back to the table. As his sneaker squeaked on the tiles, he caught the imaginary charm and placed it to his cheek and blushed. Suddenly, the would-be angel fell from Sunday's grasp and his backside bounced on the floor. He turned to see the custodian frozen in place. The few Cakery customers gasped and dropped utensils and glasses made the only sounds as Callym Rafferty pointed the nun-issued gun from the satchel directly at Sunday.

"What are you doing?" The custodian asked as he raised his hands.

The pale, young man rubbed the barrel of the pistol to his temple and replied, "To be honest, I haven't thought that far."

He leveled the gun back towards the man, who did his best to shield Gabriel who cowered behind him.

"Why don't you just put the gun down, Callym?" he asked.

"Now, why would I do that?" the boy replied, "I'm guessing that from here I could put a sizable hole in you. Don't you think?"

Sunday's throat closed up and he could not answer. Out of the corner of his eye he saw the other customers begin to crawl under their tables. Apparently, the invisible box that Jezebel Costello had trapped her self in was not bulletproof since she too slid slowly out of sight.

"I'm wondering," Callym said eerily, "Knowing that at any second, I'm going to pull this trigger right here; what do you believe in now, brother?"

Sunday's thoughts were suddenly filled with all the possibilities. Would there be a Heaven? Would he go there? It had been so long since he felt really strongly about any idea of God that he was suddenly concerned that he may not be on the guest list. Gabriel had mentioned Purgatory and Hell. Would he go there? What if nothing special happened at all? Would he just decompose back into the soil? Suddenly, that seemed anti-climactic to him and for the first time in as long as he could remember; Sunday found himself hoping that there was something bigger out there and that he was in its favor.

The front door to the Cakery swung open and Sister Rochelle rushed in, pistol drawn.

"Sweet Christ," She said as she flanked the wheelchair-bound terrorist, "What did you do?"

Callym steadied his aim on Sunday and called out to the woman, "This doesn't concern you, Sister."

"Callym, I have a gun pointed at you too." She explained, "Just put it down."

"You won't shoot me." He said, calling her bluff.

"And you won't shoot him." She said, "So, let's just put the gun down and go home."

"That sounds like a real good plan, Callym." Sunday said as he shook.

"Shut up! All of you!" The young boy demanded, "I could shoot everyone in here if I wanted to."

"That's true." Sunday quaked, "But you're not going to do that. Why don't you just set the gun down?"

Sister Rochelle edged closer to Callym, which only upset the boy and caused him to pull back the hammer of his weapon. The nun walked around the wheelchair and pointed her gun directly against the boy's head.

"It's over, Callym. Give me the gun."

Callym's hands quaked, shaking the pistol. He twitched within his seat and said, "I can't. I have to shoot him."

"Then do it." Sister Rochelle insisted.

"What!" Sunday cried.

The patrons screamed as Rochelle continued, "Do it, then give me the gun and we can leave."

Callym steadied his arms, pointed the barrel directly at Sunday who held his hands out pleadingly, mere feet away. He looked to the nun, hoping to see her wink at him, noting that some kind of rescue plan was in place. Perhaps at any moment, the windows would shatter by repelling S.W.A.T. members or maybe the safety was still set. However, the nun looked on coldly as the creepy teen squeezed his bandaged fingers around the trigger. Sunday felt a chest-splitting force that took him off of his feet. Screams ceased to an abrupt silence and blackness blanketed his eyes as three successive booms cracked through the air.

reject reject reject reject reject reject reject reject reject reject
reject reject reject reject reject reject reject reject reject reject i
hate my life reject reject reject reject reject reject reject reject
reject reject reject reject reject reject reject reject reject reject
reject reject reject reject why wont these voices stop reject
reject reject reject reject reject reject reject reject reject reject
reject reject reject reject reject reject reject reject reject reject
reject reject reject reject reject reject reject reject reject reject
reject reject reject reject reject reject reject reject reject reject
reject reject reject reject reject reject reject reject reject reject
reject can not understand reject reject reject reject reject reject
reject reject reject reject reject reject reject reject reject reject
reject reject reject reject reject reject reject reject reject reject
reject reject reject reject reject how I can just kill a man
reject reject reject reject reject reject reject reject reject reject
reject reject reject reject reject reject reject rage reject reject
reject reject reject reject reject reject reject reject reject reject
reject reject reject reject reject reject reject reject reject reject
reject reject reject reject reject reject reject reject reject reject
reject reject reject hate reject reject reject reject reject reject
reject reject reject reject reject reject reject reject reject reject
reject reject reject reject reject reject reject reject reject reject
reject reject reject reject reject reject reject burn burn burn
reject reject reject reject hate hate reject reject reject reject
reject reject reject reject reject reject reject reject reject I see a
red door reject reject I want to paint it black reject reject reject
reject reject reject reject reject since I cant die reject I wish
everybody else would   reject reject reject reject reject reject
reject reject reject reject reject reject I would love reject reject
reject reject reject reject reject reject reject reject reject
nothing more reject reject reject reject reject reject reject reject
than reject to reject watch reject reject reject reject reject
reject reject the whole world burn reject reject reject reject
reject watch the whole fucking thing burn reject reject voices
voices voices

Welcome to my world

Yet another **brainless** shrink matriculates from the community colleges and tells me to keep a **notebook**

Brilliant doctor. Truly a genius suggestion. Revo**fuckin**lutionary.

I woke up in back in this new 'hospital'... if you can call it that.

It seems that **I broke** my leg yesterday.

I don't completely remember. **Another** episode. **Another** fit.

Whatever you want to call it, **I hate** it.   **DEAD**

...but **only on the inside**.

Unfortunate

I do recall speaking with the old monk. I told him that it felt like something evil was **trapped** inside. Something wicked. I wanted him to try to rid it via **exorcism**. At first, he was reluctant. I remember that. I remember 'persuading' him with a little help from my emergency needle...

Amazing what a little **blue juice** can do.

I remember feeling **something**...

Something that I can only describe as **hate**, but thats not quite the right word... it **tore** at me; stabbing sensations from under my skin. I was sure that the exorcism would work. Clearly the **evil** in me was displeased by the ritual.

Ive been told that when the old monk notified me that nothing more could be done is when I blanked out and went into my fit of **blind fury**.

The monks will probably never permit me back on their grounds.

It's a shame. Having a holy man around could have **proved** handy.

I watched as the Lamb opened the first of the seven seals. Then I heard one of the four **living creatures** say in a voice like thunder, "**Come!**" I looked, and there before me was a white horse! Its rider held a bow, and he was given a crown, and he rode out as a conqueror **bent on conquest**.

I need a few **friends**.

I'll **get by with** a little help from my friends.

Morphine More fiend Morphine **Morphine** **Morphine** Reject **Morphine**

CHAPTER EIGHTEEN

When he finally came to his senses, something within him seemed magical; a blissful joy that he had never felt before. His entire body tingled as if wrapped in a warm, plushy blanket. He cooed comfortably, struggled to open his eyes but only squinted to avoid the harsh light that attempted to penetrate his stinging retinas.

He felt completely at peace. The regular bitterness that usually lined his every thought he had was gone, replaced with lollipops and roses. He inhaled and took in the sweet, musky scent that loomed about him in an aura. The last thing that he remembered was the gun shots. Three gun shots. Had someone been shot? Did he shoot some one? Had he been shot?

The scene suddenly replayed from his memory. It was he who had been shot; three times in the chest. The custodian attempted once again to open his eyes but the light was still far too much for him. He wondered if he were in a hospital. It did not smell like a hospital. More importantly, he wondered why there was only a dull ache around his chest.

Have I died?

I must have died.

...Neat!

He forced his eyelids apart and rose from his position; unable to cease his smile even if he wanted to, which oddly enough... he did not. He adjusted to the light and saw that he lay upon the couch in the WonderKids nurses' lounge. The second-hand sofa had never felt so cozy. Sunday could feel the thin, worn foam inside the cushions form to his body and it felt like home to him. Everything about WonderKids suddenly felt like home to him.

"He's awake!" Kylie Court cheered from beside him as he rose fully.

Little Molly Rollins rushed to the custodian's side and threw her small arms around him. He returned her embrace, held her tightly and patted her back.

Sister Rochelle sat at the small break room table and she read a file. She set it down, looked over the custodian and asked, "How do you feel?"

"A little achy;" He said, still smiling, "but really good, actually."

"I was so worried about you." Kylie said as she clutched his hand.

Sunday looked to her endearingly and set his other hand on top of her gloved one.

"Hand sandwich." He teased and began to laugh hysterically. Once his chuckles died down, he asked, "I was shot, right?"

"Yes." The nun replied.

"Three times?"

"Yes."

"Wait… you *told* him to shoot me; didn't you?"

Sister Rochelle responded coolly and unemotionally, "Yep."

Sunday knew that he should have been furious. He knew that he should have wanted to yell and scream in outrage. Kylie Court and Molly Rollins also must have thought this as they both remained silent and waited to see what the custodian's reaction would be. Strangely, he found that he was not furious; he did not want to yell or scream. He simply shrugged and once again began to laugh incessantly.

"What the hell happened to me?" He giggled as his cheeks began to sting from the constant smiles.

Sister Rochelle set down the file, rose from her seat, walked over towards the sofa and removed her pistol from its holster. She took a bullet from the clip and handed it to him. The casing was silver and had three tiny, cross-shaped prongs, while the projectile that was held in place by the prongs appeared to be a thin, clear casing with a crimson dust inside.

"These bullets are specially made and issued by my Organization. Inside is a fine Ketoret powder."

"What's that?" Kylie asked.

"A mix of minerals and such: stacte, onycha, frankincense. It's common church incense."

Sunday joyfully said, "Awesome."

Sister Rochelle explained, "Incense has a calming effect on people and the fine powder hitting a target at such velocity causes the olfactory sensors to release an overload of pleasure-inducing endorphins. Tell me, Mr. Sunday, how does the room smell to you?"

Sunday took a happy breath and said, "Marvelous."

"He smells the incense." She explained.

"Incredible." Kylie said, "So, you can stop someone without causing any harm at all. Heck, just the opposite."

"Yes." The nun explained further. She turned to Sunday and added, "That's why I wanted you to keep the bag on you."

Sunday nodded and said, "I know… I'm sorry…I love you."

The nurse shook her head and said, "That's just the Ketoret. The fine powder is all over you and in your nose and lungs. You took three shots… You should level out a bit in a few minutes, but you'll be on cloud nine for a good forty-five minutes unless you shower before then."

Sunday goofily shook his head that he understood as he continued to clutch Kylie's latex-gloved hand.

"Listen, Sunday." The nun continued, "Things have gotten a little hectic downstairs. A lot of the directors are here now. We managed to sneak you all back in unnoticed and Mr. Stewart is retrieving your van. It's important that nothing is mentioned in regards of any of this. You can't even let on that your chest hurts, okay?"

"Okey dokey." He said with a thumbs-up.

Kylie became excited and explained, "Your phone call worked! They actually showed up!"

Sunday gleefully leaped from the sofa like an overjoyed child and ran from the room, dragging Kylie by the hand behind him. He ran to the railing and looked down unto the main floor. Trailing chords and wires behind them, two small, local news crews were setting up their equipment below.

"I can't believe they actually showed up!" He cheered.

Sunday pulled Kylie closer to him, put his arm around her waist, spun around with her and sang, "I believe in marigolds, since you came along."

She laughed and said, "I think that it's 'miracles'."

"I think you're a miracle." He said as he dipped her.

Swept up in the moment, Kylie gazed up to meet the custodian's eyes and hoped that he would kiss her. Sunday leaned in closer as she pursed her lips and prepared for one of the rare times in which she craved physical contact as opposed to cringing over the thought of it. She closed her eyelids and waited, only to feel the custodian's wet lips on her forehead.

Looking up, she saw Sunday's elfish expression and incense-induced, crooked smile. A little disappointed, she stepped out of their dance and teased him, saying, "You're high."

Molly Rollins joined them in the hallway and said, "Sunday, Sunday! I made a plan too!"

The pig-tailed girl recounted her prank to the custodian and noted that Mr. William Augustus Augustine-Chrystine had yet to be seen since he had first entered the restroom.

Sunday chuckled and then led the girls skipping hand-in-hand-hand down the spiral staircase to better appreciate their collective handiwork.

— ◉ —

"*P*reposterous!" William Augustus Augustine-Chrystine roared as he threw open the door to the first floor conference room. Hunched over, his body weak and flush of color from his sudden stomach ailment, the rat-faced man joined the associates already deep in discussion at the table. Taking part in the conversation were the Swindles, Marvin Snell, Wayland Puttey and Head Physician Margo Levine-Alonzo. The Head Physician was aided by Dr. Randall Shayam, Kylie Court and a still jubilant custodian. Although Sunday had eagerly and vigorously shook every hand upon his entrance into the room, he found no desire to greet the group's newest arrival with a colloquial handshake; instead he stuck out his tongue and made a 'pfft' sound.

Mr. Augustine-Chrystine paid little attention to the custodian as he continued his diatribe, "The vote *will* go on as planned! Small-time news coverage or not, this little scheme to buy time will not work. At the very best you'll get a 'feel-good' story about the kids of this place. And I've been here all day; believe me when I say that there is nothing 'feel-good' about this place."

"The coverage on the advancements with the progress for the young coma patient could merit some recognition in the medical community. That shouldn't be ignored, Boss." Dr. Shayam noted.

His mouth still fixed in a permanent grin, Sunday stared at the doctor and whispered to him, "I never noticed that you have a mole right here."

The custodian pressed the dark brown spot on the man's chin as if it were a button and said softly, "Boop!"

Dr. Shayam swatted his hand away, rather irritated.

"It definitely merits consideration." Mrs. Swindle suggested.

"He's a *vegetable*!" The rat-faced director retorted, "You know what, check that... he's not even a vegetable, *vegetables* are more responsive. And you talk about progress? Progress? Ha! You have nothing and anyone who wants to dump more funds into this place on the off chance that progress can be made in maybe bringing the boy to vegetable status is out of their mind."

Thomas Swindle scowled and rose from his seat, angrily. He glared across the table and warned, "I suggest you choose your next words carefully." He touched his wife's shoulder and continued, "That *boy* is our grandson."

The room grew uncomfortable and silent. Marvin Snell leaned back in his chair and said mordantly, "I'm waiting for the tumbleweeds to roll through."

Sunday giggled and began to whistle the classic *High Noon* chime. Kylie Court slapped him across the chest in an effort to get him to behave. Dr. Levine spoke through the corner of her mouth and asked, "What is into you, Mr. Sunday?"

Kylie Court leaned over the Head Physician's chair and explained the custodian's current condition. Meanwhile, Mrs. Swindle had turned her attention to the custodian and asked, "Did you say that this is Mr. Sunday?"

The joyful man replied cheerfully, "Yes ma'am, I am."

The silver haired woman lit up with delight, "You're the one who suggested the theories that are being used to help out little lamb, yes?"

Sunday blushed and Kylie Court answered for him, "Yes, he is!"

Mrs. Swindle rose from her seat and wrapped her arms firmly around the custodian. He put his arm around her lovingly as her husband extended his hand and said, "Son, I can't begin to thank you enough."

Sunday took the man's hand and said, "Thank you, sir."

"I expect you to go far, young man. I expect you to go far." Mr. Swindle said as he released his firm grip.

A tapping came from the other side of the door; Stew cracked it open and slyly sneaked his head in. He excused himself and said, "Sorry to interrupt, Head Physician Dr. Levine-Alonzo, but I just saw a Channel 5 News van pull up…"

The Head Physician shot from her seat and beamed with glee, "Is it…"

Stew smirked and confirmed the woman's suspicions, "Channel Five's own Tabitha Townsend!"

Dr. Levine screamed like a giddy concert groupie, sprinted from the room and said winningly to Mr. Augustine-Chrystine on her way out, "Tabitha Townsend. How's that for coverage?"

She pushed past Stew and joined the line of children who made their way out to the van to greet Atlanta's most successful newswoman, who also happened to be Dr. Levine's personal hero. Stew regained his balance and tossed Sunday the black satchel and said, "I put the keys in there too."

Sunday smiled warmly and walked up to his co-worker. He put his palms to Stew's cheek and said, "Stew, Stew, Stew… You are my friend."

Stew stepped back and asked, "What's gotten into you?"

"I got shot with like… love bullets, man." Sunday giggled, "Love bullets. What a great band name… Dude, we should *totally* start a band!"

Kylie rushed over to interject and said, "I'll explain later."

The Board of Directors decided to continue their meeting at another time and left the room to greet the local celebrity. On her way out, Sunday grabbed Kylie Court by the wrist and prompted her to lag behind.

"Wait." He said, "I have something for you."

Kylie smirked, blushed and asked, "You got me something? Why?"

Sunday searched the contents of the black satchel and produced the tiny bag, "Because you're just amazing, I guess."

Kylie took the gift graciously and pulled the ruffled crepe-paper that lined the bag to the side. She slid her hand inside and pulled out a package of elbow-length, latex gloves with large smiley faces printed all over them. The young woman laughed and held the gift to her chest.

Sunday smiled and twirled his foot in a circle on the floor. He bashfully asked, "Do you like them? I know… I mean… I thought that…"

Under the influence of endorphin inducing powders or not, Kylie could not help but to be enamored with the custodian. She stepped closer and kissed him sweetly.

"Perfect." She said as she wrapped his arms around her waist.

— ◎ —

A decade ago, Tabitha Townsend made her debut on Channel 5's *Late Night News Report*. That evening she detailed stories about the conflicts in Bosnia, a lady that raised her pet pig on diet soda, the latest antics of Roseanne Barr and most importantly, the Olympic Park bombing. Instantly, the fledgling broadcaster had become the voice of the city. Dr. Margo Levine-Alonzo watched the report that night and she, like many of the other citizens of the city, immediately became a devoted fan of the young reporter. As the years passed, Tabitha Townsend's popularity grew and grew; before long she was referred to in the journalistic community as a local Oprah.

Standing at almost six feet tall, her fiery, orange hair cut into a smart bob and dressed in a sleek grey and red ensemble, Tabitha Townsend commanded respect. Followed by her entourage of production crew and make-up personnel, she marched into the facility and immediately took charge as she pointed out where she wanted lights to be set and what angles she preferred for the shots that they were soon to capture. The crowd that had rushed to meet the celebrity swarmed her as she took in her surroundings. Even one of the lesser known news crews began to film the reporter's entrance like paparazzi.

"So what's the deal here?" The reporter asked, "Some kid is going to be saved thanks to some miracle cure, right?"

"Yes ma'am," Dr. Levine stuttered, completely awestruck, "I'm Head Physician Dr. Margo Levine-Alonzo. We have a patient who has been in a coma for over ten years and we believe that we are very close to curing him."

"Close? So he's not awake? We can't interview him?" Ms. Townsend inquired.

Dr. Levine's throat went dry as she answered, "Unfortunately, no."

Tabitha Townsend motioned for her crew to turn back towards the van and said, "If there's no one to interview then there is no story. Let's go."

Kylie Court rushed to stop the reporter and her entourage and cried, "Wait! There is a story here. There are many stories here; all you have to do is pick one."

Ms. Townsend paused, quite intrigued, "We're already here, tell me what you have."

"Well," Kylie began, "Every child here has an unusual ailment, one of them is sure to interest you. Gene, the coma patient is only one of the kids here, and did we mention that his cure was discovered by the staff custodian? There's bound to be a story in the WonderKid's staff. Everyday they try their best to take care of these poor kids medically and mentally through creative games and songs. You can't just turn and leave with out looking around."

The reporter did not respond, but clearly she agreed with the young phlebotomist because she began to once again look around the facility and at the children who crowded around her. She turned to the only member of her entourage who wore a tie and said, "Okay Phil, here's what I'm thinking. Establishing shot of the hospital from outside. We'll interview a couple of the cuter kids, real heart wrenching shit about how they can't be cured. Have the staff sing a little song."

She turned to Kylie and confirmed, "You did say there would be singing?"

"Yes, of course." Kylie agreed.

"Okay, so they sing a little song. Then we move onto the 'possible cure' of the coma kid, there's a little hope, we interview the person in charge and the janitor- it'll appeal to the red-necks, another little clip with the cute kids, I'll pass out hugs, get everyone to say the call letters and there you go."

"It sounds genius, Ms. Townsend." The producer replied.

"Great." Tabitha Townsend continued. She pointed to Molly Rollins and said, "You, pig-tails. How would you like to be on TV tonight, cutie?"

Molly Rollins blushed and nodded. The reporter looked around the room for a second child to interview and her eyes were drawn to the two floppy wings that protruded from Gabriel's back.

"You," She called to the boy, "Are you sick?"

Gabriel giddily replied, "No ma'am, I'm an angel."

"Perfect." The reporter exclaimed, "Phil, get those kids prepped."

The producer rounded up his team and began to put them to work. The reporter looked to Kylie and asked, "Now who is in charge here?"

Before the woman could answer, a voice came from within the crowd that said, "I am."

William Augustus Augustine-Chrystine began to make his way through the group as he pompously attempted to take charge. The rat-faced man pushed past Peter Tertiary who in turn elbowed the man hard in the lower abdomen. Mr. Augustine-Chrystine's body quaked and gurgled and he doubled over. He felt a mass within him drop to his colon and suddenly he struggled to maintain his bowels. He hurried past the crowd and almost knocked over the famous reporter as he trotted back to the men's room.

The children instantly pointed to the Head Physician and informed Tabitha Townsend that she was in charge. Dr. Levine shook her hero's hand and said, "Pleased to meet you. I am a huge fan."

"That's great." The reporter replied and instructed the star-struck physician that she would need to meet up with the Channel 5 make-up artists to prepare for the camera. A glow of immeasurable glee surrounded Dr. Levine as she released Ms. Townsend's hand and watched the woman continue with her preparations.

The physician held her hand to her mouth to try to conceal her joy and the children in the crowd began to break apart and went back to playing their games and riding the carousel. Dr. Levine spotted Sunday and approached him. The custodian beamed at his boss and waved to her emphatically.

"Pretty cool, huh?" He said.

The doctor nodded and replied, "I can't believe I'm going to be on TV with Channel Five's own Tabitha Townsend."

She gave a moment's pause to ensure that she was not dreaming and then continued, "I know that I've been rough on you the last few months. I just wanted you to know that I know that you had a lot to do with all of this."

The Head Physician took Sunday by the hand and said, "I just wanted to say thank you. This is the best day ever. Ever."

Sunday nodded and replied, "I love you too."

—◉—

Little Molly Rollins and Gabriel sat in chairs in the hastily thrown together make-up table. Around them, the lesser news crews had already begun to film various children at play and interviewed doctors and board members. The Channel 5 stylists applied make up to the children and redid Molly's pigtails using big silky bows.

Callym Rafferty rolled towards the children and said, "So, you are both going to be on the television? Congratulations."

"Thanks!" Gabriel replied cheerfully.

Callym wheeled closer and slyly asked, "Are you nervous?"

"Why would we be nervous?" Molly asked.

"Oh, there are plenty of reasons. You could get in front of the camera and forget what you were going to say or sometimes when people get nervous their throats dry up and their voices crack."

The children grew anxious as the pale, young man continued, "She seemed like a professional reporter too; she could end up asking you questions that you can't answer or worse… what if she makes you cry on TV? Millions of people would see it. I don't know. *I* would be nervous."

Molly's eyes widened and she exclaimed, "I can't swallow all of the sudden! My throat is closing up, it's happening!"

Gabriel attempted to calm the young girl, but to no avail. Molly had worked herself into an anxiety attack, which triggered a scream that filled the room and caught the already taping newscasters off guard. Gabriel watched, helpless, as the WonderKids staff scattered to move Molly to her soundproofed room and to locate something to bring down her anxiety.

Kylie Court ran up the spiral staircase and down the hallway until she reached Pill Alley. Nurse Durby sat at the counter, entranced in her game of Suduko. Kylie lightly tapped on the counter and said, "Excuse me, Nurse Durby; we are having an issue with Molly, as you can probably hear."

She chuckled kindly and continued, "We were wondering if you had anything that we could give to her?"

The pharmacist did not look up from her number game, nor did she speak. She simply shook her head 'no'.

"There's no valium? Nothing to calm her down?"

Once again, the nurse merely shook her head.

"How about a tiny bit of the Lithium Vali…"

The nurse proceeded to fill in the tiny boxes of her game with 7's and 3's without responding. Kylie became frustrated and debated jumping the counter to look through the bottles and vials herself; however, just then the muffled, shrill cries suddenly ceased.

"I guess… nevermind." She said, rather confused; and turned head back downstairs.

It was only after Kylie turned away, muttering insults such as 'bitch' and 'wrinkled sea cow' under her breath that Nurse Durby finally looked up from the small book of puzzles. Had the phlebotomist glanced back before she descended the staircase to join Stew and Sunday, she would have seen the nurse's blank-eyed, iris-less stare. Instead, she found the custodians in the soundproofed room as they watched Molly Rollins slowly drink a large glass of water.

"Drink it slowly." Stew guided as the young, pig-tailed girl chugged gulp after gulp.

"What happened?" Kylie asked, "Did you find something?"

Sunday shut the door behind her and squealed, "We found some Valium."

"Where?" Kylie asked.

Stew tossed her the little orange vial. Kylie read the label and looked up dumbfounded, "Channel Five's own Tabitha Townsend?"

Sunday smirked and held a finger to his mouth and said, "Shh, I found them in her purse."

"The dosage is all wrong for her, so we just gave her a half of one, but it is still going to knock her on her ass." Stew noted.

"We're going to need to find another kid to be on the TV." Kylie replied.

"I have an idea!" Sunday shouted and threw the door back open. He shouted out to the main room, "Austin Olsen! Come here, now!"

The tubby child jiggled his way to the soundproofed room and sniffled, "What's up? Did you hear that Gabriel gets to be on TV? How cool is that?"

Kylie turned to the boy and asked, "How would you like to join him?"

Austin Olsen was filled with so much delight that he could not help but to jump and down as he screamed, "I'd love to! I'd love to!"

Kylie flagged down Phil the Producer and motioned for him to join them. The well-dressed man made his way to the room and asked, "What is going on?"

"We are going to have to switch one of the kids for the interview." Sunday explained.

"This is Austin Olsen, he's volunteered to help." Kylie added as she rested her hands on the round child's shoulders.

The producer looked over the boy, made a disgruntled, sour expression and then shrugged, "I guess he will have to do."

"Sweetness!" Austin exclaimed.

"Just promise that you won't freak out like Molly did." Stew said.

"Freak out? What do you mean?" Austin gulped.

"Yeah, stage fright, what-have-you" Stew explained, "It got to Molly and she lost her cool. Can you keep your cool?"

Austin flashed a Billy Idol snarl and a 'hang loose' sign with his hands and said, "I'm cool."

"No dry mouth?"

"Nope."

"No sweaty palms?"

"Nope."

"No pre-show puking?"

"What?" Austin asked.

"Some people get nervous and throw up before having to do any public speaking." Stew explained.

"Oh crap, really?" Austin gurgled.

The boy suddenly felt a large knot form in his stomach. A thin stream trickled from his nose. He tried to wipe it away with his sleeve but it was no use. The yellow-greenish goo continued to flow. A rumble twisted its way through his intestines and into his stomach and built pressure as its path was blocked by the troublesome knot. Austin's eyes welled and he began to belch uncontrollably.

"What is happening now?" Phil the producer asked.

Austin Olsen clutched his stomach as various liquids trickled from his body, "The quickening!" he choked.

"Good for you!" Sunday cheerfully supported.

"Fuck." Stew growled as he lifted the child and rushed him to the men's room, leaving disgusting trails in their wake.

"Everything is under control sir; I assure you." Kylie said and frantically, "We just need to find you another child to interview."

"I'll grab Heavy Paul." Sunday said and skipped from the room.

"Perfect!" Kylie replied. She turned back to the producer and said, "You'll love this kid, sir. He's in high school, he's a star athlete and he's blue!"

"Blue?"

"Blue."

The producer thought for a moment and said, "I like it!"

He left the room and called to his star reporter, "Tabitha, we're going to use a blue kid for the interview. It will be fabulous!"

Kylie Court slumped on the edge of Molly's bed and the two girls flopped back onto the mattress and listened out into the hallway to the sounds of children playing, reporters reporting, Stew kicking the door open to the men's room and to the horrified cries of William Augustus Augustine-Chrystine from the men's room of, "Oh Jesus, No!"

CHAPTER NINETEEN

*T*he men's room held a stench that nearly knocked Sunday backwards once he opened the door. He lost his footing on reddish, chunky sludge that trailed into the door, over the garbage can, to the first sink, across the counter to the second and third sinks and finally into the last stall. The custodian gripped the wall and steadied himself.

"Sunday, is that you?" Stew called from behind the last stall's filth covered door.

"Yeah." Sunday called, "How is it?"

"What is going on over there?" Mr. Augustine-Chrystine called from within his stall.

"It's Chinatown, guys." Stew said.

Austin made a horrible noise and a series of gurgled, bubbly splashes followed. Stew stuck his head out from the stall and gasped for fresh air but found none as the dense stench filled the room.

"I'm going to have to shave his head; I don't think that we can wash the stink out." Stew cried as he took a deep swallow of air to keep from vomiting. A tiny, orange chunk fell from his sparse hair.

"You may have to shave your own head." Sunday giggled.

Stew looked at his greasy, vomitous hair in the mirror and screamed.

"And on that note," Sunday said, "You are on your own. I have to go take a shower before they film us."

"You can't leave! You have to help me!" He begged.

"Ooh, it burns," coughed Austin between retches.

"I have to," Sunday explained, "It's fucking Chinatown."

The custodian exited the restroom and skipped merrily towards the showers. On his way, he approached Kylie Court, who straightened the wrinkles in Gabriel's shirt. Maybe it was the way the light hit the glitter on the fabricated wings, maybe it was the way the make-up softened his features, maybe it was the incense but something strange suddenly struck Sunday. He stopped by the pair and knelt down next to the winged boy. The two exchanged cheerfully expressive smiles.

Sunday reached out and grabbed the child's shoulder and said, "I'm probably never going to feel this way again; so, I just wanted to tell you…that I think that you are amazing."

Gabriel hugged the custodian and whispered, "Thank you, Sunday."

"I love you, kid." Sunday replied.

Gabriel took a step back and beamed, "I love you too, sir."

Sunday looked up at Kylie and said offhandedly to the boy, "I love her too."

Kylie turned a raspberry shade and replied, "I think you need to go take that shower."

—◎—

At first, the custodian enjoyed his shower as if he were a child. He lathered a foamy beard, used the shampoo to spike up his hair and even laughed at the sight of the three bruises that formed a triangle in his chest from the Ketoret capsules. However, somewhere in the middle of his bathing, the bliss that he had experienced washed off of his body and twisted down the drainpipes below. He once again began to lament. He pouted, knowing that he would soon have to help clean the Austin mess. Once again, everything was back to normal; and every thought was tinted with something bitter or negative.

Sunday stepped out of the shower, got dressed and readied himself for his appearance on the news. Despite the return of his pessimistic mood, he was still pleased at the way that things had started to shape out. He had made Dr. Levine's day, things were going well with Kylie and he was complimented by board members. Not a bad day in the least, he thought as he brushed his teeth.

The custodian expected to see the news crews hard at work when he walked back into the main room. He expected bright lights and action all around. Instead, he saw only the children at play, per usual and the board members had retreated to the small conference room. The chords had been rolled up, the lights packed away. The news crews had left. Sunday searched for someone who could bring him up to speed. He found Kylie Court as she sat at the foot of the spiral steps, her head buried in her hands.

"Hey, what happened to the news crews?" He asked.

Kylie looked up and propped her cherubic chin in her open palms. She sniffled and despairingly said, "Shortly after you left Dr. Levine got a phone call, then told them all to get the footage that they needed and to get out… that is, after she got Channel Five's own Tabitha Townsend's autograph and tried to make a future lunch date."

The phlebotomist smiled halfway, but her disheartened feelings pulled her cheeks frownward, "She's looking for you."

Sunday shrugged and wondered what other accolades could be coming his way. Perhaps he would be getting a raise or perhaps they would next be considering another one of his theories or maybe they were finally taking his request for a skating rink seriously.

"Is it true?" Kylie asked sullenly.

Sunday was confused. "I don't know what you're talking about?"

He finally pieced together that the phone call, the news crews leaving and Kylie's current state were all tied to him. "What is it?" he asked.

Kylie did not answer him. She did not look back up at him. Instead, she said, "You should go see Dr. Levine."

Then she turned to walk away.

—◉—

*T*he Head Physician sat behind her desk, alone. Sunday entered the office as the woman framed her new autograph from Tabitha Townsend. She ran her finger over the glass and traced the two large looping T's. Sunday knocked on the open door and took another step inside.

"How did the reporting go?" Sunday asked as casually as he could.

"Kylie filled in for you. We will see how it turns out when they air it." The Dr. Levine replied and set the frame down onto her desk. She turned to face the custodian, but did not look up from the stacks upon stacks of papers.

"I meant what I said today;" She began, "Today was one of the best days that I can remember... and what you did today will more than likely save this place."

Sunday blushed and said, "It's the least I can..."

"That being said..." the woman continued. She tapped her fingers on the desk until she found the nerve to continue, "I talked to Hope."

Heavy, heavy things weighed on Sunday's chest and he found it difficult to breathe without forcing himself to inhale. He gulped and asked, "What did she say? Did she get detention? Did she take off on another road trip?"

Dr. Levine finally looked up, her eyes bloodshot red and replied, "She told me Sunday. She told me."

When he finally found his voice, Sunday asked meekly, "Where is she?"

Dr. Levine snapped angrily, "That's none of your concern!"

The Head Physician looked back to her files and calmed down a bit before she continued, "She told me at first that nothing happened, but I knew it was a lie."

Sunday might as well have turned to stone. He could not move, could not speak and was fairly sure that his heart had stopped beating.

"How could you?" She proceeded to scold, "And don't tell me she started it. She already admitted that. How *could* you?"

"I...I..." Sunday stuttered.

The Head Physician reached into a manila envelope, pulled out a notarized document and slid it across the desk. Sunday glanced over and peered at it.

"It's a restraining order, Mr. Sunday." Dr. Levine explained.

Sunday wished that he could vanish. He wished that if he closed his eyes tight enough, he would disappear. It did not happen.

She tapped at the form, "As her legal guardian, I could have you arrested. Right now, I feel like I *want* to have you arrested."

"But according to the courts she's..." Sunday tried to argue.

"Don't you dare bring age into this! God forbid I did press charges and they reopen that case as well. Jail time. Child abuse. Do you have any idea how thoughtless...?"

Once again, the Head Physician stopped to regain composure. She looked back at the new autograph and continued, "Like I said, you did save this place today. I did not forget that. I told them that you were simply harassing the girl. Stalking and what-not; it seemed the least that I could do."

Sunday was completely caught off guard by the slew of information and uttered a disheveled, "Thanks?"

"It shouldn't affect your ability to find a new job." The woman added as she looked back to her desk and began to look through the top drawer.

"New job?" Sunday asked, "What are you talking about?"

Dr. Levine pulled an object out of the desk and said, "She told me that she left this behind for you and asked me to give it to you. At first I was just going to burn it."

She placed the troll pen in the custodian's shaking hand. He looked at the happy, plastic creature and asked again, "What did you mean about a new job?"

The Head Physician looked up and softly uttered, "Sunday, you're fired."

Sunday did not know what to say. He wanted to argue, to fight for his job, but he did not know how to begin. He looked at the restraining order and his pen and nodded in defeat.

"Dr. Levine…" He whispered.

The Head Physician closed her eyes and said, "If you stay, you run the risk of putting us in far more trouble than we've ever been. Unless you want to see all the good you've done today go to waste, please, just go."

As Sunday neared the door, he realized that if Kylie Court already had this information, it was likely that the others did as well. He turned back to the woman and asked, "They are all going to hate me aren't they?"

Dr. Levine did not answer for she had already turned her chair away from him and began to sob.

—◦—

On his way to gather his belongings, Sunday noticed that some of the children and staff members in the main room had already started to look at him sideways. He hung his head and hurried his pace to the employee break room. Sunday cleaned what little he had in his locker and made his way to exit the facility for the last time.

Gabriel and Austin Olsen met him halfway across the room. Austin was out of breath and covered in a caked-on layer of his own insides. Both of the boys looked terribly concerned.

"Sunday, Sunday! I heard someone say that you were fired. What is happening?" Gabriel cried.

"It's a lie, right?" Austin pleaded, "Say it's a lie."

Sunday set down his belongings and knelt down between the children.

"I'm afraid it's true, guys." He said.

The children threw their arms around the custodian and hugged tightly as they both began to cry.

"What will we do?" Austin asked between tears.

Sunday forced a smile and said, "You're going to do what you always do. Do your best."

He made a fist and chipped it off of the chubby child's chin, "...And study your Bob Marley."

"What?" Austin asked and rubbed his puffy eyes.

"He's a musician. He says '*don't worry about a thing; cause every lil' thing is gonna be alright.*'"

The boys hugged Sunday once again and stepped back as Stew approached from the bathroom, dripping in goo. The bottoms of his pants were soaked through, as was his arm from the wrist down. Errant flecks of nastiness were scattered about his face and hair.

Sunday rose to meet his friend and tried his best to smile and teased, "You look horrible..."

Stew did not say a word and did not return the smile. He walked up to Sunday, looked him up and down and shook his head.

"I guess you heard, huh?" Sunday asked.

Once again, Stew said nothing. Instead, he answered Sunday with a slimy, cold-cocked, right hook across his temple. Sunday stumbled backwards and fell to the ground. He looked up at his best friend, mortified. From over the second floor railing, Callym Rafferty peered down and cackled. Gabriel and Austin Olsen ran off hurriedly while Stew glared at the custodian. Sunday braced himself to be kicked or something, but the beating never came. Stew closed his eyes, spit on him and marched away furiously.

Sunday picked up his belongings to the sounds of Callym's laughter. He took one last look around the main room before he made his way out. As he passed by the ball pit, the children that swam in the spheres froze and stared. He crossed the floor to the carousel and touched the poles as they circled by him while the riders of the plastic ponies flinched as they passed by.

He walked between the double, stone, spiral stairways and pushed open the front doors. It was not until he had gotten halfway to his van that he heard the front door being thrown open behind him. He turned to see Kylie Court in the entranceway. Sunday stepped back towards her.

"Sunday there are a lot of rumors. What is happening?" She asked.

"I can explain…" he began.

"They are saying you were stalking her. Harassing her. Is it true?"

Kylie noticed Sunday's red, swollen eye and looked down at all of his personal effects that he bundled in his arms and the document and troll pen clutched in one hand. It was all the evidence that the young woman needed to know that all of the allegations were true. Her temperament quickly changed and she scowled at Sunday.

"It *is* true!" She gasped, "You monster!"

Sunday pleaded, "Let me explain."

But it was to no avail. Kylie Court, red with rage and devastated, disheartened and disappointed summoned all of her anger and released them in one latex covered slap across Sunday's face and then turned back towards the door.

"Kylie! Wait! Please!" he begged.

Kylie spun around and said sternly, "Don't. Just don't. Not ever. Ever."

May 22

Diane,

I have been thinking. I should have never have taken that shower.

I keep thinking about how **happy** I felt before I took that shower.

Every thing fell apart after that shower.

I guess if I really think about it there's a lot that I probably never should have done.

Clearly, I should have handled Hope differently — the very start — Years ago. I should have never let her crush get so out of control. I just couldn't do it. It felt too good to be liked. **Fucking** egos, huh?

> Today's haiku sucks
>
> I know it's true, I'm sorry—
>
> just not in the mood.

If I could go back☺ I guess the best thing would be to go back to me when I was 12. I could tell him everything that I know. Change *everything*.

Now that I think about it, that's not a bad idea.

Excuse me for a moment, Diane,

I'm going to compose a letter to my 12 year old self

PS. Enjoy the new notebook. I must have left the old one at WonderKids when I left.

Dear Sunday at age 12,

This is future you. If you are reading this then that means that technology has made incredible advances. Way to go technology!

Listen, I know that you probably don't believe that this is really you so☺

Remember, when you were like 7 years old and every night before bed you would kiss that poster of Princess Leia? See it's really you.

It's important that you pay attention to everything on this list. It's up to you to change our future, and believe me— your future sucks right now. But you can make it right☺

- In high school you are going to end up taking Tiffany Dali out for dinner and a movie. Even though you have known her for years, I assure you; this is a date. Don't be afraid to kiss her.

- Feel free to skip the vest fad that everyone else goes for your senior year☺ it ruins your yearbook photo.

- Never stop taking your guitar lessons.

- Cars need oil changes. I cannot stress this enough.

- If you ever stumble upon a place called WonderKids, never go inside.

- If you do happen inside and should you work there, do not grow attached to anyone there.

- Stay away from a girl named Hope— together you will ruin your life.

- Stay away from a girl named Kylie— She will break your heart.

- In fact, if you end up at WonderKids longer than 6 months— as future you, I give you permission to move to Brazil and become a vagrant. Trust me, it's better than the way we feel right now.

- Never buy a van.

- Watch out for a guy named Stew's punches (they hurt)

- If you ever meet a kid named Gabriel with wings☺ run.

- Do something more with our life than sweeping floors and cleaning puke. Do something more than I did

Sincerely,

Future Sunday

May 24

Diane,

I saw Talitha Townsend's story on WonderKids on Channel 5 tonight— not bad at all.

It was strange to see everyone on the television. They started with like a helicopter shot or something above the Pavilion. Then Talitha Townsend did that thing where she summarizes the story as she walks in front of the building. They had intermittent clips of some of the kids playing around, riding the carousel, doing homework.

They showed footage of one of the younger kids getting a routine check-up and then they cut to Kylie Court. She was singing along to the player piano. Talitha Townsend was talking over her, so it was hard to tell what she was singing— but it sounded a lot like Steely Dan's Only a Fool Would Say That.

Then they had small clips of interviews that she held with Dr. Levine, Kylie, Gabriel and Heavy Paul. They even showed footage of last year's track meet.

They interviewed the Swindles and they talked about the progress with Steve (Gene).

By the end of it, I'll admit that I was crying a little.

It's true. You don't know what you have until it's gone.

Once I had a job
Pretty sure I had friends too
But that was all once.

May 30

Diane,

According to the news today, unemployment is way up.

That sucks, because I've been thinking that maybe I should try to apply myself, you know? Get a desk job or something. Something with a 401k plan.

Something respectable. I wonder: do how people get those jobs?

I'm definitely going to need a tie.

JOBS

HR coordinator (find out what this really is) - 770-771-2331

Account Executive- Contact Chris Turner - 101-121-1132

Account Recruiter- Joan Amber - 770-178-7700

Other possibilities

Coke (free soda!)

Would I make a good banker?

Flower Delivery- no one ever complains about getting flowers!

Auto repair (do you need a license or anything?)

So, I've been watching a lot of old movies.

You know, I'm starting to think that movies, TV, these stories we share☺ maybe they have caused us to set the bar way to high. Maybe we can't ever be happy because we are all looking for that romantic happy ending. And let's face it, that kind of thing doesn't really exist.

I started thinking about endings to movies like Roman Holiday and The Children's Hour. Maybe being alone isn't all that bad.

My small apartment

It has become the fortress—

Of my solitude.

It's like a cocoon

And I'm a caterpillar—

Hoping to grow wings.

June 6

Diane,

Still no job.

The news says that the job market is a mess.

At least I'm not the only one going through this.

The news also says that everything sucks.

Why do they have to make things so depressing?

I wonder what things would be like if at the end of each day we weren't reminded of all the terrible things we missed.

Or if we didn't have to worry about money?

I've been thinking about it and just about all of history's biggest conflicts were caused by money, war or media spiraling out of control and more often than not, religion is involved too. It's a shame that the same causes of our plight are the very things we count on to correct it.

Vicious circles, indeed

Diane,

I don't know why, but today has been incredibly tough. All I have wanted to do all day is to call someone to talk☺ But there's no one. I can't call Steve. I can't call Kylie. I can't call Hope. I'm starting to think that there's a very good chance that I no longer have any friends.

Maybe I will swing by the Cakery today.

It's hard to be down on yourself when sweets are involved. And I need that, because today I am down.

> There's a little blue light
>
> That stays lit in our hearts
>
> I'm not sure why it shines
>
> But it's guided me so far—

There's a little brief moment

When I'll feel your glance

Our eyes may never meet

But I will be looking right back—

> There's a little piece of starlight
>
> That got caught in your eye
>
> And while you float above me
>
> I'll be in the wings, if you want to stop by—

> There's a little bound book
>
> That tells your life's story
>
> And I'm hoping the next chapter
>
> Is named after me—

There's a little soft whisper

That speaks only two words

And I'm not sure what it's saying—

And I wonder if you heard.

> And there's still a little whisper
>
> That repeats just two words
>
> It's speaking our names together
>
> And I can't help but wonder
>
> Have you noticed?
>
> Have you heard?

Everyone's an artist when they are depressed.

June 18

Diane,

I haven't changed out of my sweat pants in days.
I'm seriously starting think that I am going stir crazy.

I have watched just about every movie I have. I can hardly watch any more TV. I can actually feel my brain turning to a soup from it all.

I'm starting to think maybe I need to take a long look in the mirror to see where I went wrong and what I need to do to get myself back on some kind of path.

Any path.

I keep trying to think about what I want to do. But I just don't know.
It's not that I ever wanted to work at WonderKids© it wasn't a childhood dream. And god knows that I wasn't always happy there. But it fit.

Hell, no one likes change.

I just don't know what I want to do.
What I am supposed to do.
I wish I had a clue.
Or maybe like a set of cliff's notes for my life.
That would be cool.

July 3

Diane,

I'm still feeling kind of bummed, so I decided to list out my happiest memories:

Christmas— age 8— remember getting a toy spaceship that I really wanted, but never thought I would get. I played with that thing everyday.

Birthday— age 10— got my first record player. Knew right away that I was destined to love music.

Christmas— age 12— I played Joseph in the church's pageant. It was my only time ever on a stage.

First Concert— Age 16— An all day show. I saw Blind Melon, Ramones, Silverchair and other acts that I can no longer remember. It was eclectic and brilliant.

First Real Kiss— Age 16— At the all day show. Mandy Buttons. She kissed me during Rock Away Beach. I'll never forget it.

May of this year— Shared a few moments and a kiss or two with Kylie Court. Momentarily thought everything was working out in my favor.

Wow, Diane!

That's a small and sad list.

I'm going to go grab a piece of cake or something.

(sigh)

Trust me, I'm not okay.

July 7

Diane,

Take me off of the unemployed list! I got a new job!

It's nothing glamorous, but it's a job. Starting next week I will be working at an auto repair shop off of Interstate 85.

I got the impression that most of the guys who work there speak Spanish, but that's okay by me. Less socializing I will have to do. Less potential for drama.

I've decided that since I am turning over a new leaf of sorts, I am going to try to stay as far away from drama as I can.

See how that works for me for a while.

I have a new job
Pay checks and health insurance
Look out, here I come!

I do keep thinking about WonderKids, though.

I keep wondering how this new job will compare to the old one.

I keep wondering how everyone is doing. It's been over a month since I spoke to any of them.

It's amazing how easy it is to avoid people who live in your community when you live in a city.

I wonder if they think of me?

August 1

Diane,

Things are going pretty smoothly. I've been at the new job a little over a month and I am learning lots.

I'm learning a bit more about cars day by day. It's greasy, lonely work— but it's an honest living and I'm sure not to fuck it up.

What's more is I am starting to learn Spanish. I am the only guy at work who doesn't speak it, and I've grown tired of having to speak in a make-shift Tarzan speak to convey my thoughts. I have made a new friend at work and he has offered to help me.

His name is Ricky and he does the oil and fluid flushes. His family is from South America and he offered to teach me some basic phrases to help me out.

Me llamo Sunday

Me encanta musica

Y pop-tarts de grape

I'm not an expert☺ but hey it's a start.

Brand new job, brand new friends, brand new languages— brand new life.

It's not the best, but it's a start. I'm actually starting to feel good again.

Diane,

I just remembered that tomorrow is Heavy Paul's big track meet.

I really would like to go and cheer him on.

I wonder if enough time has passed.

Probably not.

If I go, I guess I should keep a low profile.

I'm curious to see if Hope's prediction so long ago will come true. I can't believe it has been over 6 months. Amazing.

The minute hand ticks

And takes away more from us

Til seconds remain

Do you think that they miss me like I miss them?

Probably not, I guess?

Then again, if the Nile river can learn to change its flow,

Maybe any of us can☺ maybe it will be an opportunity for a new start.

I'll dress inconspicuously just in case.

They fired the custodian today.

Everyone was very upset.

People were crying in every corner of the hospital.

It made me laugh.

I must say though, that I will miss him.

Something about that guy that I really liked.

TV crews were also here filming stuff all day. Many of the children had a chance to say something on the cameras.

I wasn't one of those kids.

But it did get me thinking of what I would say if they asked me to be on TV.

What would I have said?

Gabriel tried to use his time to prepare everyone for the coming of the savior and the uttering of the word, but the producer squelched that pretty fast and changed the subject to his school work. All of it will end up on the editing room floor I am certain.

I would probably have had the same problem.

No one wants to be told that the only way to save them is to tear down all they have learned to care for.

No one wants to hear about the truth.

Because they are all afraid of pain.

But Pain is one of God's greatest gifts.

It reminds you that you are alive.

I take back everything I said about pain.

I have decided that Physical Therapy is the working of the devil and should only be used to torture tormented souls.

I guess that means it is only appropriate that I have to deal with it 3 times a week.

An hour long session in which my mangled leg is twisted, pulled and stretched its limit- all in the name of recovery.

An hour long session in which my body burned and my muscles ached.

Even the metal sleeve in my leg aches.

She pulled the leg to extend the muscles, and I swear that I could hear fibers tearing. She made me lift weights with it and would not let me stop, even after the limb quivered from the agony. Then she tried to make me support my own weight on it. I could hardly bring myself to stand before I was screaming.

The therapist said that if I don't work out the leg in this excruciating manner, I may never walk again.

I wanted to watch her die.

I wanted her to share my pain.

She says it's all about steps. Baby steps to your goal, she said.

Why have all my steps been painful?

When do I get to reach the top?

If I have to feel this way, everyone should.

IF you had to choose between having Jesus love you and everyone else hate you

Or Everyone love you and Jesus hate you

Which would you choose?

I dreamed last night that it was the 1800s again.

I dreamed that I was afloat on a few boards lashed together with fraying rope.

My family had died due to the rotten potatoes that plagued all of Ireland.

I remembered the stiff blue faces of my cousins.

Frail thin frames

I too was malnourished. Sun-scorched

I remembered burying my family on the now barren and useless plot of land.

I dreamed I sailed away from all that I knew for a small chance to escape the death that blanketed our valley.

The first few weeks aboard my tiny sailboat, things were good. I had enough rations. Every morning I would wake and eat my fill of beans. In the afternoon I would fish and each evening would enjoy what I had caught.

It was a lovely cycle.

I dreamt that on the third week I encountered a storm. A terrible storm that soaked through and ruined more than half of my rations. I battled through the weather, but sacrificed my sail.

From that moment on, I was a slave to the tides.

I would spend days at a time, barely moving. I tried to row, but the vessel was far too large for one man to navigate.

At week six I ran out of food completely. I relied only on what I could catch each day.

At Week ten a second storm came. Heavy waves tossed me around. Numerous times I thought that I would die. I lashed myself to the stern and waited it out.

When the rain finally stopped and the waves calmed, I saw that my ship had been heavily damaged. It would not last another week.

I got to work constructing a raft out of what ever materials I could pull free from the boat and began stockpiling cooked fish.

At week twelve I set adrift on the raft, leaving the boat to finish its slow but destined descent into the sea.

I dreamed I died on that raft. I dreamed that I ceased to exist in this world except as a meaty shell.

I did not wake up. My soul did not ascend and the dream did not continue in a fanciful setting.

For the remainder of my slumber, I dreamed that I was a hollow corpse afloat on the Atlantic Ocean.

At week nineteen, I dreamed of the sea birds that pecked and ate at my flesh.

I dreamed that the sun bleached my skin a leathery white.

By week twenty two I had rotted away on that raft. Yet I experienced every moment that occurred to my corpse until the eaten, mangled remains finally slipped off of the raft and into the sea at week thirty-six.

I wonder what that means?

I'll be back!

Ker-POw

The fat boy smuggled in a copy of **THE TERMINATOR** last night.

What an **AMAZING** movie!

The world ends, people die, cars explode, buildings explode... **everything** explodes.

It was the greatest thing I have ever seen. **Ever**.

I watched again this morning.

I want to see something explode. How cool would that be?

I could tape it and watch it over and over and over on the fat boy's VCR.

After I watched the movie again, **Brother Linus** called and asked if I wanted to stop by again to discuss my feelings, religion what-have-you.

I think he thinks that he is saving me.

That or he has the 'blues'... nothing my needle can't fix.

We talked about Job and how everything was taken from him. I felt a great deal of satisfaction with that story. Its not often that God makes himself out to be the bad guy. The ending sucked though.

At least at the end of **the terminator** you know that the world is still going to end.

Hasta La Vista, Baby.

The **unclean spirit** returns and brings with it 7 other spirits more **evil** than itself

And the last condition of that person is worse than the first

Thus it will be with this **evil generation**

262

Had to go to the **physical terrorist** today.

The good news is that I AM ON **CRUTCHES**!

The **terrorist** says that I will never be able to have the metal guards removed, but since all my clothes are made to fit the rods that hold them in place, its okay by me.

Ive decided it's creepy enough to be cool.

They also said that after the crutches I can move onto a cane. They say I will probably always walk with a cane. Classy!

As soon as I am on a cane I am going to walk into the terrorist's office and im going to **impale** her with the tip of my cane.

The bad news is that she worked me so hard I bled out around the metal rods and now I am stuck in bed for the rest of the day.

I gave myself a shot of my emergency **syringe** just to pass the time.

As soon as I can figure out a way to **destroy** something from this bed, I am going to do it just so they will give me another dose.

Bored, bored, bored, bored, bored, board, bored, bored, **bored**.

Idle hands are what?

The scribes said we want to see a sign

He said only an evil generation needs a sign save that of Jonahs

How cool would it be to be an **EVIL** genius?

(I think I would be good at it)

Ive been doing some thinking and I think that I have found the perfect way to help myself

And the best part is all I have to do is be me

If all goes well then I will have **saved** a soul (and returned the fear of God in the hearts of hundred others). If that doesnt put me back in his **graces**
I dont know what will

One of the 3rd graders found the custodian's old notebook
We've been taking turns reading it
A lot of sad ramblings
And an odd affection for toaster pastries
Im going to need to do a bit more research and the whole thing is going to rest on the actions of **the custodian**. But I think if I can find the perfect distraction then this plan is **foolproof**.

At least I hope it is. I'm surrounded by **fools**

And I saw as it were a sea of glass mingled with fire
Behold! I come as a thief
And he gathered them together into a place called
Armageddon

She settles into slumber
A short lived hibernation
REM soon sets in
Suddenly she is sitting
Dressed for the occasion
Sullen white sundress
Torn tattered tennis shoes
She is not yet a woman

Wearing makeshift war paint
Lipstick and MAGIC markers
At the front of the building
Which will soon resemble
Ancient tribal burial ground
She laces up her shoes
And enters the structures mouth

She only inhales after
Safely passing each doorway
She pauses as she reaches
A Parthenon of fear
Bells sound and she saunters inside

Nineteen wide eyes stare

Mouths agape snickering

She walks to the table

Next to the black board it reads:

YOU ARE HERE TO LEARN. BEHAVE

How could she be Have?

She had never met him before

It was time to begin her play

Standing on chairs

Shouting in tribal tongues

She opens her light pink

HELLO KITTY lunch box

It holds no peanut butter

It holds no thermos of milk

She raises her father's

Gleaming

Screaming

Handgun

Was that a Dream?

Maerd a taht saw

Nugdnah gnimaercs gnimaelg

Tomorrows the day!

We are taking a field trip to go see Heavy Paul compete

It's the perfect time to

Do something amazing!

Hasta La Vista

Baby

Things I need

GASOLINE

Ammonia

Mothballs

Alcohol

Metal piping

Something for fuses

So I say to **hell** with this

If Gods not going to show these people the way

I will **SCARE** it into him

If it does not get me in his graces at least i had some fun

Ive got a bus schedule and I know exactly where I need to go to get all my supplies

The only thing that could stop me is a soldier from the future

Im more unstoppable than **the terminator**

Im the most unstoppable force ever

I wasn't sent from the future to ensure the apocalypse

I was sent from hell to ensure it

I am **Callym Rafferty**

Behold! I stand at the door

And I knock

Part Three

Shakin' the Blues

Heavy Paul focused on the dirt path ahead of him. He tuned out the hoorahs that rang in his ears from the spectators that filled the stands and tried not to think about the pressure that mounted on his shoulders to win this final medal which would assure Our Lady of the Holy Spirit High School's victory. A thin bead of sweat trickled down his tinted skin; he closed his eyes, controlled his breathing and tightly gripped the long pole that he held tightly in his left hand.

The WonderKids' news story that Tabitha Townsend aired had suddenly made Paul a local phenomenon and word had soon reached many of the nation's top colleges. This resulted in a surge of ticket sales for the National Track and Field Championship and a record-setting number of college scouts attending the event. Amid the crowd, hundreds of Heavy Paul supporters donned blue t-shirts and hats, as well as face and body paint. Heavy Paul tried to push all of this from his mind as he quietly recited a prayer.

BANG!

The official's starting gun fired into the air and mechanically, the teenager raced to the end of track. He pumped his legs as hard as he could; his feet left divots in the dirt behind him as the weight supported by his running shoes slammed into the ground with each step. Heavy Paul leveled the long pole as if it were a medieval jousting staff and leaned his body forward as he gained speed. He neared the end of the track, lowered the long staff to the ground, its tip trenched a straight line through the earth until it reached the hard block that rested at the end. The pole arched in a large misshapen semi-circle and somewhere in the wood Heavy Paul heard the splintering sounds of wood cracking.

"It's over." The teen thought as he anticipated the staff's inevitable snapping, "I knew I was too heavy to do this."

To his dismay, his feet lifted from the ground and the pole began to pull itself back into shape. Paul sailed through the air and approached the horizontal bar that had been set to 6.02 meters- a height that had yet to be cleared. He twisted his blue body around, arched his back and threw his head towards the ground. As he descended to the mat below him, his feet barely cross the beam, the space between them no more than the width of a penny. With a harsh *TWACK*, Heavy Paul crashed onto the mat and landed on his back. He looked up to see that the bar was still in place. He had cleared it!

The stadium erupted in commotion and the OLHSHS Track Team joined their star player as he rolled awkwardly off of the mat. It took almost the whole team to lift the teen onto their shoulders to carry around the field. Heavy Paul held his arms up in victory as he passed by overjoyed classmates, clapping teachers, cheering parents and one proud, former custodian who sat in the back of the bleachers and tried his hardest not to be seen.

Sunday pulled the hood to his sweatshirt over his head, lowered his ball cap so as not to be noticed and stood up to applaud the young champion as he was carried by. While he stood, Sunday searched the bleachers for familiar faces. A handful of sections to his left, he spotted a large group of Wonder Kids towards the front of the stands. Among them was Austin Olsen, who sported a blue sweater and a new crew cut and azure-winged and jubilant Gabriel. They jumped up and down with glee, clutched each other and waved around flags that touted the high school's insignia. He noted little Molly Rollins and Peter Tertiary, as well as Callym Rafferty; but as he searched the joyous faces, he did not see Hope in attendance. Sunday watched from afar as Kylie Court laughingly passed out high-fives to the ecstatic children and he wished that he could be in the middle of their celebration.

Sunday wanted nothing more than to go to the group, to have them hug him, tell him that they missed him, that they needed him. He wanted to, but he knew that he could not. He looked down at his watch, yelled, "Way to go, Paulie!" one last time and snuck down from the bleachers while he knew that he was unlikely to be noticed.

— ◉ —

*O*ver the months, Kylie had grown into her role as the children's main mentor and had proven to be responsible, fun and well respected by the children and staff alike. She had put her own unique twists on Sunday's games and songs and made them far more safe and organized. The phlebotomist had reaped the recognition for curing the Swindles' grandchild in the custodian's absence; which ascended her higher and higher in not only the Head Physician's favor, but the Board of Director's as well. She performed a quick head count of the children while they gathered around Heavy Paul to congratulate their sweaty, blue victor.

"Callym, I don't want you straying too far away." Kylie Court called to the boy who mingled alone by the hotdog stand.

"I'm just hanging out by the hotdog cart." Callym Rafferty replied coarsely. He leaned upon his simple, black, maple wood cane and tapped rounded silver tip with his gloved fingers. Since he had received the swanky accessory, the strange, pale boy had acquired a penchant for wearing full suits, ties and gloves; the latter of which also prevented him from constantly biting around his fingertips. He was clad in a black coat with tails, a white collared shirt with a red tie and black pin-striped slacks that had metal rivets fashioned to them for the rods that entered his leg. He continued his conversation with the vendor and ignored Ms. Court as she announced her instructions.

"Okay, kiddos." Kylie called out, "We are going to give Paul time to talk to some of the college recruiters and the reporters and then we are off to get pizza. Everyone find a buddy and make sure that you are back here in twenty minutes."

The children paired up and began to head towards the various stands and back to the field to play on the track, now that it had been cleared of actual athletes. With a snap of his wrist, Callym's cane blocked the skipping duo of Austin Olsen and Gabriel. The boys stopped and happily looked to the overly dressed teenager.

"We're going to get some Heavy Paul t-shirts; you wanna come along, Callym?" Gabriel asked.

"No, children; I do not." Callym shook his head as if it were the last thing that he wanted to do, "But I do have an offer for you. How would you like to make twenty-five dollars, Lunch-Box?"

The children's eyes twinkled at the thought about all the goodies that twenty-five dollars would bring them.

"What do we have to do?" Gabriel asked.

Callym Rafferty tapped his cane twice to the ground, grimaced and explained, "Well, in this hotdog cart is at least... I dunno, what would you say, brother? Thirty-five hotdogs?"

The hotdog vendor replied, "Fifty."

"Fifty hotdogs;" the teen corrected himself and continued, "That have to be thrown away because they are at least an hour past their expiration. That's a whole hour just stewing in their juices."

The hotdog vendor slid open the metal door and a hot waft of wet and old processed pork assaulted the boy's nostrils.

"Okay, it's kinda gross. What's your point?" Austin asked.

"I bet this guy one-hundred dollars that *you* could eat all of them in less than fifteen minutes." Callym said, "Do it, and I'll give you a cut."

Austin Olsen thought about it and looked down into the pink-tinted frank water. It did not smell appetizing, but Austin was hungry, and Austin had eaten much worse.

"Are they at least hot?" he asked.

"Not in the slightest."

"Anything to drink?"

"There's hotdog water."

"I want thirty dollars." The chubby child negotiated.

Callym reached out his gloved hand, shook Austin's and said, "Deal."

The vendor laughed, started to slide the lukewarm wieners into stale buns and noted, "No one can eat fifty hotdogs."

"You're about to eat those words." Austin said surely and added cockily, "Go ahead and grab me a glass of that water too."

The child stretched out a bit, leaned to the left and then to the right and finally as forward as his round body would allow. As he jogged in place he said confidently to the vendor, "You just say when."

The vendor checked his watch and shouted, "Go!"

Austin quickly began to shove the hot dogs down his mouth in rapid succession. One after another, he hardly stopped to chew and only paused to take brief gulps out of the glass of colored liquid. While the vendor watched in amazement at the child's feat, Callym Rafferty pulled Gabriel aside.

"I need your help Gabriel." The teen began, "And please remember that I am asking."

"What is it?" the winged boy asked.

"I have a plan to help someone very special, but I need your assistance and we are going to have to sneak out of here."

Gabriel reluctantly said, "I don't know, Callym. I don't want to get in trouble."

"Isn't it worth it, though, if it's going to help save someone's soul?"

"Fifteen, sixteen, seventeen!" the vendor cried in astonishment.

Gabriel contemplated and asked, "What will we have to do?"

Callym leaned upon his cane and replied, "All you have to do is help me trail them for a minute and then we have to do a bit of shopping. I can handle the rest."

It sounded simple enough to Gabriel, but he was still hesitant, "Can't we just ask Ms. Kylie if she'll stop at the store on the way back home? I'm sure she would."

"It's gotta be this way, Gabriel." Callym replied and began to tap on the tip of the emergency syringe in his coat pocket.

"Twenty-five!"

The ghoulish teen could see that he was going to have to work a bit harder to get Gabriel to assist him. He perused the crowded area and said, "Would it help if you knew who we were helping?"

"I guess." Gabriel responded, still uneasy.

He extended his black cane across the crowd and said, "There."

"Thirty!"

Gabriel followed the path of the cane and saw Sunday as he snuck across the concession area towards the parking lot. He had his hood pulled over a ball cap and walked quickly with his head hung low. Gabriel gasped with glee and started to run towards the former custodian, only to be blocked by Callym's wooden extension.

"Forty-five!"

"No, no." He said, "He can't know we are following him."

The winged child did not understand why he should not say hello to Sunday. He did not understand why it was necessary to follow him or how any of it was going to help save him; but he did know that the former custodian needed to be rescued from his mundane and pessimistic lifestyle.

"Okay, I'm in." Gabriel agreed, "What do we do?"

"We wait for the distraction, and then we sneak away in the commotion." Callym replied.

"Holy shit! Fifty!" The hotdog vendor announced in shock.

"What are we going to use as a distraction?" Gabriel asked inquisitively.

"Leave that to me." Callym Rafferty smirked as he graciously accepted the baffled vendor's money.

—◉—

"*Un* momento, amigo." Ricardo Nunez said as he removed the filter and a steady stream of blackened oil poured from under the Honda Civic that rested above him and splashed into the funnel. Ricardo was in his mid-thirties and a rugged-looking, Latino lothario. Nightly, his three piece punk-core band, *Eczema Overdrive*, would play in whatever dive bar would have them and he would leave each night with whatever woman he chose. By day, he was the shift-manager for Esteban's Automotive.

"Lo sentos." Sunday replied.

"Lo siento." The mechanic corrected.

"Lo siento." Sunday attempted again, "Thanks, Ricky."

"De nada." Ricky replied and leaned back, "So, we're going to wait until this drains and then we pour clean oil in it, just to flush the rest of the gunk out. Then we put a new filter on and fill it up."

"Easy enough." Sunday said."

"Muy facil." Ricky replied.

The mechanic wiped his hands off on a dirty rag from his back pocket and asked, "So, where were you today, again?"

"One of the kids from that hospital I worked at competed in the Nationals for Track and Field." Sunday explained as he inspected the flow of the oil.

"Ah, los ninos extranos, eh?" The mechanic replied, "Did I ever tell you about that girl that I knew back in Rio de Janeiro?"

"Si." Sunday said as he screwed the new filter into place.

"I swear to you, man; that girl could fly."

"That's what you've said." Sunday laughed.

"So, did the kid win?" Ricardo asked as he began to fill the Civic with new oil.

Sunday grabbed the edges of his hoodie, like a proud father and boasted, "First place."

The mechanic nodded in approval and completed the car's maintenance.

"You still want to fix that window in that piece of shit you are driving today?" He asked.

"Definitely." Sunday replied.

Just then, Esteban Ortez came into the garage from his office. Esteban Ortez was the owner of Esteban's Automotive and was a large and temperamental man who only spoke in loud, angry Spanish insults.

"Salte de abajo del pince' carro y barre el piso, Blanco!" The hefty, sweaty man screamed and then retreated to the office with a furious slam of the door.

Sunday stared blankly at the door and asked curiously, "What did he say about the white boy?"

Ricky laughed and said, "He wants you to get back to work, bro."

"Fine." Sunday sighed and slid out from under the vehicle. He wiped his hands off on the handkerchief that he now kept in his back pocket at all times and grabbed the broom and dustpan that were propped against the wall next to large stacks of tires.

"I feel for you." Ricky chucked, sympathetically; he crawled out from underneath the car, began to work inside the hood and added, "What was it that you did at the hospital before you got here? Doctor? You were a Neurosurgeon, right?"

Sunday smirked and raised his middle finger, "You're not funny."

"Once a janitor, bro..." The mechanic laughed and slammed down the hood.

The well-dressed teen and the winged boy did not have to wait long for the rancid hotdogs to reach Austin Olsen's stomach. Within minutes of receiving his earnings, the round child turned three shades of green and began to clutch his cringing belly. He stumbled over to Kylie Court who was in the middle of mentally checking-off the children who had already returned to the checkpoint.

With a weary, "I don't feel so good." Austin Olsen began to expel the fifty expired hotdogs, fifty stale buns and a few glasses of pork water.

Large and small putrid, pink chunks splattered to the concrete with a sickening, wet splash. The child fell to his hands and knees while more and more vile liquid spewed from his mouth. A number of spectators with weaker stomachs began to feel flush and nauseous. A couple of people made dashes to nearby garbage bins, where they too vomited.

Kylie Court, as well as the rest of the children and just about everyone in the vicinity of the ever widening pool of wretch was more concerned with the disgusting on-goings than the status of the children's attendance. Instantly, the boys were free to escape to the parking lot. At Callym Rafferty's signal they slipped around the corner and out of sight of their chaperone.

The boys trailed Sunday all the way to Esteban's Automotive and staked out at a dilapidated Laundromat across the street. Gabriel watched out the window intently as Sunday walked into work. The young boy giddily turned to his companion who reviewed hand-scribbled notes that he had retrieved from his breast pocket.

"What's the plan? What are we doing?" Gabriel inquired.

Callym looked up from his sheet, stared across at the automotive shop and said, "Ultimately, we are going to teach Mr. Sunday that it's time for him to start his life. If we are lucky, he will find a little faith as well. We are going to show him that there is more to life than just getting by, that there is more to life than just living."

Gabriel clapped his hands together and exclaimed, "I like the sound of that!"

"I thought you would." The pale teen responded.

"How are we going to do it?" Gabriel pried.

"Leave that to me." Callym coolly replied.

"What do we do next?" Gabriel asked.

Callym folded the paper and placed it back inside his coat and replied, "Next we go shopping."

— ◉ —

Arms loaded with grocery and hardware store bags, Gabriel stood on the side of the sleazy, off-ramp motel and confusedly watched Callym Rafferty fumble in his pockets for the remaining winnings from the hotdog bet. Once he retrieved the crumpled wad of bills, the well-dressed teen handed the money to the homeless man that he had recruited to assist them in checking into a room.

"It has to have a kitchen." Callym instructed to the shabby, unshaved man as he released the cash.

While the homeless man walked around the corner and into the lobby, Gabriel took the opportunity to inquire further about Callym's plan.

"What are we doing here?" he asked.

Callym rummaged through the bags that Gabriel held and said mysteriously, "Shh."

A few moments later, the homeless man returned with a key attached to a red, plastic diamond and a couple of bills worth of change. Callym took the key and insisted that the man keep the remaining cash for booze or what-not and instructed Gabriel to follow him as he hobbled around the building and into their room.

Room 66 was one of the select rooms that the motel rented at hourly rates. The small space consisted of a bed that was well past its prime and covered in stained, floral sheets, a tiny dining table that barely had room on it for anything more than two plates and a bar-style counter that separated the sink and the out-of-date stove that made up the kitchen. The room was decorated in a yellow, brown and orange motif with matching carpet that only would have been fashionable in the seventies.

Callym walked past the bed and to Gabriel's surprise did not even suggest that they jump on it. He led the winged boy purposefully into the kitchen and they unloaded the contents of the bags onto the kitchen table. From the hardware store bags, they set out three metal pipes, six metal caps for the pipes, a roll of thin twine and a hacksaw. They set a canister of gasoline on the table and from the grocery bags they set out mothballs, rubbing alcohol and a large jug of ammonia.

Callym immediately went to work screwing the caps onto the end of each pipe and shoved mothballs down inside. Gabriel looked on perplexed while the teen began to boil a combination of ammonia and alcohol. He dropped a couple of mothballs into the mixture for safe measure.

"Why does this set up look familiar?" Gabriel asked.

"It's from *The Terminator.*" Callym replied and began to pour gasoline haphazardly into the ends of the tubes, which splashed the liquid across the bubbled laminated countertops.

Gabriel recalled the scene from the movie in which the protagonist began to mix the ingredients into pipe bombs that would later be used against the killer robot. It occurred to him that whatever it was that he had gotten involved in was more dangerous and sinister than he had been led to believe. He watched his companion toil over the tubes as he packed more and more flammables into the metal cylinders.

"What are we doing, Callym?" He panicked.

Callym propped up the piping on the counter and began to stir the boiling concoction. He pulled his shirt and tie over his nose to avoid some of the fumes as he explained nonchalantly, "If I am doing this right, I am making explosives. If I'm wrong then they will be very elaborate Molotov cocktails."

Gabriel gasped, "Why are you doing that?"

Callym turned the down the burner on the stove, removed the pot from the heat and went back to stuffing mothballs into the tubes. He fought the urge to test the substance by lighting a match and moved out of the kitchen and over to the bed, where he began to cut lengths of twine.

"We are making explosives so that we can blow up that terrible place that Sunday is working in, so that he will be forced to come back." He explained.

"That won't bring him back and that won't save him!" Gabriel objected, "It will only cause hurt!"

"Trust me;" Callym debated as he measured another piece of thin rope, "Even if doesn't bring him back… *which it will*, he will still be forced to find the path that's been set for him."

"You're crazy! You're going to kill yourself!"

"You and I both know that's the one thing that I can't do." Callym said cryptically.

"And what if he's inside when you do this?" Gabriel asked.

Callym grinned, "That's where the saving comes in."

"This is madness. You can't do this!" Gabriel said as he watched in horror while the teenager limped into the kitchen and began to pour the contents of the pot into the tubes.

"I *am* doing this." Callym replied, "*We* are doing this."

Gabriel knew that he had to do something to prevent the teen from completing his plan. He had to warn Sunday. He stepped towards the door and said, "I'm going to stop you. I'm going to tell him what you are doing. It won't work."

Callym laughed and without looking up from his work replied, "Go ahead."

He reached in his pocket, pulled out his hand scribbled notes and tore off a section of it which he offered to the winged child.

"Here, take this." he said, "It's his address."

— ◉ —

The cardboard window had been retired from the van and a brand new piece of glass filled its space. Sunday repeatedly checked his blind spot though the translucent pane; pleased that his vehicle was no longer pieced together with old boxes and duct tape. With no whistle of the wind outside to drown out the sound, he cranked the volume to the radio and relished the clean, crisp music for the first time in almost a year.

As he sang along, Sunday pondered what the WonderKids were doing to celebrate Heavy Paul's achievement. If he were still employed by the facility, he would have orchestrated something extravagant, he was sure. Perhaps he would have hired a rock band and constructed skateboarding ramps in the parking lot or taken the children to someplace entertaining like those restaurants where everyone dresses like knights. The thoughts of the children began to depress him so that his cheery singing trailed off into a sullen silence.

He spent the remainder of his night lounging on his sofa, lamenting in his notebook and watching classic films on television. The feelings of loss and remorse that he had spent months upon months ridding his heart of came flooding back to him as he thought about the cost of his past mistakes. He reminisced over fond memories of his time at WonderKids- the children's faces when they were happy, the way that they looked up to him, his friends. It was more than the former custodian could bear. He helped himself to half a bottle of red wine, without bothering with a glass and somewhere in the middle of *Love in the Afternoon*, his head became fogged and his eyes began to droop.

He tipsily hummed the movie's theme, "*Fascination*" and collapsed into a laying position. He sighed and thought about how little he had. A crappy apartment, a job as a janitor at a crappy automotive shop, maybe one friend- and he couldn't understand half of what he said. His hum broke into a series of sniffles as he attempted to stifle his desire to cry. He had lost so much and gained so little. While he beat the cushion with his fist, he thought to himself;

Why can't I just stay happy?

What am I doing wrong?

What seemed like mere moments later; he was disturbingly woken by a frantic knock on his door. Sunday sluggishly tossed his legs off of the sofa and onto the floor and lagged to his front door. The knocking started once again, harder and faster this time.

"I'm coming, I'm coming." Sunday somberly shouted.

He undid the chain latch, flipped the dead bolt lock and opened the door. Gabriel stood in the doorway; fear painted across his expression. Sunday looked down at the child and for a moment was torn between wanting to hug the boy and closing the door on his face.

"What are you doing here?" Sunday yawned.

The winged child forced his way inside and cried, "You have to help me. Callym and I snuck off and I think that he is about to do something very, very bad!"

Sunday wanted to tell the boy that it was no longer his problem; that he should call Kylie or Dr. Levine to help him; but the tears that pooled in the child's eyes told him that the situation was serious and Gabriel truly did need his assistance.

"Okay." He sighed as he opened the door to let the child wait inside as he grabbed his coat and made a quick cup of sobering coffee.

CHAPTER TWENTY-ONE

*T*he van raced down the wet highway and cast waves of street-water upon the sidewalk. Light, sprinkles of precipitation illuminated in the headlights and beaded upon the windshield. The engine backfired, the vehicle jostled and a black plume rose from the tailpipe. Sunday fought the wheel to keep the van on course while Gabriel sat next to him with his eyes closed and prayed that all would be okay.

"I don't understand what in hell you were thinking." Sunday declared as he flipped on the windshield wipers. His head pounded from the alcohol, which he had begun to regret drinking.

Gabriel kept his hands folded and his eyes closed as he answered, "I was trying to save you."

"From what?" Sunday demanded.

"From yourself." The child replied, "Callym said he had a plan to help you find your path. Your faith. I didn't know what he was planning!"

Sunday took his eyes off the road and leered at the boy. Furiously, he hit the steering wheel and shouted, "See? This is what I was talking about. I told both of you to let the other-worldly stuff go because it would only lead to trouble…and here we are!"

He punched the wheel again yelled, "God damn it, Gabriel!"

The child gulped but did not say a word. He only looked disappointingly at the man and shook his head. As Sunday maneuvered the van off of the interstate ramp, he saw the black pillar of smoke which billowed from Esteban's Automotive. The stench of burning rubber hung in the air; flames climbed out of the doorways and the windows and engulfed the building. Sunday pulled the van to a stop in front of the shop and stared in awe at the destruction.

"You don't think anyone is inside, do you?" Gabriel worried aloud and began to cry.

"Fuck! Ricky." Sunday muttered to himself and climbed from the van. He knew that on occasion the mechanic would stay late so that he did not have to go home before his band's gigs. Sunday watched as the blaze brought down an interior beam from within the building.

Maybe he's not in there.

The flames reached one of the oil barrels and intensified the fire. Sunday could feel the heat from the asphalt where he stood as the white hot intensity of the blaze lit the darkness around him.

He's probably not in there.

Gabriel sobbed from within the van and prayed as hard as he could, "Please don't let anyone be in there. Please don't let anyone be in there."

Please God, don't let any one be in there.

From underneath the sounds of popping and scorching wood, the crackle of sheetrock as it burned and crumbled came the pleading screams from within the building, "Ayúdame!"

Fuck! Someone is in there.

Sunday turned to the praying child and said, "Wait here."

He sighed and looked to the heavens in hopes that somehow, some heavenly body would help him. He received no such assistance and reluctantly ran into the flame enveloped doorway. No corner of the garage was safe from the fire; it surrounded Sunday and a hellish heat sucked the air from all around him. He searched the room for signs of life and shouted, "Hello?"

The thick smoke stung at his eyes and clogged his lungs. He held his handkerchief to his mouth and continued to look around the room. The Civic that he had been working on was on fire, the seats and dashboard just melted masses and the paint had begun to bubble. Sunday saw the fire extinguisher on the wall and thought about attempting to battle the blaze. A burning piece of the ceiling fell to the ground and knocked over a barrel of oil. Sunday decided that it was not wise to stay in the room longer than he had to and left the extinguisher alone.

He heard the cries again and followed them into the manager's office. Esteban Ortez lay on the floor, barely mobile. His face was covered in soot and were it not for his weak coughing, Sunday may have suspected him dead. He tied the handkerchief over his nose, grabbed the large man by the wrists and began to slowly drag him from the office.

"You have to help me, sir." He said while he struggled to pull the man through the flaming garage.

More pieces of the ceiling dropped around them and another support beam collapsed. It fell on top of the Civic and sent it falling off the lifts with a twisted, metallic crash. Shelves toppled over and spilled their contents onto the fiery, oil covered floor. The black, burning pool lurched towards Sunday and blocked the path that he had used to enter the building.

His body was covered in sweat and his eyes stung to the where he could hardly see. He looked around the room for a new path to take, but he saw none. Behind him, what was left of the ceiling had caught on fire. Sunday had run out of willpower. He found it hard to think clearly and even harder to breathe. It felt as if the smoke had clenched his lungs and he began to cough uncontrollably. His bones seemed to have softened into a quivering, rubbery substance and he released the large man's arms and collapsed to the floor.

This is it.

This is how where I die.

Please, please; don't let me die.

A large hose snapped and began to spray flammable fluids about the garage. Soon the fire caught up to the stream, causing long flames to spout from the whipping hose; setting fire to the walls, the inventory and everything else in its path. Sunday watched as everything around him charred. Mr. Ortez was no longer moving, no longer coughing and the puddle of oil crept closer to them. Sunday eyes grew heavy and his body longed to rest. He curled into a fetal position and closed his eyes.

No!

Something within him willed Sunday to open his eyes. He forced himself to his feet, grabbed the large man's wrists and once again inched his way towards the door. Slowly dragging Mr. Ortez, he exited the building shortly before the volatile canisters caught fire and finally exploded in a bright, hot blaze.

Sunday sunk to the ground beside Mr. Ortez's large mass. He took in a deep lung-full of the cool and moist night air. Exhausted, he threw his arm atop the man to check to see if he was still alive. Not only did the man have a pulse, but Sunday could feel that he was breathing.

"Mr. Ortez, was Ricky in there?" Sunday asked.

The fat man slightly shook his head no.

"Are you sure you were the only one in there?"

The fat man slightly nodded yes. From inside the van the winged child raised his palms to the sky and exclaimed, "Thank you, Jesus."

Off in the distance the sirens of fire engines roared. Sunday looked over his employer and whispered, "You're gonna be okay, sir. Help is coming."

He turned back to Gabriel and shouted, "What the fuck were you two thinking? Where is he, Gabriel?"

Gabriel shrugged and once again felt as though he may cry. However, his tears were halted when a terrible thought occurred to him.

"Sunday," he gasped, "He knows where you live."

— ◎ —

Esteban Ortez had been left on the sidewalk for the trained professionals to tend to and Sunday and Gabriel sped off in the van back the way they came in hopes of stopping Callym Rafferty's diabolical scheme. They flew past the fire trucks and ambulances that raced their way to the fire.

"Should we call the cops?" Gabriel asked.

Sunday pushed the accelerator as far down as he could and refused to take his focus from the saturated road. Without breaking his gaze, he replied, "We're trying to get to him before we'd need to do that."

The man then mumbled incoherently under his breath. The only thing that Gabriel understood was, "...all because he thinks he's an angel."

Gabriel had been so preoccupied with his concern for the innocent people that could be hurt from Callym's actions that upon hearing the custodian's jab, his emotions finally reached a tipping point.

"You know what, Mr. Sunday?" He shouted, "I have had enough!"

Taken by surprise, Sunday briefly and blankly stared over at the boy, who had begun to huff with anger.

"You want proof?" The boy asked, "You never knew your father, he moved to Arizona when you were only a few months old. But *you* didn't know that. I do."

Sunday eyed the child, suspiciously. Gabriel grew red in the face and continued, "When you were young you wanted to be a pilot when you grew up; or a priest because they only work on the weekends, as you cleverly noted to the sisters who taught you in elementary school."

Sunday listened, astonished at all the intimacies that the child seemed to know about him. Gabriel sniffled, wiped his nose upon his coat sleeve and continued.

"You have a scar on your forehead from when you fell off a porch at a birthday party when you were seven. You don't like the idea of airplanes, but you love the idea of traveling. You keep a notebook, just like all of us do; but you name yours Diane. You tell yourself it's because you don't take the daily writing seriously, but really it's because you don't have any one you have ever been able to open up with because you close yourself off and you are scared!"

A part of Sunday suddenly wanted to believe that the child was indeed divine. It was the only way that he could rationalize all the knowledge that the child had on him; but still the bulk of what he believed was that this simply could not be possible. He accelerated at speeds unsafe for the waterlogged streets as the van neared his apartment and asked, "How do you know all of this?"

Gabriel's crying had stopped. He sat upright and clung tightly to the handle mounted in the door; his body slid to and fro in his seat as the van weaved between the other cars on the highway that moved at much safer speeds. Without taking his eyes from the windshield, the boy answered, "You don't want to hear it."

"Tell me."

The van turned off of the highway and Sunday slowed to more temperate speed. Gabriel relaxed his grip on the handle and explained, "I'll start from the beginning, but only if you promise not to interrupt."

Sunday ran a red light at a four-way intersection and reluctantly agreed. The young child adjusted his posture in his seat and began, "Everyone who believes a higher power believes in the same entity. Call it God, Yahweh, Allah, Vishnu- it's all the same."

Sunday turned the van sharply to the left and said, "I think most people know that."

"They know it, but they forget." Gabriel continued, "See, that higher power just wants you to believe in it and to be happy. It doesn't care what you believe it is, or how you believe it operates; just believe and do everything you can to find what makes you happy."

The van approached another intersection as the light changed from yellow to red. The young boy braced himself for Sunday to send the vehicle through the light. Sunday, however saw this and hesitantly brought the vehicle to a stop. Gabriel took a sigh of relief and continued;

"See, in their heart of hearts, there are a ton of things that people *know*. But they pile on so many other things until they just forget. Like you. You strayed so far away from everything that you know in your heart of hearts to the point where nothing can ever go right for you."

The words struck Sunday like shotgun shells. He wondered if it could have been possible that he had spawned his own vortex of despair from his own pessimism. He wondered if it could have been possible that he didn't simply 'grow-out' of his belief in a higher power like he did the Tooth Fairy or Santa Clause but instead just drowned himself in all the wrong things.

What do I believe?

Anything at all?

"You aren't the first person that this had happened to;" Gabriel explained, "People are funny, fickle creatures and sometimes they get a little too lost and God steps in to send a message to put you all back on track. He did it with the great flood and the Ten Commandments, Sodom and Gomorrah... Jesus."

Sunday was not sure he believed any of what the child was saying, but he was shocked to find himself captivated by the tale. He turned onto his street and attempted to sum up his estimation of the boy's remarks, "So, every time we get too fucked up, God steps in with a miracle that teaches us how to fix things?"

"Yeah, kinda." Gabriel replied, "There's a system. He sends a witness and a messenger first. Then there's a sign; like the burning bush, doves of peace and what-have-you to prepare everyone to be ready for the message is delivered... *I'm* the witness."

Sunday was skeptical, "So, you're saying that things are so fucked up right now that God's about to send a message so that we can fix things?"

As he said it out loud, it suddenly did not sound so far fetched. The van pulled up to the apartment building and Sunday parked illegally across the street. The pair stepped out and observed the building. There was no sign of smoke or flames coming from any of the visible windows. Sunday identified his room; everything seemed to be fine as well. Relived, he felt his nerves begin to calm down and his heartbeat ended its fluttering.

"Of course, everything is fine." He thought, "What was I thinking?"

One act of arson seemed completely plausible to Sunday, but a full strategic plan of fiery terrorism designed just to get him to believe in God again suddenly seemed ridiculous. He felt slightly embarrassed that he momentarily bought into Gabriel's ranting and pushed the thoughts aside. As he deduced that all was safe, he decided that he had his fill of his involvement. He resigned that he would take Gabriel back to the facility and would call the police to let them all handle it. He had more pressing concerns now anyway. He had to find a new job in the morning.

"Get in, we are leaving." Sunday said to his winged passenger.

"You think its okay?" Gabriel asked.

"I think all of this has gone way too far." He replied and pulled his cell phone from his pocket to dial 9-1-1.

A dull blast split the air and startled the duo. Sunday looked across the street to see the glass from his living room window shower to the ground below. Flames filled the frame and the building's fire alarm began to sound.

"No!" Sunday cried and fell to his knees.

Gabriel looked on, speechless as the residents began to rush from the entrance and onto the sidewalk where they looked on and hoped that the fire did not reach their homes. Sunday searched the crowd for signs of Callym Rafferty.

"…my apartment…" Sunday muttered in disbelief.

"He can't be too far from here." Gabriel said and looked up and down the sidewalk for signs of the young man.

Gabriel took two steps back and sat on the sidewalk. He put his hands to his head and tried to unravel the psychotic teen's way of thinking. He stared blankly at the ground and said, "He manipulated me. He brought me along because he knew I would come to find you and that I would make you leave your apartment."

Sunday looked on as the boy proceeded to think things through. Meanwhile, he inventoried all of the items that he would have to replace. He no longer had his old couch, his television, his classic movie collection. His clothes were surely ablaze, his favorite books and music; all of it was gone now. Across the street, many of his neighbors were already on their phones contacting Emergency Services.

"He had three pipes…" Gabriel said aloud, "If you were Callym and you could set off one more explosion, where would it be?"

Just then, the cell phone in Sunday's hand began to vibrate, notifying him that he had just received a text message. He flipped open his cell phone and looked down at the screen, which read:

Oh, Mary Don't You Weep

Sunday looked around for signs of Callym, and said, "He has to be watching us."

He tossed the phone over to Gabriel who was still deep in thought. The child read the message, lit up with excitement and said, "I think I know where he's going next!"

—◎—

$\mathcal{N}$ovember breezes whipped through the monastery dogwoods and the rain muddied the fields. The van slowly rolled past the lake and Sunday saw that many of the monks had hurried by the water to ensure that the peacocks had been placed in their pins to shield them from the storm. He parked the van, left the engine running and instructed Gabriel to wait inside.

"No, this is partly my fault. I need to come with you." The boy pleaded.

Sunday opened his door and replied, "It's possible that we got here before he did; I need you to stay here and keep an eye out… You're like B-Team."

Gabriel was pleased with this and began to scout through the windows and whispered to himself, "I'm B-Team."

"That's right;" Sunday said as he stepped out of the van, "Now wait here."

The cathedral appeared grim under the dark, blackened sky. Rain pelted down sideways onto the stone path. Sunday ran up the wet, marble steps and took cover under the giant archway. He pulled the drenched hood down from over his head and stood in front of the large doorway. He remembered the last time that he entered the cathedral; how aggressively the young man had attacked the white-toothed monk, how easily he broke his own body to do so, and it now appeared that his capabilities were limitless. Fear paralyzed him and the part of him that wanted to believe that Gabriel was indeed an angel wondered if it was possible for the opposite to occur. Could he be chasing a devil?

Sunday summoned all of his courage and opened the heavy doors. As he stepped inside the empty building, he heard a raspy voice call out from somewhere inside, "I was wondering when you would arrive."

Sunday walked into the church and looked across the vacant pews. The altar appeared undisturbed underneath the watchful eye of the hanging statue of Christ. Lightning flashed from outside and lit the church up in the blues, reds and violets of the stained glass windows. The gravely voice echoed once again through the room.

"Join me, Sunday."

He spun around and saw Callym Rafferty lean over the stone balcony. In his gloved hand, he held out a metal pipe with a crudely fastened, twine fuse. He made a motion with his finger for the man to meet him. Sunday ran towards the staircase, taking two at a time and threw open the door. Panting, he stood in the small aisle and faced the wily-eyed, young man.

"It's over, Callym." Sunday demanded, "Put down that thing and let's go."

The boy laughed menacingly and replied, "It's only just beginning, brother."

He reached in his pocket and produced a book of matches and held out the pipe explosive to prevent Sunday from stepping any closer to him.

"What do you want, Callym?" Sunday asked.

"I want to know something." The young man answered, "Did it work?"

"What are you talking about?"

"Were you saved?" Callym asked, "Do you believe?"

Sunday was perplexed to learn that the winged child had told the truth. All of this destruction was committed in the name of Sunday's salvation. He shook his head in disbelief and replied, "You're insane!"

"No!" he screamed, "I finally know what I am. I'm a raksha; a demon. I was born as a human, just like Gabriel. That's why I don't feel things like real people. That's why I am the way I am."

Sunday eased closer and replied, "You aren't a demon, Callym. Truth be told, of all of the children that I have worked with over the years, you are the most normal. You aren't a devil, just like any other angst-ridden kid. You just need help."

Callym cackled, looked Sunday dead in the eye and inquired cynically, "Doesn't that strike you as sad?"

Callym tapped his cane as he paced the front row of pews and continued, "Call it what you want, brother, the fact is- I'm damned. I don't have a conscience. If I did, it is long gone, so there is no chance of me ever being sorry for what I do; but I thought that if I could get you to believe in God, then maybe that God would forgive me. Maybe this pain will stop."

"That's ludicrous." Sunday gasped.

"Is it?" Callym stepped closer and asked, "Tell me, how many times tonight did you seek out your God?"

Sunday thought about the multiple times during the course of the evening that he asked God for assistance of some kind. The realization shocked him. He could not remember the last time that he had prayed or spoken to the higher power in anything more than exacerbated curses. Not wanting to admit this, Sunday shrugged.

Unpleased, Callym pulled out a match, lit it and asked again, "How many?"

Sunday quickly answered, "A few, okay? A few."

The young man waited until the flame reached his finger tips and blew out the match. He bared his teeth, turned away from Sunday and looked across at the churches pleasant solitude and pleasingly replied, "Then I succeeded."

"Did you really have to burn down everything to prove that?" Sunday cried, astonished.

Callym coldly answered, "Nope."

Sunday was speechless. He had no idea what to say or do; instead he stood, lock-kneed and stared at the bewildered teenager. Callym turned back towards the large crucifix and said softly, "But he's not going to ever forgive me either, is he? Nothing's ever going to change, is it?"

Callym slammed his cane to the ground and smiled maliciously, "And that's why you and I are going to burn down this church."

"We are going to do no such thing!" Sunday objected.

Callym whipped back towards Sunday, glared at him and growled, "Why shouldn't we? You admitted it, you believe in a God now. But he let you lose everything tonight."

"You did all that." Sunday argued.

"And he *let* me do it!" Callym rebutted back and removed another match, "He let you lose your job, your house... Kylie Court...everything. He took everything from me too. We're just evening the score."

Callym's gloved fingers raked the head of the match along the granulated surface, lighting the small stick. He held it to the twine which caught fire and quickly began to burn. The crazed teen pulled his arm back and prepared to throw the explosive towards the altar. Sunday's adrenaline took control of his reflexes and he charged at the young man with all his force.

His tackle took Callym from off of his crippled limbs and knocked both his black cane and the pipe bomb from his hand. The two men stumbled forward, hit the railing of the balcony and clumsily fell over. Callym Rafferty's face clipped the stone overhang as he flipped over backwards and crashed to the ground, landing on top of a pew. He shrieked in pain as his good leg folded back behind him and his body came to rest. Sunday, meanwhile, fell straight to the ground; the impact knocking the wind out of him.

Once he regained his senses, Sunday struggled to his feet and limped over to the boy, whose cries of agony had subsided as he had passed out from shock. Sunday looked down at him, his face had split opened in a broken, straight line across the bridge of his nose and under his right eye. His leg certainly was broken; the bone shredded through his skin, just below his knee. Sunday approached the still lit pipe bomb that had rolled across the marble floor. He picked up the crudely fashioned weapon and pulled the loose fuse from its place and fell back to his knees. He looked up at the large, sculpted Jesus and said breathlessly, "Thank you."

CHAPTER TWENTY-TWO

*S*unday loaded Callym Rafferty's unconscious body into the back seat of the van, placed the fuse-less pipe explosive in the glove box and climbed into the driver's seat. Gabriel looked on with a concerned expression and asked, "Is he dead?"

Sunday fished in his pocket for his cell phone and replied, "No, he's knocked out."

He dialed WonderKids and waited. There was no answer. This confused Sunday. Surely, by now someone would have discovered that the children were missing and someone would have been waiting by the phone. He disconnected the call and tried to call Kylie Court and immediately the voicemail picked up. Baffled, Sunday left a message;

"Kylie, this is Sunday. I found Gabriel and Callym. I'm on my way to bring them back now. Call me when you get this."

He hung up the phone and asked the winged child who sat next to him, "Do you know where they could be?"

Gabriel scratched his head and replied, "Kylie was taking some of the kids out for pizza- I assumed it would have been cancelled because of Callym and me…" A look of despair washed over the child, "Oh my! I ruined every one's day!"

Gabriel looked as though he may begin to cry again. Sunday pulled the van out of the parking lot and replied, "Hey, you did a good job. You did the right thing when you came and got me and you were a great B-Team captain, so cheer up."

The child sniffled, wiped his nose on his sleeve and stuttered, "Okay"

"C'mon," Sunday said and patted the boy on his shoulder, "I'll buy you a treat while we wait."

Gabriel brightened up and sat upright in his seat. He turned to his driver and looked as though he had something to say. Sunday looked back at him and waited for the child's diatribe which never came. Instead, Gabriel turned up the radio and began to sing along. Sunday grinned and joined them as the van pulled out onto the main road.

Sunday did a lot of soul searching as he navigated the wet roads. A lot of what he had heard from Gabriel made sense to him. It did seem like the world was heading on the wrong track and he thought of how nice it would be if God would step in and help everyone right all of the problems. At the same time, Callym was right. Even though Sunday had made the first steps in reconnecting with God, it was true that his shamble of a life was still a mess and even more so now.

What am I supposed to do, now?

Amid all of his contemplations and questions, Sunday's cell phone rang. He pulled the device from his pocket and looked to see that Kylie Court was the caller.

"Hello?" he answered.

"Hey you." She said in return. It was the first time in months that Sunday had heard her charming, southern voice. She continued, "I saw you called."

"Yeah I did. I wanted to let you know that I have Gabriel and Callym and I will be bringing them to you soon. We are just going to grab a bite to eat first." Sunday said into the receiver.

"Thank Jesus!" Kylie exclaimed, "We have Sister Rochelle looking for them, I felt so bad, Sunday. I was so scared. Thank you!"

Sunday could not help but laugh at her overzealousness.

"I tried looking on my own but we had to race back to the hospital." She explained.

"Is everything alright? No one answered when I called at the facility." Sunday asked as he pulled the van into the Cakery parking lot.

"Yeah, everything is fine, thanks to you. Just bring the kids to St. Joe's and not WonderKids. We are all over here because Hope is in labor."

The words hung in Sunday's ears and he didn't respond. He thought that if he did not respond to the comment, then maybe some strange force would make it as if he never heard it; and maybe if he had never heard it, it would never have been true. But he could not shake the echo that loomed.

Hope is in labor.

Hope is in labor.

SMASH!

Sunday thoughtlessly ran the van up over the Cakery's concrete parking barrier. Gabriel was jostled towards the dashboard and Callym rolled from the backseat, which woke him and he woozily grumbled. From the other end of the phone, Kylie heard the commotion and asked;

"Is everything okay over there?"

Sunday lied and said, "Yes, of course. Everything is fine. We will see you soon." He hung up the phone and sat completely still.

Gabriel climbed from the passenger seat and viewed the damage. There were minor scratches on the lower bumper and the hubcaps, but ultimately the van was fine. The ten-speed bike that lay twisted under its front tires, however, did not fare as well. Jezebel Costello, the flack jacketed mime ran through the entrance way of the Cakery and into the parking lot. She stared in dismay at the condition of her bicycle and threw up her arms in a grand questioning gesture.

Sunday stepped out of the van and took stock of the wreckage. The tires of the bicycle were beyond repair, the frame was bent in half. Sunday walked up to the mime and apologized, "I am so sorry; I guess that I wasn't paying attention."

Jezebel did not look satisfied. She crossed her arms, tapped her foot and scrunched up her face.

"It's been a long night." Sunday explained, "I'll replace the bike, how's that?"

The woman shook her head.

Upping the ante, Sunday added, "How about I replace the bike and I give you a ride to where ever it is that you are going after we leave here?"

Once again, Jezebel Costello shook her head.

"Okay." Sunday said, "I replace the bike, I give you a lift and I buy you anything you want from inside?"

Sunday hoped that the woman would accept his offer. His mind still reeled from the news that he had just received and he was in no mood to negotiate with someone who refused to speak. Jezebel put her finger to her chin, tapped it and rolled her eyes. After a second of pondering, she extended her hand and nodded. Sunday shook the mime's hand, opened the sliding door, tossed Callym over his shoulder and said exasperatedly, "Let's go."

—◎—

The clinging of dishes and clanging of skillets drowned out the sounds of "*Sentimental Journey*" on the Cakery's vintage juke box. The orange string lights that outlined the wood panels had all but burned out, and the vinyl records that lined inside each looked dusty and worn. The needle scrapes could be heard through the speakers as it gently followed the wavy grooves. There was the thick heavenly smell of maple syrup that filled the air, but provided little comfort to Sunday.

Elbows firmly on the table, his hand propping up his weary head; Sunday stared at his coffee and mindlessly attempted to pour sugar into the cup- missed and mounded a heap of sugar onto the Formica table top. Gabriel and Jezebel sat across the booth from him and Callym lay slumped in against the booth's wall. The young woman took massive bites from her slice of chocolate crème pie ala mode and watched in amazement as the little winged boy squeezed half of the contents of a ketchup bottle onto his Shepard's pie and fries.

"That's disgusting." Sunday said. Jezebel, her mouth full, nodded in agreement.

"What? I love tomatoes. They are so sweet, like a dessert that's good for you." Gabriel insisted defensively, squeezing more of the condiment onto his finger and sucking it off, "They are like nature's apple pie."

"I thought apples were in nature's apple pie." Sunday replied dryly. Jezebel coughed to keep from laughing. Tiny bits of crust sprayed from her mouth.

Sunday could not stop thinking about the four words Kylie Court had said:

Hope is in labor.

He wondered if he was the father. If so, why did she not tell him? If he was the father, what was he to do then? Would she want him to be involved? Did he want to be involved? And what if he was not the father? Who was it? Was she pregnant the night that they were together? After? Because of her condition, it was not outside of the realm of reason that a full term could only last a matter of weeks. As all these questions whirled about in Sunday's brain, he came to terms with the reality that there was only one way that he was going to learn the truth.

You have to go talk to Hope.

He buried his head in his hands and sighed.

"Cheer up!" Gabriel chimed, "It's not that bad."

"What?" Sunday asked and looked up, defeated.

The boy took a bite of his food; a trickle of red dropped down his chin and with his mouth full he explained, "I haven't learned everything. But I do know this." He swallowed and reached for his tall beverage, "People have been given the opportunity to do what ever they want, but they focus on all the things that keep them from it." He pointed at Sunday with a ketchup covered fry, "That's what you are doing right now."

The man had no response; he merely drank his coffee and wished that he were back on his nasty sofa and that none of the night had ever occurred. Gabriel began to arrange the salt and pepper shakers in a row. He grabbed the ketchup bottle and laid it on its side.

"Look at it this way," he began as he moved the little pieces around as if he were devising some elaborate football play, "If this is you,"

He pointed to the pepper, "and the salt is Hope, and over here... this is Kylie."

He grabbed a handful of napkins and scattered them across the table, "And this is all of the things that you need to stop worrying about."

He fidgeted with the objects, "See, it's like the Bible says, 'When you need someone to hold you, but you wait for something more; you have to have faith.'"

Sunday shook his head and mumbled, "Not the Bible, Gabriel."

"Really?" The boy asked, astonished.

Jezebel nodded her head and stared intently and tried to figure out what the little boy was getting at. He edged the shakers across he table and stopped them just short of the big sugar mound. Jezebel looked at Sunday for a clue as to what was going on; but he was just as lost as she was. Gabriel looked back up, a bit embarrassed, "Yeah, then maybe you shouldn't look at it like that."

Sunday's eyes did loops in his head as Jezebel began to fish in her tote bag. The contents jangled and knocked up against each other as she rooted around and pulled random items out of it. A tangled yo-yo, loose sticks of gum, a large loop of keys, one of those little wind up monkeys with the tiny cymbals, the "M" edition of the Encyclopedia Britannica, and a little troll pen. Sunday snatched it off of the table.

"Is this MY pen?" He demanded.

Jezebel gave Gabriel a strange look and the little boy said, "Um, yeah. I was going to bring it back to you, but then... I kind of..."

Sunday knew that the girl had stolen it from him and that the boy was covering it up; however, the drive to drill a life lesson onto the child had escaped him.

"I don't care anymore." he said and slid the pen securely in his jacket pocket.

Jezebel finally reeled out her cigarettes and offered Sunday one, which he declined. She shrugged and offered it to Gabriel. Before he could take it or refuse it, Sunday yanked it from her and threw it at her head.

"He's eight!" he scolded.

Jezebel shrugged again, picked up the cigarette and lit it.

"Now, can we all just finish so I can drop you both off and go back to figuring out what I am supposed to do for a home?"

Jezebel nodded sorrowfully and Gabriel said, "Sure, Sunday."

For an instant Sunday actually thought that he had gotten through to them. He drank slowly from his cup and listened to the "*Tsk, Tsk*" from the jukebox needle as it began to play "*Crazy*". Gabriel took another slathered bite and all but sang, "So, anyways; do you want to hear more about me being an angel?"

Sunday slammed his head onto the table and cried, "Oh, my Christ!"

Jezebel jumped back, shocked and repelled by the *THUNK* of his skull on the Formica.

"Ouch. Don't do that Sunday..." Gabriel began.

Mrs. Lovett passed by with a coffee pot, and as she topped off the mug, finished the haloed boy's sentence, "Yeah, you may break my table."

Sunday apologized and asked for the check, ready for but not anticipating his return to St. Joseph's Medical Pavilion.

—◎—

$\mathcal{G}$abriel had spent the ride in the van turned around in his passenger's seat and informed the mute mime all about his experience as and angel and how he was reborn as a human child so that he could witness the new message that would be sent down from God. Sunday tried to tune it all out, his mind already made into a putty over his thoughts about Hope and her pregnancy and how his return would be received by people like Dr. Levine, Stew and of course, Kylie Court.

Although the clouds still hung low overhead, the raining had stopped. Sunday drove the van around a large puddle and continued down the street. Meanwhile, Gabriel explained the signs, the messengers and how Callym Rafferty, the demon-child fit into things.

"He's just like me, see?" He said, cheerfully to the woman, "It's just he was sent from somewhere else to witness it all."

Jezebel nodded as though she understood. She pointed at her wrist as if to ask the time then she shrugged her shoulders.

"Oh, we don't know when it will happen." The child answered.

A strong gust of wind blew through the trees that lined both sides of the two-lane road. Dying leaves pulled from the branches and swirled trough the air. Sunday turned his wipers on to brush away the wet, brown leaves that clung to his windshield. The wind continued to blow and more leaves fell to the glass. First a brown leaf, then a small yellow one, another brown one, a blue flower petal, a brown leaf, a blue flower petal and then another blue flower petal. Soon, the entire sky was full of floating blue petals.

"Holy fucking shit!" an unfamiliar voice shouted from behind Sunday.

He turned around and saw Jezebel Costello stare out of her window up to the sky, her eyes wide and mouth agape.

"You spoke!" Sunday exclaimed.

"Well, it's goddamn raining flowers! It's a miracle!" She shouted in amazement, "I'm making an exception."

"I thought you said no miracles, Gabriel?" Sunday asked.

Gabriel shot up from his seat and pressed his hands and face to his window. A fluttering wall of blue was all he could see as thousands upon thousands of petals filled the sky and collected onto the ground. Suddenly, it became hard for Sunday to maneuver the van over the silky terrain. Gabriel straitened his halo and whispered excitedly, "It's the sign!"

He spun in his seat and shouted to the back of the vehicle, "Callym! Wake up! It's the sign!"

Sunday could not believe his eyes. All around him was beautiful, velvet blue. Even from within the van he could smell the floral scent. He looked up at the tree line to see if perhaps the petals had fallen from their fruits. However, nowhere on any of the trees did he find anything similar to the petals that trickled to the ground. He could not explain it. Perhaps it was indeed a divine act.

Callym Rafferty opened his eyes and gazed out of the back window. He too saw the strange occurrence and became ecstatic.

"It's the sign." He cried and then began chanting in a strange phrases and dialects, "Yarthsa na ni der a Ekil, yarthsa na ni der a Ekil! Killer! Maker! Killer! Maker! Yarthsa na ni der a Ekil, Yarthsa na ni der a Ekil!"

He started to twitch and convulse and Jezebel panicked from the center seat.

"This kid back here is all fucked up, man!" She screamed.

Callym began to flail his limbs about, shouting his chants at the top of his lungs, ""Yarthsa na ni der a Ekil, yarthsa na ni der a Ekil! Killer! Maker! Killer! Maker! Yarthsa na ni der a Ekil, Yarthsa na ni der a Ekil!"

His metal brace that wrapped around his leg connected with the van's new window and shattered it into millions of tiny pieces. Mortified, Sunday turned in his seat and looked behind him at the gaping hole that had just been fixed earlier that day.

"Son of a-" He started to shout.

His curses were cut short by Jezebel's screams. Sunday turned his attention back to the road just in time to see a pick-up truck that had lost control on the blossoms that littered the asphalt headed straight for them. He cut the steering wheel hard to the right and barely avoided an accident. No sooner had the passengers of the van sighed a breath of relief, the vehicle slipped from Sunday's control and veered straight into a telephone pole with a nightmarish smash that thrust everyone violently forward.

—◎—

The van was totaled. The front end had been bent inwards in the shape of the pole and steam flumed from the crumpled hood. The passengers crawled out, lucky to have escaped with only the mere scrapes and bruises that they had acquired. Sunday slumped out of the vehicle and reviewed the damage. All around him petals fell from the clouds.

"Is everyone okay?" He asked.

Jezebel Costello released a barrage of obscenity, "Motherfuckinggoddamnbitchshits, I thought we were goners."

Gabriel nodded and peered back into the vehicle at Callym Rafferty, who was still twisted inside the van, chanting.

"He's going to need help." The boy noted.

Sunday examined the busted side window and then and there blamed Callym for the accident. He replied coldly, "He's not getting it from me."

Sunday left the winged boy and the young woman to pull the broken teen from the wreckage and began to walk the remaining mile to St. Joseph's Medical Pavilion. Gabriel and Jezebel propped Callym up with his arms around their necks and together they hobbled down the street, dragging teen's dangling feet behind them.

Sunday intermittently sulked and stressed. The flower petals fell even heavier and gathered in piles that covered his ankles as he traipsed through them. He wondered if it was in fact, a sign from God. If so, what did it mean?

"What am I supposed to do?" He asked aloud, "Am I just supposed to go find another shitty job?"

Gabriel and Jezebel caught up to him and the haloed child replied, "That's horrible thinking, Mr. Sunday. You can be anything; if you really want. What kind of job do you really want?"

"Yeah, and I've got some magic beans if you want them." Sunday said sarcastically. He thought back to the words spoken to him earlier that day and added sadly, "Once a janitor, always a janitor."

Gabriel snapped back defensively, "For crying out loud, Sunday! Haven't you learned anything tonight? If you can't open yourself up to the possibility that there is something better for you, then you are never going to find what you are looking for! Never. Ever."

Sunday was reminded of all the decisions he had made over the years that he would have changed if he could; all the easy answers he chose and how his lack of effort had kept him in nowhere jobs, with little self esteem and little to show. He wondered if it was even possible that was destined for better things; excitement, joy, maybe even love. If there were truly something greater than all of us sending down the unusual precipitation to let everyone know that help was on the way, did it even care enough about Sunday to show him how to obtain these elusive things? He let the child's lecture sink in and held out his hand. A single, silky blue petal fluttered into his palm.

Please tell me what I'm supposed to do.

CHAPTER TWENTY-THREE

*T*he emergency waiting room for St. Joseph's Hospital was packed with people; some were sick, some had broken bones, others had lacerations, but all were fascinated by the strange flowers that fell from the sky. Many of the lingering patients had moved to the windows to watch the streets slowly fill with the tiny petals. Others had gathered around the television to watch Tabitha Townsend's live coverage from the Channel 5 rooftop. The buzz around the room ranged from talk of miracles to El Nino to global warming as the cause of the odd occurrence.

Sunday carried Callym Rafferty over his shoulder and across the room to an empty green, cushioned chair in the corner by the radiator. He slumped the boy down into the seat and Jezebel pulled the small magazine table closer so that they could elevate his leg. Sunday eyed the young woman's enormous bag and asked, "Do you have like a rope or something in there?"

Jezebel opened the sack and rummaged around inside. She pulled out a long red ribbon and a pair of fur covered handcuffs. Sunday dismissed the ribbon, and but took the leopard printed restraints and shackled the mumbling, pale boy to the metal coils of the radiator. He rose from the rows of seats and said, "Keep an eye on him for me. I'll be back."

Sunday led Gabriel to the receptionist's desk and said to the nurse that sat behind the computer, "Hi. Do you see that creepy kid over there?"

The nurse glanced over and took note of the bruised and battered boy. "Heavenly Father!"

She gasped as she reached for the phone to call an emergency team to tend to the boy. Sunday leaned over the counter and pressed the disconnect button.

"Hang on, ma'am; there's no rush. There are plenty of good people who need help before him." Sunday said, "I just wanted to let you know he has multiple face lacerations and a severely broken leg. He's also responsible for the arsons tonight. Feel free to contact whatever officials you deem necessary."

He did not wait to see what the nurse's reaction would be. Instead, he took Gabriel by the loop of his backpack and led him towards the maternity ward. They passed by a room with opened double doors marked "Chapel". As they walked by, Sunday began to worry once again about what he was supposed to do. He had no home, no job, no car and it was possible that he was about to learn that he was a father. He fretted that he would be a terrible role model, that he would fail as he always had. He felt lost and as though he had no one to rely upon. He had no one to confide in and to top it off; he also feared the reaction from his old friends and co-workers once they saw him. He hung his head wearily and pressed the button to queue the elevator.

Please, let me do the right thing.

They found Stew with a group of Wonder Kids in the maternity waiting area. His head was freshly shaven, not a hair upon it and it made him appear much more rugged. The room was nicer than the emergency waiting room. It was clean and the people who lounged in the chairs did not look sickly or weakened. The walls were painted a soothing yellow and there were plenty of magazines and simple toys to occupy the time. As soon as Molly Rollins saw Sunday, she rose from her Connect Four board and rushed to hug him. She was quickly joined by Austin Olsen and a number of the younger children. They wrapped their tiny arms around his waist and legs and eventually pulled him to the ground.

He hugged the children back and staggered to his feet. For a moment, there was an awkward silence between Sunday and his old friend. Both men were unsure of what to say to the other, until Stew finally said, "Look, about the last time I saw you…"

Sunday stopped the apology and replied, "It's cool. It's cool."

The two friends embraced, patted each other on the back and watched as Gabriel reunited with his peers as well.

"You look good." Sunday smiled and rubbed Stew's bald head.

"I think it's a good look for me." He agreed, laughingly.

A different kind of silence fell between the two men. They each knew what the other wanted to say, but neither had any idea as to how to properly begin. Sunday finally found the courage to ask, "So, Hope is having a baby?"

"Yeah," Stew sighed and then pseudo-teasingly added, "Is it yours?"

Sunday sort of chuckled uncomfortably and answered, "I honestly don't know."

"She hasn't told anybody much of anything." Stew replied consolingly.

Just then, Head Physician Dr. Margo Levine-Alonzo appeared in the doorway. She stopped mid-step at the sight of her former custodian and for a moment Sunday was afraid that she was going to call an officer to enforce the terms of the restraining order that she had taken out on him. He gulped, nervously as the doctor inspected the children.

"Stewart, can you please take the children back to the facility. We will be back shortly." She calmly and quietly requested.

Stew nodded, rounded up the kids and turned to Sunday and said, "It was good to see you. Really."

"It was good to see you too." Sunday replied.

The men shook hands and wrapped their free arms around each other.

"Don't be a stranger." Stew whispered.

"Definitely."

Stew ushered the kids from the room and after wishing him good luck, left Sunday alone with Dr. Levine. Sunday stood motionless and waited for her to begin.

"Thank you for bringing the children back." She said after some time.

Sunday nodded, and said truthfully, "Callym's a bit roughed up and he's waiting in the E.R."

He hesitated and then added, "He set fire to two buildings tonight and attempted a third. I'm pretty sure that the authorities have been notified."

Dr. Levine walked further into the waiting room and watched her heroine cover footage on the television of the blue petals that had blanketed the city. She picked a red checker, and slid it into the yellow, Connect Four board, completing a diagonal pattern.

"I've spoken to Hope," She began.

"Is she okay?" Sunday worriedly asked.

The Head Physician nodded and added, "She's in room three-thirteen. She'd like to see you."

Sunday graciously thanked her and asked, "Are you okay with that?"

Dr Levine turned back towards him and sincerely approved with a simple and soft, "Yes."

As Sunday turned to leave for Hope's room, the doctor stopped him before he could exit the waiting area, "Sunday, wait."

He paused and turned back to the woman, who added, "I've also spoken with the Board of Directors. We would like you to come back."

Sunday was stunned and honored. It would be easier to care for a new child if he worked in the same building. He was amazed to learn that he was so appreciated, but something inside him wanted more.

"Can I think about it?" He asked.

"Of course." Dr. Levine answered, batted her eyes and added purposefully, "But it would mean a lot to me personally if you did."

Sunday chuckled and said, "Thanks, Dr. Levine. I'll consider it."

—◉—

Decals of pastel ducks and bunnies lined the yellow walls. Halfway down the hallway, Sunday stopped at the long window that shown into the newborns' nursery. He perused the line of medical cradles until he found the one that was marked with a pink stork sticker that read:

BABY MARGO

Sunday stood on the tips of his shoes, but he could not find a vantage point that allowed him a view of the child. He hopped up and down, but even at his apex, he could only make out the fuzzy pink ball atop the child's tiny cap. He was immediately filled with possible-paternally love and he could not help but to beam proudly at the bassinette.

I have a daughter.

He continued down the hallway to room 313 and motioned to knock on the door. Before his hand could hit the wood, he heard a voice from inside call out, "Come on in, Sunday."

Sunday opened the door and slowly walked inside. Hope sat up in her bed, propped up by pillows. She lay underneath the white hospital issued sheets and stared out the window at the petals that slowly drifted by. On the television in the background Tabitha Townsend announced that the phenomenon was happening all around the world. Hope turned to face Sunday as he silently closed the door behind him.

"You look like shit." She said.

The woman in the bed was hardly the Hope that Sunday had remembered. She wore little make-up, which he knew to be a rare occurrence and around her now wise eyes were the beginnings of wrinkles and crow's feet. A grey streak ran through her chestnut, shoulder-length hair. She looked frailer and as though she was in her early to mid-forties.

"So do you." Sunday teased, "And don't say 'shit'."

Hope patted the side of her bed and motioned for Sunday to join her. He walked across the room and sat on the edge of the mattress.

"It's raining flowers; did you see?" She asked softly. She turned her attention back to the window and stared contently.

"Yeah. Weird huh?" Sunday responded, unsure of what he was thinking, much less what she was.

"They are for her." Hope said.

Finally finding courage, Sunday asked, "Why didn't you tell me?"

"Honey, she isn't yours." She said solemnly and without looking at him.

Although he had not been granted a great deal of time to come around to the idea, all of the dreams he had built for being a father to the baby were suddenly crushed. Sunday shook his head in disbelief and said, "That's a lie; you know it is."

Hope turned back to Sunday and held him tightly, buried her head in his chest and started to cry, "She's not mine either. I'm giving her up. I couldn't do it if you knew. I knew you would talk me out of it."

Sunday stopped breathing. He was the father, but she had decided to put the child up for adoption. He had seen how hard life could be for the children of WonderKids and Hope had lived it first hand. He could not believe what he had heard and the notion tore at him.

"You're damn right I would!" He exclaimed, "Why would you do that?"

Hope sat back and wiped her eyes, "Look at me, Sunday. I'm aging so fast. I'm so much older than you now. How long do you really think that I'll be able to care for her?"

"I would be there to help." Sunday stated, pleadingly.

She took his hand and began to trace his fingers with her pruning thumb. Her tired eyes met his and a tear rolled down her face, "Sunday, I love you; but you can't even take care of you."

He wanted to argue but he could not. He knew that she was right and he began to sob. He once again felt like a terrible failure. It was just one more thing in a long line of things that he could not do right or that had been taken from him. Hope held him close as Sunday kissed her forehead and begged, "Hope, please. It can work."

She shook her head and pushed him away. They were now both in tears and she sobbed, "I love you; I always have."

She placed her hand on his heart and added, "But it can't work. We aren't supposed to be together. It's like I said before, you know your heart belongs to Kylie. Go to her."

There was then a knock on the door and a nurse that wheeled a medial cart behind her interrupted their conversation. Hope sat back and dried her eyes and Sunday sniffled and stood up. The nurse began to check Hope's drip bag and said, "Ms. Hope has to run a few tests now; she's going to need a moment."

Sunday nodded and hugged Hope again. Her breath warmed his neck, and she pressed her soft lips to his skin one last time. Sunday slowly turned to the door and opened it. Before exiting, he turned around and said, "Just tell me one thing?"

Hope looked up and sadly said, "Anything."

"Tell me you aren't naming her Margo Daylily Margo."

A giggle forced its way through Hope's tears and she replied, "I'm kind of partial to Audrey."

—◎—

I have a daughter.

I don't have a daughter.

She could have been my daughter.

She isn't my daughter.

*She **should** have been my daughter.*

*S*unday stared at the bassinette and wished that he could see the little girl who lay inside. Down the lonely hallway, he heard the familiar rattle of keys. He turned to the left and saw the night shift janitor who pulled his broom and dustpan from the utility closet. Knowing that the janitor likely had keys to the room, Sunday approached him and said, "Sorry to bother you."

The janitor looked Sunday up and down and said, "Do I know you?"

"No," Sunday replied, "I used to work at WonderKids, though. I was hoping you could help me. My friend just had a baby and I was hoping to get a peek at her, but I can't see from the window."

The janitor lit up and said expressively, "You're the custodian from down there aren't you?"

Sunday nodded and the man instantly began to laugh. He slapped his hand across his knee and exclaimed, "I knew it! Man, you're a legend up here. Is it true that you spiked Mr. Augustine-Chrystine's latte with laxative?"

Sunday attempted to deny his involvement but the janitor would not hear it. He flipped through his keys, led Sunday to the door and said, "Anything for you! I can't wait to tell the guys you were here. They aren't going to believe it."

Sunday shook the man's hand and thanked him. The janitor smiled and replied, "Hey; once a janitor, always a janitor, right?"

Sunday gave a thumb-up and walked inside the nursery. He crept softly as not to disturb the slumbering newborns and placed his hands on the side of the bassinette. He looked inside and saw the peaceful infant wrapped in a pink blanket and matching stocking cap. Her pink cheeks dimpled as she situated herself in her woolen cocoon.

"For a kid who's not supposed to be mine," Sunday said, caressing her face with his index finger, "You sure do have my nose. You poor thing."

He began to whisper baby garble to her. Audrey opened her big green eyes and gave him a gummy smile. Sunday instantly fell in love with her and the thought of never seeing her again already began to pain him. He lifted her gently from her crib and held her to his heart. The infant nestled into him and cooed.

"Hey, so you know what?" He said, as she clutched hold of his finger and he struggled not to cry, "You are so tiny. So cute and so tiny."

He wiggled his finger in the girl's grasp and she squeakily laughed.

"Yeah, you got Daddy's finger. Yes you do." Sunday said and started to cry, "You are so cute and tiny. So tiny and you aren't going to remember any of this. You aren't going to remember Daddy... and that sucks."

Sunday kissed her head softly, and whispered, "But you have to remember that Daddy will always love you."

He sniffled, and began to sway back and forth and softly sang:

If you said goodbye to me tonight,

There would still be music left to write.

What else can I do?

I'm so inspired by you;

That hasn't happened for the longest time...

By the end of his song, Sunday had lulled the child back to sleep. He placed her softly in the cradle, kissed her and breathed deep her powdery scent. She smelled just how he thought something so brilliant should. He wished that he could wrap her up and take her with him. He reached into his coat pocket and set his troll pen next to her. He looked up to see that Gabriel and Austin Olsen stood in the hallway and looked at him through the long window. He ignored them and turned back to the infant.

"Remember." He whispered.

—◎—

The hospital chapel was little more than six rows of benches, a small altar and a few candles and flowers placed about for aesthetics. Behind the altar stood a nondescript, simple cross in front of two stained glass windows. Sunday walked inside and found a seat in the middle pew. He stared at the cross, sighed, wiped his eyes dry and fell to his knees.

Sunday could not remember the last time that he had prayed, but he felt so lost and alone that he did not know what else to do. He was used to having luck turn on him, but this night proved to be more than he could take. Hands folded and looking to the sky, Sunday said aloud;

"God, it's me Sunday. If you are out there, please… please show me what I need to do."

He prayed and prayed. He tried to recall the prayers that he learned when he was a child and when he reached the parts that he could not remember, it prompted him to pray even harder. He asked for guidance to find the path that he was supposed to be on. He wanted things to feel right in his life and he prayed for it until he cried.

Sunday wept until he felt a soft hand gently touch his shoulder. He turned around and saw Kylie Court standing behind him. She was still wearing her OLHSHS regalia with matching blue latex gloves and to Sunday looked absolutely beautiful. She forced a smile for him and walked around the pew to sit next to him.

"Hi." She whispered.

"Hey." Sunday sniffled.

"Are you holding up okay?"

"She said she's not mine." Sunday repeated. He gazed upon the cross and continued, "You know, for a minute there… For a minute I really wished that she was mine, you know?"

Kylie did not answer; instead she took his hand, wrapped her gloved fingers around his and said, "I wish that there was something I could say…"

Sunday wiped an errant tear from his cheek and added, "I think that I owe you an apology…"

Kylie shook her head no and placed a finger to her lips, "Let's just both agree that we forgive each other. Is that okay?"

"I'd like that." Sunday replied and tried to smile.

They sat quietly, hand-in-hand, happy to be reunited. After she had taken in enough of the moment to be satisfied; Kylie placed a black and white notebook onto Sunday's lap and said, "We confiscated this from the kids not too long ago. I thought you might want it back."

Sunday flipped through the pages of the notebook, each one addressed to Diane. As he skimmed the lines of his old journal, he realized that most of the information that Gabriel used to convince him that he was an angel could be derived from his scribings. He once again felt used and lied to and no longer knew what to think or what to believe. He looked back to the cross, confused.

"Nothing makes sense any more." He said.

"Maybe nothing ever does." Kylie contemplated. She tried to change the subject for him and said, "I heard that they offered you your job back. That's good."

Sunday shrugged and mumbled, "Yeah, I guess."

"Aren't you going to take it?"

"I just don't know."

"If you don't take it, where would that leave us?" She asked.

Hollow and defeated, Sunday looked at her and replied, "Where would we be if I stayed?"

Kylie Court stared at him and tried to read what he was thinking. She answered softly, "I don't know."

Sunday held his hands out as if he had nothing else to offer, "I guess that leaves you here and me elsewhere."

Tears rolled down Kylie's face as she tremblingly asked, "Where will you go?"

Sunday stood up from his seat and began to slide his way out of the pew. He shrugged and said, "Where the day takes me, I guess. With a little luck I'll find my path; and if it brings me back here maybe we can see what happens then."

He did not look back until he had reached the double doors. When he did, he saw that Kylie sobbed into her latex-clad hands. He took two steps back inside and for an instant contemplated accepting his old custodian position just to see how things played out.

There's more for you out there than mops and brooms.

He knew that he could not stay, even for Kylie. In a broken voice he called out, "Pickle."

Kylie turned to him and tried to clear away the mascara that trickled down her face like black teardrops with her glove. She sniffled and softly answered, "Yes?"

"I just wanted you to know that where ever it is that I end up, I'll be thinking of you... I love you."

—◉—

Callym Rafferty laughed hysterically as Sunday exited the chapel morosely. Jezebel Costello no longer looked after him as two large security guards had taken her place. Sunday tried to walk past the taunting teenager without paying him any attention, but the boy screamed out, "Getting some God are you, brother? How's that working out?"

He cackled and kicked his metal braced leg about and continued, "You know what's sad, Sunday? Do you want to know what is really sad? It's never going to work. It's never going to work because you're bitter to the bone and you will never get to have anything. Nothing will ever change for you. Ever. Ever."

"I'm not listening to you, Callym." Sunday said as he approached.

"You are just like me, brother!" The boy screamed, "And I will show you."

Callym lunged at Sunday as far as the handcuffs would allow and gripped him by his wrist. He pulled Sunday closer so that his head was locked into his arm. The security guards flanked him and pointed their mace canisters at him. Callym made an attempt to prod Sunday with the emergency syringe that he had concealed in his hand and growled through gritted teeth, "Bitter to the bone, brother! Bitter to the bone!"

Sunday struggled in the teen's locked arms and felt the metal tip of the needle poke slightly at his neck. Before Callym could break the skin, Sunday sent his elbow upwards and into the boy's jaw. Callym stumbled backwards and further pushed the bone through his leg. He collapsed in the chair and the two security guards braced him with riot sticks.

Sunday brushed himself off and checked his neck to see if he was bleeding. Once he determined that he was alright, he turned from the boy and continued towards the exit. He walked through the sliding glass doors as the pale, creepy child screamed behind him, "You're just like me! You are just like me!"

—◉—

The petals had piled at least four inches on top of the wet ground. Sunday kicked through them as he wandered across the hospital parking lot. He had no where to go and no way to get there. He was not in the mood to look for a hotel for the night and he did not want to kill time at the Cakery. He had a long list of things that he did not want to do, but for the life of him, he could not decide what he wanted to do, or what he should do.

I'll go where the day takes me.

He glanced down the road towards the nearby bus stop and saw Jezebel Costello sitting alone on a bench and walked to her.

"I don't get this shit." She said and caught a petal in her hand as Sunday sat down next to her.

"There's not much I do get anymore." Sunday replied.

Jezebel rummaged through her bag and pulled out a pack of cigarettes and offered Sunday one. He accepted and held it towards her lit Zippo lighter. She exhaled a puff of smoke and said, "I think the kid's right. I think it's a miracle."

Just then, Gabriel and Austin Olsen came screaming from across the parking lot, "Wait! Wait!"

When they had reached the bus stop and had caught their breath; Gabriel panted frantically, "Where are you going?"

"I don't know." Sunday replied, "Away."

"What about everything that's happened?" The crying boy asked as he motioned to the blue barrage from above, "What about all of this?"

Sunday took another long drag from his cigarette and looked down at the boy and replied, "You said it yourself. It's about making me happy. I can't be happy here. I have to leave."

"But you are there. In my vision of when the Savior speaks the word, you are with us. I dreamed it!" He yelled.

Sunday replied, "Maybe your dream is just a dream."

Gabriel wept uncontrollably and gulped for air between howls. Sunday knelt down next to him and said, "For what its worth; I think I was an ass to you. I tried to clip your wings; and you know what? It doesn't matter that I don't believe you. You've made so many people happy; you're an angel to them."

He hugged the winged child, fixed his halo and said, "You bug the hell out of me, Gabe; but I will miss you."

He swallowed his sobs and said, "I'll miss you too."

Sunday hugged Austin Olsen as well, assured the boys that it would be okay and sent them back inside. As the children walked away Sunday heard them talking.

"Do you really think that everything will be okay?" Austin asked.

Gabriel sniffled the last of his tears away and happily replied, "I think every little thing is going to be alright."

Jezebel looked down the empty stretch of road ahead of them, flicked her cigarette into the sea of blue, and said, "What's next?"

"I don't know" He replied.

Jezebel searched through her bag and tossed her miming books into the trash. She looked to the sky at the last of the falling petals that had begun to lessen in quantity, "You know, I think this is God telling me it's time to move on."

Sunday looked at the like-minded woman and asked, "You too? Where are you thinking of going?"

Jezebel shrugged and said, "Anything's going to be better than amateur miming in this shit town."

A roar of an engine came from around the corner and a black Royal Enfield with a sidecar pulled to a stop in front of them. To Sunday's astonishment, Sister Rochelle piloted the vehicle. She took off her helmet and said to the duo that sat listlessly on the bus stop bench, "Planning on going somewhere?"

"Yes ma'am." Sunday replied.

"I've seen you save these people at least twice in the short time I've known you. It's going to be a shame for them to lose you."

Sister Rochelle shook her head and motioned for him to join her, "Why don't you just come with me?"

Sunday remained seated, flicked his cigarette to the petal covered sidewalk and said defiantly, "I'm not going back."

"I don't want you to." The nun replied, "I think you would be a great addition to my Organization. What do you think?"

"What would I be doing?" He inquired.

Sister Rochelle turned down the southern rock that blared from the motorcycle's custom speakers and explained, "You'll travel around with me and we will find kids like these."

Sunday liked the idea of traveling; it sounded adventurous. Toiling it over, he asked, "And I never have to come back here?"

The nun shook her head. Sunday looked to Jezebel to see what she thought. The young woman shrugged as if to say that she had no answers for him. Sunday looked to the sky, but he knew he would find no answers there either. Perhaps Gabriel was right; he had to open himself up to possibilities. The job sounded appealing enough and if God were indeed telling him that he was heading on the right path, what better chauffeur than a nun?

"Okay." Sunday said, and climbed onto the back of the motorcycle.

The nun reached down into the sidecar, removed the familiar black satchel and handed it to Sunday. He peeked inside at the contents and slid it around his shoulder.

"Keep it on you at all times." The nun instructed and the man nodded in acknowledgement.

Jezebel approached the bike and asked, "Do you mind giving me a lift?"

The nun waved the young woman on, she hopped gleefully into the side car and they sped down the road, casting a swirling trail of petals behind them. The farther they pulled away from the facility, the more Sunday felt at ease. Suddenly, it did not matter that he had no home, he would find another. It was not important that his job burned to the ground, all that was important was that his boss was safe. He felt a comfort from within that let him know that all would be alright and he relaxed and watched as the trees rushed by him and the wind tousled his hair.

The motorcycle approached the mangled wreck of Sunday's van and he tapped the nun on the shoulder and asked her to stop. The bike came to a rolling halt and the disturbed blue petals fell back to the ground. Sunday stepped from the seat and walked towards his vehicle. He opened the door, leaned inside and opened the glove box.

"What are you doing?" Sister Rochelle yelled.

Sunday turned and called back, "Starting from scratch."

He pulled the metal pipe from the compartment and with it a crinkled Hallmark card fell to the floor. Sunday picked it up and read it over. He cherishingly placed the card in his coat pocket and smiled. He unscrewed the cap of the pipe; the scent of flammables burned his nose. He lit the end, tossed it through the window and casually walked back towards the road.

As they sat and watched the van burn, Sunday inspected his black satchel and removed the notepad and a regular black ball point pen. He flipped through the blank pages and began to write:

Dear Diane,

Sunday tapped the pen to his tooth and pondered as he stared into the blaze. He daydreamed about where his travels would take him, the places we was to see, the children he would help and all the unthinkable things that he would do. He looked back towards St. Joseph's Medical Pavilion and could see the faint outline of the WonderKids building peeking from behind the grand hospital. He thought about the people that he would miss while on his travels. A smile swept over his face as he scratched out his inking on the page and wrote instead:

Dear Kylie,

Yes, it was true that one day Sunday's path may return him to his city, to his friends and to his WonderKids; maybe even one day the path would lead him back to his love, but until then, Sunday thought, he would follow the path so that he could become the man that he knew that he could be. Sister Rochelle signaled that it was time to go and they all walked through the miraculous petals back to her bike. Sunday tucked the notebook back into his satchel and contemplated stealing one last look at his skyline. He resigned to keep his head straight; to only look ahead, to keep focused on his path, on his destination, on his future. The possibilities astounded him. Sunday raised his eyes upwards and said unto the heavens,

Oh, sweet Serene, thank you. I'm having a good time.

*W*eeks had passed since the day it had miraculously rained flowers. Piles upon piles of petals were pushed onto the sidewalks and corners in high mounds. Light gusts of wind carried others as they spiraled across the streets and through the crisp air. The gleeful chirps of birds greeted the pleasant afternoon and a young fawn darted quickly through the woods beyond the barbed-wire fence that encompassed the maximum-security juvenile detention center. It was a magnificent moment and one that would have been enjoyed by any of center's residence, if only the building's windows had not been bricked over.

Callym Rafferty's head hung lifeless from his neck. Both of his legs had been fitted with the crescent guards and were strapped in place to the padded rests under them. His arms were treated similarly, each with three straps; one at the wrist, the elbows and just below his armpit. His chest was bound twice across the ribcage and numerous tubes ran in and out of his body. His nails had grown dingy and long from unkemptness and his pants were stained from his own urine. His white, clouded eyes stared blankly to the ground as excessive amounts of Lithium Validemerethyzine pumped through his body and filled his mind with never-ending nightmares.

Even though the boy was completely catatonic and immobilized, his white room was heavily padded and the objects allowed in the room were highly regulated by the supervising staff. The heavy door opened and two men walked inside. Callym did not have the energy nor the will to raise his head to see who they were, but he tried to listen to them talk to take his mind from the hellish visions had tormented him.

"…Your weekly tutoring of the child and continued concern for his well being played highly into the judge's decision."

Callym recognized the man's voice as that of Mr. Roger Skinner, the head of the center.

"You have no idea how much that pleases me."

"You understand that if you claim the child as a ward, your corporation will be responsible not only for his well being, but also his actions?"

"Yes."

"And I assume that you have read the child's file?"

"I have."

"Well, everything else is in order; so I see no reason why we can't have the boy released into your care no later than Thursday."

"That sounds superb. Thank you."

Even though Callym was too weak to glance upward, he heard a pair of footsteps near him and felt the presence of someone standing quite close. There was a brief lull in the conversation between the two men as the young teen inhaled the familiar odor of homemade soap.

"I have to ask; if you've read his file and you know his history, why would you choose this boy, Mr. Linus?"

"Actually, son; it's Brother Linus."

Callym raised his eyes to see the white-toothed monk standing before him. The monk touched the boy's cheek and said, "Let's just say that we believe in saving those who can't save themselves."

Brother Linus smiled a large, gleaming grin at the young teen, lowered his glasses and revealed to the child his own clouded, white eyes...

…Sunday and the children of WonderKids will return in:

RIPPLE

The Author would like to thank:

My parents… what else can I do? I'm so inspired by you.
My brothers, my sisters and my dearest friends…You are my good time.
And you…

Special Thanks To:
Brigitte Clifton
Valerie Manson
&
Mike Farris

Mike Farris' music can be found at www.mikefarrismusic.net.

If you too would like to see the revival of Grape Flavored Pop-Tarts (With Icing, No Sprinkles); please send your request to www.kelloggsgreatideas.com and support the effort.